Elsewhere....
III

Elsewhere Volume I . . . Winner of the 1982 World Fantasy Award for Best Anthology:

"*Elsewhere* boasts 384 pages and an all-star lineup, including Yeats and Márquez; Graves and Kotzwinkle; John Gardner, Ursula K. Le Guin, and W. S. Gilbert. Evangeline Walton contributes a lyric myth; Márquez, a one-sentence epic whose run-on technique lulls you into alpha-appreciation; Gardner, an adult Alice-in-Wonderland romp; Kotzwinkle, a poignant tale of eons-old lost love; and Michael Moorcock, a lighthearted adventure of 'Elric at the End of Time.' Poems and illustrations too."

—The *Los Angeles Times*

"*Elsewhere* is one of the best fantasy literary values of any year. . . . Refreshingly, the editors have largely eschewed the well-traveled swords-and-sinews route. Instead, an atmosphere of wistful, gentle magic pervades many of the stories and poems."

—*Library Journal*

"*Elsewhere* is a work of considerable quality. . . . Stories reveal a wide range of emotions, such as whimsy, treachery, revenge, gentle love, and haunting tragedy. Highly recommended."

—*V. O. Y. A.*

"Apart from providing large chunks of good reading for almost any taste, this book will be among the handful of fantasy anthologies valuable for classroom use."

—*A. L. A. Booklist*

"In short, this is a book to be read, savored, reread—and saved. In it are the sorts of stories you'd like to read to wise children, or share with friends."

—*Science Fiction Review*

Elsewhere Volume II:

"Here's another example of how good fantasy can be if you just look in the right places. . . . There's an Eskimo chant, a poem from ancient China, a story from *The New Yorker,* and another from *The Atlantic, etc.* A little more than half the contents are original, though. Represented are Joanna Russ, Robin McKinley, Patricia McKillip, Fritz Leiber, Evangeline Walton, Somtow Sucharitkul, Jane Yolen, and Paul Hazel. . . . Buy this book. If you're tired of all those nondescript fantasy trilogies, this is what you should be saving your money for."

—*Science Fiction Review*

"Here is an anthology that will give you a better idea of the sheer richness of modern fantasy than any random selection of novels. . . . The level of craftsmanship is very high. The contributors between them have won virtually every conceivable literary award, including the Nobel Prize. Contributors are virtually a who's who of the fantasy field. . . . Here there be dragons. Two or three anyway. Here there be (thankfully) very few Tolkien imitations or brainless barbarians."

—*The Philadelphia Inquirer*

"*Elsewhere* II: The second in a trilogy of what promises to be an extraordinary treasure trove of literary fantasy. Recommended."

—*A. L. A. Booklist*

"The landmark fantasy anthology series for the eighties is unequivocally *Elsewhere.* . . . Most of the hot new talent in what the editors call 'high fantasy' are published here; in today's conservative fantasy market it's a relief to find some genuine vision—that is, after all, what fantasy's all about, isn't it?"

—*Heavy Metal Magazine*

TALES
OF
FANTASY

ELSEWHERE

Vol. III

EDITED BY
TERRI WINDLING &
MARK ALAN ARNOLD

INTERIOR ILLUSTRATIONS
by Terri Windling

ACE FANTASY BOOKS
NEW YORK

The editors would like to thank the following for their help, suggestions, and/or moral support in the editing of this volume: Betty Ballantine; Professor Bernth Lindfors; Patricia McKillip; Robin McKinley; Darrell Schweitzer; Baird Searles; Regi Wells; Betsy Wollheim; Jane Yolen; The SF & Fantasy Department of Berkley/Ace Books—Susan Allison, Beth Meacham, Melissa Singer, Sue Stone; Ace Production Editor Nancy Wiesenfeld; and the judges of the 1982 World Fantasy Award.

ELSEWHERE VOLUME III

An Ace Fantasy Book/published by arrangement with
the editors

PRINTING HISTORY
Ace Original/April 1984

ISBN: 0-441-20405-8

Ace Fantasy Books are published by The Berkley Publishing Group,
200 Madison Avenue, New York, New York 10016.
PRINTED IN THE UNITED STATES OF AMERICA

Table of Contents

INTRODUCTION

There is a great deal to be said for reality (indeed, I revel in the world we live in), but the fact is, the yardstick by which reality is most often measured is fantasy.

Life itself is fantastic—all life—an incredible coincidence of events and happenstance, the more incredible because it tried, and still tries, to repeat, and has *learned* to repeat, to adapt to circumstances that change, producing countless millions of forms so far. And *Homo sapiens*, at any rate, is just at its beginnings. Who knows where we will really end up? So there's no escaping it. It is reality that is truly fantastic. Just in the past hundred years, many miracles once regarded as threateningly magic have emerged as simple realities, i.e., miracles which have rational explanations. Does this make them any less of a miracle? But if rational definition is the thin line between fantasy and reality, will we, somewhere down the pike, everything rationalized, all explained, (O dreary world) run out of fantasy altogether? No, and again, no. Not ever.

Fantasy exists not only in reality, but in the limitless reaches of the human psyche. No matter how much joy and delight and even exaltation we experience in the world we live in, the mind stretches and pulls and demands more—more wonder, more mystery, more enchantment—at all levels of the human (and non-human) condition.

Consider. With the whole world of marvels that daily open up to the eyes of a growing child, why the fascination with fairy stories, with fable, myth, legend, wizardry and witchery, unicorns, dragons, magic swords and all the other paraphernalia of the classic children's tales of wonder. With such a fantastic real world to entrance the attention, why this driving need for un-reality? Why the long, delicious games of "Let's pretend—"? And later, the avid absorption in weird worlds, terrifying adventure? Well, of course, the prosaic answer is that the whole thing is simply a learning process. Yet long after children have learned to distinguish between fantasy and the mundane (and, with hope, to cope with the latter) they continue to create their own unrealities and to read about, watch, share in, other people's unrealities. For most of us, indeed, dreamworlds continue deep into maturity and, if we are lucky, for all of our lives. And some of us, to the unbounding joy of the rest, continue to share them.

Because we *are* the dreamers, the animal that can think in abstracts, use creative imaginings as a learning process, as practice, as an absorbing, vital, joyful, fearful opportunity to figure what we would do if—, and if—, and if—. Even if, as now, we must imagine nightmarish real worlds, then so be it; perhaps our imaginings, given that we can make them sufficiently vivid, will force us to find the way to avoid their realization. And that is only one, rather solemn role, of the many that fantasy can play.

For love, joy, fear, terror, risk, all have a place in dreams. Far from being an escape, indeed, fantasy is a vast challenge and a region of huge hopes; it is at once a lodestone, something magnetically attractive, and a seething cauldron of creativity. It gives us books, music, art, adventure. It makes us creatures of power—and perhaps that is its ultimate and basic function. It makes us boundless, limitless. No matter what future discoveries are made, no matter how many miracles explained, no matter how far we go, in space, inner or outer, someone, somewhere, somewhen, entranced by the power inherent in fantasy, will be creating wonders in who knows what forms, feats of draconian imagination to entrap, terrorize, enchant and delight. We, the dreaming laughing animal, cannot live without fantasy, for in a very real sense we depend upon it, and it is ours—a multi-creation of the gut, the heart, the mind and the sheer, joyous, exuberant fun of being *Homo sapiens.*

—Betty Ballantine
(Co-founder of Ballantine Books and The Ballantine Adult Fantasy Series)
Bearsville, New York, November 1983

God Is Alive, Magic Is Afoot

God is alive, Magic is afoot,
God is alive, Magic is afoot,
God is afoot, Magic is alive, alive is afoot.
Magic never died.
God never sickened. Many poor men lied.
Many sick men lied. Magic never weakened,
Magic never hid, Magic always ruled.
God is afoot, God never died.
God was ruler though his funeral lengthened.
Though his mourners thickened, Magic never fled.
Though his shrouds were hoisted the naked God did live.
Though his words were twisted the naked Magic thrived.
Though his death was published round and round the world,
The heart did not believe.
Many hurt men wondered. Many struck men bled.
Magic never faltered. Magic always led.
Many stones were rolled but God would not lie down.
Many wild men lied. Many fat men listened.
Though they offered stones Magic still was fed.
Though they locked their coffers God was always served.
Magic is afoot. God rules. Alive is afoot.
Alive is in command. Many weak men hungered.
Many strong men thrived. Though they boasted
Solitude God was at their side.
Nor the dreamer in his cell, nor the captain on the hill.
Magic is alive. Though his death was pardoned
Round and round the world the heart would not believe.
Though laws were carved in marble they could not shelter men.
Though altars built in parliaments they could not order men.
Police arrested Magic and Magic went with them for Magic
loves the hungry.
But Magic would not tarry. It moves from arm to arm.
It would not stay with them: Magic is afoot.
It cannot come to harm. It rests in an empty palm.
It spawns in an empty mind. But Magic is no
instrument.
Magic is the end. Many men drove Magic but Magic
stayed behind.

Many   strong men lied.   They only   passed through
    Magic and out the other side.
Many   weak men lied.   They came to God in secret and
    though they left
Him nourished they would   not tell who healed.
Though mountains danced before them   they said that God
    was dead.
Though his shrouds were hoisted   the naked God did live.
This   I mean to whisper   to my mind.   This   I mean
    to laugh with   in my mind.
This I mean my mind to serve till service is but Magic
Moving through the world, and mind itself is Magic coursing
    through the flesh.

And flesh itself is Magic dancing on a clock,

And time itself the Magic Length of God.

*—Leonard Cohen
(adapted to verse by
Buffy Sainte-Marie)*

The Stagman

Robin McKinley

She grew up in her uncle's shadow, for her uncle was made Regent when her father was placed beside her mother in the royal tomb. Her uncle was a cold, proud man, who because he chose to wear plain clothing and to eat simple food claimed that he was not interested in worldly things; but this was not so. He sought power as a thing to be desired of itself, to be gloated over, and to be held in a grasp of iron. His shadow was not a kind one to his niece.

She remembered her parents little, for she had been very young when they died. She did remember that they had been gentle with her, and had talked and laughed with her, and that the people around them had talked and laughed too; and she remembered the sudden silence when her uncle took their place. The silence of the following years was broken but rarely. Her maids and ladies spoke to her in whispers, and she saw no one else but her uncle, who gave her her lessons; his voice was low and harsh, and he spoke as if he begrudged her every word.

She grew up in a daze. Her lessons were always too difficult for her quite to comprehend, and she assumed that she was stupid, and did not see the glitter of pleasure in her uncle's eye as she stumbled and misunderstood. She could only guess her people's attitude toward her in the attitude of the women who served her, and none ever stayed long enough for her to overcome her shyness with them; and she had never in her life dared to ask her uncle a question. But as she grew older it crept into her dimmed consciousness that her people had no faith in what sort of a queen she might make when she came to her womanhood; she could feel their distrust in the reluctant touch of her waiting women's hands. It made her unhappy, but she was not surprised.

The country did well, or well enough, under her uncle; it did not perhaps quite prosper, as it had done in her parents' day, but it held its own. Her uncle was always fair with a terrible fairness in all his dealings, and the edge of cruelty in his fairness was so exact and subtle that no one could put a name to it. He was severe with the first man who dared question the health of the princess—too severe, with the same brilliant exactitude of his cruelty. Thus the tales of the princess's unfitness grew as swiftly as weeds in spring, while he sat silent, his hands tucked into his long white sleeves, and ruled the country, and gave the vague, pale princess the lessons she could not learn.

He might have been Regent forever, and the queen banished to a bleak country house while her spinsterhood withered to an early death. But it was not enough for him; he wanted the country well and truly in his own hands, not only in the name of the princess, his niece. She might have died mysteriously, for his scholarship included knowledge of several undetectable poisons. But that was not sufficient either, for there would be those who felt pity for the young princess, and a wistfulness that had she lived she might have outgrown the shadow of her childhood and become a good queen, for her parents had been much beloved. There might even have been a few—a very few—who wondered about the manner of her death, however undetectable the poison.

He pondered long upon it, as the princess grew toward her womanhood and the season of her name day celebration approached. He spent more time in his tower study, and when he emerged he looked grimmer even than was his wont, and muttered of portents. The people who heard him looked over their shoulders nervously, and soon everyone in the country was saying that there were more thunderstorms than usual this year. The Regent looked more haggard as the season progressed, for he was not a very good magician—he claimed that he knew no magic, and that magic was a false branch of the tree of wisdom; but the truth was that he was too proud and secret to put himself into a master mage's hands to learn the craft of it—and the thunderstorms wearied him. But his increasingly drawn and solemn appearance worked to his advantage also, for the people took it as a sign that he grew more anxious.

The princess also was anxious, for on her name day she should be declared queen. She knew she was not fit, and she watched the sky's anger and feared that it was, as her uncle declared, a portent, and that the portent warned against her becoming queen. A relief, almost, such would be, although she was enough her parents' daughter to be ashamed of the relief, as she had long been ashamed of her lack of queenly ability. She would have gone gladly to the bleak country house—a wish flickered through her mind that perhaps away from the strict, tense life of her uncle's court she might find one or two women who would stay with her longer than a few months—and left her uncle to rule.

Then the sightings began. Her uncle was sincerely shocked when the first countryman rushed into the royal hall to babble out his story—half a man, this thing was, half a beast. But no one had seen the Regent shocked before, and those who looked on believed that the tale only confirmed the worst of his fears. But the Regent knew, hidden deep inside himself, that he was a very poor magician, and the thing he truly feared was that in his rough calling-up of storm he had set something loose that he would not be able to control.

He withdrew to his high, bare room to brood. He had ordered another storm, and it had come willingly; but he was too shaken, now, to command it, and so it loitered uncertainly on the horizon and began to break up into wandering, harmless clouds. He did not know what to do. All that night the people saw the light in his room, and told each other the story the countryman had brought—that the thing had been seen more than once; that the farmers for fear of it would not go alone to their fields—and trembled. With a wildness born of panic, at dawn the Regent collected the scattered clouds and gave the land such a storm as it had never seen; and he descended to the great public hall again, pale but composed, his hands tucked into his sleeves, while the thunder crashed and the lightning ripped outside.

That day two more messengers came, despite the storm, with stories of sightings in two more villages; that the creature was not even half a beast, but a monster, and huge; that the women and children were afraid to leave their houses even in daylight. And these villages were not so distant as was the first man's.

Even the princess heard the rumors, although she was not told what precisely the sightings were of; perhaps the women did not know either. But she understood that the sightings were of some evil thing, and that her people shrank from her the more for them. She dismissed her women, trying not to notice the relief in their faces, asking only that her meals be sent up to her private room. Even her last claim upon the royal economy was poorly delegated, and occasionally she missed a meal when no one remembered to bring her her tray; but someone remembered often enough, and she needed little food.

One day the door of her room opened, and she looked around in surprise, for she had been utterly alone for so long. Her uncle stood upon the threshold and frowned, but she was accustomed to his frowns, and saw nothing unusual.

"It is your name day," he said.

She started. "I had forgotten."

"Nonetheless, there is a . . . ritual . . . that must be performed. A ritual of . . . purification, most suitable for this day that you should have come into your queenship."

She thought she understood him, and she bowed her head; but for all the years of her uncle's domination she had a brave heart still, and it shrank with sorrow. "So be it," she whispered. When she raised her head again she saw there were people with him; and a woman she did not recognize laid a white robe at the foot of her bed, and stepped behind the Regent again at once, as though his shadow were a protection.

"Dress yourself," said her uncle, and he and his attendants left her.

Four of the royal guard escorted her punctiliously to the great hall where her uncle was; and with him waited many other people, and she shrank from their eyes and their set, grim faces. Almost she turned and ran back to her empty room; but she was her parents' daughter, and she clenched her fingers into fists beneath the too long sleeves, and stepped forward. Her uncle spoke no word to her, but turned to the doors that led outside; and she followed after him, her eyes fixed on the back of his white gown, that she did not have to look at all the people around her. But she heard the rustle as they followed behind.

The Regent led them out of the city, and the crowd that accompanied them grew ever greater, but none spoke. The princess kept her fists clenched at first; but she had eaten so little, and been in her small room so long, that she soon grew weary, and no longer cared for the people who followed. But her pride kept her eyes on her uncle's back, and kept her feet from stumbling. On they went, and farther on, and the sun, which had been high when they set out, sank toward twilight.

The sun was no more than a red edge on a slate grey sky when they stopped at last. It was a clear night, and one or two stars were out. Her uncle turned to face his niece and the people. "Here is the place," he said. "The place shown me in my dream, as what is to be done here was shown me." He dropped his eyes to his niece and said, "Come."

The princess followed numbly. They were in the hills beyond the city, beyond the place where her parents and their parents were buried. Beyond these hills were the farmlands that were her country's major wealth, but just here they were in wild woodland. There was a small hollow in the gentle rise of the hills, and within the hollow were standing stones that led to a black hole in one hillside; and suddenly she knew where she was, and her exhaustion left her all at once, for the terror drove it out. "No," she whispered, and put her hands to her face, and bit down on the cuff of one sleeve.

Her whisper was barely audible, but her uncle wheeled round. "I beg you," she whispered through her fingers.

"I do only what is necessary—what I was ordered to do," her uncle said, loudly, that the crowd might hear; but his voice was not low and harsh, but thin and shrill.

Desperately she turned round and stared at her people. There was light yet enough to see their faces palely looking back at her. They watched, mute and grim and expressionless. She dropped her hands and turned back to follow her uncle; oblivion seized her mind. The crowd waited at the edge of the hollow; six courtiers only followed the Regent and his niece, and at the mouth of the tunnel these courtiers paused to kindle the torches they carried. Then they entered the dark hole in the hillside.

When they reached the end of the short tunnel the princess stopped and stared dully at the chain pegged into the rock wall; the links were rusty with disuse, for her great-grandfather had ended the sacrifices which had once been a part of the twice-yearly Festival. The only sacrifices for generations had been the sheaf of corn burnt at every threshold for the winter solstice. Dully she turned her back to the low, rough wall and leaned against it, and raised her arms, the huge sleeves belling out around her like wings, that her uncle might the easier fasten the chains to her wrists. How long? she wondered, and did not know. In the old days, she had read, the priests killed the victim when he or she was chained, that he might not truly suffer the agonies of thirst and starvation; and then left him there for the seven days tradition said it would have taken him to die. When the waiting was done they took the body away and buried it honorably. She thought, wearily, that she doubted her uncle would have the mercy of the old priests.

One torch they left her; one of the courtiers tipped it against the wall, where it trailed soot up to the ceiling; then the seven of them turned and left her, never looking back, as she, wide-eyed, watched them go, and listened to the echo of their footsteps fading into silence, into the grass under the sky beyond the stony cavern in the hill.

Then she broke, and screamed, again and again, till her voice tore in her throat; and she hurled herself at the ends of the chains till her wrists were cut and bleeding; but still she pulled at her fetters and sobbed, and clawed backwards at the indifferent wall, and kicked it with her soft slippered feet. Then she sank to her knees—her chains were too short to permit her to sit down—and turned her cheek against the rock, and knew no more for a time.

The ache in her shoulders and wrists woke her. The torch had nearly burnt itself out, and what light there was was dim and red and full of shadows. She sighed and stood up, and leaned against the wall again. She closed her eyes. Almost she could imagine that she heard the hill's heartbeat: a soft thud, thud. Thud.

Her eyes flew open. I am no Festival offering, she thought. I've been left for the monster—the monster has come for my name day. That is why I am here. A ritual of purification—if it is my fault the thing came then perhaps I do belong to it—gods, I can't bear it, and she bit down a scream. Thud. Thud. Please make it hurry. She gave a last horrible, hopeless jerk at her chains, but her mind was too clear for this now, and the pain stopped her at once. The torch flickered and burnt lower yet, and for a moment she did not recognize the antler shadows from the other shadows on the low, smoky wall. Then she saw his great head with the wide man's shoulders beneath it, the stag pelt furring him down to his chest. But it was a man's body, naked and huge, and a man's huge hands; and panic seized her and she screamed again, though her voice was gone and the noise was only a hoarse gasp. But the stag head's brown eyes saw the cords that stood out on her neck, and saw the terror that pressed her against the wall. He had taken soft, slow steps thus far, but now he hurried, and his huge hands reached out for her. She had just the presence of mind to be able to close her eyes, though she could not avoid the warm animal smell of him; and she felt his hands close around her bleeding wrists, and she fainted.

She came to herself lying stretched out on the ground. She was not sprawled, as though she had fallen, but rested peacefully on her back, her poor sore wrists laid across her stomach. She blinked; she had not been unconscious long, for the torch still burnt, guttering, and by its light she saw an immense shadow looming over her, that of a stag, with antlers so wide he must turn his head with care in the narrow tunnel. She raised herself to her elbows, wincing at her shoulders' protest. Surely . . . ? The stag looked gravely down at her. She sat up the rest of the way, and gingerly touched one wrist with a finger. The stag stepped forward and lowered his nose between her hands; his eyes were so dark she could not see into them, and his breath smelled of sweet grass. "Yes, they are sore," she said to him stupidly, and he raised his great head again, the heavy, graceful neck proudly balancing his crown. How did I . . . ? Did I imagine . . . ? She looked at the wall. The chains had been pulled clear out of the wall, their staples bowed into broken-backed arches; they lay on the floor near her, flakes of rust mixing with smears of fresh blood.

The stag dropped his nose again, and touched her shoulder as gently as a snowflake landing, or a mare greeting a new foal. She stood up as shakily as any foal; her head swam. Then she took an eager step forward, toward the other end of the tunnel, toward the grass and the sky—but the stag stepped before her, and blocked her way. "But . . ." she said, and her eyes filled with the tears of final exhaustion, of desolation of spirit. The stag knelt before her. At first she did not understand, and would have stepped over and around him, but he was stubborn. She seated herself meekly on his back at last, and he rose up gently and walked out of the cave.

She shivered when the first breath of air from the hill touched her face, although it was a warm night. She looked up in wonder at the sky, and the stars twinkling there; she could not believe she had spent so little time in the tunnel, leaning against the rock wall, with her arms aching and her mind holding nothing but despair. She looked uncertainly back the way her uncle had led them, though she could not see far for the trees that ringed the small valley. But it seemed to her that the shadows under the trees were of more things than leaves and stones, and some of them were the shapes of human watchers; and it seemed to her too that a low murmur, as from human throats, rose and mixed with the gentle wind; but the murmur was a sound of dismay. The stag paused a moment a few steps beyond the cave's threshold, and turned his fine head toward the murmur, toward the path to the city; then he turned away and entered the forest by a path only he could see.

They stopped at dawn, and he knelt for her to dismount; she stretched her sore limbs with a sigh, and sat stiffly down. The next thing she knew it was twilight again, the sun setting, and a small fire burnt near her, and beside that lay a heap of fruit. There were several small apples, and sweet green gurnies, which must have come from someone's orchard, for the gurny tree did not grow wild so far north. She did not care where they had come from, though, and she ate them hungrily, and the handful of kok-nuts with them. She recognized the sound of a stream nearby, and went toward it, and was glad of a drink and a wash, though she hissed with pain as she rubbed the caked scabs on her wrists. When she returned to the little fire the great stag was standing beside it. He stamped the fire out with his forefeet and came to her and knelt, and she trustfully and almost cheerfully climbed onto his back.

They travelled thus for three nights. Each evening she awoke to a fire and to a small offering of fruit and nuts; but she had never eaten much, and it was plenty to sustain her. Even though she did not know it, her eyes grew brighter, and a little color crept back to her pale face; but only the stag saw, and he never spoke. On the third morning, though she lay down as she had done before, she did not sleep well, and once or twice she half awoke. The second

time she felt a flickering light against her closed eyelids, and
sleepily she opened them a little. A huge man knelt beside
a small fire, setting down a small pile of fruit beside it, and
then prodding it with a stick to make it burn up more
brightly. He stood up beside it then and held his hands out
as if to warm them. He was naked, though his heavy hair
fell past his shoulders, and his thick beard mixed with the
mat of hair on his chest and down his belly. His hair was a
deep red brown, like the color of a deer's flank, and the
bare skin beyond was much the same color. If this were not
enough to know him by, the antlers that rose from his
human head would have reassured her. She closed her
eyes again and drifted peacefully back to sleep; and when
she awoke at twilight, the stag lay curled up with his legs
folded neatly under him and the tip of his nose just resting
on the ground.

That night they climbed a hill face so steep that she had
to cling to his antlers to prevent herself from sliding backwards; the incline did not seem to distress him, although
she could feel the deep heave of his breathing between her
knees. About midnight they came to a level place, and she
saw that a vast lake stretched to their right, and the moon
shone silver upon its untroubled surface. She could not see
its farther shore; the silver faded to blackness beyond the
edge of her eyesight. The stag stood for a few moments till
his breathing calmed, and then took a path that led them
away from the lake, through more trees, and then to a
broad field that smelled sweetly of grass and sleeping
cattle; and then into more trees. But something now twin-
kled at them from beyond the trees; something too low
and golden for a star. Her heart sank. She had thought as
little as she might for the past four nights; she knew irresist-
ibly that she must be being carried to somewhere; but she
was sorry that the somewhere was so close. She reached
out and grasped a silky-smooth horn. "Stop," she said.
"Please."

He stopped and turned his head a little that he might roll
one brown eye back at her. She slipped off his back and

stood hesitating. Then she laid a hand on his shoulder and said, "Very well." He stepped forward and she kept pace at his side.

The golden twinkle resolved itself into a ring of torches set on slender columns in a semicircle around a small, bare courtyard before a great stone hall. The stag walked without pause up the low steps to the door, a door high and wide enough even for his branching crown. Still she kept pace; and before her was a vast chamber, dimly lit by a fire in a hearth at its far end. There were several tall chairs before the fire, and from the shadows of one of them a tall narrow man with pale hair stood up and came toward them. "Welcome, child," he said to her; and to him, "Thank you."

She did not care for the big hall; it was too large and too empty, and the shadows fell strangely from its corners; and the last roof she had stood under had also been of stone— she shuddered. She would not pass these doors. The man saw the shudder and said gently, "It's all over now. You're quite safe." She looked up at him—he was very tall—and wanted to say, How do you know? But if she asked one question a hundred would follow, and she was tired, and lonely, and had been trained never to ask questions.

She did not remember if it was the stag or the tall man who showed her to the long narrow room with the row of empty beds in it; she woke up burrowed in blankets in the bed nearest the door, with sunlight—late morning sunlight, she estimated, blinking—flaming through the row of windows high above her head.

Her sleeping hall, she discovered, was built out from one wall of the great central chamber she had peered into the night before. The tall man sat on the front steps she had climbed, her hand on the stag's shoulder, the night before; his long hands dangled idly between his bent knees. He looked up at her as she stepped from the sleeping hall; his hair blazed as yellow as corn in the sunlight. He wore a plain brown tunic over pale leggings and soft boots; and around his neck on a thong was a red stone. She turned away from him; around her on three sides were trees, and on the fourth side, the great grey hall; overhead the sky was a clear, hard blue. She lowered her eyes, finally, and met the man's gaze; he smiled at her.

"I am Luthe," he said.

She did not answer immediately. "I am Ruen. But you know that, or I would not be here." Her voice—she could not help it—had a sharp, mistrustful edge to it.

Luthe spread his fingers and looked down at them. "That is not precisely true. I did not know your name till now, when you told it to me. Your . . . difficulties . . . were brought to my attention recently, and it is true that I asked, um, a friend if he would help you out of them. And I asked him to bring you here."

"A friend," she said, the edge to her voice gone. She closed her eyes a moment, but there was little she cared to remember and she opened them again, and tried to smile. "It is pleasanter to thank you—and him—without thinking about what, and how much, I have to be grateful to you for." She paused. "I would like to declare, here, today, that I have no past. But then I have no future either. Have you a use for me?"

"Yes," said Luthe.

"I suppose you will now tell me that I may not forsake my past so? Well. I am not surprised. I never learned so much as . . . my uncle wished to teach me, but I did learn a little."

"You learned far more than he wished you to," Luthe said grimly. "Had you cooperated to the extent of idiocy, as would have pleased him best, he would not have had to disturb the weather for half the world to invent portents for his insignificant corner of it."

She smiled involuntarily. She had never heard anyone speak with less than complete respect of the Regent; and these few words from this strange man reduced her uncle to nothing more than a nuisance, a bothersome thing to be dealt with; and suddenly her past was not the doom of her future. "That awful weather was *his* . . . ?" She sobered. "But I am still a poor excuse for a queen, even if he is not a—an entirely honorable Regent."

Luthe laughed. "You are wrong, my child. Only a real queen could call that poison-worm only 'not entirely honorable.' The defects in your education can be mended." He stood up, and bowed. "Which is the first item on our agenda. We will do our poor best to look after certain historical and philosophical aspects. . . ." He paused, for she was looking at him uneasily.

"Truly I am not good at lessons," she said.

"You wouldn't know," Luthe said cheerfully. "You've never had any. With me you will have real lessons. And your . . . um . . . lesson in practical application will be along presently."

"Will I—may I—see my . . . the stag again?"

"Yes," said Luthe. "He will return. Come along now."

She sighed, but the custom of obeying orders was strong.

She had no way of knowing it, but visitors to Luthe's mountain often found themselves a little vague about the passing of the days. There was something about the air that was both clearer and fuzzier than the air she was accustomed to; she slept heavily and dreamlessly and woke up feeling happy. She learned a great deal in a very short time, and was astonished to discover she could.

"Do stop giving me that fish-eyed look," Luthe said irritably; "I'm not magicking anything over on you. You have a perfectly good brain, once you are permitted to use it. Your uncle's absence provides permission. Now pay attention and don't brood."

One morning Luthe announced, "No lessons today. I anticipate visitors." She looked up in alarm. She had seen no one but Luthe since the stag had brought her here; and she knew at once that the visitors would have something to do with her future. She tried not to be dismayed, but she

was still enjoying the novelty of enjoying anything, and
dreaded interruption; the habit of pessimism was not easily
shaken, even by Luthe's teaching.

Soon she heard the sound of . . . something . . .
making its way through the trees around the courtyard
where they sat. Just before she saw the great stag separate
himself from the shadows of the trees Luthe stood up. The
stag's footfalls were soft; the noise was made by someone
who staggered along beside him, one arm over his neck.
This man wore tattered leggings under a long white tunic,
now torn and dirty, the left side matted brown and adher-
ing to his side. The stag stopped just inside the ring of trees.
"Oof," said the man, and fell to the ground.

"You needn't have half killed him," Luthe said. "You
might also have carried him here."

The stag looked at Luthe, who shrugged. "Perhaps.
Perhaps not. Well, he is here, which is what matters."

Ruen stared at the stag, who turned his head to return
her gaze; but if he said anything to her, she did not hear it.

"*Ruen*," Luthe said, and she realized by his tone that he
had repeated her name several times.

"I ask pardon," she said, and snapped her eyes away
from the stag's.

Luthe looked at her and smiled faintly. "Here is the
practical lesson I promised you."

She blinked, and glanced down at the man on the
ground. He stirred and moaned; the moan had words in it.
She knelt beside him, and his eyes flickered open, saw her,
tried to focus on her. "Ugh?" he muttered. "Uh. Oh." His
eyes closed again.

"I suggest you get him to the nearest bed in the nearest
sleeping hall," Luthe said briskly, "and I will join you in a
little time and tell you what to do next."

The man on the ground was a lot bigger than she was,
but she lifted one of his arms to drag it around her shoulders. He feebly tried to help, and she managed to get him
to his feet. "Sorry," he muttered in her ear. "Not feeling
quite . . . well."

They stumbled the few steps to the nearer of the two long sleeping rooms, and she hauled him up the few steps to the doorway, and tried to lower him gently onto the first bed; but his weight was too much for her, and he fell with a grunt. Luthe arrived then, and handed her warm water in a basin, and herbs and ointment, and long cloths for bandages, and a knife to cut away the stained tunic. She'd never dressed a wound before, but her hands were steady, and Luthe's patient voice told her exactly what to do, although he did not touch the man himself. The wound, or wounds, were curious; there were two neat round holes in the man's side, one of them deep and the second, a hand's-length distant, little more than a nick in the skin. She stared at them as she bathed the man's side; they might have been made by a blow from a huge stag's antlers.

When she had done all she could to Luthe's satisfaction and could at last leave the man's bedside, the stag was nowhere to be found.

She slept in the bed next to his that night, with a fat candle burning on a little table between them, but he slept peacefully, and when she rose at dawn and blew the candle out she stood looking down on the man's quiet face, and noticed that he was handsome.

Later that morning he awoke and, when he discovered her sitting beside him, said, "I'm hungry." When she brought him food, he had pulled himself nearly to a sitting position against the bedhead, but his face said that it had not been a pleasant effort; and he let her feed him without protest.

On the second day he asked her name. She was tending his side and she said, "Ruen," without looking up.

On the third day he said, "My name's Gelther." She smiled politely and said, "My honor is in your acquaintance."

He looked at her thoughtfully. "Where I come from we say, 'My honor is yours.' You must be from the south. And you must be of high blood or you wouldn't be talking of honor at all."

"Very well. I am from the south, and I am of high blood. Both these things I would have told you, had you asked."

He looked embarrassed. "I apologize, lady. It's a habit, I believe. I've been told before that I'm better at doing things than I am at making conversation. Although I'm not sure if talking to the lady who binds your wounds and feeds you with a spoon when you're too weak to sit up is making conversation." She said nothing, and after a moment he went on, "The only Ruen I know of is a princess who disappeared mysteriously a few months ago. . . . I'm doing it again, aren't I?"

She nodded, but asked with a careful casualness, "What kind of mystery was she supposed to have disappeared in?"

She could see him considering what to tell her. "The tales vary. She was old enough to be declared queen, but she—there was something supposed to be wrong with her. This, um, ritual, might have cured it. . . ."

She laughed: the noise startled her, for she would not have thought that such a description of her uncle's perfidy would have struck her so. "I ask pardon. That ritual, had it been completed to expectation, would certainly have cured her."

Gelther eyed her. "They do say the rite went awry somehow. And we always did think there was something a little odd about the Regent."

"Yes." She frowned.

Gelther said, half-desperately, "*Are* you that Ruen?"

"Eh? Oh, yes—of course." Satisfaction and puzzlement chased each other across the young man's face. "But you heard that that Ruen had the mind of a child who could never grow up, which is why her name was not given her properly upon her name day, as a queen's should; but I seem quite normal?" Now embarrassment joined the puzzlement, and satisfaction disappeared. "I would not have grown up had I not been rescued and brought here. . . . But I almost wish I had not."

Gelther said, astonished: "Why ever not?"

She looked at his open, bewildered face. "Because I do not know what I must do. When I believed in my uncle and not in myself, I needed do nothing. I see that my uncle is not as I believed; but I am not accustomed to practical matters—to action—and I am afraid of him." She sighed. "I am terribly afraid of him."

"Well, of course you are," said Gelther stoutly. "I have heard—" He stopped, and smiled crookedly. "Never mind what I have heard. But perhaps I can help you. This is the sort of thing I'm good at—plotting and planning, you know, and then making a great deal of noise till things get done."

She looked at him wistfully and wished she could feel even a little of his enthusiasm for what such a task was likely to entail.

Gelther was walking, slowly and stiffly, but walking, in five days, and had his first independent bath in the bathhouse behind the stone hall on the sixth. Luthe was never around when Gelther was awake; Gelther had asked, on that fifth day, when he went outside the sleeping room for the first time and saw nothing around him but trees, "Are you alone here?" His tone of voice suggested barely repressed horror. "No, no, of course not," she responded soothingly. "But our host is, um, shy." She found the solitude so pleasant that she had to remind herself that not everyone might find it so.

But she did wonder at Luthe's continued elusiveness; she saw him herself every day, but always, somehow, just after Gelther had nodded into another convalescent nap. That fifth day, she taxed him with it. He replied placidly, "He's your practical lesson, not mine. We will meet eventually. Don't worry. You shan't have to explain my vagaries much longer."

She showed Gelther the way to the wide silver lake, and they walked there together. "Where is your country?" she asked, a little hesitantly, for fear that he might think she was taking a liberty.

He laughed. "I thought you were never going to ask me that," he said. "No—I'm not offended. I'm from Vuek, just north of your Arn—I meant only that I cannot understand how you have not asked before. I asked you at once—indirectly perhaps, but I did ask."

She nodded, smiling. "I remember. That is different, somehow. You were the one in bed, and I was the one standing on my feet. You needed to know."

He looked at her. "I always need to know."

They came to the lake, and found a log to lean against, and sat down, Gelther very carefully. Then she asked the question that she had wished and feared to ask since she first saw the wounds in his side. "How . . . how did you happen to come here?"

He frowned, staring off over the lake. "I'm not sure. I don't remember much of it. At home, I hunt a lot when there isn't anything else to do, and the tale was brought to me of a huge stag that had been sighted a way off, and I thought to track it. They said it had a rack of antlers the like of which had never been seen anywhere; and they knew I would be interested. I'm a good tracker, I would have found it anyway; but it was so damn easy to find you'd think it was waiting for me. . . ." His voice trailed off. "So, I found it, and it led me a fine dance, but my blood was up and I would have followed it across the world. And it turned on me. Deer don't, you know—at least not unless one is wounded to death, and cornered. And this great beast—I'd been following it for days by then, and we were both pretty weary, but I'd never gotten close enough to it to even try to put an arrow in it—and it turned on me." His voice was bewildered, and then reminiscent. "It did have antlers like nothing I've seen. It was a great chase. . . . I don't remember after that. I woke up—here—and there you were, the little lost princess from Arn." He smiled at her and it occurred to her that he was trying to be charming, so she smiled back. "Maybe I'm supposed to help you," he said.

It was her turn to look out over the lake. That, I suppose,

is what Luthe has had in mind all along, she thought, and suddenly felt tired.

The next morning Luthe presented himself to Gelther for the first time. "Prince," said Luthe, and bowed; and Gelther glanced sidelong at Ruen to make sure she regis tered the title before he bowed back. "Forgive my long delay in greeting you."

Gelther accepted the lack of explanation with what seemed to Ruen uncharacteristic docility; but after Luthe had left them, he said to her accusingly: "You didn't tell me he was a mage."

"I didn't know," said Ruen.

"Didn't . . . ? By the Just and Glorious, can't you read the mage mark?"

"No," she said, and he shook his head; and she thought that for the first time he understood the boundaries of her life with her uncle; it was as though she had said she had never seen the sky, or never drunk water.

Luthe said, at their next meeting, "I am glad to see you recovering so quickly from your hurt."

"I have had excellent care," said Gelther, and smiled at Ruen, who fidgeted. "And I thank you, sir, for your hospitality—"

"You are welcome to all that my house may afford you," Luthe interrupted smoothly. "And as soon as you are quite healed—for you are a little weak yet, I believe—I will set you on your way home again."

Prince Gelther, however forthright he might be to common mortals, had the sense to leave mages well enough alone, so he did not inquire how he happened to be here or where here was. Ruen could see these questions and others battering at each other behind his eyes, and she could guess that Luthe saw them too; but none escaped Gelther's lips, and Luthe offered nothing but a smile and a bright blue glint from half-shut eyes.

"Sir," said Gelther carefully. "I would ask—perhaps a great favor."

"Say it," said Luthe, with the careless generosity of a

great lord who may instantly retract if he chooses.

"I would beg leave to take the lady Ruen with me, for I believe that I might help her, and her country and her people, escape the heavy reign of the false Regent."

"An excellent plan," said Luthe. "I applaud and bless it."

Ruen sighed.

They set out a few days later, on foot, bearing a small, heavy bundle each, of food wrapped up in a thin blanket; it was nearing summer, and travel was easy. Luthe bid them farewell in the small court before his hall; he was at his most dignified with Gelther, although his words were cordial. But he set his hands on Ruen's shoulders and stared down at her with almost a frown on his face. "Gelther is a very able man," he said at last; "you and your country are fortunate to have gained him as an ally."

"Yes," Ruen said dutifully.

Luthe dropped his hands. "You were *born* to be queen," he said plaintively. "There is a limit to the miracles even I can produce."

"Yes," repeated Ruen. "I thank you for all you have done."

"Ah, hell," said Luthe.

Gelther and Ruen went downhill all that day, and the trees were so tall and thick they could not see the sun but in occasional flashes, useless to give them a sense of direction; but Luthe had told them to go downhill, and that they would not lose themselves, and Luthe was a mage, so they did as he said. They went downhill the second day as well, sliding on the steep bits and holding on to convenient branches; and in the afternoon the trees grew thin and the slope eased, and Gelther said, "I know where we are!" and strode off purposefully. Ruen followed.

She did not know what she was expecting from Vuek, or from Gelther's family; but they greeted her with pleasure—almost with relief, she thought, for Gelther was a third son, and it was obvious, although perhaps not to

Gelther himself, that his father, mother, and eldest brother had begun to wonder how much longer their small kingdom could contain him. Everyone believed her story at once; or if any had doubts, they were swiftly set aside, for several aristocratic Arnish families, tiring of the Regent's inelegance if not his tyranny, had emigrated to Vuek, and the manner in which her subjects-in-exile greeted Ruen left no room for question. There was even one woman among these who had borne brief service as the young princess's waiting maid; and if Ruen felt that the woman's eagerness to prove her loyalty now was a little overemphatic, she did not say so aloud.

Soon Gelther, and a few of the Arnish men, were out rousing the countryside; and sooner than it took Ruen to wonder what the next step should be, there was an army, forming up for drill in the fields surrounding Vuek's capital city.

A week before they were due to march to Arn, Gelther and Ruen were married. Gelther's mother planned and arranged it; Ruen stood quietly where she was put while gowns were pinned on her and shoes cut and fitted, and hairdressers tried for the style best suited to her small solemn face. When the day came, Gelther took a few hours off from enthusiastic drilling to stand at Ruen's side while the priests muttered over them and the girls of the royal family threw flowers over them, and all the aristocracy available from Vuek and Arn and the other small kingdoms and duchies who were providing soldiers for Gelther's army made obeisances at them; and then he rushed back to his military maneuvers. Ruen retired to a handsome, well-furnished room that her new mother had set aside for her; for she was to have no part in the restoration of her throne.

Gelther was preoccupied on their wedding night, but then so was Ruen.

But Arn was taken without a sword's being drawn. Vuek had a common border with Arn, if a short one, and Gelther's soldiers marched directly to the Regent's palace; they saw few farmers in the fields, and those they saw avoided them; the streets of the city were empty, and when they reached the palace itself the few guards they found were sitting or wandering dazedly, and when ordered to lay down their weapons they did so without demur. Gelther and his captains strode through the front doors without any to say them nay; and when they reached the great hall where the throne stood, and where the Regent was accustomed to meet those who would speak with him, it was empty but for a few courtiers. These courtiers only turned to look at the invaders.

One shook himself free of the vagueness that held everyone else; and he came toward them, and bowed low. He wore no sword or knife. He said to Gelther, who was obviously the leader, "You will be Prince Gelther, husband of our beloved queen, whom we look forward to welcoming soon, when she returns to her land and her people. We wept when she left us, and turned our faces from the Regent, and have hoped upon each dawning that it heralded the day she would come back to us."

Gelther exchanged looks with his captains, and all grasped their sword hilts in expectation of a trap. But there was no trap.

The Regent's body they found, as the courtiers had found it two days before, bowed over a long table in the high tower room where he had called the storms and watched for portents. His lips were writhed back over his teeth in a grimace, but it appeared to be a grimace of anger; he did not look as though he had died in pain, and there was no mark on him. His captains shivered, but Gelther said, "The man is dead, and he was Regent, and my wife's uncle; and that is all we need now remember. The people have declared that they wish to welcome us; so let us allow ourselves to be welcome." They buried the Regent with restrained pomp and the respect that might have been due a queen's uncle who had stood by her and cared for her when her parents died while she was yet too young to rule herself. Gelther, who knew much more about the Regent than he would ever have admitted to his wife, would let no man say a word against him. None ever knew if he had died naturally, or been slain, by his own hand, or another's; perhaps even by a portent he had wrongly tried to call up.

Her people did indeed honor their queen when she returned to them; they could not leap quickly enough to do her bidding, smile quickly enough when her eye fell upon them, clamor loudly enough to serve her, spread quickly enough the tales of her evenhanded justice, of her kindness to the weak and patience with the confused. But their hearts were perhaps particularly captured by the prince, who was loud and strong and merry—it was noticed that the queen never laughed—and who refused to be crowned king in deference to his wife, who, he said, "is the real thing." And of course the people of Arn had seen Gelther only in triumph, and the fact that the queen did not find anything in her native land to rouse her to laughter perhaps stirred memories they wished to forget.

Gelther also made Arn's army the finest in the whole of the Damarian continent, and all the countries near Arn were very careful to stay on the most cordial terms with it; and the Arnish families' greatest pride was to have a son or two or three in the prince's army. A goodly number of the young men who flocked to carry the Arnish prince's banner came from other countries, for tales of the prince's greatness travelled far.

Ruen bore four children, all sons; and she was kind and loving to them, and they responded with kindness and love. But, although there was perhaps no one to notice, her maternal kindness was little more exacting than the kindness she gave the least of her subjects who pleaded for her aid. But perhaps it was only that she had so little in common with her children; for while her sons treated her always with respect, they thought of nothing but the army once they were old enough to be propped up on their first ponies.

The people did notice that the queen seemed most at

ease with folk young enough not to remember the days of the Regent's rule; but her people chose to tell each other that many women are happiest in the company of those they may pretend are their children, and such a one was their queen. It had been only a very short time after Gelther accepted the Arnish welcome in the queen's name that all her subjects were eager to tell her that they had forgotten the Regent entirely—and the longer anyone had lived under him, the more eager he was to proclaim his complete lack of memory—if she had asked; but she never asked.

Her youngest son was eleven years old and would soon outgrow his third pony the morning that her eldest burst in on his parents' quiet breakfast. "Father! We go hunting today! There are sightings of a great stag—as large as the one that gored you when you met Mother—to the northwest. *Several* sightings. He's been showing himself to different villages but everyone's been afraid to mention it—seems they think he's half man or something, and an ill portent—some nonsense about something my stupid great-uncle did. You'd think they'd have forgotten by now."

"No." It was so unusual for the queen to say anything when the conversation turned to hunting that both Gelther and their son gaped at her.

Gelther swallowed. "No . . . er . . . what?"

"No, you will not hunt this stag. I insist." She opened her wide eyes wider and fixed them on her handsome husband. "You shall *not* go."

It was a struggle for Gelther, for he loved hunting best of anything when there were no wars to be fought; but he was fond of his wife, and she had never asked him such a thing before. Indeed she asked him little enough at any time—and, well, she was a woman, and the Regent had been very queer to her for many years, and it was perhaps understandable that she should be a little, well, superstitious about something that reminded her so suddenly of the bad old days. She'd been the one who'd patched him up then too; it had probably been worse for her. And the villagers were probably exaggerating the beast's size anyway. "Very well," he said, a little wistfully.

She smiled at him, and there was such love in her eyes that he smiled back, thinking, I could not have had a better wife; four sons she's given me. Then he rose from the table and slapped his eldest on the shoulder and said, "So, my son, we must find our amusement elsewhere; have you tried the new colt I bought at the Ersk fair? I think he'll just suit you."

Two days later the queen walked out of the palace in the early afternoon, alone. She often did; she liked to visit the tomb of her parents on the hill beyond the city by herself; and her waiting women and royal guards, who would rather have made a parade out of it, had grown accustomed the queen's small eccentricity, and no longer thought anything of it. But this time she did not return. A great hue and cry went up, in Arn and in Vuek and everywhere that messengers could go, from the mountains east, north, and west, even beyond the desert in the south to the great sea; but she was never seen again by anyone who brought word back to her mourning husband and country.

The villagers who had been frightened by the reappearance of the great stagman, as they had first seen him twenty years ago, were relieved when he disappeared again; and since news travelled slowly and erratically to them, none noticed that the stagman vanished for the second and final time two days after the Arnish queen walked out of her palace and did not return.

Harvest Child

Steve Rasnic Tem

Two months ago I was doing volunteer work at a refugee camp in Somalia. I've done quite a bit of that—going where lives were so bleak, so devastated, no one but a handful could stand to witness it—since I retired from the army. Lieutenant colonel. World War II, Korea, Viet Nam. I suppose if I'd paid more attention to soldiering and less to sight-seeing disaster areas I'd have done much better than lieutenant colonel. But I stumbled across a harvest child in each of those places. The last one in Somalia.

I had just gotten off the phone with the United Nations people again. Trying to get food, seeds, anything we needed. We were getting practically nothing; the U.N. had really dropped the ball on that one. None of the refugees had received food rations in two days, and we had no idea when the next truck would arrive. The starving were lying in huts made of thornbush branches, animal skins, and rotten pieces of cloth. No blankets, and only two small hand-dug wells to provide water for 76,000 people. We soon discovered that the two wells were contaminated.

The mothers' breasts were no longer giving milk. The children's bellies were swollen, their eyes more vacant than the worst cases of shellshock I witnessed in my military years. So many unable even to cry, the encroaching starvation a slow, silent death.

The Somalis have an age-old tradition of caring for kinspeople; they will take any number of refugees in, despite the devastating cost to themselves. It was frustrating, watching the armies of starving continue to pour into land already virtually depleted of resources. I understood why the Somalis were doing it, perhaps more than most; my own people back in the Midwest would have done much the same. But that made it all the more painful for me.

There wouldn't be a harvest that year; I had thought about that a great deal the past few days. A terrible drought, almost no rain in nearly five years. Overgrazing, indiscriminate cutting of trees, intertribal war, wind and water erosion: it all aided the desert as it slowly took over more and more of the crop and grazing land. I had seen it happen before; the burning dust brought with it an indescribable chill.

I was walking toward a new group of arrivals, mostly old men and women, when she stepped out of the crowd: dark liquid eyes, glistening hair, mouth and cheeks that added up to the look which promised so much: green crops in the ground, flowing streams, corn, barley, wheat. A harvest child. She brought me back to the Kansas of my childhood—1934; I was nine years old. And just for a moment she brought back the dust storms that seemed a mile high, that swallowed the horizon and turned the sun rust-colored at noon, that made you afraid you'd be buried in your sleep. So you woke up every few hours from nightmares of suffocation, bothering your mother too many times with it. But one night when you awakened it had grown still outside, the wind gone off somewhere. Everyone else asleep. That was the night she came.

We'd spent most of the day indoors. In my daddy's house, the house my daddy and grandpa built with their own hands, when grandpa was still alive. Straightening nails and wiring up the rafters with bailing wire. A real roughshod affair; I can still remember the lopsided corners and the way the boards met off-angle in places, as if the wind had thrown them there and by some natural process they'd just grown together. I loved that house, even back then. It showed where my daddy's hands had been. My daddy who couldn't touch me, hold me, any of us really, or say more than an occasional kind word.

You couldn't even see to the edge of the front yard for the blinding dust. One of my uncles was due to come in that day but we really didn't expect him; we'd heard they were having to plow several feet of dust drift off the roads to clear them. We'd had to wear goggles over our eyes and handkerchiefs over our mouths and noses the past few days to walk outside at all. Even then the mucus in your nose dried out so bad it formed a rock-hard crust that burned your skin. When you could smell the dust it smelled burnt. "Hell," my daddy would say, and we all knew he meant that was where we were. It didn't seem much like we were in Kansas anymore.

That day had been especially bad, I remember. The wind howled like some big thing lost out there in the dust. Cornstalks hit the side of the house like bones. I'll never forget the way the corn had died: brown spreading from the tips down a dead vein in the center of each leaf, spreading 'til it bronzed the plant completely, the dry stalks leaning in the direction of the wind. When the winds started picking up topsoil they took the corn with it.

The dust seemed more persistent in getting into the house this time. Mama was frantic. Usually you could keep most of it out by stuffing sheets and rags against the door frame and the windowsill. Even then a little bit of it would slip in and gradually build up in the air, so that a fine layer covered all the furniture and you were always having to brush it off your clothes. Mama had to keep a cloth over the food. But this night the wind blew the rags out of the cracks and chinks and the dust just poured through. Mama ran around crying, trying to stuff the rags back in. Daddy made us put our handkerchiefs up over our faces, said it wasn't healthy to breathe that air.

Things calmed down some after supper. And Grandma told us another one of her stories before bed. Mama didn't approve of her tales, because Grandma believed things a good Christian woman just did not believe. She'd listen to anybody's tales and repeat half of 'em, Mama always said to my daddy. But Grandma was my daddy's mama, so Mama never could say too much. When Grandma was telling her stories my mama would just sit in her rocker and knit. And frown.

"Won't be a harvest this year, I'm afeared," Grandma was saying. "Guess it'll be a good time for the good Lord to give somebody a harvest child."

"What's a harvest child?" I asked my grandma. I didn't say too much back then, usually. I guess that's why Grandma looked up at me a little surprised.

"Why that's a gift, youngun, usually a girl. She'd be a sister for you boys." My brother Jack made a face and she laughed. "The Lord—or whatever does sech things—" She looked at my mama quickly. Mama just frowned some more and kept rocking. "He gives it to you, to make up for the lost harvest, and just maybe to help bring the harvest back to you someday, all things willing."

"Some gift!" my daddy said. "Just givin' you 'nother mouth to feed."

After we went to bed I thought about that a long time. I'd always wanted a sister, and I knew Jack did, too, although we were both too embarrassed to admit it. There had always seemed something missing in the house, something out of whack. I always figured that somehow a sister would put things right again. Not somebody to take care of, really, but a special friend. Somebody to talk to in a way you couldn't talk to your daddy or your brother or other male kin, even your mother, I guess. I just knew things would be better with a sister around.

When I woke up I stared all around the little house. I couldn't figure what had disturbed me. Everybody else was asleep. And so still—I suddenly realized the wind had stopped blowing. No more whistling, or shaking. And the way the windows glowed, all silver, I could tell that the moon had come out from behind the giant dust clouds.

But then there was a tapping, and I nearly jumped out of bed. I listened hard. Maybe it had just been a tumbleweed blowing against the door. But there it was again, and I knew this time it had to be a knock.

I got up out of bed and padded to the front door, trying not to wake up anybody else. I turned the knob and pulled, just a little bit.

Her face and shoulders were dark, shadowed, as if they were covered with the brown dust. But her hair . . . golden, like it was glowing on its own, moving on its own like the way the wheat heads seemed to sometimes even when there wasn't any wind. The color was like wheat heads, too, I realized, so gold and full and ripe, just before harvest time.

My grandma was suddenly there beside me, pulling the little girl in. That's what she was, I could see as she passed me so quietly. About eleven years old, same age as Jack.

Soon the whole household was up and surrounding her, wondering who she was and where she'd come from. But she couldn't seem to remember any of that. My mama took to her, and held her, but it was hard to tell if that was helping any. "Poor baby," my mama kept crooning. "Lost out in the storm."

My grandma stood back and looked at her. "Harvest child . . ." she whispered.

Mama looked up at her sharply and no one else said a word. Then we all gathered around the newcomer again, just looking at her. Daddy scratched his head, it seemed like the whole time.

After a while I caught sight of my grandma standing by the window, looking out. I went over to her. She was rubbing her hands, making them look raw.

"What's the matter, Grandma?" I said.

She looked down at me a little funny. Then she tried to smile, but not doing it too well. "A harvest child means many things, child. Most of 'em good." She gripped my shoulder. "But sometimes that means there's a lot more bad got to come first."

She didn't know her name, so we called her Amanda. That was Daddy's youngest sister who died of the croup when he was just a boy. Mama looked at him funny when he came up with the name; that was an unusual thing for him to do, taking that kind of interest. I guess it surprised us all.

There was a time at first, the first month I guess, when Amanda kept pretty much to herself, staying close to Mama and keeping out of the way of the rest of us. Not that she was afraid; more like she was shy. Except with my grandma. I do think she was a little afraid of my grandma. I'm not sure why, but she was even quieter than usual when Grandma was around, keeping behind Mama's skirts and staring at the old woman like a cautious little animal. Of course, that made things even worse between Mama and Grandma. Mama seemed sure that Grandma meant our new sister harm, although even she didn't know why. I never thought that about Grandma. It seemed to me she was just a little nervous about Amanda, as if she didn't know what was going to happen because of Amanda, and that scared her.

That changed a little. Amanda started bringing Grandma fresh-picked flowers, putting them in a vase by her bed, and making such a smile as I've never seen. Even Grandma, for all her nervousness around the child, had to laugh when she saw that smile. Funny thing was, none of us had seen blooming flowers under that dust for some time. We couldn't figure out where she was finding them.

After a while, though, Amanda started acting just like any other little girl her age, laughing and playing with dolls and chasing the hens and chattering away the whole time about all kinds of nonsense. It was hard to believe she hadn't always been with us. She even had fights with my brother Jack like most sisters and brothers do. Catcalling and crying and both of them running to Mama, who just shooed them out the door again.

I couldn't tell any difference at first between her and any other girl. Except that she was my friend.

First time I knew that was when she took the blame for something I'd done. Daddy used to take the things his boys did pretty seriously, with very little humor. He really expected us to be men. With times so hard he seemed to think that was necessary; there just wasn't enough easy time to indulge a childhood. He expected us to grow up fast. "Only way you boys are gonna survive is to be men jes' quick as you can," is the way he used to say it, but not looking at us. That's how we knew something was bothering him; he'd always looked at us.

I'd been playing around the root cellar. I knew I wasn't supposed to be there, but I liked it so much down there—it was so dark, and cooler than anywhere else around. You

could pretend it was a cave, or an Egyptian tomb. I day-
dreamed a lot down in that old cellar. It was harder to
daydream out in the open air; everything was so flat, it
used to seem that your daydreams and fancies had nothing to hold on to. The wind just picked them up and blew
them away, left them crumpled on the ground, covered
with a fine layer of dust.

I'd found a sack with a few potatoes in it. Dried out a
little, but not too bad. The eyes were already long as little
garden snakes; I figured Mama had just forgotten about
them. Or maybe that was just wishful thinking. I picked up
one and stared at it. And thought I recognized a face. From
some storybook or dream, maybe. Without thinking I
pulled Grandpa's old pocketknife out of my pants and
started carving into the potato, trying to uncover the face
that was hiding there. Sharp, crooked nose and high
cheekbones and slash of a mouth framed by long mouth-
lines. After a while the potato looked like some sort of witch
or evil goddess, the eyes making long snakes for hair,
wriggling in a disgusting way as I put in the finishing
touches: cleft chin and wrinkled neck.

I stared at her. I vaguely remembered a woman like her
in one of the school books, turning people to stone with
just a look. Only with her gritty feel, the way the leftover
peel made streaks in her face and hair, I figured she
probably turned people into dust. Like the itinerant
preacher who passed through occasionally used to say,
"Dust unto dust." That was her. She could turn you, your
brothers and your sisters, your whole world into dust with
just one look. You had to be careful. Had to watch out. Or
she'd turn on you.

That night my mama came into the house carrying the
sack of potatoes. I wanted to run out; I didn't know what to
do. She started to cry, pulling out the ruined potato. Daddy
went over and grabbed it out of her hand, then turned and
looked at me.

At the time I wasn't sure why everybody looked so upset
over one potato. I guessed it was because we had so little
left, even one potato meant more hardship. And then

realizing they were upset over just one little potato made them even more upset. Because it told them just how bad off we were.

Amanda stepped up to Daddy and said, "I did it." She didn't even have to look at me. She knew. I listened to Daddy whipping her out past the barn that night with a feeling I'd never had before. Like I was almost devastated with guilt, but that there was something happy about the feeling, too. I never knew if she cried when he whipped her; I couldn't hear her and I couldn't ask Daddy. I was too embarrassed to ask her.

The next day Amanda came home from playing out in the dust with her arms full of potatoes. She wouldn't say where she got them, just that she'd found them in the dust. Daddy and Mama didn't know what to believe. They knew it couldn't have happened the way she told it, but they couldn't come up with a better explanation either. No one lived close enough to us for her to have stolen them. So they finally just took them, and Mama cooked them a little bit at a time, although I think it always bothered her the way we got them.

The next few years things were hard. Us kids knew, although Mama and Daddy would never say we didn't have any money, or that we didn't have enough food. We just didn't talk about it. So I guess in a way we were a little protected from it, and for the most part played and went to school the same as we always had.

Except some of our friends had to go away. We were lucky; we owned the land and house. A lot of the other families were tenant farmers, and the big land companies decided tenant farming didn't pay in a drought and started kicking people off the land they'd farmed for years, that they had kin buried in.

The land companies sent giant earth movers and tractors to knock the old houses down and plow up everything including the front yards. They planted cotton: green and dry. Daddy said it would ruin the land; the big land companies were just trying to get the most out of it before they sold it to somebody else.

So a lot of our friends had to leave, going to California and other places. That next school year there was just a handful of us left.

Amanda did well in school, although she was still pretty quiet. She still brought vegetables and other things home from playing, and one time a new shawl for Mama. Daddy and Mama had given up asking her about it a long time ago. And always bringing Grandma fresh-picked flowers, even when they weren't in season, even when there weren't any flowers to be had anywhere, the dust having killed them all. Amanda still brought them, giving them to Grandma with a smile.

Grandma asked where she got them, sometimes, shaking her head when Amanda said she couldn't remember.

Of course, Daddy didn't care to ask much of anything by that time. That's when he'd first started drinking. Sometimes he even dragged Jack along to a neighbor's place to drink. To have somebody to help carry him home, I guess. No matter what, he insisted on passing out and sleeping in his own bed, not at a saloon or somebody's place miles away. Mama and Grandma kept saying that was bad for Jack, that the boy would get to be just like him, but he didn't seem to listen.

I wasn't growing up to be like Daddy, or Jack. I realized that that year. I was different. I used to be like Jack, I know; used to like all the same things: hunting and fishing and scaring the livestock every chance we had. We spent most of our time together. That changed pretty quickly. I started spending a lot of time with Amanda: talking to her, listening to her. Soon I spent all my time with her. Jack stayed with Daddy.

"You gotta be careful," she said to me one day. We'd been about a mile from the house, on a little rise, one of the few places around there that hadn't changed much the past few years; it was still green as ever.

"Careful of what?" I said. She talked . . . abstractly, a great deal of the time. Like she was telling a riddle. I didn't like it all the time.

"Of your anger. . . ." She brushed grass and seeds off her dress.

"Anger? I ain't angry!" I felt anxious. "You know I 'most never lose my temper!"

"We all have anger," she said in a quiet voice. "Even me. You've seen lots of folk angry around here, haven't you?"

I nodded. There were a lot of bitter people. First they got pushed off their land, then for them to get to California and other places they had to sell most of what they owned. And there were always people around to take advantage, offering them far less than what their belongings were worth, just because the people were desperate. I saw one man shoot his horse rather than sell it for far less than what it was worth. The two men had just been standing there with the horse in front of the house, arguing, when the poor farmer went into the house, came back with a shotgun, and stopping on the porch took aim and shot his own horse. I'd never seen anybody as mad as that other fellow, standing there looking down at the fine piece of horseflesh he'd intended to buy.

Mirrors and pictures and good pieces of furniture passed down from grandparents to parents to children, valuable pieces brought over from the old country, cherished items once owned by dead relatives—I saw them stacked up in people's yards and burned, burned in anger because they couldn't bear to sell them for such shamefully low amounts. Kids' toys and mama's best linen, daddy's tools and grandpa's cedar chest. Anger striking the match. Smoldering. That was the scariest thing about it all: They were all so angry, but quiet about it. Lots of them never said a word. Just lit the match and stepped back, staring blank-eyed and pale.

They left their old houses to the wind and stray animals—birds and mice and skinny dogs and cats. Jack used to go out and break windows, tear down boards, wreck anything he could get his hands on. A lot of our schoolfriends did the same. Jack more than anybody else, though. He'd just spend hours tearing up a place. It worried Mama and Grandma; I don't know how Daddy felt.

I felt strange about it. For some reason I thought Amanda understood what Jack was up to.

I did have the anger, deep down, but I knew Amanda was changing that. With her there, there just seemed to be less reason to be angry.

One night a year later Jack came home from town by himself. Pale and angry and trying not to cry. "Daddy's hole up down the saloon! They can't get him to leave!"

We all went down, even Grandma. All the men were standing in the street, quiet. No one said a word. They all stared at the saloon. A few young boys ran around the street bumping into people, but nobody really paid them any attention. I listened carefully. I could hear Daddy inside the saloon, screaming, busting things up. I looked at Amanda. She had sat down on an old log, her hands folded. She seemed to be waiting.

Nobody would go in. When Grandma tried, it took three men to stop her.

Suddenly, we all saw Amanda walking up the sidewalk toward the saloon. Mama began to scream. A couple of the men tried to catch her, but before they could reach the door she had walked in.

It was quiet for just a minute. Then I could hear my daddy yelling again. "Get away from me! Who asked you to come anyway?" Then I could hear things breaking up in there again. What if he hurt her? I'd never forgive him. . . .

Then we heard him scream. "Get away from me, witch!"

And a shot. My mama began to moan to herself.

It seemed like a long time, but then Amanda walked out alone.

No one said anything. Except my grandma. I can still hear her whisper, so low it was almost as if she hadn't intended to say anything and a little breeze just came and picked her thoughts up out of her mouth and turned them into words. "Harvest child. . . ." Those were the words; I do remember.

No one doubted Daddy'd killed himself. Lots of people said they'd seen it coming for a long time. My grandma never replied, except one time to say, "It was time. Time for the harvest," but she was tired, so nobody paid much attention.

Mama never would talk about it, so I don't know what she thought.

Things changed after that. Jack settled down some, enough that we stopped thinking he'd turn out like Daddy. He started doing better in school. And he fell in love with Amanda.

He had the right, I know; she wasn't really our sister. And I'd never thought about her romantically myself; she was my friend. Although I never saw her encourage him, she didn't seem to want to stop him, either. I couldn't blame him—she'd grown into a beautiful young woman, her hair even more golden than when she'd first come to us.

But I still felt it wasn't right. No good would come of it. And I knew Grandma felt the same way. When she looked at the two of them, it was with sadness.

There's something else, too, I realized at the time, although I couldn't quite think it out. My mind seemed to clamp shut when the idea was only halfway in focus. Jack was better without Daddy. Mama and me were, too. We all were. I still hate to think that, but it's true.

Things were getting better all over the Midwest by that time. It was 1940. The government had started a grass-seeding program back in '35 that was showing good results; a good deal of erosion cover had been replaced. Farmers had started using a three-year rotation of wheat and sorghum and a fallow year. There was increased contour plowing, terracing, and strip-cropping. You could see shelter belts of trees on the horizon now, planted to break the high winds. A lot of politicians were saying that the dust bowl years would never happen again.

And old neighbors were returning from California. They were coming home.

I'd noticed that Amanda had grown restless the last few months before school that year. She was seventeen; it'd be her last. But it wasn't the same kind of hurry-up-to-be-grownup I saw in Jack. It was as if she were waiting, and not too happy about what she was waiting for. And each time a storm came up she seemed anxious, sharp with the rest of the family for the first time I could remember. She'd spend long hours out on that little rise where she'd warned me about anger, just staring off into the distance. She looked sad, as if something were ending. I couldn't sleep most nights thinking about her, the way she was acting, and when I'd get up at night to use the bathroom I'd see her sitting out on the porch, looking toward the moon, watching, waiting.

Grandma seemed to be waiting, too. "Things are lookin' better," she'd say, talking about the way the land was now, and the old neighbors coming back, and all the things the government was doing for us. Then she'd stare off into the distance, just like Amanda, waiting.

Tornado season begins around March in Kansas. The old-timers say you can usually tell a few hours before one hits; the livestock seem restless, people's tempers flare, and the whole countryside seems to hold its breath.

That year the waiting seemed to drag on forever. I thought Jack and I were going to kill each other before school was out, always snapping at each other and quarreling over every little thing. Grandma had to separate us several times when we got into it at home. She was looking more and more worried herself; she and Mama weren't even speaking that spring.

Amanda wasn't paying too much attention to Jack anymore, or me either for that matter. We'd both try to talk to her, but she usually wouldn't reply, just sit there, staring at the dark fingers of cloud reaching down, raking the earth. Fake tornadoes, I used to call them. Those clouds looked a little like tornadoes to a youngster I suppose; they just didn't spin. I used to imagine they did that for protective camouflage, so that airplanes wouldn't fly into them and tear them apart. Self-preservation—back then I figured everything must value that.

Amanda had changed Jack all right. Despite our quarrels, I could tell he really cared about things. He had grown. He was sprouting new things just about all the time. Maybe that's why she didn't pay as much attention to him anymore, or to the rest of us; her work was done.

It was almost time for school to let out that day when the first twister hit. What strikes me the most now that I look back on it is how pretty it had seemed at that first sighting, like a giant gray feather off in the distance, one of those plumes The Three Musketeers might have worn in the book I'd read in school the year before. I said that to Jack and he frowned, poked me, and said it looked just like a big old tree in a heavy rain. One of the girls said it was like spigot water when dust got in the pipe, kind of muddy gray.

We all stood at the windows watching it jump over Thompson's barn and climb over the little rise separating the Thompson place from the school. We watched it coming closer and closer. Some of the kids were getting nervous. The teacher was from back east—our old teacher had stayed out in California with the rest of her family—and I don't think she had ever seen a tornado before. She stood there staring like the rest of us. Some of us recognized the danger, I guess, but we'd been seeing twisters all our lives; they were like old, friendly landmarks. You never really thought about one attacking you. That always happened to other folks.

Then I noticed Amanda.

I have never seen, before or since, such a look. She seemed to be straining upwards on her feet. A tenseness in her back; for a second I was afraid it was going to snap. But the odd thing about it, despite her painful appearance, I was convinced that she was almost thrilled with the approach of the tornado.

"There's another one!" Bobby Collins shouted, and I remember, clearly, the shrill panic in his voice.

Kids scrambled away from the windows and started for the stairs that led to the shelter beneath the school. The teacher shouted, urging them to safety, but they didn't have to be told. I think I may have been the only one who heard her.

"Another one! Three!" Jack yelled, and I thought my brother was going to cry.

Jack and I started down the stairs behind the others. Two of the tornadoes were almost at the schoolhouse. Then I remembered Amanda. "Jack!" I shouted, almost sobbing, and twisted back around, away from his hand.

Amanda had opened the door, and was walking slowly outside.

Jack must have turned around right after me, because he was shouldering past, then running toward the open door.

I'm not sure I'll ever know why I did it, if I was afraid Jack was too late and he'd just get himself killed going out there, or if I sensed Amanda was finally going home, her work completed, and we had no right to stop her. Sometimes I wonder, God forbid, if maybe I just wasn't a little scared of Amanda, and the way she had changed things in our lives, all of our lives. I do know it broke my heart, what I did. I leaped after Jack and grabbed him, held him away from the door, held him away from Amanda, then I knocked us both under the large oak table as the twister thundered past.

My brother finally forgave me. I think maybe after a few years he realized what Amanda was, and understood why I'd done what I'd done. He sent me a painting of a young girl harvesting wheat one year, right about the same time Amanda had disappeared. Her hair golden, a distant look in her eyes.

Everybody said she'd been killed, but no one ever found a body.

I searched all over the Somali refugee camp for the beautiful young black girl, that harvest child. But like my Amanda, I never saw her again. I figured there would be other chances, though. Besides, I now knew the bad times would eventually pass for these people, as they had for my own. It made the work a bit easier, the suffering a little more bearable to watch.

My grandma died in that storm. They found her in bed, looking out the window. They figured her old heart couldn't handle all the excitement.

But she was smiling. And there were newly picked flowers in a vase on her bedtable.

I think about Grandma a lot these days, now that I'm getting older. I wonder about what she saw. I wonder if it was anything like what I saw while I was pulling Jack away from the schoolhouse door. Out in the swirling dust, a young golden-haired girl lifting up her arms.

And three tornadoes bending down, surprisingly gently, to lift her.

When I'm older, Amanda, just a bit older. Bring me fresh-picked flowers. Come smile at me.

And When the Green Man Comes

The man is clothed
in birchbark,
small birds cling to his limbs
and one builds
a nest in his ear.

The clamor of bedlam
infests his hair, a wind
blowing in his head
shakes down
a thought that turns
to moss and lichen
at his feet.

His eyes are blind
with April,
his breath distilled
of butterflies
and bees, and in his beard
the maggot sings.

He comes again
with litter of chips
and empty cans,
his shoes full of mud and dung;

an army of shedding dogs
attends him,
the valley shudders where
he stands,
       redolent of roses,
exalted in
the streaming rain.

—John Haines

Simpson's Lesser Sphynx

Esther M. Friesner

Later we all agreed to share the blame. We should have known Simpson was just not our kind. On the basis of blood alone we admitted him to the Club. His father was good stock: Boston, Choate, and Yale; his mother similarly Philadelphia, Miss Devon's, and Skidmore. But nature delights in sports. Who can depend on biology? We are still writing notes to next of kin, and the Club Secretary claims he will resign if those *Enquirer* reporters don't cease hanging around the Pro Shop, putting him off his game.

It was August and we were bored. The market had been sluggish, and so were we. Sterling went so far as to suggest a trip to the local massage parlor to take our minds off our portfolios before he was hissed down and sent to the bar for another round of G&Ts. As he shuffled from the room, he bumped into Simpson.

That is, he afterwards learned it was Simpson he'd encountered. The man's face was hidden behind the bulky wooden crate he bore before him. He heaved it onto the sideboard, scraping the mahogany ruinously, and blew like a draft horse.

"There!" He wiped his brow. "That's done."

We stared at the crate. It was riddled with air holes, and through these a pungent, unpleasant reek began to fill the room. Something inside hissed.

"Simpson," said Dixwell severely, "no pets."

Simpson's eyes crinkled. "Pets?" he echoed, laughing. The thing in the crate hissed again, and we heard a scrabbling sound. The smell was stronger, overwhelming the room's comfortable aura of oiled leather and good burley.

"Here I am, back from Greece with something a sight more interesting to show than slides, and what happens?" Simpson went on. "Dixie quotes Club scripture at me. Well, it's *not* a pet I've got in here. It's a present; a present to the dear old Club. Now, I'll need a hammer."

Wilkes was at his elbow on the moment, hammer graciously proffered. Wilkes is—or was—such an integral part of the Club that old members have long forgotten whether he was hired as butler, waiter, confessor, or handyman. New members were wisely too overawed to ask.

Simpson pried the lid off the crate. Hard pine splinters flew everywhere, and the feral stench intensified. When the lid lay grinding sawdust into the Aubusson, Simpson stood back, made a dramatic flourish, and was actually heard to remark, "Ta-*daah!*"

She did not respond to vulgar fanfare. Simpson had to rap sharply on the side of the crate before the tiny, exquisitely modelled head peeped over the wooden rim. It was no bigger than a man's hand, a head with the face of a Tanagra figurine framed by clusters of dark curls such as old Cretan priestesses wore. She opened her delicate lips and a third, more tentative hiss escaped.

"Come on, Bessie," cried Simpson, seizing the crate and dropping it to the floor with a jarring thud. "Don't make me look bad. Come out and show yourself." He tipped it over and the sphynx spilled out in a tumble of feline body, bare breasts, and goshawk's wings.

"Isn't she a beauty?" Simpson demanded. The sphynx looked at each of us in turn as he spoke, her bosom heaving and her eyes wild. You could trace the ripples of fear on her tawny flanks. Her eyes were blue. "Don't ask me how I got her through customs. Trade secret. The things I do for the Club! Wilkes, bring me a Scotch. I want to toast our new mascot."

"Simpson, you're mad," objected Haskins. "This . . . this creature is a miracle! A myth come to life! It can't—it *shouldn't* exist, and yet . . ." He stretched out a hesitant hand. The sphynx sniffed it warily, cat-fashion, then allowed him to stroke her fur. Slowly an enchanting smile spread across her face; she closed her eyes and thrummed.

"Where did you find it? How? . . ." demanded Dixwell.

Simpson shrugged. "That's a story I'm saving to dine out on."

It was Chapin, as usual, who cast a sopping-wet blanket over the whole affair. "We cannot keep it . . . her . . . here," he decreed from the height of three hundred years of Puritan ancestry. "Quite aside from an obvious violation of U.S. Customs law, we cannot. This is a dangerous animal, Simpson. A monster!"

"Don't you know what sphynxes eat?" put in Hobbs.

Well, of course we'd all suffered through the Oedipus tale in the original Greek at prep school. However, none of us really liked Chapin, and it was hard to ignore how prettily the little sphynx purred and snuggled when Haskins scratched between her wings.

"Oh, for God's sake!" Simpson spat in exasperation. "She's never taken a bite out of me, if that's what you mean. Besides, this one's purebred; can't eat manflesh unless it's gotten according to the code. I watched them for at least a week before I nabbed Bessie, and the only time I saw one of them chow down on a local boy was when he got stupid and arrogant enough to try his hand at the Riddle." You could tell Simpson meant the Riddle to be capitalized by the way he said it.

"What riddle?" Chapin asked in minuscule. We had long suspected his education lacking. Who has not heard of the immortal riddle the sphynx propounds? What is it that goes on four legs at morning, two at noon, three at night? We also had to supply Chapin with the answer: man.

"So you see," Simpson went on, "she's harmless. A, she can only ask the Riddle in Greek—doesn't speak a word of English, besides making cat sounds. B, she can't hurt a fly with it since every schoolchild knows the answer to that old chestnut. And C, unless the victim's willing to be questioned, she can't touch him. Now have we got a mascot?"

We did. We all grew rather fond of Oenone, as she was renamed. Only Simpson would call a sphynx "Bessie." She lived in a kennel in the woodsy clump off the eleventh tee and never needed leashing. It was great fun to do a round of golf and stop by to visit our unique Club pet. She bounded from the kennel or the woods when called and perched on a large boulder, like her famous man-eating ancestress. There she would jabber at us in flawless Greek, cocking her head expectantly, her rose-petal tongue darting out to lick needle-sharp fangs.

"Sorry, Oenone"—we all chuckled—"no riddles today; and the answer is man." This sent her slinking back to the kennel where Wilkes fed her 9-Lives mackerel and changed the newspapers lining the floor.

When winter came, it was Wilkes who offered to take Oenone to live with him in the groundsman's cottage. We saw little of her until spring, although I once surprised the two of them in the Club library. Wilkes was reading, and Oenone, perched on the wing chair's back, almost appeared to be following the text. When he turned a page too quickly, she hissed. He became aware of me and hastily stood up.

"Just relaxing a bit. I do enjoy a good book," he said. I glanced at the book, a paperback mystery. Despite his polished facade, Wilkes was hopelessly addicted to tales of ruthless women, spies, and blackmailers.

Oenone leaped from the chairback and rubbed against his legs. "She looks well. You're taking good care of her, Wilkes," I remarked.

"Oh, she's no trouble. Very affectionate, she is. And smart? Personally"—he lowered his voice—"I've never cared much for cats. But she's different."

I looked at Oenone's human face and pert breasts. Wilkes was innocent to the obvious. So were we all.

That spring the disappearances began.

The first to go were Reynolds and Kramer, a pair of busboys, to be followed in rapid succession by Thomson, Jones, and Green, caddies. At first no one missed them; a certain turnover in personnel is expected at any club.

Then it was Wilkes.

The police were little help. Theories flew, but the Club remained beyond implication. Or so it did until the bright May morning when Dixwell announced he was going out to cure his slice and did not return.

"This is atrocious," fumed Chapin, consulting his watch every five minutes as we sat in the bar. "Dixie swore he'd give me advice on my IBM holdings; said he had private news. Must be keeping it to himself, make a killing and leave his friends out in the cold."

Wearily I stepped down from the stool. "If it's so important to you, we can seek him out on the greens."

Chapin took a cart; I opted to walk. It was better for my health, especially in view of Chapin's driving. So it was natural that he got to the eleventh tee ahead of me by nearly ten minutes. When I came trudging over the bank shielding the sand trap I heard the whine of Chapin's voice from the woods and assumed he'd found Dixwell. Only when I came nearer did I realize that the second voice was female.

"I'll tell you honestly, Chapin," she said, "I don't like you; never have. Don't think I don't know who proposed feeding me generic tuna at the last Club board meeting. Why should I tell you if Dixie's come this way?"

"You're doing just fine on 9-Lives, from the look of you." Chapin's voice was harsh. "Mackerel's brain food; how long have you known English?"

Oenone's reply—who else could it be but Oenone?—came calm and measured. "I don't owe you answers. You have it all wrong. It's you who must play with me; by the old rules."

Chapin's barking laugh was so loud I thought I'd come upon them soon, but I only found the golf cart. They were deeper in the woods, and as I pressed on I heard him say, "And if I don't, you won't help me find Dixie before the market closes, is that it? Dying to ask that stupid riddle after all these years, aren't you?"

"Call it an ethnic whim."

"I call it blackmail; but okay." I could imagine Chapin's fatuous grin. "Ask. What have I got to lose? But the answer is man."

"Is it?" Oenone purred. The rumbling shook the blackberry bushes. I was at the edge of her kennel-clearing, about to announce myself, when I tripped over something and sprawled out of sight just as the sphynx propounded her riddle. "Who was that lady I saw you with last night?"

"Man!" snapped Chapin automatically, then goggled. "*What* did you say?"

I raised myself on my elbows and saw her. She had grown, our sweet Oenone. She was as big as a Siberian tiger, and her steel grey wings fanned out suddenly with a clap of thunder. There were blots of dried blood on her breasts.

"I said," she replied sweetly, "you lose." She pounced before he could utter another word.

I lunged away, sickened by the scream that ended in gurgles and then silence. Something snagged my feet a second time, and I went down in a deafening dry clatter, falling among Oenone's well-gnawed leftovers. I spied Dixwell's nine iron among them. Gorging, she ignored me as I tottered off.

We mounted an armed hunt, but in vain. Sphynxes are smart, as witness Oenone's quiet scholarship, learning English and—no doubt—a more suitable set of riddles. She knew she'd never make her full growth on 9-Lives mackerel. She was gone; literally flown the coop. Where she went is anyone's guess. America is larger than Greece, and there is wilderness still.

Perhaps there will come reports of backpackers unaccounted for, campers gone too long in the high country, mysterious vanishments of hunters and fishermen. Will they chuckle, as we did, and dare her to ask her silly riddle? Arrogance is never the answer to the sphynx's question. Oedipus himself was never educated at Yale.

Of course, look where it got him.

Simpson has been blackballed from the Club. Under the circumstances it was the least we could do.

Intruder

Some morning, while you and I are dozing,
Puss, not puling outside like most mornings,
will try the handle, and finding himself
denied entrance, will kick in the door.

His monstrous head will enter first, next
his vacant grin and his body weighing
four stone. Then, my fair
but furless one, he will seize
you by the scruff, and boot you out.

Maybe I should never have started feeding
him those sides of liver, those fresh eggs,
those vast stinking salmon. But what's done
is done. Puss, clumsy still on two feet,
but eager to please me, reaches into the cupboard
to take down the Limoges, that we too
may enjoy our filets of mackerel, our dishes of cream.

—*Susan Feldman*

The Duke of Orkney's Leonardo

Sylvia Townsend Warner

The child, a boy, was born with a caul. Such children, said the midwife, never drown. Lady Ulpha was cold to the midwife's assurances; the same end, she said, could be reached by never going near water. She was equally indifferent to the midwife's statement that children born with a caul keep an unblemished complexion to their dying day. Lady Ulpha had long prided herself on her unblemished decorum. The violent act of giving birth, the ignominy of howling and squirming in labor and being encouraged by a vulgar person to let herself go, had affronted her. Seeing that encouragements were unwelcome, the midwife did not mention that cauls are so potent against drowning that mortals making a sea voyage will pay a great price for one. The child was washed and laid in the cradle, and a nurse given charge of it. As for the caul, by some mysterious negotiation it got to Glasgow. There it was bought by the captain of a whaler and subsequently lost at sea.

Sir Huon and Lady Ulpha were fairies with a great deal of pedigree, pride to match it, and small means for its upkeep. On the ground that it does not do to make oneself cheap, they seldom appeared at the Court of Rings, a modest Elfin kingdom in Galloway, preferring to live on their own estate, small and boggy, and make a merit of it. When the boy was of an age to be launched into the world, it would be different.

He was still spoken of as The Boy, because he had been named after so many possible legacy leavers that no one could fix a name on him, except his nurse, who called him Bonny—a vulgar dialect term which would get him nowhere. He was the most beautiful child in the world, she said, and would grow into the handsomest elfin in all Scotland. Looking at her child more attentively, Lady

Ulpha decided that though he was now an expense, he might become an asset.

His first recollection of his mother was of being lifted onto her high bed to have his nose pinched into a better shape, his ears flattened to the side of his head, and his eyebrows oiled. As time went on, other measures were imposed. He had to wear a bobbing straw hat to shield him from getting freckles, and was forbidden to hug his pet lamb in case he caught ticks. In winter a woollen veil was tied over his face. This was worse than the hat, for it blinded him to his finer pleasures: the snow crystal melted in his hand, the wind blew the feathers away before he had properly admired them. Baffled by the woollen grating over his eyes, he came indoors, where sight was no pleasure. The veil was pulled off and he was set to study an ungainly alphabet straddling across a dirty page.

It was in summer that he got a name of his own. A trout stream ran through the estate, and as he couldn't be drowned he was allowed to play in it, provided he kept his hat on. Sir Glamie, Chancellor of the Court of Rings and an ardent fly-fisher, had permission from Sir Huon—who knew he would otherwise poach—to fish there on Wednesdays, provided he threw back every alternate fish. Having scrupulously thrown back a small trout, Sir Glamie approached a pool where he knew there was a large one. A ripple travelled toward him, and another. He saw a straw hat, and advanced on the poacher. Under the hat was a naked boy, whose limbs trailed in the pool. The boy was not even poaching, merely wallowing, and scaring every trout within miles; but as Sir Glamie drew nearer he saw that the boy was winged. "Are you young what's-his-name?" he asked. The boy said he thought so. Sir Glamie said he was old enough to know his name. The boy agreed, and added, "It used to be Bonny." Sir Glamie replied that Bonny was a girl's name, and wouldn't do. Overcome by the boy's remarkable beauty, he had a rush of benevolence, and casting round in his mind remembered the worms, small and smooth and white, that fishermen call gentles, and impale on the hook when the

water is too cloudy to use a fly. "I shall call you Gentle," he
declared. By force of association, he took a liking to the
boy, extricated him from Lady Ulpha's clutches, and took
him to Court, where he was made a pet of and called
Gentil.

It was not the introduction his parents had intended: it
was premature, since clothes had to be bought for him and
he would outgrow them; it was also patronizing, and made
their heir seem a nobody. But as none of the legacies they
invoked had responded, they submitted, called him Gentil, made him learn his pedigree by heart, and loyally
attended banquets.

Gentil was scarcely into his new clothes before he grew
out of them. A fresh outfit was under consideration when
the need for it was annulled: the Queen made him one of
her pages, and a uniform went with the appointment. For
the first time in his life he was aware of his beauty, and
gazed at his image in the tailor's mirror as though it were a
butterfly or a snow crystal—a snow crystal that would not
melt. At intervals, he remembered to be grateful to his
parents, but for whose providence he might still be admiring the veined underwater pebbles without noticing his
reflected face. It needed no effort to be grateful to his new
friends at Court: to the Queen, who stroked his cheek; to
her ladies, who straightened his stockings; to his fellow-
pages, who shared their toffees with him; to Sir Glamie,
who chucked him under the chin with a fishy hand and
asked what had become of the hat; to Lady Fenell, the
Court Harpist, who sang for him

> I love all beauteous things,
> I seek and adore them

—an old-fashioned ditty composed for her by an ad-
mirer, which exactly expressed his own feelings. For he,
too, was a beauty lover, and loved himself with an untroubled and unselfish love.

Fenell's voice had grown quavering with age—she had
actually heard Ossian—but her fingers were as nimble as

ever, her attack as brilliant, and young persons of quality
came from all over Elfindom to learn her method. The
latest of these was the Princess Lief, Queen Gruach's
daughter from the Kingdom of Elfwick, in Caithness. She
had the air of being assured of admiration, but there was
nothing beautiful about her except the startling blue of her
eyes: a glance that fell on one like a splash of ice-cold
water. During the reception held to celebrate her arrival,
the glance fell on Gentil. It seemed like a command. He
came forward politely and asked if there was anything she
wanted. After a long scrutiny, she said, "Nothing," and
turned away. He felt snubbed. Not knowing which way to
look, he caught sight of Sir Huon and Lady Ulpha, whose
faces expressed profound gratification. He knew they did
not love him, but he had not realized they hated him.

If it had not been for Lady Ulpha's decorum, she would
have nudged Sir Huon in the ribs. All that night they sat up
telling each other that Gentil's fortune was made. There
could be no mistaking such love at first sight. Gentil would
be off their hands, sure of his future, sure of his indestructi-
ble good looks, with nothing to do but ingratiate himself
with Queen Gruach and live up to his pedigree. And, as the
castle of Elfwick stood on the edge of a cliff, the caul would
not be wasted. The caul might count as an asset and be
included in the marriage settlement.

It was just as they foresaw. Lief compelled Lady Fenell
into saying she had nothing more to teach her (the formula
for dismissing unteachable pupils), assaulted Gentil into
compliance, and bore him off to Elfwick, where, after a
violent set-to with Queen Gruach, she had him proclaimed
her Consort and made a Freeman of Elfwick.

The ceremony was interrupted by the news that a ship
was in the bay. Every male fairy rushed to the cliff's edge.
Narrowing his eyes against the wind, Gentil was just able to
distinguish a dark shape tossing on the black-and-white
expanse of sea. He was at a loss to make out what the
others were saying, except that they were talking excitedly,
for they spoke in soft mewing voices, like the voices of
birds of prey. Gulls exploded out of the dusk, flying so

close that their screams jabbed his hearing. They, too, sounded wild with excitement. The sea kept up a continuous hollow booming, a noise without shape or dimension, unless some larger wave charged the cliff like an angry bull. Then, for a moment, there seemed to be silence, and a tower of spray rose and hung on the air, hissed, and was gone. Ducking to avoid a gull, Gentil lost sight of the ship. When he saw it again, it was closer inland. He saw it stagger, and a wave overwhelm it, emerge, and be swallowed by a second wave. There was a general groan. A voice said something about no pickings. A flurry of snow hid everything. He heard the others consulting, their voices dubious and discouraged. They had begun to move away, when a shriller voice yowled, "There she is, there she is." They gathered again, peering into the snow flurry. When it cleared, the ship was plainly visible, much smaller and farther out to sea. Everyone turned away and went back to the castle, where the ceremony was resumed, glumly.

When he said to Lief that he was glad to see the ship still afloat, and hoped no one on her was drowned, she said, embracing him, that he would never be drowned—that was all she cared for. He learned that Elfwick had rights over everything that came ashore—wreck, cargo, crew: the east wind blew meat and drink into Elfwick mouths. Next day she walked him along the cliffs, and showed him where the currents ran—oily streaks on the sea's face. A ship caught in a certain current would be carried, willynilly, onto a rock called the Elfwick Cow, which pastured at the entrance to the beach, lying so temptingly in the gap between the cliffs. She pointed to a swirl of water above the rock, and said that at low tide the Cow wore a lace veil—the trickle of spray left by each retreating wave. He clutched at his retreating hopes. "But if a sailor gets to shore alive—" "Knocked on the head like a seal," she said, "caul or no caul. Cauls have no power on land." Seeing him shiver, she hurried him lovingly indoors.

Her love was the worst of his misfortunes. He submitted to it with a passive ill will, as he submitted to the inescapable noise of the sea, the exploitation of a harshly bracing climate. Wishing he were dead, he found himself at the mercy of a devouring healthiness, eating grossly, sleeping like a log. "You'll soon get into our Elfwick ways," Queen Gruach remarked, adding that the first winter was bound to be difficult for anyone from the south. She disliked her son-in-law, but she was trying to make the best of him. If Gentil had inherited his parents' eye for the main chance, he could have adapted himself to his advantages, and lived as thrivingly at Elfwick as he had lived at Rings—where everyone liked him, and he loved himself, and was happy. At Elfwick, he was loved by Lief, and was appalled.

The first winter lasted into mid-May, when the blackthorn hedges struggled into bloom and a three-day snowstorm buried them. The storm brought another ship to be battered to pieces on the Elfwick Cow. This time, the cold spared her plunderers the trouble of dispatching the crew. The ship was one of the Duke of Orkney's vessels, its cargo was rich and festive: casks of wine and brandy, a case of lutes (too sodden to be of any use), smoked hams (none the worse), bales of fine cloth. In a strong packing case and wadded in depths of wool was an oval mirror. Lief gave it to Gentil, saying that the frame—a wreath of carved ivory roses, delicately tinted and entwined in blue glass ribbons—was almost lovely enough to hold his face. She was in triumph at having snatched it from Gruach, who had the right to it. He thanked her politely, glanced at his reflection, saw with indifference that he was as beautiful as ever, and commented that he was growing fat. The waiting woman who had carried the mirror stood by with a blank face and a smiling heart. To see the arrogant Princess fawning on an upstart from Galloway was a shocking spectacle but also an ointment to old sores.

Baffled and eluded, Lief continued to love her bad bargain with the obsession of a bitch. She beset him with gifts, tried to impress him by brags, wooed him with bribes. She watched him with incessant hope, never lost patience with him, or with herself; she was so loyal she did not even

privately make excuses for him. If anyone showed her a
vestige of sympathy, she turned and rent him. This and
quarrelling with her mother were the only satisfactions she
could rely on.

At first, she hoped it was winter that made him cold.
Summer came, and Gentil was cold still—cold like a sea
mist and as ungraspable. If she had believed in witches,
she would have believed he was under a spell; but Caithness was full of witches—mortals all, derided by rational
elfins. He was healthy, could swim like a fish, leap like a
grasshopper—and none of this was any good to him, for
he was without initiative, and had to be wound up to
pleasure like a toy. The only thing he did of his own accord
was sneak out and be away all day. Sometimes he brought
back mushrooms, neatly bagged in a handkerchief.
Otherwise, he returned empty-handed and empty-
headed, for if she asked him what he had seen, he replied,
"Nothing in particular."

And it was true. He could no longer see anything in its
particularity—not the sharp outline of a leaf, not the polish
on a bird's plumage. It was as though the woollen veil had
been tied over his face again, the woollen grating that had
barred him from delight. He saw his old loves with a listless
recognition. Another magpie. Another rainbow. More
daisies. They were the same as they had been last summer
and would be next summer and the summers after that.

It was another April, and Gentil, wandering through the
fields, was conscious only that a cold wind was blowing,
when he heard a whistling—too long-breathed for a
thrush, too thoughtful for a blackbird. The whistler was a
young man, a Caithness mortal. He was repairing a tumbled sheepfold. Each time he stooped to pick up a stone, a
lappet of black hair slid forward and dangled over one eye.
Gentil was accustomed to mortals, took them for granted,
and never gave them a thought. At the sight of the young
man he was suddenly pierced with delight. The lappet of
hair, the light toss of the small head that shook it back, the
strong body stooping so easily, the large, deft hands nes-

tling the stones into place were as beautiful and fit and complete as the marvels he had seen in his childhood. Weakened by love, he sat down on the impoverished grass to watch.

He went back the next day, and the morning after that he got up early and was at the sheepfold in time to collect some suitably sized stones and lay them in a neat heap at the foot of the wall. Love is beyond reason, and when the young man took stones from the heap as though they had been there all the time, Gentil was overjoyed. Civility obliged him to attend the celebrations on Gruach's birthday, telling himself furiously that no one would notice if he was there or not. On the morrow, he woke with such a release into joy and confidence that he even dawdled on his way to the sheepfold. It was finished, the young man was gone. Gentil took to his wings and flew in wide circles, quartering the landscape. A flash of steel signalled him to where the young man was laying a hedge.

This task had none of the scholarly precision of mending a dry stone wall. It was a battle of opposing forces, the one armed with a billhook, the other armored in thorns. It was an old hedge, standing as tall as its adversary; some of the main stems were thick as a wrist, and branched at all angles with intricate lesser growths. Here and there it was tufted with blossoms, for the sap was already running. The young man, working from left to right, chose the next stem to attack, seized it with his left hand, bent it back, and half severed it with a glancing blow of the billhook. The flowing sap darkened the wound; petals fell. Still holding the upper part of the stem, he pressed it down, and secured it in a plaited entanglement of side branches, lesser growths, and brambles. Then he lopped the whole into shapeliness with quick slashes of his billhook. The change from dealing with stone to dealing with living wood changed his expression: it was stern and critical—there was none of the contented calculation which had gone with rebuilding the sheepfold.

It changed Gentil too—from a worshipper to a partisan. He hovered above the hedge, watching each stroke, studying the young man's face—how he drew down his black eyebrows in a frown, bit his lip. Secure in his invisibility, Gentil hovered closer and closer. They were moving on from a completed length of hedge when a twig jerked up from the subdued bulk. "Look! Here!"—the words were almost spoken when the young man saw the twig and slashed at it. The bright billhook caught Gentil in its sweep and lopped off half his ear. Feeling Gentil's blood stiffening on his hand, the young man licked the scratch he had got from a thorn and went on working. Another length of hedge had been laid before Gentil left off being sick, and crept away.

Several times he trustingly lay down to die. The trust was misplaced; the cold of shock and loss of blood forced him to rise from the ground into the clasp of the sunny air and walk on. When he tried to fly, he found he could not: the loss of half an ear upset his balance. He walked on and on, vaguely taking his way back to Elfwick and wondering how he could put an end to his shamed existence. He could not drown, but he remembered a place where a ledge of rock lay at the foot of the cliff, and if he could get that far he could let himself drop and be dashed to pieces. But he must make a detour, so that no one from the castle would see him.

Lief, impelled by her bitch's instinct, was there before him, not knowing why but knowing she must be. In any case, it never came amiss to look seaward: there might be another ship. He went past without seeing her. She grabbed him. As they struggled on the cliff's edge, she saw the bloody stump of his ear but held him fast.

As time went on Lief sometimes wondered whether it would not have been better to let him have his way. But she had caught hold of him before she saw what had happened, and her will to keep him was stronger than her horror at his disfigurement. So she fought him to a finish, and marched him back to the castle.

The return from the cliff's edge was perhaps the worst thing she had to endure. There were no more people about than usual but it seemed to her that every Court elfin was there, gathering like blowflies to Gentil's raw wound, turning away in abhorrence. It was natural, she accepted it. Elfwick had never lost the energy of its origin as an isolated settlement, embattled against harsh natural conditions: cold and scarcity, wind and tempest. Its savagery was practical, its violence law-abiding. Though it had grown comfort-loving, it had never become infected with that most un-Elfin weakness, pity. She herself nursed Gentil through his long illness without a tremor of pity traversing her implacable concern. She risked her reason to save him, exactly as the wreckers risked their limbs to snatch back a cask from the undertow, and she recognized the rationality and loyal traditionalism of the public opinion she defied. The mildest expression of it was Gruach's. "He must be sent back to Rings." While he was thought to be past saving (for the stump festered and his face and neck swelled hideously) there was hope. But the swelling went down and Gruach visited the sickbed to remonstrate in a motherly way against Lief's devotion. "I chose him. I shall save him," said Lief.

"But have you considered the future? It's not as though you were saving a favorite hound. He is your Consort, remember. How can you appear with such an object beside you? How could you put up with the indignity, the scandal, of his mutilation?" Lief replied, "You'll see." She put a bold front on it, but at times she despaired, thinking that if Gentil once left her keeping, public opinion would soon do away with him.

As it happened, this problem did not arise. No one was more horrified by his deformity than Gentil himself. He refused to be seen, he would have no one but Lief come near him. If she had to make an appearance at Court, he insisted that she lock him in and keep the key between her breasts. She still did not know what had happened. When she questioned him he burst into tears. She did not ask him again, for by then she was as exhausted by his illness as he, and only wanted to sit still and say nothing. They sat together, hour after hour, saying nothing, she with her hands in her lap, he fingering his ear.

The oncome of winter was stormy; two profitable ships

were driven onto the Cow, the castle resounded with boasts and banquetings. Then for months nothing happened. A deadly calm frost clamped the snow, waves crept to the strand and immediately froze, the gulls flew like scimitars through the still air. Gentil sat by the fire, fingering his wound.

The smell of spring was breathing through the opened casement when he suddenly raised his head, looked round the room and on Lief, and said passionately, "Everything is so ugly, so ugly!" Casting about for something to please him, Lief remembered her mother's gold and silver beads, which the Duke of Orkney had thought to hang round a younger neck. Schooling herself to be daughterly and beguiling, she persuaded Gruach to unlock her treasure chest, questioned, admired, put on the gold and silver beads, and asked if she could borrow them. And though Lief had never shown the least interest in the Duke of Orkney's importations, except when she carried off the oval mirror, Gruach thought she might be returning to her right mind, and handed over the beads and some other trifles. Gentil tired of running the beads through his fingers; a jewelled bird trembling on a fine wire above a malachite leaf and a massive gold sunflower with a crystal eye were more durable pleasures. Later, he was spellbound by a branching spray of coral. At the first sight of the coral, which to Lief was nothing to marvel at, since there was no workmanship about it, he gave a cry of joy that seemed to light up the room.

But this, too, eventually went the way of the sunflower and the bird. And when she brought fresh rarities to replace it, he thanked her politely and ignored them. Except for sudden fits of rage, when he screamed at her, he was always polite. The fits of rage she rather welcomed; they promised something she could get to grips with. It never came. He sat by the fire; he sat by the window; the maimed ear had thickened into an accumulation of flaps, one fast to another, like the mushrooms, hard as leather, that grow on the trunks of aging trees and are called Jew's-ears. A scar extended down his cheek. The rest of him was lovely and youthful as ever.

Nothing deflects the routine of a court custom. The Freemen of Elfwick had no particular obligations except to wear a badge and have precedence in drinking loyal toasts at banquets; but in times of emergency they were expected to rally and attend committee meetings. Gentil was now summoned to such a meeting. Naturally, he did not attend. The emergency was still in the future, but it was inevitable, and must be faced with measures of economy, tightening of belts, and finding alternative sources of supply. For the Duke of Orkney was mortal, and over sixty— an age at which mortals begin to fall to bits. His heir was a miserly ascetic, always keeping Lents; there would be no more casks of wine and brandy, no more of those delicious smoked hams, no more candied apricots from Provence, fine cloth from Flanders, spices to redeem home-killed mutton from the aroma of decay; the Cow would advance her horns to no purpose, the Elfwick standard of living would fall catastrophically. The meeting closed with a unanimous recommendation to make sure of the Duke of Orkney's next consignment.

It could be expected before the autumnal equinox. Spies were sent out for hearsay of it, watchers were stationed along the cliffs, where they lolled in the sun, chewing wild thyme. It had been an exceptionally early harvest; rye and oats were already in stooks, rustling in the wind. It was a lulling sound, but not so to the Court Purveyor. For it was a west wind, and though it was gentle it was steady. Of all the quarters the wind could blow from he prayed for any but the west. With a west wind keeping her well out to sea, the Duke's ship would be safe from those serviceable currents that nourished the Cow. Elfwick would get nothing.

Subduing his principles, consulting nobody, the Purveyor put on a respectable visibility and sought out the nearest coven of witches. They were throwing toads and toenails into a simmering cauldron; the smell was intolerable, but he got out his request, and at the same time got out

a purse and clinked it. "A wind from the east?" said the
head witch. "You should go to my sister in Lapland for
that." He answered that he was sure a Caithness witch
could do as well or better. She threw in another toad and
said he should have his will. Handing over the purse, he
asked if there was anything else he could supply. A
younger witch spoke up. "A few cats . . . seven, maybe."
"Alive?" "Oh, aye." He carried the hamper of squalling
cats to the place they commanded, and fled in trust and
terror.

The storm which impaled the Duke of Orkney's ship on
the Elfwick Cow did so at a price. Hailstones battered
down the stooks and froze the beehives. A month's washing was whirled away from the drying yard. Shutters were
torn from their hinges, fruit trees were uprooted, pigs went
mad, the kitchen chimney was struck by lightning, the
Purveyor, clutching at his heart, fell dead. Lief stepped
over him on her way out. The clamor of wind and voices,
the reports of a superb cargo, of a cargo still at hazard, had
been more than she could withstand. Settling Gentil with a
picture book, she locked him in, put the key in her bosom,
and ran to the cliff's edge. Bursts of spray made it difficult
to see what was going on. She caught sight of a Negro,
fighting his way to shore against the suck of the undertow.
He was down, he was up again, still grasping an encumber-
ing package. It was wrenched from him by the undertow;
he turned back. When she could see him again, he had
retrieved it. Curious to know what it was he guarded so
jealously, she descended the path. By the time she
reached the strand, he had been dispatched, and lay
sprawled over his package—an oblong wooden box, lat-
ticed with strips of iron—as though he would still protect it.
She tried to pull it from under him, but it was too heavy for
her to shift. More and more plunder was being fetched
ashore. She stood unnoticed in the jostle till one of the
Freemen tripped over the Negro. He started at seeing Lief
there, and panted out felicitations: never had the Cow
done better for Elfwick. She told him that the Negro's box
was hers, under the old law of Finders Keepers; he must

call off one of the wreckers to carry it after her to the castle.

On the cliff's summit she stopped to look back. Twitches of lightning played incessantly over the sea. Remade by wind and tempest, she felt a lifetime away from Gentil; when the grunting porter asked what to do with the box, she had forgotten it existed.

Yet in the morning the box was the first thing in her mind. Gentil had a cat's pleasure in anything being un-packed: had a crate been large enough, he would have jumped in and curled up in it. The box was brought to her apartment, the castle's handyman called in. Practiced in such duties, he made short work of it. The iron bands were eased and tapped off, screw after screw withdrawn. At intervals he remarked on the change in the weather. The wind had fallen as suddenly as it had come up, and when he had finished the box he would see to the shutters, and then the pigsties, which the pigs in their frenzy had torn through like cannonballs. This box, though, was a different matter. Made of solid mahogany, it would baffle the strongest pig in Scotland. He laid the screws aside and raised the lid. Whatever lay within was held in place by bands of strong twine and wrapped in fold on fold of waxed linen. The handyman cut the twine, bowed, and went away. Gentil came out of hiding. Kneeling by the box, Lief lifted the oblong shape and held it while Gentil unwound the interminable wrappings. The oblong turned into a frame, the frame held a padding of lamb's wool. Gentil folded the linen and smoothed it affectionately. Pulling away the lamb's wool, he was the first to see the picture.

It was the half-length portrait of a young man, full face and looking directly before him. Behind him was the land-scape of a summer morning. Wreaths of morning mist, shining in the sun, wandered over it. Out of the mist rose sharp pinnacles of mountain, blue with distance yet with every rocky detail exactly delineated. A glittering river coiled through a perspective of bronzed marshes and meadows enclosed by trees planted in single file, each tree in its own territory of air. It was as though a moment before

they had been stirring in a light wind which now had fallen.
Everything lay in a trance of sunlight, distinct, unmoving,
and completed. Only the young man, turning his back on
this landscape, sat in shadow—the shadow of a cloud,
perhaps, or of a canopy. He was not darkened by it, but it
substantiated him, as though he and the landscape belonged to different realities. He sat easily erect, with his
smooth, long-fingered young hands clasped like the hands
of an old man round a stick. His hair hung in docile curls
and ringlets, framing the oval of his face. He had grey eyes.
In the shadow which substantiated him, they were bright
as glass, and stared out of the canvas as though he were
questioning what he saw, as smilingly indifferent to the
answer as he was to the lovely landscape he had turned his
back on.

Lief tired under the effort of holding up the picture. She
propped it against a chair, and went round to kneel beside
the kneeling Gentil and discover what it was he found so
compelling. The likeness was inescapable: Gentil was gazing at himself in his youth, at the Gentil who had come
forward and asked if there was anything she wanted; she
had said, "Nothing," and nothing was what she had got.
Tears started to her eyes and ran slowly down her cheeks.
She shook her hand impatiently, as if to dismiss them. He
turned and looked at her. The sun shone full on her face.
He had never seen her cry. The glittering, sidling tears
were beautiful, an extraneous beauty on an accustomed
object. He shuffled nearer and stared more closely, entranced by the fine network of wrinkles round her eyes.
She heard him give a little gasp of pleasure, saw him
looking at her with delight, as long ago he had looked at an
insect's wing, a yellow snail shell. Cautiously, as though
she might fly away, he touched her cheek. She did nothing, said nothing, stretched the moment for as long as it
could possibly last. They rose from their knees together
and stood looking at the picture, each with an arm round
the other's waist.

Love—romantic love, such as Lief had felt for Gentil,

Gentil for the young man at the sheepfold—was not possible for them. In any case, elfins find such love burdensome and mistrust it. But they grew increasingly attached to each other's company, and being elfins and untrammelled by that petted plague of mortals, conscience, they never reproached or regretted, entered into explanations or lied. This state of things carried them contentedly through the winter. With the spring, Gentil astonishingly proclaimed a wish to go out-of-doors, provided he went unseen. Slinking out after midnight, they listened to owls and lambs, smelled honeysuckle, and ate primroses chilled with dew.

After the sweetness of early morning it was painful to return to the stuffiness of the castle, its oppressive silence shaken by snores. Gentil planned stratagems for escaping into daylight: he could wear a sunbonnet; they could dig an underground passage. But the underground passage would only deliver him up to the common gaze, the sunbonnet expose him to a charge of transvestism—more abhorrent to Elfwick than any disfigurement, and certain to be more sternly dealt with. Seeing him again fingering his ear and staring at the morning landscape behind the young man in the painting, Lief racked her brains for some indoor expedient which might release him from those four walls. Build on an aviary? Add a turret? The answer swam into her mind, smooth as a fish. The court library! It was reputed to be a good one, famous for its books of travel. And was totally unvisited. She had heard that some of the books of travel were illustrated. Gentil enjoyed a picture book. The midsummer mornings which had curtailed their secret expeditions now showed a different face: no one would be about at those unfrequented hours of dawn.

No one was. The snores became a reassurance and even a blessing, since they could be timed to smother the squeaks of the library door. Gentil sat looking at the travel books and Lief sat listening to the birds and looking at Gentil. One morning, he gave a cry of delight, and beckoned her to come and see what he had found. It was a woodcut in a book about the Crusades—a battle scene with rearing horses and visored warriors. It was unlike

Gentil to be so pleased with a battle scene, but he was certainly in a blaze of joy. He pointed to a warrior who was not visored, whose villainous dark face was muffled in a wimplelike drapery, whose eyes rolled from beneath a turban. "That. . . that. . . that's what I need, that's what I must have!" She said it would be ready that same evening.

Having embraced Islam, Gentil found a new life stretching before him. Turbaned and wimpled, he appeared at Court, kissed the Queen's hand, sat among his fellow-Freemen, studied sea anemones. This was only an opening on wider ambitions. It seemed excessive to go to Mecca, and Lief did not wish to visit his parents. But they went to Aberdeen, travelling visibly and using the alias of Lord and Lady Bonny. From Aberdeen they took ship to Esbjerg and inspected the Northern capitals. As travellers do, they bought quaint local artifacts, patronized curiosity shops, attended auctions. One has to buy freely in order to discover the run of one's taste. They discovered that what they most liked was naturalistic paintings. They concentrated on the Dutch School, Lief buying seascapes, Gentil flower pieces, and by selling those which palled on them they made money to buy more. In course of time, they acquired a number of distinguished canvases, but never another Leonardo.

The Unknown

María Luisa Bombal

I am privy to much that is unknown.

Of sea and earth and sky I know an infinity of small and magic secrets.

This time, however, I will tell only about the sea.

Miles down, below the deep, dense zone of darkness, the ocean again illuminates itself. A golden light radiates from gigantic sponges, yellow and resplendent as suns.

Numberless plants and cold-blooded creatures live within this layer of light, buried eternally in the brightness of a glacial summer.

A profusion of green and red anemones blossom on the wide sandy lawn, amid schools of transparent jellyfish, dangling like umbrellas, which have not yet set out in quest of their wandering destiny through the seas.

Hard white corals entwine like bushes, through which glide dark velvet fish, opening and closing like flowers.

Sea horses there are: tiny thoroughbreds of the deep moving at a silent canter with radiant algae manes rising slowly round them like halos.

And only I know that underneath certain deformed conch shells burrowed on the bottom there sits a little mermaid, weeping.

Surely you remember when as children we would leap from rock to rock, stopping short to balance with our arms widespread like wings on the edge of a narrow crevice carved by the sea—a jagged inlet where the waves crashed and then, retreating, left in their wake a long, foaming mantle: iridescent, gliding through the spectrum on its reluctant return, hissing, hissing . . . whispering something like a message.

But did you understand the meaning of that message? Well, I did.

For in fact the foam was trying with its dying breath to whisper in our ear the secret of its noble origins. . . .

"Far, far away, deep in the ocean depths," sighed the

foam, "there exists a submarine volcano erupting ceaselessly. Night and day the crater boils, blowing dense bub-
bles of silver lava toward the surface. . . ."

But I digress. My primary objective in these brief lines is
to acquaint you with something strange and until now
unknown which likewise took place down there in the
abyss.

It is the tale of a pirate ship trapped centuries ago in the
vortex of a whirlpool that sent it spinning to the bottom
amid uncharted currents and buried reefs.

Time passed. Giant octopuses tugged gently at the top-
masts as if to set a new course. Starfish came to nestle in
the hold.

Recovering at last from his long swoon, the pirate captain roused his crew with a roar and gave the order to
weigh anchor.

And as the dazed seamen raced to man the capstan, the
captain went to the bridge—where no sooner had he taken
in his surroundings than he began to curse.

For the ship had run aground on an endless beach
bathed in dark green moonlight.

To make matters worse, regardless of what direction he
turned his telescope, there was no sign of water.

"Damned sea!" he shouted. "Blasted tides driven by
the devil himself. Thunder take them for leaving us
stranded so far inland. . . . Who knows how long before
they'll lift us off this bloody beach."

He turned, training the telescope overhead to inspect
the sky, the stars, the position of the eerily glowing moon.

But his eyes encountered neither sky nor stars nor visible moon; rather, what he saw was the exact inverted
reflection of that demonic, sandy desert on which the ship
was marooned. "In the name of Satan," he whispered,
"am I going mad?"

And then, to top things off, he noticed one final oddity:
the luxuriant black sails—the pride of his ship—though
motionless and silent, were bellying full from every mast
. . . yet not a breath of wind was blowing.

"Ashore all hands!" rang suddenly throughout the ship.

"Load weapons, keep your cutlasses at the ready, and scout this cursed coast!"

The gangplank promptly lowered, a groggy crew disembarks, followed by their captain with a pistol in his hand.

They sank ankle-deep in the fine, cold, silky sand. Two groups they formed: one plodding east, the other west—both in search of the sea.

Then abruptly, "Halt!" the captain bellowed. "Chico will stay here to guard the ship. Now the rest of you swabs hop to it. On the double!"

And Chico—a mere lad, son of an honest fisherman, who had run away from home in search of adventure and mischief—upon hearing the command trudged back to the ship with his head bowed, as if counting each one of his steps.

"Dunderhead! . . . bandy-legged son of a Dutchman! . . . turtlebrain!" the captain ranted when the boy stood before him—so small, in spite of his fifteen years, that he scarcely reached the solid-gold buckle on the captain's bloodstained belt.

Children on board, he thought to himself, struck by a sudden uneasiness.

"Captain," the boy said quietly, "have you noticed that our feet leave no tracks in this sand?"

"Nor do the sails throw any shadow," the captain added in a dry, cruel whisper.

Then, his anger seeming to abate before the boy's naïve and puzzled gaze, he laid his rough hand on Chico's shoulder and said, "Let's go, son. The tide will be in soon."

"Aye aye, sir," the boy murmured, as though he meant "thanks."

Thanks. Forbidden word among pirates. Sooner burn your lips than utter it.

Did I say thanks? Chico asked himself, startled.

I called him son, the captain realized in amazement.

"Captain," Chico began, "at the time of the shipwreck . . ." He faltered as the captain bristled, blinked, raising himself to his full height. "I mean, the accident . . .

well, I was in the hold. When I came to my senses, what do you think I found? Myself surrounded by the most disgusting creatures I've ever seen."

"What kind of creatures?"

"Well, starfish . . . but alive. And gross. Quivering like the insides of someone just disemboweled . . . slithering from one side to the other, piling up in slippery mounds, even trying to fasten onto me. . . ."

"Ha! And you were frightened, eh?"

"Quick as an eel I jumped up and jerked open the doors and the aft hatchways, kicking them and swatting them with the broom as I swept them out. How like crabs they scuttled across the sand! But one thing I must tell you, sir, is that *they* left tracks."

The captain makes no reply.

And for a time both stood there side by side under that deathly green light, amid a silence so complete that suddenly they began to hear.

To hear and feel within themselves the surge and rise of an unknown tide, the pull of a sentiment neither could give a name to, a sentiment far more destructive than anger or hatred or dread—an orderly sentiment, nocturnal, gnawing, to which the heart, patient and resigned, surrenders.

Like one entranced, Chico at last whispers, "Sadness," as though it were a new word just breathed in his ear.

And then the captain, trying to shake off the nightmare, reverted to his loud voice. "Enough, Chico. Let's talk plain. With us you learned to fight, to wield a dagger, to sack and burn . . . but I've never heard you blaspheme." He paused and then, lowering his voice, asked: "Tell me, you must know—where do you believe we are?"

"Exactly where you think we are, Captain," the boy answered respectfully.

"In that case," the pirate said with a loud and scornful laugh, "thousands of fathoms beneath the sea and damned." A second later the laughter died in his throat.

Because what he had intended as mirth echoed like a terrifying moan, a cry of affliction from someone desperate, burning with desire for something irrevocably lost.

In the Court of the Crimson King

The rusted chains of prison moons
Are shattered by the sun.
I walk a road, horizons change,
The tournament's begun.
The purple piper plays his tune,
The choir softly sings;
Three lullabies in an ancient tongue,
For the court of the crimson king.

The keeper of the city keys
Puts shutters on the dreams.
I wait outside the pilgrims door
With insufficient schemes.
The black queen chants the funeral march,
The cracked brass bells will ring
To summon back the fire witch
To the court of the crimson king.

The gardner plants an evergreen
Whilst trampling on a flower.
I chase the winds of a prism ship
To taste the sweet and sour.
The pattern juggler lifts his hand;
The orchestra begins;
As slowly turns the grinding wheel
In the court of the crimson king.

On soft grey mornings widows cry,
The wise men share a joke;
I run to grasp divining signs
To satisfy the hoax.
The yellow jester does not play
But gently pulls the strings
And smiles as the puppets dance
In the court of the crimson king.

—*Ian McDonald & Peter Sinfield*

The Warrior's Daughter

Susan Heyboer-O'Keefe

*If victorious in battle, Aswarth of Millead vowed to sacrifice
whoever first met him from his household. And the Lord
Oreht, god of blood oaths, delivered the enemy into Aswarth's hand.*

*Then Aswarth returned to his house at Katl, but alas,
his daughter came out to meet him with piping and with
dancing. She was his only child; beside her, he had neither
son nor daughter, neither from wife nor from concubine.
And when he saw her, he rent the white robe of victory and
sat in the dust of the roadside and said:*

*"Daughter, what thing is it that you do to your father?
You have brought me low, to the very earth, and are the
cause of a great trouble in my heart; for I have opened my
mouth to my Lord Oreht, and I cannot take back my vow."*

*And she said to him, "My father, if you have made a
pledge, do with me accordingly, as your Lord Oreht has
indeed avenged you on your enemies. I ask to have only
this: Let me alone for a month that I may wander through
the mountains, I and my companions, and bewail my
virginity; for I go to be bride to Oreht without knowing
man. Then I shall return, and as the words you spoke with
your mouth, so shall it be done."*

And he said, "Go."

*And he sent her away for a month, and she left, she and
her companions, and bewailed her virginity upon the
mountains.*

From *The Book of Taath's Obedience*

The child is sweet like a field at harvest, but trembles like
a wheat stalk in the wind. She takes no arm. She walks
ahead alone into the mountains. From behind, the women
whisper, *Samara, Samara, Aswarth's daughter, Oreht's*

bride. She stops and looks at them and asks, *Why do you call?*

There is no break in her voice, but her skin is pale and her eyes are the color of cold ashes. The women close around her. They stroke her thick, black braided hair. They cluck and coo softly with all their mother tongues. She walks now in their midst, no longer alone.

Come, they say. *We will hide you in the mountains.*

How? My father Aswarth made a vow.

The women speak their single word. She answers in her turn. The word is bare, clipped, dry. It cannot tell what mute contractions of the heart intend and fail.

My father Aswarth is a mighty warrior whose vow was heard by the great Lord Oreht. My father is the chief of Millead. The elders elected him to rescue the land from the enemy, to bring the land to peace. And so he has, even with a vow, even for a people who hate him.

He has told me many times how he was turned out in his youth by his own half-brothers. No son of a strange woman, they said, would inherit in a house of Millead. So he fled to the land of Bod, and there gathered rough men about him.

Late one evening he returned to Millead, bringing his men with him. Aswarth, the harlot's son, returned. His coming was sighted from afar; every door was locked against him by the time he entered the village, all except the gate lock, which the gods broke open before the true ruler of Millead. He and his men entered through the gate and walked the empty streets to the house of his half-brothers.

And there my father stood, holding a torch high against the evening dark. Many times he has told me how his eyes flamed wildly, his muscles twitched in wrath, his spittle sprayed contempt as he shouted at the windows.

"I am Aswarth of Millead, born of Millead."

He flung his arms upward with a great showering of sparks from the torch.

"See these veins that throb with Millead's blood. I de-

mand my full fair measure from you, or you have my word,
you will take back by forced battle this blood you say is
yours alone. Then my dead body will have no claim on
you!"

My father Aswarth stood for long minutes, his arms held
up to the silent house. He waited for an answer from the
tongue of Millead. He waited for a word from brother to
brother. But finally the fire in his hand grew too heavy with
silence and he hurled the torch upward into the dark.
Round and round the torch spun, with a long red tail that
haloed the night, round and round and round, my father
says, streaking the sky like a dead star to be wished on.

The balsam breaks clear to a little grassy stretch and
beyond it a spring. Samara dips her hand into the water
and drinks, lets fall her hand, and shatters the reflection. As
she stands looking downward, the women come, one by
one in turn, to press two fingers upon her brow. One
woman afterwards goes off alone to weep.

What does it mean, she asks herself, the vow of this one
man? What of the child's own word, the young woman's
promise?

Several times this older woman, who had gone off alone
to weep, had watched Samara at the city gate. Samara
would stand in the cool shadow of a seller's booth and
there meet with young Zaleb of Raanoth-Rena, who had
come from west of the river to march against the enemy.
They met there frequently the three weeks he prepared to
march. Zaleb talked, Samara listened. From the sweep of
his hands, the woman knew he was telling Samara of his
home west of the river, so strange to the girl and yet a part
of the same land, the same people. She questioned him
briefly, he answered with long stories, and sometimes her
upturned palm brushed his gesturing hand as question and
answer collided.

On the day before he left, Samara gave him a token.
She unfastened the ivory toggle at her girdle and pinned it
at the neck of Zaleb's cloak. Looking at each other, they
did not see her sash unwind and fall till it was caught up in

the hooves of a runaway ass and nearly carried away. The
two of them chased after the brightly colored cloth. The
older woman remembers the sight: Zaleb running, calling
out, one hand stretched toward the strip of cloth, one hand
clapped tight against the toggle at his neck; Samara skip-
ping slowly behind him, her ungird tunic billowed out like a
sail on a ship that sailed the Great Sea. A hawker stepped
into their path right after them. From his sleeves, he drew
out finely wrought hair combs. He cried out his price, the
crowds surrounded him, and the couple disappeared. It
was the last time the woman saw them together.

If young Zaleb of Raanoth-Rena had been slain, the
woman would know why the child would not hide. But
Zaleb was alive. He had survived the march against the
enemy, some say protected by Aswarth's own hand during
battle. But even though Aswarth's vow was known to all,
even on the very day the women journeyed into the
mountains, Zaleb had been seen at the city gate, waiting in
the shadow of a seller's booth.

The women draw close against the coming dark. The
sun is nearly set. It spins out gold on the plain beneath.
Long metallic threads of heat-risen dust slowly rise and
slowly fall like waves on a molten sea. The waves wash up
from the plains below, wash up the sides of the mountains
to where the women are, wash up until the wavelike
motion stops and swirls in place, and fills up a pool of
sun-sparked air. It is here that the women pause.

Among them is a nursing mother. She sits in the pool of
light to suckle her infant, her full rich breasts yellowed by
the sunset. She looks like a woman from the east in the
golden light, a graven image, or a lustrous envoy of the
sweet goddess Tela.

Samara stands forward and reaches out, the long thin
shadow of her hand touching the baby from a distance.
She holds the shadow steady at the baby's cheek. From
behind the women make sudden angry noises.

The dead child can have no child, they say.

The warrior's blood dries up. Your womb quickens with

fear, not life. It gives us nothing of the hero's strength. You were once the daughter of our single heart. Now you are dead, childless, unremembered. In one month's time you will have no name except that of Aswarth's daughter, and Aswarth will be known for his vow, nothing more.

And yet . . .

She is still Samara this month upon the mountain. She is their own Samara. Her life is an immeasurable thing.

The child looks round at all their faces, her head cocked to the silence, her mouth gently closed. Smiling, she turns, takes the baby from its mother, and holds it to herself. The baby gives a low cry. Samara whispers in its ear, then begins to sing. Some of the women cover their heads with their cloaks and disappear into the newly fallen darkness.

My father Aswarth, the mighty warrior, has received the Lord Oreht's own legacy, the land of our people. My father takes it in place of his own rightful inheritance. He accepts this land. He loves it. The land is his recompense for the people who deny him.

From the home of his exile in Bod, before the elders of Millead called him back, my father traveled the length and the breadth of this land. All around was beauty to be wondered at. All around were the unknown ancients moving upon the earth, and for this my father has no name. He can only tell me of what he saw.

From the home of his exile he journeyed with the sun to the great northern forests of cedar. It is in this same region that the mountains wear a white crown all seasons of the year. We are like the mountains, he tells me, forever white with victory against the foe.

Then my father traveled southward down the red-soiled plains of Pilim with its thick oak and luscious rose; and along the coastal cliffs with no sweet safety of harbor; and down to the south where the summer rains flood the land like desperate tears from an unforgiven soul; and north again, up along the river where the palm trees root in the long deep wound of the water's path. And then across the innermost lands, those most blessed lands, where the tilled earth swells gently, and olive trees stand close, and the mountains rise one by one like lone gods who would be worshipped. And finally back, back against the sun's path, to the point of his beginning. He had to see finally his own, his lovely Millead.

Such was his journey. But with every sight he saw, near every place he traveled, and in most of all that was in between, there was the desert. There is always the desert.

The desert is the struggle of our people, my father says: the tiller closes his eyes and breathes and wipes his brow and thinks of the day when it shall be done for him, and when he opens his eyes, there is sand beneath his feet. The desert is why *this* land is ours. For the land itself teaches the lessons we most need to learn. The land itself is a rebuke to our rashness. Good and patient husbandry makes blossom a king's garden from even a patch of dust. Rashness makes blossom only an unfilled hunger for bread.

And yet, my father says, even the desert has its harvest.

When the elders asked my father to help fight against the enemy, he had to struggle against the wish to destroy them there in the meeting tent. He had known what they would ask, for no word left Millead that Aswarth did not hear. But when they spoke the words before him, he could only walk the length of the tent, trembling and silent. The elders watched him, my father says, and readied the guards to seize him if he should turn.

"You are the people who drove me from my father's house. Where is your hatred now?"

The elders did not answer his question. They told him only that Millead needed a fierce defender, Millead needed his might.

"What shall I say to you?" my father asked. "I gave you my word once that you would take back the blood you said was yours alone. But you take it back to spill on strange ground, as though my blood were a charm against the enemy. I tell you now my blood has a new price. I swear this time it will be paid. I am no longer a youth, content to fling words at the stars. I am a man. I have a child. I have made a home for myself.

"My price is this: I shall fight in your battle for Millead's sake. I shall lead you because it is Millead we are both defending. But I swear to you I will receive what's mine. The Lord Oreht will give me victory, and you will give me Millead. That is my price. I am to be chief over the land."

The elders agreed. Then my father brought his household to Katl where we would be safe during the war, and there at his new home he spoke these same words, naming his price, this time in the sacred oath to Lord Oreht.

In the darkness, the women hug the fire's warmth, and the velvet of their sisters' skin, and the comforts of their own flesh. Cheeks rest on arms, waists are encircled. It is the night touch of a shared journey. And the women, staring into the fire and murmuring softly, are like young girls whose loves have gone away. They are without men.

But they have memories girls do not have. The ache within them has its focus. It is not diffuse and full of wondering. It is needle sharp. The ache remembers the moment and the man, and the exactness of the two. The ache remembers the giving and the holding back, the dream melted by a stroking palm, the anger, the exhaustion, the passing glance caught and held and kept. The ache remembers, and the women murmur softly to ease it. The quiet, soothing whispers blend in the night until there are no single names and no single faces. There is only one woman. She has only one lover. She sighs for him in the darkness.

Then Samara moves—brushes back her hair, inches toward the fire. She is not one of them. This is the worst of all, in the women's private thoughts.

One woman leans close to Samara and asks about the soldier who waits, asks if they should send for him. Who would know?

Yes, who would know? the others agree. Let it be a woman's vengeance. Return to your father after obeying

yourself. Go to be bride to Oreht after wedding yourself to
your love. Or do not return at all. Let us send for the soldier
who waits for you. He will take you away.

My father Aswarth made a vow.

The women rise up angrily.

*Aswarth has made many vows. Let him keep them
himself.*

Come, let us send for the soldier, let us hide you both.
Peace is ours already. The Lord Oreht will not strike us
with war if you hide. The Lord Oreht does not care for one
girl's life. If he does, then surely we are meant as your
rescue. Come, listen. If we haven't captured you with silk,
we will take you with hemp. The soldier waits. He wants
you for his bride. He has fought bravely and won, the
image of your face an amulet against death. He returns
triumphantly, only to discover his bride is a burnt offering
to his triumph. If you obey this foolish vow, you carry
Zaleb's despair with you.

Let us save you, the women plead.

Samara does not answer.

My father sent for us after his meeting with the elders,
and our whole household traveled down from Bod to Katl
to make our home in Millead. My uncle said we looked like
a caravan of foreign merchants crossing the desert.
Perhaps he thought I would make a game of it, but I did
not.

The first days were a strangeness to me. The desert wind
blew against my face, crept inside the windings of my
headcloth, and opened my skin into thousands of tender
cracks. The wind had many voices. After a few days I could
listen to the voices and understand the words. Why do you
always look out over the land? the wind asked. There is
nothing to see. If I find something, I level it down to the dry
scrub and to the burrows of the night creatures, and to the
small stones that have not yet been ground to dust, but are
waiting their time. Men come. Not all of them leave. Do not
look for them. You will see nothing but what I want.

And still I looked. My gaze rolled outward over the

stretch of land, weary for the sight of a tree or a spring or a color. The sight of the people ahead did not satisfy me. The desert made my eyes impatient for something other than men.

The journey grew long and difficult. Before we had left Bod, we had been told of wells along the way, but the directions no longer seemed clear to memory. The water-skins hung loose and nearly empty, and the men argued whether to continue to Millead or search for other wells. Some wanted to continue. Water was on the way, on this very route. If they had not found it in so many days' journey, it was because an entire household moved more slowly than men alone. Others wanted to detour east, where there was a well, drunk from within the week, whose location had been described by a friend. It was perhaps two days away, longer if we continued to move toward Millead. I listened to the men argue and passed my tongue over the sweat on my upper lip. My tongue burned with salt.

In the light of the dying embers, Samara is small and sweet, a child at the hearth who dreams of bread. An old woman sits opposite her in silence, a neighbor from Bod who on this journey receives only a stranger's kindness from the girl. They keep watch, together and apart, as the embers cool. They do not break the air with words.

My mother rose from the bed where she'd been sleeping. I was a child then, and she took me by the hand to walk outside in the rain. She said the coolness soothed her fever. She held my hand tight and she walked looking upward.

She led me to a cluster of fruit trees near our house. She went to the tree in the middle and put both arms around it as though to embrace a man. She laid her cheek on the trunk. I shall always remember how pale her skin was against the bark, and how her arms were as thin as the frailest branch.

Samara, she whispered, stand here and look up into the

leaves and tell me—do you see the fruit? The tree was only flowering, but I told her yes because I was afraid. Good, she said. Good. She held her palm up. Pick one for me, she asked, so I may hold it. I told her no. She was very quiet now, and she nodded. You're right, she said, leave it till it's ripe.

She held my hand instead. We moved away from the cluster of trees, stood in an open space, and lifted our faces to the rain. We waited out the storm. My mother's hand stayed in mine the whole while, hot and trembling.

The strongest finally forced a decision, and we continued our journey to Millead. The next morning we sighted the well. We stayed there all that day, filling the waterskins, watching the children play in the dark, foul water.

The edge of the desert is its most dangerous point. There, with water and family so close behind, we stand and look and everything from our eyes to the horizon is the same. We see a place that man cannot take and hold and lay his mark upon. We see a kind of peace, something that seems to whisper forever, and we shut our eyes and know desire.

But our eyes do not see the secret movements made toward us, our family, our water. The desert is not a place to visit in order to reclaim our souls. It wants to take us as its own, to make us stony inhabitants. The desert wants us to surrender.

At all times we must keep watch. We must test the desert by entering it. Only then can we know its strength. We may even have to live there for a time to draw its forces away from the edge and back into itself. We must fight it always, in order to know we are always ready to fight.

Having seen the desert once, we know it lies under all things. It lies under every loose word, every quick thought, every simple act greened with a surface like slick oil. It lies waiting for our moments of sleep, waiting for our sigh-ladened wish that it all be done for us. Then we half-wake ourselves and take once more the plough to turn the earth, and there is sand beneath our feet, and we don't remember who we are.

When I see my father's face again at the end of this month, I shall remember the morning of his march. I set the pipe at the threshold and said, "See, Father, how we wait for victory." He nodded, smiling. "Will you play it for your father as well as for young soldiers?" Then he held out his hand and his eyes spoke many words. "I shall bring peace to this land. I will try to protect my men, all of my men, Samara, but Millead must have peace."

And when I see my father's face again, I shall remember the first time I saw him after the battle. The runner came with the news. Even as he was on the road shouting, I had the pipe up from its ready place at the threshold and was outside the city. When I saw the first of the soldiers, I sounded the pipe, stamped my feet, and sang to the Lord Oreht. The Lord is severe yet just, I sang. He demanded a fierce battle, yet he gives us victory.

Then I saw my father among the soldiers and saw how he looked at me. I dropped the pipe and knelt at his feet. "I thank the Lord Oreht for your safety," I whispered. From behind me I heard my name being called, Samara, Samara. I knew the voice and was glad, but did not raise my head, for I had seen my father's face.

My father Aswarth stood close. "Must you be first in your eagerness? Daughter, you have brought me very low." Dropping to his knees beside me, he was silent for many minutes, and his men drew quietly around us. Then a terrible sound rushed from his mouth, and he rent the cloak and tunic of his victory. On his chest were scars of the lifelong warrior.

And when I see my father's face again when my month of wandering has ended, I shall think of no other faces, nor of lives I might have known. I am the warrior's daughter, she who has conquered the desert. If I have no name, I have at least the peace of Millead. If I have no name, I have at least the pride of Aswarth.

It is near dawn. The sky has lightened to grey. Around the cold fire is a ring of black, the huddled shapes of sleeping women. One of them stirs, yawns, rises. Samara sits across the ring from her, knees drawn up under chin, staring into the ashes. During the night her cloak had fallen to the ground. Her bare shoulders are white in the grey morning. The woman goes to her and fastens the cloak around her neck. One by one the women wake and rise. The first helps Samara to her feet. The girl holds her for a moment, steadying herself, then gently pulls back, stands straight and smiles her thanks, then begins to walk deeper into the mountains again. The women gather their belongings, stir the ashes, and leave to follow the girl. It is not yet dawn, but they have far to go.

And at the end of one month, she returned to her father who did with her according to the vow which he had made to Oreht. She had never known a man. And it became a custom that the women of Millead went year by year to the mountains to lament the daughter of Aswarth the warrior.
From *The Book of Taath's Obedience*

Gretel in Darkness

This is the world we wanted.
All who would have seen us dead
are dead. I hear the witch's cry
break in the moonlight through a sheet
of sugar: God rewards.
Her tongue shrivels into gas . . .

                Now, far from women's arms
and memory of women, in our father's hut
we sleep, are never hungry.
Why do I not forget?
My father bars the door, bars harm
from this house, and it is years.

No one remembers. Even you, my brother,
summer afternoons you look at me as though
you meant to leave,
as though it never happened.
But I killed for you. I see armed firs,
the spires of that gleaming kiln—

Nights I turn to you to hold me
but you are not there.
Am I alone? Spies
hiss in the stillness, Hansel,
we are there still and it is real, real,
that black forest and the fire in earnest.

—*Louise Glück*

Rocinante

Steven R. Boyett

The city had decided to make the clouds green again that day. It does that sometimes. There's something dark about the city, something as dirty and unknown as a theater floor.

Wandering the dead streets that day, staring at my reflection in department-store windows—a reflection only I could see—I met a man. He'd composed a poem, and the poem had no words. He recited it to me. I can't reproduce it here; you have tissue and bone and chemical reaction to feel things. A signal is sent along a particular nerve channel, a well-worn neural pathway. You, in your roundabout but acceptable way, receive the signal, interpret it, and react—or choose not to react, as you will. But the dead don't have tissue and bone and chemical reaction, and the feelings the poem evoked weren't meant for the living.

The man finished reciting it, smiled at me, bobbed his head, turned, and walked toward a wall of a corner drugstore until he merged with it. I hurried to Rocinante while the impressions were fresh.

Rocinante is one of those mechanical horses you can ride for a dime. She's made of plastic and sits in front of the Army-Navy store downtown. Rocinante had been the name of Don Quixote's horse. She'd picked it for herself. She couldn't remember what her real name had been. I couldn't remember mine, either. She called me Nemo. She used to cry and tell me things, things I can't mention here. They were private things.

I recited the poem to her in my own inadequate way. She liked it. We were both silent a long time after I finished. I scratched at the concrete of the entrance way to the closed and wooden-windowed Army-Navy where I knelt in front of her.

"Sometimes I wonder why I'm here," I said, breaking the silence.

(My father killed me. I didn't take out the trash that last night and he beat me to death with a garden hose. It never entered my mind to hit him back, to make him stop, and he beat and beat, and the feel of the blows tearing into my back blended into one steady rhythm that slowly faded away. I can forgive him, I guess. Death's not so bad.)

"It's a punishment," she said. Her breath was a bourbon you could barely smell, and the corsage I pinned on my prom date long ago. You felt it rather than smelled it.

"I didn't do anything that bad when I was living," I protested. "Not bad enough to deserve this."

"This isn't bad," she countered. "It's just boring."

"More for you than me."

She snorted. "Maybe you're here for something you *didn't* do."

I frowned at the dark green sky. "Shit."

"That's a useful word for you, isn't it, Nemo? It gives you something you can hold on to."

"Shit," I breathed. Louder: "Shit, shitshitshit."

Daylight came and I went away.

Next day I brought Rocinante a flower. It had died, so I could pick it up and walk through the motionless city with it clasped in fog-solid hand and lay it at her plastic hooves.

She cried. I could hear the sobs behind the plastic, echoing things like a mother in a cave looking for her lost child.

I often wondered what she'd done to be put there. I couldn't bring myself to ask her much about her life. I do know that Rocinante had been dead far longer than I. She talked of things I knew as history. I loved to hear her talk.

"I have a lot of time to think during the day," she said after her crying had subsided. "Sometimes I think about stupid things. The other day it was merry-go-round horses." Her laugh was bitter. "Always the happy ride, the children's ride. But you know, I think the horses on carousels are like me—I think they're trapped there, always circling for their past lives." She was quiet a moment. "Sometimes I think about my life, about embarrassing things that happened to me, or about people I loved. I often think the reason we're here has something to do with love. I don't know what. But it fits; I think it and a part of me says yes, that strikes a chord somewhere. The funny thing—no, the *tragic* thing— is that, even if I'm right, if all the loves I had have put me here, I wouldn't repent any of it. I still would have loved."

I heard what she said without feeling it. I'd never loved. Not really.

"You see, Nemo," she continued, "you aren't the only one who spends a lot of time thinking about why we're here."

"Oh? And that's what you've decided, huh?"

Her tone carried the smile her plastic lips couldn't form. "No. It's just . . . conjecture. The only thing I feel definite about is that the way you end up is always fitting. Unjust, perhaps, even ironic—but always fitting."

(I am an intangible shadow, able to touch but not move, unreachable and unseeable to all but the dead.)

"How does this fit me?" I asked.

"I don't know. I don't know you well enough," she answered. "And even if I did, you might not be acting the way you did when you were alive. What were you like?"

How to answer that? There was so much I couldn't remember. "I . . . was in high school," I said slowly. "I don't remember the name of it. A high school . . . like any other." It was hard to get to, sealed behind something. "I really didn't get involved much in what was going on; I . . . read books . . . and stayed away from most everybody. I liked . . . *debate!*" I remembered it as I said it. "I went out sometimes . . . but not often . . . tried to learn to play guitar and never quite managed it, started a short story . . . and never finished . . . sang with rock groups until they found better singers . . . and couldn't dance. I never misspelled words, ever, and I couldn't add or subtract. I was happy, I guess. I hated most of it."

The sun began to appear in the small, light patch of sky preceding it, settling into the grid of the city.

"You're interesting, Nemo," said Rocinante as the sunlight touched me and I began to fade away. "I hope you can make it back tomorrow."

I guess it was inevitable that Rocinante and I become close. We each had stories to tell, and there were few of the dead in the city besides ourselves. I don't know why not. I don't even know what city it is. It could be the one I was born in, the one I grew up in, the one I died in: they were all different. I don't remember their names.

"Being alive doesn't seem like such a big deal anymore," I told Rocinante next day.

"Hindsight's such a wonderful thing," she muttered dryly. "I wish I could move."

"I'm sorry," I said. "I wish you could, too. I wish there were something I could do."

"*I* don't miss being alive. I don't understand why not, because I don't like *this*, whatever it is."

"Nothing ever comes by here." I sat at her base with knees drawn to chest, hugging them. "You ever notice that? No cars, no people walking by, nothing. No city's like this. Where are we really, I wonder?"

"I don't know, Nemo. I've been here as long as I can remember."

I turned my shadow-head to look up at her. "During the day, when I'm gone wherever it is I go, is this just a regular city? Do husbands go to work while their wives in their nightgowns get the paper from their driveways? Do bakery trucks make their rounds? Does anybody ever ride you?"

"No."

"No little kid ever comes by and drops in a dime?"

"Once." She was quiet a moment, remembering.

"Once, a child came by, a little boy, and dropped in a dime, and rode me. Nothing else, before then or since."

The sun opened its hangover eye, a gargantuan Peeping Tom looking through the skyscrapers. "See you later," I said, beginning to dim. As I faded out I saw a glint of something lying in the gutter in front of the store. It was a silver-gold flash, winking between pull tabs and wrinkled Lay's Potato Chips wrappers beside the curb. A dime?

I bent forward to look closer, and it was next day.

I'm usually allowed a half hour, maybe forty-five minutes. A day, I mean. There's no break between days for me; one segues to another without night's intervention. The time goes on, but I don't go with it.

Each day begins with me in a new place in the city. I've had a lot of time to get to know the place, even with me spending long stretches with Rocinante. Today I faded in in the middle of a street. I looked up: dawn was glimmering straight ahead. I turned around and began walking. I was at the edge of town; the Army-Navy was in the center. I had just sighted it down the street when the rising sun sent its light through me.

Another part of town. Got my bearings. Walked. Didn't even get to the store before the sun got to me.

"You bitch!" I yelled. I flipped it a disappearing finger—

—and completed the gesture in front of a stop sign on a curb. I stepped around a corner; the building to my right had hid the sky, which looked like it had been scoured with steel wool. I was on the edge of town. I tried to walk a straight line out of the city, though I didn't expect to make it. What I expected was to run into some kind of invisible barrier, a wall designed to keep me from leaving, but no, I just ended up stepping into another part of the city. I was willing to bet the place I ended up was on the exact opposite side of town. To find out, I turned around and stepped forward again. I was at my starting point.

It took the rest of the day's time to discover that the perimeter was roughly circular, and three more days' time to find out it was about three miles in diameter. Every time the sunlight hit me and I reappeared the next day, I was near the perimeter, no time to reach Rocinante before the next sunrise. The city sometimes plays its little jokes.

So I spent the allotted slots of my days learning the geometry of the city as I'd known the back of my hand. Sometimes for days on end I'd try to reach Rocinante. A couple of times I even got within hailing distance before the sun hit me.

Only once did I see anybody else.

The city grew cold with the season's change; then winter flew swiftly away on Pegasus' wings. Summer came again, and rain pelted me in the morning's half-light. In a flash of lightning I saw a figure in a raincoat, gray and shabby. He was leaning against the brick wall of a plasma donors' building, bristle-brush jaw moving as he mumbled to himself. A flash of lightning showed his face in purplish white. He turned, and his rheumy eyes went wide. The brown paper bag he'd been clutching dropped from his hand. I heard breaking glass as he ran away.

I walked across the street and kicked the bag. My foot wouldn't move it. He must have been alive. Another of the city's jokes, I guess.

I liked walking around the city that day. The rain pattered my closed eyelids, tickled the inside of my open mouth with the same feeling your leg gets when it's gone to sleep and sensation is just returning. I think I got in two hours that day, until a shaft of sunlight poked through a gap in the dark clouds and speared me into the next day.

The ground was dry; I was still soaked. Ahead of me on the road where I'd appeared was a large book. Its blue binding was weathered and moldy. I bent over and looked at the cover:

SOUTH DADE '55

A high school yearbook. *My* high school yearbook.

I touched the thing as if it were a dead animal, pulled my hand quickly from the coolness beneath my fingertips. Reached out again. Opened the cover. Pushed the book away and yelped aloud when I realized that I'd moved it, I'd *moved* it, and I hadn't moved anything in a very long time. I approached it again, warily, and reread the date.

If I'd lived another year, it would have been my senior class yearbook.

I turned the pages.

Athletics. Prom Queen. Superlatives. Clubs. Everything I'd had nothing to do with. Senior portraits—familiar faces leapt up. I could match them to names along the side. It was something to hold to, tangible memories like a fresh, green vegetable, a peapod snapped and the odor rising, right there and real.

The last page before the supporters' ads:

In Memory of Janice Fountenot and Daniel Larexis.

And pictures below that.

A smiling girl, a senior portrait she'd probably never seen. I hadn't known her. Her smile was the kind you expected to see foil braces attached to.

The other picture—another familiar face. I saw it reflected often in the windows of lonely department stores.

I clutched the yearbook to my chest and ran

into tomorrow. The area was familiar; not more than two blocks away from the Army-Navy. I ran with the yearbook and stopped in front of Rocinante. She looked the same; nothing at all had changed. The CLOSED sign was still behind her in the dusty store window; a piece of chewing gum was still stuck beneath her left front plastic hoof. I didn't have to look to see these things; I knew.

Though I'd run, I wasn't out of breath. I didn't need air for anything. If I thought about it I could billow my lungs like Mylar balloons, feel my diaphragm tighten, feel the air rush into my nose, out my mouth: cool, warm, cool, warm. All by remembering.

"Nemo," said Rocinante mildly. "Where have you been?"

"I couldn't get back to you. The city kept me away."

"Ah. I've been thinking—mostly because I'm unable to do anything else. I think the city's alive. I think it's a real city, the kind you and I know, but it only shows one face to us. It holds things, won't let us see the people within its walls, its doors. Sometimes it tosses out morsels—my little boy, the yearbook I see there in your hand."

I looked at the blue thing, sudden memory returning the feel of its weight to my grasp. "Yeah. Rocinante, I've found my name." I opened the book to the memorial page. "Daniel Larexis."

"Bring back any memories?"

I frowned. "No. It's like . . . discovering a mole on your arm. It was there all along, you just never knew it. Just another piece of information to file away about yourself, that's all."

"Mmm."

I sat at her base and leafed through the yearbook, telling her stories about remembered friends pictured in the strange pages. Remembering them led to memories of my family, as though I were exploring a house whose rooms contained doors that led to more rooms, more doors.

I told her about my mother, about how I'd ask her for five dollars so I could go out, and how she'd turn away from the supper she was required to cook, or from running the sweeper over the tattered carpet, and walk down the hall into her bedroom, emerging after loud words with my father with a five-dollar bill in her hand. She would give it to me without a word and I'd take it, fold it, shove it into my back pocket, and go out. Usually I'd come in and complain because I'd had a lousy time.

The city let me come back to Rocinante for seven days, and I spent all of it telling her stories inspired by the yearbook. Sunlight hit me at the end of the seventh day and it became the eighth, and I ran down the familiar street—they were all familiar now—and stopped.

There was no yearbook in my hand.

On the way to Rocinante a year or so later—the city had kept me away again—I found a box in the middle of the road. It was the end of summer, a nice nip in the air—too cold for most people, considering the time of day, but I'd got used to it. The box was white, with a clear plastic window on top and an orchid inside, a light purple thing with color smooth as fine powder. A corsage.

I opened it and smelled.

Yes. Rocinante's breath and a distant prom. There were still little drops of moisture on the inside of the clear plastic, as if it had just been removed from the refrigerator.

I looked at the orchid, at the purple-fringed and fragrant vagina-lips. "Why are you doing this to me?" I whispered, talking not to the orchid but to the city. I didn't get an answer, of course.

I took the flower to Rocinante. It died before I got to her, becoming brown and burned-looking. My eyes stung with imagined tears. I told Rocinante about the prom: junior-senior prom; my date had been a lovely, quiet girl I had thought I was in love with. Dinner, dancing, a ride to the beach in my parents' car, and I saw her wondering why I'd grown cold to her as the evening lengthened. I couldn't tell her it was because she wasn't what I'd imagined her to be. At her doorstep she turned to give me the perfunctory good-night kiss and I stopped just short of her lips and pulled my head back, gazing without expression into her surprised eyes. I'd turned away and driven off without another word.

The orchid made Rocinante cry. I worked up the courage to ask her why.

"You brought me a rose once," she said. "It did the same thing: it gave me memories. I get them in fragments sometimes, no matter how hard I try to forget. There was a man once, long ago, who took me dancing through the

night. We got tipsy on champagne and rode on horseback
to the lake to watch clouds race across the full moon. I
leaned over and kissed him, and never touched him again,
not in any romantic way. He thanked me gravely and we
remained the best of friends."

She paused. "I hate thinking about those things. I'm
convinced the key to getting away from here, from this city,
is to get away from our past. I want to forget but I can't. If I
can remember what happened to me yesterday, or even
five minutes ago, then I have a past and I can never get
away."

I scratched at the concrete by her base.

"Nemo, do you know you're the only diversion I have
from my thoughts all through the day?"

I didn't bother to correct her. Nemo, Daniel, what's in a
name? I stared at the dead corsage in my hands.

We were both silent until the sun took me away.

Weeks later it was hot. Dry, dusty-hot, Texas-drought
hot. The sun had caught me in midstride and the step
I'd begun up a flight of stairs was completed beside a
curb. The slight breeze was a devil's breath across my
face.

I stepped onto the sidewalk and walked away from the
smear of sunlight that was already beginning to appear.
Today I'd beat the sun, I vowed, watching sidewalk lines
pass beneath my feet. Today I'd remain in shadow behind
a skyscraper and see if the sun could take me then.

When I first saw it I thought it was a green snake in front
of my foot and I jumped up. And then I landed and saw
that it wasn't a snake at all, it was . . .

I remembered my heart and it froze.

It was a garden hose. Hollow, green plastic tube with
metal head. Eighteen inches long. Dark brown stains on
the metal end and first six inches: dried blood.

One hand strayed to my back.

I looked at the thing as though it *were* a snake, one that
would strike any second. The yearbook, the corsage, my
name, the faces—my *past*—I could face those.

But not this. God, not this.

I made myself look up from the garden hose. The Army-Navy was three blocks down the street. I could see the outline of Rocinante's front half—head, neck, and curled front legs—by the entrance.

Moving through chest-deep molasses, I backed up a step. Sunlight glinted on the head of the hose. I looked over my shoulder at the way I'd come. The sunlight seeped into me

and I walked into the next day at exactly the same spot. That had never happened before. It was dim twilight, a little cooler than the day before.

The hose was still there.

Forcing an insubstantial throat to swallow, I willed my left leg to move. I stepped down onto the street, circled the garden hose, and stepped onto the sidewalk again on the other side of the thing. I turned my head away and ran to Rocinante, feeling it behind me all the way.

Fear caused me to remember enough of my body to make me breathless when I stopped before the Army-Navy. "Rocinante," I gasped, falling to her metal base. "Rocinante, I've got . . . to talk . . . to you." I closed my eyes. "There's . . . so much . . . I don't understand."

She said nothing.

"My past," I said. "These pieces, all coming back." I sat up and opened my eyes.

Silent Rocinante.

"Rocinante?"

I stood. Blinked. Looked at the dead glass eyes, the right one chipped.

No, not Rocinante. A mechanical plastic horse. Rocinante was gone. Paid whatever penance she was supposed to pay, learned what she was supposed to learn. Forgotten what she was supposed to forget.

I glanced to the dirty gutter. Yes, the thing that had gleamed: a dime.

I looked at the box on the pole at Rocinante's side, at the coin slot on top of it. To ride Rocinante. . . .

On my knees I reached out to grasp the dime. My fingers touched it, felt nothing, moved it not one bit. It was nailed to the center of the earth. I shut my eyes and kept my fingers where they were.

The dime, think about the dime! You can feel its cold metal on your fingers, the serrated edge. Pick it up, pick it up.

But I couldn't move it.

The dime gleamed gold and I was on another street in the city.

It's been a long time since then. The city hasn't let me back near the Army-Navy. Sometimes it rains, sometimes it's hot. It never snows. The clouds, every so often, are a pale sort of green. The city plays its little jokes.

I spend a lot of time thinking about what Rocinante said. About how the way you end up is always fitting.

There is a feeling the living have, a sudden shudder, a sort of twitch of the body that occurs for no apparent reason. People speak of cats walking across graves.

I think it's me in my world, walking through you in yours.

Springsong in East Gruesome, Vermont

Little Miss Pingry answered demurely
when asked how Mamma was, "Thank you, poorly,"
in gingham and sunbonnet lowered her eyes
to her pinafored lap with its shin-sharp thighs
and did her daintiest not to drool
as she gnawed on the ulna of a ghoul
with neat little teeth so pointed and bright
that I think I shall not sleep tonight.
      (And the wind slinks down from Mount Horrid
        to rattle the corncrib slats.)
Miss Lettie Grigsbee's eldest pig
was named Doremus. Who gives a fig
for the tittletat spite that her neighbors vent
of the grunt he uttered and what it meant
when, leaning his elbows over the sty,
an itinerant butcher offered to buy
and of how she began to jerk and slaver—
as she has ever since—at the shock it gave her?
       (And the wind scuttles over the stubble
        snatching the scarecrows' hats.)
Deacon Bigelow, whiskers aflame
from a leaky lantern, bellowed a name
that only once in a thousand years
had ever been heard by human ears.
The weathervane squealed, the lightning-rods
writhed on the lawn, peas popped from their pods,
swallows dropped dead from the crackled sky,
and three hump-shouldered owls trudged by.
       (And the wind is fretting the mortar
        out from the chimney bricks.)
Old Mrs. Dreed, marshamallow fat,
kept a prim white mouse and an albino bat.
Her hope was to mate them just to see
what manner of beast their get would be.
When nothing happened, in despair
she fashioned an image and said a prayer.
She fashioned it out of gingerbread
that she pricked with a needle until it bled.
       (And the wind went whimpering over the hill
        knowing the end of such tricks.)

—Ramon Guthrie

"Banju Wangi! By golly! Remember that
pack of cannibals? Inky lot of blokes, what?"

The Idol's Eye

James P. Blaylock

I won't say that this was the final adventure of Professor Langdon St. Ives and his man Hasbro—Colonel Hasbro since the war—but it was certainly the strangest and the least likely of the lot. Consider this: I know the Professor to be a man of complete and utter veracity. If he told me that he had determined, on the strength of scientific discovery, that gravity would reverse itself at four o'clock this afternoon, and that we'd find ourselves, as Stevenson put it, scaling the stars, I'd pack my bag and phone my solicitor and, at 3:59, I'd stroll out into the center of Jermyn Street so as not to crack my head on the ceiling when I floated away. And yet even *I* would have hesitated, looked askance, perhaps covertly checked the level of the bottles in the Professor's cabinet if he had simply recounted to me the details of the strange occurrence at the Explorers Club on that third Thursday in April. I admit it: the story is impossible on the face of it.

But I was there. And, as I say, what transpired was far and away more peculiar and exotic than the activities that, some twenty years earlier, had set the machinery of fate and mystery into creaking and irreversible motion.

It was a wild and rainy Thursday, then, that day at the club. March hadn't gone out like any lamb; it had roared right along, storming and blowing into April. We—that is to say, the Professor, Colonel Hasbro, Tubby Frobisher, John Priestly (the African explorer and adventurer, not the novelist) and myself, Jack Owlesby—were sitting about after a long dinner at the Explorers Club, opposite the Planetarium. Wind howled outside the casements, and rain angled past in a driving rush, now letting off, now redoubling, *whoosh*ing in great sheets of grey mist. It wasn't the sort of weather to be out in, you can count on that, and none of us, of course, had any business to see to anyway. I was looking forward to pipes and cigars and a glass of this or that, maybe a bit of a snooze in the lounge and then a really first-rate supper—a veal cutlet, perhaps, or a steak and mushroom pie and a bottle of Burgundy. The afternoon and evening, in other words, held astonishing promise.

So we sipped port, poked at the bowls of our pipes, watched the fragrant smoke rise in little lazy wisps and drift off, and muttered in a satisfied way about the weather. Under those conditions, you'll agree, it couldn't rain hard enough. I recall even that Frobisher, who, to be fair, had been coarsened by years in the bush, called the lot of us over to the window in order to have a laugh at the expense of some poor shambling madman who hunched in the rain below, holding over his head the ruins of an umbrella that might have been serviceable twenty or thirty years earlier but had seen hard use since, and which, in its fallen state, had come to resemble a ribby-looking inverted bird with about half a dozen pipe-stem legs. As far as I could see, there was no cloth on the thing at all. He had the mannerisms correct; that much I'll give him. *He* seemed convinced that the fossil umbrella was doing the work. Frobisher roared and shook and said that the man should be on the stage. Then he said he had half a mind to go down and give the fellow a half crown, except that it was raining and he would get soaked. "That's well and good in the bush," he said, "but in the city, in civilization, well . . ." He shook his head. "When in Rome," he said. And he forgot about the poor bogger in the road. All of us did, for a bit.

"I've seen rain that makes this look like small beer," Frobisher boasted, shaking his head. "That's nothing but fizz-water to me. Drizzle. Heavy fog."

"It reminds me of the time we faced down that mob in Banju Wangi," said Priestly, nodding at St. Ives, "after you two"—referring to the Professor and Hasbro—"routed the pig men. What an adventure."

It's moderately likely that Priestly, who kept pretty much to himself, had little desire to tell the story of our

adventures in Java, incredible though they were, which
had transpired some twenty years earlier. You may have
read about them, actually, for my own account was published in *The Strand* some six months after the story of the
Chingford Tower fracas and the alien threat. But as I say,
Priestly himself didn't want to, as the Yanks say, spin any
stretchers; he just wanted to shut Frobisher up. We'd
heard nothing but "the bush" all afternoon. Frobisher had
clearly been "out" in it—Australia, Brazil, India, Canton
Province. There was bush enough in the world; that much
was certain. We'd had enough of Frobisher's bush, but of
course none of us could say so. This was the club, after all,
and Tubby, although coarsened a bit, as I say, was one of
the lads.

So I leapt in on top of Priestly when I saw Frobisher point
his pipe stem at St. Ives. Frobisher's pipe stem, somehow,
always gave rise to fresh accounts of the ubiquitous bush.
"Banju Wangi!" I half shouted. "By golly!" I admit it was
weak, but I needed a moment to think. And I said it loud
enough to put Frobisher right off the scent.

"Banju Wangi," I said to Priestly. "Remember that pack
of cannibals? Inky lot of blokes, what?" Priestly nodded,
but didn't offer to carry on. He was satisfied with simply
recalling the rain. And there *had* been a spectacular rain in
those Javanese days, if you can call it a rain. Which you
can't, really, no more than you would call a waterfall a
faucet or the sun a gas lamp. A monsoon was what it was.

Roundabout twenty years back, then, it fell out that
Priestly and I and poor Bill Kraken had, on the strength of
Dr. Birdlip's manuscript, taken ship to Java where we met,
not unexpectedly, Professor St. Ives and Hasbro, themselves returning from a spate of very dangerous and mysterious space travel. The alien threat, as I said before, had
been crushed, and the five of us had found ourselves deep
in cannibal-infested jungles, beating our way through
toward the Bali Straits in order to cross over to Penginu-
man where there lay, we fervently prayed, a Dutch
freighter bound for home. The rain was sluicing down. It
was mid-January, smack in the middle of the northwest

monsoons, and we were slogging through jungles, trailed
by orangutans and asps, hacking at creepers, and slowly
metamorphosing into biped sponges.

On the banks of the Wangi River we stumbled upon a
tribe of tiny Peewatin natives and traded them boxes of
kitchen matches for a pair of long piroques. Bill Kraken
gave his pocket watch to the local priest in return for an
odd bamboo umbrella with a shrunken head dangling
from the handle by a brass chain. Kraken was, of course,
round the bend in those days, but his purchase of the
curious umbrella wasn't an act of madness. He stayed far
drier than the rest of us in the days that followed.

We set off, finally, down the Wangi beneath grey skies
and a canopy of unbelievable green. The river was swollen
with rain and littered with tangles of fallen tree trunks and
vegetation that crumbled continually from either shore.
Canoeing in a monsoon struck me as a trifle outré, as the
Frenchman would say, but St. Ives and Priestly agreed that
the very wildness of the river would serve to discourage the
vast and lumbering crocodiles which, during a more placid
season, splashed through the shallows in frightful abun-
dance. And the rain itself, pouring from the sky without
pause, had a month before driven most of the cannibal
tribes into higher elevations.

So we paddled and baled and baled and paddled, St.
Ives managing, through a singular and mysterious invention of his own, to keep his pipe alight in the downpour,
and I anticipating, monsoon or no, the prick of a dart on
the back of my neck or the sight of a toothy, arch-eyed
crocodile, intent upon dinner.

Our third night on the river, very near the coast, we
found what amounted to a little sandy inlet scooped into
the riverside. The bank above it had been worn away, and
a cavern, overhung with vines and shaded by flowering
acacias and a pair of incredible teaks, opened up for some
few yards. By the end of the week it would be underwater,
but at present it was high and dry, and we required shelter
only for the night. We pushed the piroques up onto the
sand, tied them to tree trunks, and hunched into the little

cavern, lighting a welcome and jolly fire.

That night was full of the cries of wild beasts, the screams of panthers and the shrill peep of winging bats. More than once great clacking-jawed crocodiles crept up out of the river and gave us the glad eye before slipping away again. Pigmy hippopotami stumbled up, to the vast surprise of the Professor, and watched us for a bit, blinking and yawning and making off again up the bank and into the undergrowth. St. Ives insisted that such beasts were indigenous only to the continent of Africa, and his observation encouraged Priestly to tell a very strange and sad tale—the story of Doctor Ignacio Narbondo. This Doctor Narbondo, it seems, practiced in London in the eighteenth century. He claimed to have developed any number of strange serums including one which, ostensibly, would allow the breeding of unlike beasts: pigs with fishes and birds with hedgehogs. He was harried out of England as a vivisectionist, although he swore to his own innocence and to the efficacy of his serum. Three years later, after suffering the same fate in Venice, he set sail from Mombasa with a herd of pygmy hippos, determined to haul them across the Indian Ocean to the Malay Archipelago and breed them with the great hairy orangutans that flourished in the Borneo rain forests.

He was possessed, said Priestly, with the idea of one day docking at Marseilles or London and striding ashore flanked by an army of the unlikely offspring of two of the most ludicrous beasts imaginable, throwing the same fear into the civilized world that Hannibal must have produced when, with ten score of elephants, he popped in from beyond the Alps. Narbondo, however, was never seen again. He docked in Surabaja, disappeared into the jungles with his beasts, and, as they say of Captain England in Mauritius, went native. Whether Narbondo became, in the years that followed, the fabled Wildman of Borneo is speculation. Some say he did, some say he died of typhus in Bombay. His hippopotami, however, riddled with Narbondo's serum, multiplied within a small area of Eastern Java.

The explanation of the existence of the hippos seemed to whet St. Ives's curiosity. He questioned Priestly for an hour, in fact, about this mysterious Doctor Narbondo, but Priestly had merely read about the mad doctor in Ashbless's *Account of London Madmen* (a grossly unfair appellation, at least in regard to Doctor Narbondo) and he could remember little else.

Half a dozen times that night I awakened to the sounds of something crashing in the forest above, and twice, blinking awake, I saw wide, hairy faces, upside down, eyes aglow, peering at us from overhead—jungle beasts, hanging from the vine-covered ledge above to watch us as we slept. Visions of Narbondo's hippo-apes flitted through my dreams, and when daylight wandered through the following morning, I was convinced that many of the past night's visitations had not been made merely by the creatures of dreams, but had actually been the offspring, so to speak, of the misanthropic Doctor Narbondo.

We had a brief respite from the rain that morning, and, determined to make the most of it, we loaded our gear aboard the piroques and prepared to clamber in. The sun broke through the clouds about then, and golden rays slanted through the forest ceiling, stippling the jungle floor and setting off an opera of bird cries and monkey whistling. We stood and stared at the steamy radiance of the forest, beautiful beyond accounting, then turned toward the canoes. A shout from Hasbro, however, brought us up short. He'd seen something, that much was certain, in the jungle beyond the riverside cavern.

"What ho, man?" said St. Ives, anxious to be off yet overwhelmed with scientific curiosity.

"A temple of sorts, sir," said Hasbro, pointing away into the forest. "I believe I see some sort of stone monolith or altar, sir. Perhaps a shrine to some heathen god."

And sure enough, bathed now in sunlight was a little clearing in the trees. In it, scattered in a circle, were half a dozen stone rectangles, one almost as large as an automobile, all crumbling and half-covered with creepers and moss.

Bill Kraken, still suffering from the poulp madness that had so befuddled him in the past months, gave out a little cry and dashed past Hasbro up the bank and into the forest. The rest of us followed at a run, fearing that Bill would come to harm. If we had known what lay ahead, we would have been a bit quicker about it even yet.

What we found in the clearing was that circle of stone monoliths, crumbling, as I've said, with age. Dozens of bright green asps rested in the sunshine atop the stones, watching us through lazy eyes. Four wild pigs, rooting for insects, crashed off into the vegetation, setting off the flight of a score of apes which had, hitherto, been hidden away overhead in the treetops. In the midst of the circle of stones sat a peculiar and indescribably eerie statue, carved, it seemed, entirely of ivory. It was old, though clearly not so old as the monoliths surrounding it, and it was minutely carven; its mouth looked as if it were ready to speak, and its jaw was square and determined and revealed just a hint of sadness. On closer inspection it clearly wasn't ivory that it had been carved from, for the stone, whatever it was, was veined with thin blue lines.

It was uncanny. Professor St. Ives speculated at first that it was some sort of rare Malaysian marble. And very fine marble at that—marble that Michelangelo would have blathered over. More astonishing than the marble, though, were its eyes—two great rubies, faceted so minutely that they threw the rays of the tropical sun in a thousand directions. And it was those ruby eyes that not only cut short our examination of the ruined ring of altars and the peculiar idol, but which were the end of poor old Bill Kraken, a fine scientist in his own right before falling into the hands of the aliens after Birdlip's demise.

It was the flash of sunlight from those rubies that had instigated Kraken's charge up the slope and into the clearing. While the rest of us had gathered about commenting on the strange veined stone, Bill had stood gaping, clutching his umbrella, hypnotized by the ruby lights which, as the forest foliage swayed in the breezes overhead, now shading the jungle floor, now opening and allowing sunlight to flood in upon us, played over his face like the glints of light thrown from one of those spinning mirrored globes that dangle from the ceiling of a ballroom.

Suddenly and in an instant, as if propelled from a catapult, he sprang past St. Ives, hurled Priestly aside, and jabbed the tip of his umbrella in under one of the ruby eyes—the left eye, it was; I remember it vividly. He pried furiously on the thing as St. Ives and Hasbro attempted to haul him away. But he had the strength of a madman. The eye popped loose, rolling into the grasses, and Mad Bill shook off his two erstwhile friends, wild in his ruby lust. He cast down his umbrella and dived for the gem, convinced, I suppose, that St. Ives and Hasbro and, no doubt, Priestly and myself were going to wrestle him for it. What brought him up short and froze the rest of us to the marrow there in that steamy jungle sun was a long, weary, ululating howl—a cry of awful pain, of indefinable grief—that soared out of the jungle around us, carried on the wind, part of the very atmosphere.

Our first thought after that long frozen instant was, of course, of cannibals. Bill snatched up the stone and leapt down the path toward the piroques with the rest of us, once again, at his heels.

Before night fell we had paddled out into the Bali Straits, never having caught a glimpse of those supposed cannibals nor seen the hint of a flying spear. There lay the Dutch freighter the *Peter Van Teeslink*. A week later Bill Kraken died of a fever in Singapore, shouting before he went of wild jungle beasts and of creatures that lay waiting for him in the depths of the sea and of a grinning sun that blinded him and set him mad.

We buried him there in Singapore on a sad day. St. Ives was determined to bury the ruby with him—to let him keep the plunder which had, it seemed certain, brought about his ruination. But Priestly wouldn't consider it. The ruby alone, he said, would pay for the entire journey with some to spare. To bury it with Kraken would be to submit, as it were, to the lusts of a madman. And Kraken, only six months previously, had been as sane as any of us. Keep the ruby, said Priestly. If nothing else it would provide for Kraken's son, himself almost as mad as his father. Hasbro agreed with Priestly as did, after consideration, St. Ives. The Professor, I believe, had an uncommon and inexplicable (in the light of his scientific training) fear of the jewel. But that's just conjecture. In the forty-five years I've known him he's demonstrated no fears whatsoever. He's too full of curiosity. And the ruby, finally, was a curiosity. It was certainly that.

Such were the details of our journey down the Wangi River as I related them that day at the Explorers Club. Everyone present at the table except Tubby Frobisher had, of course, been along on that little adventure, and I rather suspected that Tubby would just as soon I'd kept the story to myself, he being full of his own wanderings in the bush and having no acquaintance whatsoever with eastern Java or Bill Kraken. It was the ruby, in the end, that fetched his attention.

For some moments he'd been hunched forward in his chair, squinting at me, puffing so on his cigar that it burned like a torch. He slumped back as I ended the tale and plucked the cigar from his mouth. He paused for a moment before standing up and stepping slowly across to the window to look for his stranger on the street. But the man had apparently moved along.

There was a crashing downstairs about then—a slamming of doors, high voices, the clattering of falling cutlery. "Close that off!" shouted Frobisher down the stairwell. There was an answering shout, indecipherable, from below. "Shut yer gob!" Frobisher shouted, tapping ashes onto the rug.

One of the club members, Isaacs, I believe, from the Himalayan business, advised Frobisher to shut his. Under other circumstances, I'm sure, Tubby would have flown at the man, but he was too full of our Javanese ruby, and he barely heard the man's retort. It was quiet again downstairs. "By God," said Frobisher, "I'd give my pension to have a look at that damned ruby!"

"Impossible," I said, relighting my pipe which I'd let

grow cold during my narrative. "The ruby hasn't been seen in five years. Not since Giles Connover stole it from the museum. It was the ruby that brought about his end; that's what I believe—just as surely as it brought about the death of Bill Kraken."

I expected St. Ives to disagree with me, point out that I was possessed by superstition, that logic didn't and couldn't support me. But he kept silent, having once been possessed, I suppose, by the same unfounded fears—fears that had been a product of the weird, moaning cry that had assailed us there in the jungle some twenty years before.

"It certainly has had a curious history," said St. Ives with just the trace of a smile on his face. "A very curious history."

"Has it?" said Frobisher, stabbing his cigar out into the ashtray. "You didn't manage to sell it, then?"

"Oh, we sold it," St. Ives said. "Almost at once. Within the week of our return, if I'm not mistaken."

"Four days, sir, to be precise," put in Hasbro, who had an irritating habit of exactitude, one that had been polished and tightened over his eighty-odd years. "We docked on a Tuesday, sir, and sold the ruby to a jeweler in Knightsbridge on the following Saturday afternoon."

"Quite," said St. Ives, nodding toward him.

A waiter wandered past about then with a tea towel over his arm. Simultaneously there was another crash downstairs, a chair being upset it sounded like, and an accompanying shout. "What the devil is that row?" demanded Frobisher of the waiter. "This is a club, man, not a bowling green!"

"Quite right, sir," the waiter said. "We've had a bit of a time with an unwanted guest. Insists on coming in to have a look around. He's very persistent."

"Throw the blighter into the rubbish can," said Frobisher. "And bring us a decanter of Scotch, if you will. Laphroaig. And some fresh glasses."

"Ice?" the waiter asked.

Frobisher gave him a wilting look and chewed on his cigar. "Just the filthy Scotch. And tell that navvy downstairs that Tubby Frobisher will horsewhip him on the club steps at three o'clock if he's still about." Frobisher checked his watch. "That's about six and a half minutes from now."

"I'll tell him, sir, just as you say. But the man is deaf as a stone, as far as I can make out, and he wears smoked glasses, so he's quite possibly blind too. Threats haven't done much to dissuade him."

"Haven't they, by God!" shouted Frobisher. "Dissuade him, is it! I'll dissuade the man. I'll dissuade him from here to Chelsea. But let's have that Scotch first. Did I say we needed glasses too?"

"Yes, sir," said the waiter. And off he went toward the bar.

"So this ruby," Frobisher said, settling back in his seat and plucking another cigar from inside his coat. "How much did it fetch?"

"A little above twenty-five thousand pounds," said St. Ives, nodding to Hasbro for affirmation.

"Twenty-five thousand six hundred fifty, sir," the colonel said.

Frobisher let out a low whistle.

"And it brought almost twice that at an auction at Sotheby's two weeks after," I put in. "Since then it's been bought and sold a dozen times, I imagine. The truth is, no one wants to keep it. It was owned, in time, by Isador Persano, and we all know what came of that, and later by Lady Braithewaite-Long, whose husband, of course, was involved in that series of ghastly murders near Waterloo Station."

"Don't overlook Preston Waters, the jeweler," said Priestly with an apparent shudder—a recollection, no doubt, of the grisly horror that had befallen the very Knightsbridge jeweler who had given us the twenty-five thousand pounds.

"The thing's cursed, if you ask me," I said, clearing debris from the table to make room for our newly arrived decanter of Scotch. Frobisher, sighing heartily, poured a neat bit into four glasses.

"None for me, thanks," Priestly said when Frobisher

approached the fifth glass with the upturned decanter. "I'll just nip at this port for a bit. Whiskey eats me up. Tears my throat bones to shreds. I'd be on milk and bread for a week."

Frobisher nodded, pleased, no doubt, to consume Priestly's share himself. He tilted his glass back and sucked a bit in, rolling it about in his mouth, relishing it. "That's the stuff, what?" he said, relaxing. "If there were one thing that would drag me back in out of the bush, it wouldn't be gold or women, I can tell you. No, sir. Not gold or women."

I assumed that it was Scotch, finally, that would drag Tubby Frobisher out of the bush, though he never got around to saying so. I got in ahead of him. "Where do you suppose that ruby lies today, Professor?" I asked, having a taste of the Scotch myself. "Did the museum ever get it back?"

"They didn't want it, actually," said St. Ives. "They were offered the thing free, and they turned it down."

"The fools," Frobisher said. "They didn't go for all that hocus-pocus about a curse, I don't suppose. Not the bloody museum."

St. Ives shrugged. "There's no denying that it cost them a tremendous amount of trouble—robbery and murder and the like. And it's possible that they thought the man who offered it to them was a prankster. No one, of course, with any sense would give the thing away. I rather believe that they never considered the offer serious."

"I'd bet they were afraid of it," said Priestly, who had come to fear the jewel himself in the years since our return. "I wish now that we'd buried the bloody thing with Kraken. Do you remember that ghastly cry in the jungle? That wasn't made by any cannibals."

Hasbro raised an eyebrow. "Who do you suggest cried out, sir?" he asked in his cultivated butler's tone—a tone that alerted you to the sad fact that you were about to say something worthless and foolish.

Priestly gazed into his port and shrugged.

"I like to believe," said St. Ives, always the philosopher, "that the jungle itself cried out. That we had stolen a bit of her very heart, broken off a piece of her soul. I was possessed with the same certainty that we'd committed a terrible crime that possesses me when I see a fine old building razed or a great tree cut down—a tree, perhaps, that had seen the passing of two score generations of kings and, being a part of those ages, has been imbued with their history, with their glory. Do you follow me?"

Hasbro nodded. I could see he took the long view. Priestly appeared to be lost in the depths of his port, but I knew that he felt pretty much the same way; he just couldn't have stated it so prettily. Leave it to the Professor to get to the nub.

"Trash!" said Frobisher. "Gouge 'em both out; that's what I would have done. Imagine a pair of such rubies. A matched pair!" He shook his head. "Yes, sir," he finished, "I'd give my pension just to get a glimpse of one. Just a glimpse."

St. Ives, smiling just a bit, wistfully perhaps, reached into the inside pocket of his coat, pulled out his tobacco pouch and unfolded it, plucking out a ball of tissue twice the size of a walnut. Inside it was the idol's eye—the very one.

Frobisher leapt with a shout to his feet, his chair slamming over backward on the carpet. Isaacs, dozing in a chair by the fire, awoke with a start and shouted at Frobisher to leave off. But Tubby, taken so by surprise at St. Ives's coolness and by the size of the faceted gem that lay before him, red as thin blood and glowing in the firelight, failed to hear Isaacs's complaint. He stood and gaped at the ruby, his pension secure.

"How . . ." I began, at least as surprised as Frobisher. Priestly acted as if the thing were a snake; his pipe clacked in his teeth.

There was a wild shout from downstairs. Running footsteps echoed up toward us. A *whump* and crash followed as if something had been hurled into the wall. Then, weirdly, a blast of air sailed up the stairwell and blew past us, as if a door had been left open and the winds were finding their way in.

But the peculiar thing, the thing that made all of us, in

that one instant, abandon the jewel and turn, waiting, watching the shadow that rose slowly along the wall of the stairwell, was the nature of that wind, the smell of that wind.

It wasn't the wet, cold breeze blowing down Baker Street. It wasn't a London breeze at all. It was a wind that blew down a jungle river—a warm and humid wind saturated with the smell of orchid blooms and rotting vegetation, that seemed to suggest the slow splash of crocodiles sliding off a muddy bank and the rippling silent passage of a tiger glimpsed through distant trees. The shadow rose on the stairs, frightfully slowly, as if whatever cast it had legs of stone and was creeping inexorably along—clump, clump, clump—toward some fated destination. And within the footsteps, surrounding them, part of them, were the far-off cries of wild birds and the chattering of treetop monkeys and the shrill cry of a panther, all of it borne on that wind and on that ascending shadow for one long, teeming, silent moment.

And what we saw first when the walker on the stairs clumped into view was the bent tip of an umbrella—the sprung umbrella hoisted by Frobisher's stroller. Ruined as the umbrella was, I could see that the shaft was a length of deteriorated bamboo, crushed and black with age and travel. And there, at the base, dangling by a green brass chain below the grip that was clutched in a wide, pale hand, was what had once been a tiny, preserved head, nothing but a skull now, yellow and broken and with one leathery strip of dried flesh still clinging in the depression below the eye socket.

We all shouted. Priestly smashed back into his chair. St. Ives bent forward in eager anticipation. We knew, wild and impossible as it seemed, what it was that approached us up the stairs on that rainy April day. It wore, as the waiter had promised, a pair of glasses with smoked lenses, and was otherwise clad in cast-off, misshapen clothing that had once been worn, quite clearly, by people in widely different parts of the world: Arab bloused trousers, a Mandalay pontoon shirt, wooden shoes, a Leibnitz cap. His marbled jaw was set with fierce determination and his mouth opened and shut rhythmically like the mouth of a conger eel, his breath *whoosh*ing in and out. He reached up with his free hand and tore the smoked glasses away, pitching them in one sweeping motion against the wall where they shattered, spraying poor, dumbfounded Isaacs with glass shards.

In his right eye shone a tremendous faceted ruby, identical to the one that lay before St. Ives. Light blazed from it as if it were alive. His left eye was a hollow, dark socket, smooth and black and empty as night. He stood at the top of the stairs, chest heaving, creaking with exertion. He looked, so to speak, from one to the other of us, fixing his stare on the ruby glowing atop the table. His arm twitched. He let go of Bill Kraken's umbrella, and the thing dropped like a shot to the floor, the jawbone and half a dozen yellow teeth breaking loose and spinning off across the oak planks. His entire demeanor seemed to lighten, as if he were drinking in the sight of the ruby like an elixir, and he took two shuffling steps toward it, swinging his arm ponderously out in front of him, pointing with a trembling finger toward the prize on the table. There could be no doubt what he was after, no doubt at all.

And for me, I was all for letting him have it. Under the circumstances it seemed odd to deny him. St. Ives was of a like mind. He went so far as to nod at the gem, as if inviting the idol (we can't mince words here, that's what he was) to scoop it up. Frobisher, however, was inclined to disagree. And I can't blame him, really. He hadn't been in Java with us twenty years past, hadn't seen the idol in the ring of stones, couldn't know that the sad umbrella lying on the floor had belonged to Bill Kraken and had been abandoned, as if in trade, for the priceless, ruinous gem among the asps and orchids of that jungle glade.

He stepped forward then, foolishly, and said something equally foolish about horsewhipping on the steps of the club and about his having been in the bush. A great, marbled arm swept out, *whump*ing the air out of foolish old Frobisher and knocking him spinning over a library table as if he had been made of papier-mâché. Frobisher lay there senseless.

St. Ives at that point played his trump card: "Doctor Narbondo!" he said, and then waited, anticipating, watching the idol as it paused, contemplating, stricken by a rush of ancient, thin memory. Priestly hunched forward, mouth agape, tugging at his great white beard. I heard him whisper, "Narbondo!" as if in echo to St. Ives's revelation.

The idol stared at the Professor, its mouth working, moaning, trying to speak, to cry out. "Nnnn . . ." it groaned. "Nnnar, Nnarbondo!" it finally shouted, screwing up its face awfully, positively creaking under the strain.

Doctor Narbondo! It seemed impossible, lunatic. But there it was. He lurched forward, pawing the air, stumbling toward the ruby, the idol's eye. One pale hand fell on the edge of the table. The glasses danced briefly. Priestly's port tumbled over, pouring out over the polished wood in a red pool. The rain and the wind howled outside, making the fire in the great hearth dance up the chimney. Firelight shone through the ruby, casting red embers of reflected light onto Narbondo's face, bathing the cut-crystal decanter, three-quarters full of amber liquid, in a rosy, beckoning glow.

Narbondo's hand crept toward the jewel, but his eye was on that decanter. He paused, fumbled at the jewel, dropped it, his fingers clutching, a sad, mewing sound coming from his throat. Then, with the relieved look of a man who'd finally crested some steep and difficult hill, as if he'd scaled a monumental precipice and been rewarded with a vision of El Dorado, of Shangri-la, of paradise itself, he grasped the decanter of Laphroaig and, shaking, a wide smile struggling into existence on his face, lifted it toward his mouth, thumbing the stopper off onto the tabletop.

Hasbro responded with instinctive horror to Narbondo's obvious intent. He plucked up Priestly's unused whiskey glass, said, "Allow me, sir," and rescued the decanter, pouring out a good inch and proffering the glass to the gaping Narbondo. I fully expected that Hasbro would sail across and join Frobisher's heaped form unconscious on

the floor. But that wasn't the case. Narbondo hesitated,
recollecting, bits and pieces of European culture and
civilized instinct filtering up from unfathomable depths. He
nodded to Hasbro, took the proffered glass, and, swirling
the whiskey around in a tight, quick circle, passed it once
under his nose and tossed it off.

A long and heartfelt sigh escaped him. He stood there
just so, his head back, his mouth working slowly, savoring
the peaty, smoky essence that lingered along his tongue.
And Hasbro, himself imbued with the instincts of the
archetypal gentleman's gentleman, poured another
generous dollop into the glass, replaced the stopper, and
set the decanter in the center of the table. Then he up-
righted Frobisher's fallen chair and motioned toward it.
Narbondo nodded again heavily, and, looking from one to
the other of us, slumped into the chair with the air of a man
who'd come a long, long way home.

Thus ends the story of, as I threatened in the early pages,
perhaps the strangest of all the adventures that befell
Langdon St. Ives, his man Hasbro, and myself. We ate that
cutlet for supper, just as I'd planned, and we drained that
decanter of Scotch before the evening was through. St.
Ives, his scientific fires blazing, told of his study over the
years of the history of the mysterious Doctor Narbondo, of
his slow realization that the curiously veined marble of the
idol in the forest hadn't been marble at all, had, indeed,
been the petrified body of Narbondo himself, preserved by
jungle shaman and witch doctors using Narbondo's own
serums. His eyes, being mere jellies, were removed and
replaced with jewels, the optical qualities of the oddly
wrought gems allowing him some vague semblance of
strange vision. And there he had stood for close upon two
hundred years, tended by priests from the tribes of Peewatin natives until that fateful day when Bill Kraken had
gouged out his eye. Narbondo's weird reanimation and
slow journey west over the long years would, in itself, be a
tale long in the telling, as would that of St. Ives's quest for
the lost ruby, a search that led him, finally, to a curiosity

shop near the Tate Gallery where he purchased the gem for two pound six, the owner sure that it was simply a piece of cleverly cut glass.

At first I thought it was wild coincidence that Narbondo should arrive at the Explorers Club on the very day that St. Ives appeared with the ruby. But now I'm sure that there was no coincidence involved. Narbondo was bound to find his eye, and if St. Ives hadn't retrieved it from the curiosity shop, then Narbondo would have.

The doctor, I can tell you, is safe and sound and has done us all a service by renewing Langdon St. Ives's interests in the medical arts. Together, take my word for it, they work at perfecting the curious serums. Where they work will, I'm afraid, have to remain utterly secret. You can understand that. Curiosity seekers, doubting Thomases, and modern-day Ponce de Leons would flock forth gaping and demanding if his whereabouts were generally known.

And so it was that Doctor Narbondo returned. He had no army of supporters, no mutant beasts from the Borneo jungles, no hippos and apes with which to send a thrill of terror across the continent, no last laugh. Cold reality, I fear, can't measure up to the curious turnings of a madman's dreams. But if it was a grand and startling homecoming he wanted when he set sail for distant jungle shores two hundred years ago, he did quite moderately well for himself; I think you'll agree.

The Lady of the House of Love

Angela Carter

At last the revenants became so troublesome the peasants abandoned the village and it fell solely into the possession of subtle and vindictive inhabitants who manifest their presences by shadows that fall almost imperceptibly awry, too many shadows, even at midday, shadows that have no source in anything visible; by the sound, sometimes, of sobbing in a derelict bedroom where a cracked mirror suspended from a wall does not reflect a presence; by a sense of unease that will afflict the traveler unwise enough to pause to drink from the fountain in the square that still gushes spring water from a faucet stuck in a stone lion's mouth. A cat prowls in a weedy garden; he grins and spits, arches his back, bounces away from an intangible on four fear-stiffened legs. Now all shun the village below the château in which the beautiful somnambulist helplessly perpetuates her ancestral crimes.

Wearing an antique bridal gown, the beautiful queen of the vampires sits all alone in her dark, high house under the eyes of the portraits of her demented and atrocious ancestors, each one of whom, through her, projects a baleful posthumous existence; she counts out the tarot cards, ceaselessly construing a constellation of possibilities as if the random fall of the cards on the red plush tablecloth before her could precipitate her from her chill, shuttered room into a country of perpetual summer and obliterate the perennial sadness of a girl who is both death and the maiden.

Her voice is filled with distant sonorities, like reverberations in a cave: now you are at the place of annihilation, now you are at the place of annihilation. And she is herself a cave full of echoes, she is a system of repetitions, she is a closed circuit. "Can a bird sing only the song it knows or can it learn a new song?" She draws her long, sharp fingernail across the bars of the cage in which her pet lark sings, striking a plangent twang like that of the plucked heartstrings of a woman of metal. Her hair falls down like tears.

The castle is mostly given over to ghostly occupants, but she herself has her own suite of drawing room and bedroom. Closely barred shutters and heavy velvet curtains keep out every leak of natural light. There is a round table on a single leg covered with a red plush cloth on which she lays out her inevitable tarot; this room is never more than faintly illuminated by a heavily shaded lamp on the mantelpiece and the dark red figured wallpaper is obscurely, distressingly patterned by the rain that drives in through the neglected roof and leaves behind it random areas of staining, ominous marks like those left on the sheets by dead lovers. Depredations of rot and fungus everywhere. The unlit chandelier is so heavy with dust the individual prisms no longer show any shapes; industrious spiders have woven canopies in the corners of this ornate and rotting place, have trapped the porcelain vases on the mantelpiece in soft gray nets. But the mistress of all this disintegration notices nothing.

She sits in a chair covered in moth-ravaged burgundy velvet at the low, round table and distributes the cards; sometimes the lark sings, but more often remains a sullen mound of drab feathers. Sometimes the Countess will wake it for a brief cadenza by strumming the bars of its cage; she likes to hear it announce how it cannot escape.

She rises when the sun sets and goes immediately to her table, where she plays her game of patience until she grows hungry, until she becomes ravenous. She is so beautiful she is unnatural; her beauty is an abnormality, a deformity, for none of her features exhibit any of those touching imperfections that reconcile us to the imperfection of the human condition. Her beauty is a symptom of her disorder, of her soullessness.

The white hands of the tenebrous belle deal the hand of destiny. Her fingernails are longer than those of the mandarins of ancient China and each is pared to a fine point. These and teeth as fine and white as spikes of spun sugar are the visible signs of the destiny she wistfully attempts to evade via the arcana; her claws and teeth have been sharpened on centuries of corpses, she is the last bud of the poison tree that sprang from the loins of Vlad the Impaler, who picnicked on corpses in the forests of Transylvania.

The walls of her bedroom are hung with black satin, embroidered with tears of pearl. At the room's four corners are funerary urns and bowls which emit slumbrous, pungent fumes of incense. In the center is an elaborate catafalque, in ebony, surrounded by long candles in enormous silver candlesticks. In a white lace negligee stained a little with blood, the Countess climbs up on her catafalque at dawn each morning and lies down in an open coffin.

A chignoned priest of the Othodox faith staked out her wicked father at a Carpathian crossroad before her milk teeth grew. Just as they staked him out, the fatal Count cried: "Nosferatu is dead; long live Nosferatu!" Now she possesses all the haunted forests and mysterious habitations of his vast domain; she is the hereditary commandant of the army of shadows who camp in the village below her château, who penetrate the woods in the form of owls, bats and foxes, who make the milk curdle and the butter refuse to come, who ride the horses all night on a wild hunt so they are sacks of skin and bone in the morning, who milk the cows dry and, especially, torment pubescent girls with fainting fits, disorders of the blood, diseases of the imagination.

But the Countess herself is indifferent to her own weird authority, as if she were dreaming it. In her dream, she would like to be human; but she does not know if that is possible. The tarot always shows the same configuration: always she turns up La Papesse, La Mort, La Tour Abolie, wisdom, death, dissolution.

On moonless nights, her keeper lets her out into the

garden. This garden, an exceedingly somber place, bears a strong resemblance to a burial ground and all the roses her dead mother planted have grown up into a huge, spiked wall that incarcerates her in the castle of her inheritance. When the back door opens, the Countess will sniff the air and howl. She drops, now, on all fours. Crouching, quivering, she catches the scent of her prey. Delicious crunch of the fragile bones of rabbits and small, furry things she pursues with fleet, four-footed speed; she will creep home, whimpering, with blood smeared on her cheeks. She pours water from the ewer in her bedroom into the bowl, she washes her face with the wincing, fastidious gestures of a cat.

The voracious margin of huntress's nights in the gloomy garden, crouch and pounce, surrounds her habitual tormented somnambulism, her life or imitation of life. The eyes of this nocturnal creature enlarge and glow. All claws and teeth, she strikes, she gorges; but nothing can console her for the ghastliness of her condition, nothing. She resorts to the magic comfort of the tarot pack and shuffles the cards, lays them out, reads them, gathers them up with a sigh, shuffles them again, constantly constructing hypotheses about a future that is irreversible.

An old mute looks after her, to make sure she never sees the sun, that all day she stays in her coffin, to keep mirrors and all reflective surfaces away from her—in short, to perform all the functions of the servants of vampires. Everything about this beautiful and ghastly lady is as it should be, queen of night, queen of terror—except her horrible reluctance for the role.

Nevertheless, if an unwise adventurer pauses in the square of the deserted village to refresh himself at the fountain, a crone in a black dress and white apron presently emerges from a house. She will invite you with smiles and gestures; you will follow her. The Countess wants fresh meat. When she was a little girl, she was like a fox and contented herself entirely with baby rabbits that squeaked piteously as she bit into their necks with a nauseated voluptuousness, with voles and field mice that palpitated for a bare moment between her embroideress's fingers. But now she is a woman, she must have men. If you stop too long beside the giggling fountain, you will be led by the hand to the Countess's larder.

All day, she lies in her coffin in her negligee of blood-stained lace. When the sun drops behind the mountain, she yawns and stirs and puts on the only dress she has, her mother's wedding dress, to sit and read her cards until she grows hungry. She loathes the food she eats; she would have liked to take the rabbits home with her, feed them on lettuce, pet them and make them a nest in her red-and-black chinoiserie escritoire, but hunger always overcomes her. She sinks her teeth into the neck where an artery throbs with fear; she will drop the deflated skin from which she has extracted all the nourishment with a small cry of both pain and disgust. And it is the same with the shepherd boys and gypsy lads who, ignorant or foolhardy, come to wash the dust from their feet in the water of the fountain; the Countess's governess brings them into the drawing room, where the cards on the table always show the Grim Reaper. The Countess herself will serve them coffee in tiny cracked, precious cups, and little sugar cakes. The hob-bledehoys sit with a spilling cup in one hand and a biscuit in the other, gaping at the Countess in her satin finery as she pours from a silver pot and chatters distractedly to put them at their fatal ease. A certain desolate stillness of her eyes indicates she is inconsolable. She would like to caress their lean brown cheeks and stroke their ragged hair. When she takes them by the hand and leads them to her bedroom, they can scarcely believe their luck.

Afterwards, her governess will tidy the remains into a neat pile and wrap them in their owner's own discarded clothes. This mortal parcel she then discreetly buries in the garden. The blood on the Countess's cheeks will be mixed with tears; her keeper probes her fingernails for her with a little silver toothpick, to get rid of the fragments of skin and bone that have lodged there.

Fee fie fo fum
I smell the blood of an Englishman.

One hot, ripe summer in the pubescent years of the present century, a young officer in the British army, blond, blue-eyed, heavy-muscled, visiting friends in Vienna, decided to spend the remainder of his furlough exploring the little-known uplands of Romania. When he quixotically decided to travel the rutted cart tracks by bicycle, he saw all the humor of it: "On two wheels in the land of the vampires." So, laughing, he sets out on his adventure.

He has the special quality of virginity, most and least ambiguous of states: ignorance, yet at the same time, power in potentia, and, furthermore, unknowingness, which is not the same as ignorance. He is more than he knows—and has about him, besides, the special glamour of that generation for whom history has already prepared a special, exemplary fate in the trenches of France. This being, rooted in change and time, is about to collide with the timeless Gothic eternity of the vampires, for whom all is as it has always been and will be, whose cards always fall in the same pattern.

Although so young, he is also rational. He has chosen the most rational mode of transport in the world for his trip round the Carpathians. To ride a bicycle is in itself some protection against superstitious fears, since the bicycle is the product of pure reason applied to motion. Geometry at the service of man! Give me two spheres and a straight line and I will show you how far I can take them. Voltaire himself might have invented the bicycle, since it contributes so much to man's welfare and nothing at all to his bane. Beneficial to the health, it emits no harmful fumes and permits only the most decorous speeds. How can a bicycle ever be an implement of harm?

A single kiss woke up the Sleeping Beauty in the Wood.

The waxen fingers of the Countess, fingers of a holy image, turn up the card called Les Amoureux. Never, never before . . . never before has the Countess cast

herself a fate involving love. She shakes, she trembles, her
great eyes close beneath her finely veined, nervously fluttering eyelids; the lovely cartomancer has, this time, the
first time, dealt herself a hand of love and death.

> Be he alive or be he dead
> I'll grind his bones to make my bread.

At the mauvish beginnings of evening, the English
m'sieu toils up the hill to the village he glimpsed from a
great way off; he must dismount and push his bicycle
before him, the path too steep to ride. He hopes to find a
friendly inn to rest the night; he's hot, hungry, thirsty,
weary, dusty. . . . At first, such disappointment, to discover the roofs of all the cottages caved in and tall weeds
thrusting through the piles of fallen tiles, shutters hanging
disconsolately from their hinges, an entirely uninhabited
place. And the rank vegetation whispers, as if foul secrets,
here, where, if one were sufficiently imaginative, one could
almost imagine twisted faces appearing momentarily beneath the crumbling eaves . . . but the adventure of it all,
and the consolation of the poignant brightness of the
hollyhocks still bravely blooming in the shaggy gardens
and the beauty of the flaming sunset, all these considerations soon overcame his disappointment, even assuaged
the faint unease he's felt. And the fountain where the
village women used to wash their clothes still gushed out
bright, clear water; he gratefully washed his feet and
hands, applied his mouth to the faucet, then let the icy
stream run over his face.

When he raised his dripping, gratified head from the
lion's mouth, he saw, silently arrived beside him in the
square, an old woman who smiled eagerly, almost con-
ciliatorily at him. She wore a black dress and a white apron,
with a housekeeper's key ring at the waist; her gray hair
was neatly coiled in a chignon beneath the white linen
headdress worn by elderly women of that region. She
bobbed a curtsy at the young man and beckoned him to

follow her. When he hesitated, she pointed towards the great bulk of the mansion above them, whose façade loured over the village, rubbed her stomach, pointed to her mouth, rubbed her stomach again, clearly miming an invitation to supper. Then she beckoned him again, this time turning determinedly upon her heel as though she would brook no opposition.

A great, intoxicated surge of the heavy scent of red roses blew into his face as soon as they left the village, inducing a sensuous vertigo; a blast of rich, faintly corrupt sweetness strong enough, almost, to fell him. Too many roses. Too many roses bloomed on enormous thickets that lined the path, thickets bristling with thorns, and the flowers themselves were almost too luxuriant, their huge congregations of plush petals somehow obscene in their excess, their whorled, tightly budded cores outrageous in their implications. The mansion emerged grudgingly out of this jungle.

In the subtle and haunting light of the setting sun, that golden light rich with nostalgia for the day that is just past, the somber visage of the place, part manor house, part fortified farmhouse, immense, rambling, a dilapidated eagle's nest atop the crag down which its attendant village meandered, reminded him of childhood tales on winter evenings, when he and his brothers and sisters scared themselves half out of their wits with ghost stories set in just such places and then had to have candles to light them up newly terrifying stairs to bed. He could almost have regretted accepting the crone's unspoken invitation; but now, standing before the door of time-eroded oak while she selected a huge iron key from the clanking ringful at her waist, he knew it was too late to turn back and brusquely reminded himself he was no child now, to be frightened of his own fancies.

The old lady unlocked the door, which swung back on melodramatically creaking hinges, and fussily took charge of his bicycle, in spite of his protests. He felt a certain involuntary sinking of the heart to see his beautiful two-wheeled symbol of rationality vanish into the dark entrails of the mansion, to, no doubt, some damp outhouse where they would not oil it or check its tires. But in for a penny, in for a pound—in his youth and strength and blond beauty, in the invisible, even unacknowledged pentacle of his virginity, the young man stepped over the threshold of Nosferatu's castle and did not shiver in the blast of cold air, as from the mouth of a grave, that emanated from the lightless, cavernous interior.

The crone took him to a little chamber where there was a black oak table spread with a clean white cloth and this cloth was carefully laid with heavy silverware, a little tarnished, as if someone with foul breath had breathed on it, but laid with one place only. Curiouser and curiouser; invited to the castle for dinner, now he must dine alone. All the same, he sat down as she had bid him. Although it was not yet dark outside, the curtains were closely drawn and only the sparing light trickling from a single oil lamp showed him how dismal his surroundings were. The crone bustled about to get him a bottle of wine and a glass from an ancient cabinet of wormy oak; while he bemusedly drank his wine she disappeared, but soon returned bearing a steaming platter of the local spiced meat stew with dumplings, and a shank of black bread. He was hungry after his long day's ride, he ate heartily and polished his plate with the crust, but this coarse food was hardly the entertainment he'd expected from the gentry and he was puzzled by the assessing glint in the dumb woman's eyes as she watched him eating.

But she darted off to get him a second helping as soon as he'd finished the first one and she seemed so friendly and helpful, besides, that he knew he could count on a bed for the night in the castle, as well as his supper, so he sharply reprimanded himself for his own childish lack of enthusiasm for the eerie silence, the clammy chill of the place.

When he'd put away the second plateful, the old woman came and gestured he should leave the table and follow her once again. She made a pantomime of drinking; he deduced he was now invited to take after-dinner coffee in another room with some more elevated member of the household, who had not wished to dine with him but, all the same, wanted to make his acquaintance. An honor, no doubt; in deference to his host's opinion of himself, he straightened his tie, brushed the crumbs from his tweed jacket.

He was surprised to find how ruinous the interior of the house was—cobwebs, worm-eaten beams, crumbling plaster; but the mute crone resolutely wound him on the reel of her lantern down endless corridors, up winding staircases, through the galleries where the painted eyes of family portraits briefly flickered as they passed, eyes that belonged, he noticed, to faces, one and all, of a quite memorable beastliness. At last she paused and, behind the door where they'd halted, he heard a faint, metallic twang as of, perhaps, a chord struck on a harpsichord. And then, wonderfully, the liquid cascade of the song of a lark, bringing to him, in the heart—had he but known it—of Juliet's tomb, all the freshness of morning.

The crone rapped with her knuckles on the panels; the most seductively caressing voice he had ever heard in his life softly called out, in heavily accented French, the adopted language of the Romanian aristocracy: "Entrez."

First of all, he saw only a shape, a shape imbued with a faint luminosity since it caught and reflected in its yellowed surfaces what little light there was in the ill-lit room; this shape resolved itself into that of, of all things, a hoop-skirted dress of white satin draped here and there with lace, a dress fifty or sixty years out of fashion but once, obviously, intended for a wedding. And then he saw the girl who wore the dress, a girl with the fragility of the skeleton of a moth, so thin, so frail, that her dress seemed to him to hang suspended, as if untenanted in the dank air, a fabulous lending, a self-articulated garment in which she lived like a ghost in a machine. All the light in the room came from a low-burning lamp with a thick greenish shade on a distant mantelpiece; the crone who accompanied him shielded her lantern with her hand, as if to protect her

mistress from too suddenly seeing, or their guest from too
suddenly seeing her.

So that it was little by little, as his eyes grew accustomed
to the half-dark, that he saw how beautiful and how very
young the bedizened scarecrow was, and he thought of a
child dressing up in her mother's clothes, perhaps a child
putting on the clothes of a dead mother in order to bring
her, however briefly, to life again.

The Countess stood behind a low table, beside a pretty,
silly, gilt-and-wire birdcage, hands outstretched in a dis-
tracted attitude that was almost one of flight; she looked as
startled by their entry as if she had not requested it. With
her stark white face, her lovely death's-head surrounded
by long, dark hair that fell down as straight as if it were
soaking wet, she looked like a shipwrecked bride. Her
huge, dark eyes almost broke his heart with their waiflike,
lost look; yet he was disturbed, almost repelled, by her
extraordinarily fleshy mouth, a mouth with wide, full,
prominent lips of a vibrant purplish-crimson, a morbid
mouth. Even—but he put the thought away from him
immediately—a whore's mouth. She shivered all the time,
a starveling chill, a malarial agitation of the bones. He
thought she must be only sixteen or seventeen years old,
no more, with the hectic, unhealthy beauty of a consump-
tive. She was the chatelaine of all this decay.

With many tender precautions, the crone now raised the
light she held to show his hostess her guest's face. At that,
the Countess let out a faint, mewing cry and made a blind,
appalled gesture with her hands, as if pushing him away,
so that she knocked against the table and a butterfly dazzle
of painted cards fell to the floor. Her mouth formed a
round "o" of woe, she swayed a little and then sank into
her chair, where she lay as if now scarcely capable of
moving. A bewildering reception. Tsking under her breath,
the crone busily poked about on the table until she found
an enormous pair of dark green glasses, such as blind
beggars wear, and perched them on the Countess's nose.

He went forward to pick up her cards for her from a carpet that, he saw to his surprise, was partly rotted away, partly encroached upon by all kinds of virulent-looking fungi. He retrieved the cards and shuffled them carelessly together, for they meant nothing to him, though they seemed strange playthings for a young girl. What a grisly picture of a capering skeleton! He covered it up with a happier one—of two young lovers, smiling at one another—and put her toys back into a hand so slender you could almost see the frail net of bone beneath the translucent skin, a hand with fingernails as long, as finely pointed, as banjo picks.

At his touch, she seemed to revive a little and almost smiled, raising herself upright.

"Coffee," she said. "You must have coffee." And scooped up her cards into a pile so that the crone could set before her a silver spirit kettle, a silver coffeepot, cream jug, sugar basin, cups ready on a silver tray, a strange touch of elegance, even if discolored, in this devastated interior whose mistress ethereally shone as if with her own blighted, submarine radiance.

The crone found him a chair and, tittering noiselessly, departed, leaving the room a little darker.

While the young lady attended to the coffeemaking, he had time to contemplate with some distaste a further series of family portraits which decorated the stained and peeling walls of the room; these livid faces all seemed contorted with a febrile madness and the blubber lips, the huge, demented eyes that all had in common, bore a disquieting resemblance to those of the hapless victim of inbreeding now patiently filtering her fragrant brew, even if some rare grace had so finely transformed those features when it came to her case. The lark, its chorus done, had long ago fallen silent; no sound but the chink of silver on china. Soon, she held out to him a tiny cup of rose-painted china.

"Welcome," she said in her voice with the rushing sonorities of the ocean in it, a voice that seemed to come elsewhere than from her white, still throat. "Welcome to my château. I rarely receive visitors and that's a misfortune since nothing animates me half as much as the presence of a stranger. . . . This place is so lonely, now the village is deserted, and my one companion, alas, she cannot speak. Often I am so silent that I think I, too, will soon forget how to do so and nobody here will ever talk anymore."

She offered him a sugar biscuit from a Limoges plate; her fingernails struck carillons from the antique china. Her voice, issuing from those red lips like the obese roses in her garden, lips that do not move—her voice is curiously disembodied; she is like a doll, he thought, a ventriloquist's doll, or, more, like a great, ingenious piece of clockwork. For she seemed inadequately powered by some slow energy of which she was not in control; as if she had been wound up years ago, when she was born, and now the mechanism was inexorably running down and would leave her lifeless. This idea that she might be an automaton, made of white velvet and black fur, that could not move of its own accord, never quite deserted him; indeed, it deeply moved his heart. The carnival air of her white dress emphasized her unreality, like a sad Columbine who lost her way in the wood a long time ago and never reached the fair.

"And the light. I must apologize for the lack of light . . . a hereditary affliction of the eyes. . . ."

Her blind spectacles gave him his handsome face back to himself twice over; if he presented himself to her naked face, he would dazzle her like the sun she is forbidden to look at because it would shrivel her up at once, poor night bird, poor butcher bird.

Vous serez ma proie.

You have such a fine throat, m'sieu, like a column of marble. When you came through the door retaining about you all the golden light of the summer's day of which I know nothing, nothing, the card called Les Amoureux had just emerged from the tumbling chaos of imagery before me; it seemed to me you had stepped off the card into my darkness and, for a moment, I thought, perhaps, you might irradiate it.

I do not mean to hurt you. I shall wait for you in my bride's dress in the dark.

The bridegroom is come; he will go into the chamber which has been prepared for him.

I am condemned to solitude and dark; I do not mean to hurt you.

I will be very gentle.

(And could love free me from the shadows? Can a bird sing only the song it knows, or can it learn a new song?)

See how I'm ready for you. I've always been ready for you; I've been waiting for you in my wedding dress, why have you delayed so long . . . it will all be over very quickly.

You will feel no pain, my darling.

She herself is a haunted house. She does not possess herself; her ancestors sometimes come and peer out of the windows of her eyes and that is very frightening. She has the mysterious solitude of ambiguous states; she hovers in a no man's land between life and death, sleeping and waking, behind the hedge of spiked flowers, Nosferatu's sanguinary rosebud. The beastly forebears on the walls condemn her to a perpetual repetition of their passions.

(One kiss, however, and only one, woke up the Sleeping Beauty in the Wood.)

Nervously, to conceal her inner voices, she keeps up a front of inconsequential chatter in French while her ancestors leer and grimace on the walls; however hard she tries to think of any other, she only knows of one kind of consummation.

He was struck, once again, by the birdlike, predatory claws that tipped her marvelous hands; the sense of strangeness that had been growing on him since he buried his head under the streaming water in the village, since he entered the dark portals of the fatal castle, now fully overcame him. Had he been a cat, he would have bounced backward from her hands on four fear-stiffened legs, but he is not a cat: he is a hero.

A fundamental disbelief in what he sees before him sustains him, even in the boudoir of Countess Nosferatu herself: he would have said, perhaps, that there are some things which, even if they *are* true, we should not believe possible. He might have said: it is folly to believe one's eyes. Not so much that he does not believe in her; he can see her, she is real. If she takes off her dark glasses, from her eyes will stream all the images that populate this vampire-haunted land, but since he himself is immune to shadow, due to his virginity—he does not yet know what there is to be afraid of—and due to his heroism, which makes him like the sun, he sees before him, first and foremost, an inbred, highly strung girl child, fatherless, motherless, kept in the dark too long and pale as a plant that never sees the light, half-blinded by some hereditary condition of the eyes. And though he feels unease, he cannot feel terror; so he is like the boy in the fairy tale, who does not know how to shudder, and not spooks, ghouls, beasties, the Devil himself and all his retinue could do the trick.

This lack of imagination gives his heroism to the hero.

He will learn to shudder in the trenches. But this girl cannot make him shudder.

Now it is dark. Bats swoop and squeak outside the tightly shuttered windows. The coffee is all drunk, the sugar biscuits eaten. Her chatter comes trickling and diminishing to a stop; she twists her fingers together, picks at the lace of her dress, shifts nervously in her chair. Owls shriek; the impedimenta of her condition squeak and gibber all around us. Now you are at the place of annihilation, now you are at the place of annihilation. She turns her head away from the blue beams of his eyes; she knows no other consummation than the only one she can offer him. She has not eaten for three days. It is dinnertime. It is bedtime.

> Suivez-moi.
> Je vous attendais.
> Vous serez ma proie.

The raven caws on the accursed roof. "Dinnertime, dinnertime," clang the portraits on the walls. A ghastly hunger gnaws her entrails; she has waited for him all her life without knowing it.

The handsome bicyclist, scarcely believing his luck, will follow her into her bedroom; the candles around her sacrificial altar burn with a low, clear flame, light catches on the silver tears stitched to the wall. She will assure him, in the very voice of temptation: "My clothes have but to fall and you will see before you a succession of mysteries."

She has no mouth with which to kiss, no hands with which to caress, only the fangs and talons of a beast of prey. To touch the mineral sheen of the flesh revealed in the cool candle gleam is to invite her fatal embrace; in her low, sweet voice, she will croon the lullaby of the House of Nosferatu.

Embraces, kisses; your golden head, of a lion, although I have never seen a lion, only imagined one, of the sun, even if I've only seen the picture of the sun on the tarot card, your golden head of the lover who I dreamed would one day free me, this head will fall back, its eyes roll upward in a spasm you will mistake for that of love and not of death. The bridegroom bleeds on my inverted marriage bed. Stark and dead, poor bicyclist; he has paid the price of a night with the Countess and some think it too high a fee while some do not.

Tomorrow, her keeper will bury his bones under her roses. The food her roses feed on gives them their rich

color, their swooning odor, that breathes lasciviously of
forbidden pleasures.

Suivez-moi.

"Suivez-moi!"
The handsome bicyclist, fearful for his hostess's health,
her sanity, gingerly follows her hysterical imperiousness
into the other room; he would like to take her into his arms
and protect her from the ancestors who leer down from the
walls.
What a macabre bedroom!
His colonel, an old goat with jaded appetites, had given
him the visiting card of a brothel in Paris, where, the satyr
assured him, ten louis would buy just such a lugubrious
bedroom, with a naked girl upon a coffin; offstage, the
brothel pianist played the *Dies Irae* on a harmonium, and,
amidst all the perfumes of the embalming parlor, the cus-
tomer took his necrophiliac pleasure of a pretended
corpse. He had good-naturedly refused the old man's offer
of such an initiation; how can he now take criminal advantage of the disordered girl with fever-hot, bone-dry,
taloned hands and eyes that deny all the erotic promises of
her body with their terror, their sadness, their dreadful,
balked tenderness?
So delicate and damned, poor thing. Quite damned.
Yet I do believe she scarcely knows what she is doing.
She is shaking as if her limbs were not efficiently joined
together, as if she might shake into pieces. She raises her
hands to unfasten the neck of her dress and her eyes well
with tears, they trickle down beneath the rim of her dark
glasses. She can't take off her mother's wedding dress
unless she takes off her dark glasses; she has fumbled the
ritual, it is no longer inexorable. The mechanism within her
fails her now, when she needs it most. When she takes off
the dark glasses, they slip from her fingers and smash to
pieces on the tiled floor. There is no room in her drama for

improvisation; and this unexpected, mundane noise of breaking glass breaks the wicked spell in the room entirely. She gapes blindly down at the splinters and ineffectively smears the tears across her face with her fist. What is she to do now?

When she kneels to try to gather the fragments of glass together, a sharp sliver pierces deeply into the pad of her thumb; she cries out, sharp, real. She kneels among the broken glass and watches the bright bead of blood form a drop. She has never seen her own blood before, not her *own* blood. It exercises upon her an awed fascination.

Into this vile and murderous room, the handsome bicyclist brings the innocent remedies of the nursery; in himself, by his presence, he is an exorcism. He gently takes her hand away from her and dabs the blood with his own handkerchief, but still it spurts out. And so he puts his mouth to the wound. He will kiss it better for her, as her mother, had she lived, would have done.

All the silver tears fall from the wall with a flimsy tinkle. Her painted ancestors turn away their eyes and grind their fangs.

How can she bear the pain of becoming human?

The end of exile is the end of being.

He was awakened by larksong. The shutters, the curtains, even the long-sealed windows of the horrid bedroom were all opened up and light and air streamed in; now you could see how tawdry it all was, how thin and cheap the satin, the catafalque not ebony at all but black-painted paper stretched on struts of wood, as in the theater. The wind had blown droves of petals from the roses outside into the room and this crimson residue swirled fragrantly about the floor. The candles had burnt out and she must have set her pet lark free because it perched on the edge of the silly coffin to sing him its ecstatic morning song. His bones were stiff and aching; he'd slept on the floor with his bundled-up jacket for a pillow, after he'd put her to bed.

But now there was no trace of her to be seen, except,

lightly tossed across the crumpled black satin bedcover, a lace negligee lightly soiled with blood, as it might be from a woman's menses, and a rose that must have come from the fierce bushes nodding through the window. The air was heavy with incense and roses and made him cough. The Countess must have got up early to enjoy the sunshine, slipped outside to gather him a rose. He got to his feet, coaxed the lark onto his wrist and took it to the window. At first, it exhibited the reluctance for the sky of a long-caged thing, but when he tossed it up onto the currents of the air, it spread its wings and was up and away into the clear blue bowl of the heavens; he watched its trajectory with a lift of joy in his heart.

Then he padded into the boudoir, his mind busy with plans. We shall take her to Zurich, to a clinic; she will be treated for nervous hysteria. Then to an eye specialist, for her photophobia, and to a dentist, to put her teeth into better shape. Any competent manicurist will deal with her claws. We shall turn her into the lovely girl she is; I shall cure her of all these nightmares.

The heavy curtains are pulled back, to let in brilliant fusillades of early-morning light; in the desolation of the boudoir, she sits at her round table in her white dress, with the cards laid out before her. She had dropped off to sleep over the cards of destiny that are so fingered, so soiled, so worn by constant shuffling that you can no longer make the image out on any single one of them.

She is not sleeping.

In death, she looked far older, less beautiful, and so, for the first time, fully human.

I will vanish in the morning light; I was only an invention of darkness.

And I leave you as a souvenir the dark, fanged rose I plucked from between my thighs, like a flower laid on a grave. On a grave.

My keeper will attend to everything.

Nosferatu always attends his own obsequies; she will not go to the graveyard unattended. And now the crone materialized, weeping, and roughly gestured him to be gone. After a search in some foul-smelling outhouses, he discovered his bicycle and, abandoning his holiday, rode directly to Bucharest, where, at the poste restante, he found a telegram summoning him to rejoin his regiment at once. Much later, when he changed back into uniform in his quarters, he discovered he still had the Countess's rose; he must have tucked it into the breast pocket of his cycling jacket after he had found her body. Curiously enough, although he had brought it so far away from Romania, the flower did not seem to be quite dead, and on impulse, because the girl had been so lovely and her death so unexpected and pathetic, he decided to try and resurrect her rose. He filled his tooth glass with water from the carafe in his locker and popped the rose into it, so that its withered head floated on the surface.

When he returned from the mess that evening, the heavy fragrance of Count Nosferatu's roses drifted down the stone corridor of the barracks to greet him, and his spartan quarters brimmed with the reeling odor of a glowing, velvet, monstrous flower whose petals had regained all their former bloom and elasticity, their corrupt, brilliant, baleful splendor.

Next day, his regiment embarked for France.

The Undead

Even as children they were late sleepers,
Preferring their dreams, even when quick with monsters,
    To the world with all its breakable toys,
        Its compacts with the dying;

From the stretched arms of withered trees
They turned, fearing contagion of the mortal,
    And even under the plums of summer
        Drifted like winter moons.

Secret, unfriendly, pale, possessed
Of the one wish, the thirst for mere survival,
    They came, as all extremists do
        In time, to a sort of grandeur:

Now, to their Balkan battlements
Above the vulgar town of their first lives,
    They rise at the moon's rising. Strange
        That their utter self-concern

Should, in the end, have left them selfless:
Mirrors fail to perceive them as they float
    Through the great hall and up the staircase;
        Nor are the cobwebs broken.

Into the pallid night emerging,
Wrapped in their flapping capes, routinely maddened
    By a wolf's cry, they stand for a moment
        Stoking the mind's eye

With lewd thoughts of the pressed flowers
And bric-a-brac of rooms with something to lose—
    Of love-dismembered dolls, and children
        Buried in quilted sleep.

Then they are off in a negative frenzy,
Their black shapes cropped into sudden bats
    That swarm, burst, and are gone. Thinking
        Of a thrush cold in the leaves

Who has sung his few summers truly,
Or an old scholar resting his eyes at last,
    We cannot be much impressed with vampires,
        Colorful though they are;

    Nevertheless their pain is real,
And requires our pity. Think how sad it must be
    To thirst always for a scorned elixir,
        The salt quotidian blood

    Which, if mistrusted, has no savor;
To prey on life forever and not possess it,
    As rock-hollows, tide after tide,
        Glassily strand the sea.

                              —*Richard Wilbur*

Voices Answering Back: The Vampires

Rising in lamplight dying at dawn
grim burials in sheds and cellars
the rats scuttling through holes
and the days following in their tracks
exiled here we named the hours
since you first forgot to be afraid
once departed we became
only ourselves
with the salt on our tongues
and the cold for company
so deft in escape so practiced in dying
you might have learned from us
but each time the easiest trick worked
the brandished cross the empty mirror
you could not see us our steps upon the stairs
and while you stumbled after bats in the garden
we climbed quietly
from the upstairs window down the drainpipe
and through all the parties
you never heard what we were saying
it was something about desire
what we had in common even then
in your silence you feared us
always winning at the end but do you think
nothing lingered past dawn
shadowed among the gathered elms
do not be mistaken
we heard you walking through our dreams
we felt death moving between your hands
now we are waking early
practicing with sunlight
now we pass unharmed beneath your terrible star
eyes covered hands in our pockets
for the rules have always said
if you stop believing in us
we inherit everything

—*Lawrence Raab*

Happy Dens
or
A Day in the Old Wolves Home

Jane Yolen

Nurse Lamb stood in front of the big white house with the black shutters. She shivered. She was a brand-new nurse and this was her very first job.

From inside the house came loud and angry growls. Nurse Lamb looked at the name carved over the door: HAPPY DENS. But it didn't sound like a happy place, she thought, as she listened to the howls from inside.

Shuddering, she knocked on the door.

The only answer was another howl.

Lifting the latch, Nurse Lamb went in.

No sooner had she stepped across the doorstep than a bowl sped by her head. It splattered against the wall. Nurse Lamb ducked, but she was too late. Her fresh white uniform was spotted and dotted with whatever had been in the bowl.

"Mush!" shouted an old wolf, shaking his cane at her. "Great howls and thorny paws. I can't stand another day of it. The end of life is nothing but a big bowl of mush."

Nurse Lamb gave a frightened little bleat and turned to go back out the door, but a great big wolf with two black ears and one black paw barred her way. "Mush for breakfast, mush for dinner, and more mush in between," he growled. "That's all they serve us here at Happy Dens, Home for Aging Wolves."

The wolf with the cane added: "When we were young and full of teeth it was never like this." He howled.

Nurse Lamb gave another bleat and ran into the next room. To her surprise it was a kitchen. A large, comfortable-looking pig wearing a white hat was leaning over the stove and stirring an enormous pot. Since the wolves had not followed her in, Nurse Lamb sat down on a kitchen stool and began to cry.

The cook put her spoon down, wiped her trotters with a stained towel, and patted Nurse Lamb on the head, right behind the ears.

"There, there, lambkin," said the cook. "Don't start a new job in tears. We say that in the barnyard all the time."

Nurse Lamb looked up and snuffled. "I . . . I don't think I'm right for this place. I feel as if I have been thrown to the wolves."

The cook nodded wisely. "And, in a manner of speaking, you have been. But these poor old dears are all bark and no bite. Toothless, don't you know. All they can manage is mush."

"But no one told me this was an old *wolves* home," complained Nurse Lamb. "They just said 'How would you like to work at Happy Dens?' And it sounded like the nicest place in the world to work."

"And so it is. And so it is," said the cook. "It just takes getting used to."

Nurse Lamb wiped her nose and looked around. "But how could someone like *you* work here. I mean . . ." She dropped her voice to a whisper. "I heard all about it at school. The three little pigs and all. Did you know them?"

The cook sniffed. "And a bad lot they were, too. As we say in the barnyard, 'There's more than one side to every sty.' "

"But I was told that the big bad wolf tried to eat the three little pigs. And he huffed and he puffed and . . ." Nurse Lamb looked confused.

Cook just smiled and began to stir the pot again, lifting up a spoonful to taste.

"And then there was that poor little child in the woods with the red riding hood," said Nurse Lamb. "Bringing the basket of goodies to her sick grandmother."

Cook shook her head and added pepper to the pot. "In

the barnyard we say, 'Don't take slop from a kid in a cloak.' " She ladled out a bowlful of mush.

Nurse Lamb stood up. She walked up to the cook and put her hooves on her hips. "But what about that boy Peter. The one who caught the wolf by the tail after he ate the duck. And the hunters came and—"

"Bad press," said a voice from the doorway. It was the wolf with the two black ears. "Much of what you know about wolves is bad press."

Nurse Lamb turned and looked at him. "I don't even know what bad press means," she said.

"It means that only one side of the story has been told. There is another way of telling those very same tales. From the wolf's point of view." He grinned at her. "My name is Wolfgang and if you will bring a bowl of that thoroughly awful stuff to the table"— he pointed to the pot—"I will tell you *my* side of a familiar tale."

Sheepishly, Nurse Lamb picked up the bowl and followed the wolf into the living room. She put the bowl on the table in front of Wolfgang and sat down. There were half a dozen wolves sitting there.

Nurse Lamb smiled at them timidly.

They smiled back. The cook was right. Only Wolfgang had any teeth.

Wolfgang's Tale

Once upon a time (began the black-eared wolf) there was a thoroughly nice young wolf. He had two black ears and one black paw. He was a poet and a dreamer.

This thoroughly nice wolf loved to lay about in the woods staring at the lacy curlings of fiddlehead ferns and smelling the wild roses.

He was a vegetarian—except for lizards and an occasional snake, which don't count. He loved carrot cake and was partial to peanut-butter pie.

One day as he lay by the side of a babbling brook, writing a poem that began

Twinkle, twinkle, lambkin's eye,
How I wish you were close by . . .

he heard the sound of a child weeping. He knew it was a
human child because only they cry with that snuffling gasp.
So the thoroughly nice wolf leaped to his feet and ran over,
his hind end waggling, eager to help.

The child looked up from her crying. She was quite
young and dressed in a long red riding hood, a lacy dress,
white stockings, and black patent-leather Mary Jane
shoes. Hardly what you would call your usual hiking-in-
the-woods outfit.

"Oh, hello, wolfie," she said. In those days, of course,
humans often talked to wolves. "I am quite lost."

The thoroughly nice wolf sat down by her side and held
her hand. "There, there," he said. "Tell me where you
live."

The child grabbed her hand back. "If I knew that, you
silly growler, I wouldn't be lost, would I?"

The thoroughly nice wolf bit back his own sharp answer
and asked her in rhyme:

Where are you going
My pretty young maid?
Answer me this
And I'll make you a trade.

The path through the forest
Is dark and it's long,
So I will go with you
And sing you a song.

The little girl was charmed. "I'm going to my grandmother's house," she said. "With this." She held up a
basket that was covered with a red-checked cloth. The
wolf could smell carrot cake. He grinned.

"Oh, poet, what big teeth you have," said the child.

"The better to eat carrot cake with," said the thoroughly
nice wolf.

"My granny hates carrot cake," said the child. "In fact, she hates anything but mush."

"What bad taste," said the wolf. "I made up a poem about that once:

> If I found someone
> Who liked to eat mush
> I'd sit them in front of it,
> Then give a . . .

"Push!" shouted the child.

"Why, you're a poet, too," said the wolf.

"I'm really more of a storyteller," said the child, blushing prettily. "But I do love carrot cake."

"All poets do," said the wolf. "So you must be a poet as well."

"Well, my granny is no poet. Every week when I bring the carrot cake over, she dumps it into her mush and mushes it all up together and then makes me eat it with her. She says that I have to learn that life ends with a bowl of mush."

"Great howls!" said the wolf, shuddering. "What a terribly wicked thing to say and do."

"I guess so," said the child.

"Then we must save this wonderful carrot cake from your grandmother," the wolf said, scratching his head below his ears.

The child clapped her hands. "I know," she said. "Let's pretend."

"Pretend?" asked the wolf.

"Let's pretend that you are Granny and I am bringing the cake to *you*. Here, you wear my red riding hood and we'll pretend it's Granny's nightcap and nightgown."

The wolf took her little cape and slung it over his head. He grinned again. He was a poet and he loved pretending.

The child skipped up to him and knocked upon an imaginary door.

The wolf opened it. "Come in. Come in."

"Oh, no," said the child. "My grandmother never gets out of bed."

"Never?" asked the wolf.

"Never," said the child.

"All right," said the thoroughly nice wolf, shaking his head. He lay down on the cool green grass, clasped his paws over his stomach, and made a very loud pretend snore.

The child walked over to his feet and knocked again.

"Who is it?" called out the wolf in a high, weak, scratchy voice.

"It is your granddaughter, Little Red Riding Hood," the child said, giggling.

"Come in, come in. Just lift the latch. I'm in bed with aches and pains and a bad case of the rheumaticks," said the wolf in the high, funny voice.

The child walked in through the pretend door.

"I have brought you a basket of goodies," said the child, putting the basket by the wolf's side. She placed her hands on her hips. "But you know, Grandmother, you look very different today."

"How so?" asked the wolf, opening both his yellow eyes wide.

"Well, Grandmother, what big eyes you have," said the child.

The wolf closed his eyes and opened them again quickly. "The better to see you with, my dear," he said.

"Oh, you silly wolf. She never calls me *dear*. She calls me *Sweetface*. Or *Punkins*. Or her *Airy Fair Dee*."

"How awful," said the wolf.

"I know," said the child. "But that's what she calls me."

"Well, I can't," said the wolf, turning over on his side. "I'm a poet, after all, and no self-respecting poet could possibly use those words. If I have to call you that, there's no more pretending."

"I guess you can call me dear," said the child in a very small voice. "But I didn't know that poets were so particular."

"About *words* we are," said the wolf.

"And you have an awfully big nose," said the child.

The wolf put his paw over his nose. "Now that is uncalled-for," he said. "My nose isn't all that big—for a wolf."

"It's part of the game," said the child.

"Oh, yes, the game. I had forgotten. The better to smell the basket of goodies, my dear," said the wolf.

"And Grandmother, what big teeth you have."

The thoroughly nice wolf sat up. "The better to eat carrot cake with," he said.

At that, the game was over. They shared the carrot cake evenly and licked their fingers, which was not very polite but certainly the best thing to do on a picnic in the woods. And the wolf sang an ode to carrot cake which he made up on the spot:

> Carrot cake, o carrot cake
> The best thing a baker ever could make,
> Mushy or munchy
> Gushy or crunchy
> Eat it by a woodland lake.

"We are really by a stream," said the child.

"That is what is known as poetic license," said the wolf. "Calling a stream a lake."

"Maybe you can use your license to drive me home."

The wolf nodded. "I will if you tell me your name. I know it's not *really* Little Red Riding Hood."

The child stood up and brushed crumbs off her dress. "It's Elisabet Grimm," she said.

"Of the Grimm family on Forest Lane?" asked the wolf.

"Of course," she answered.

"Everyone knows where that is. I'll take you home right now," said the wolf. He stretched himself from tip to tail. "But what will you tell your mother about her cake?" He took her by the hand.

"Oh, I'm a storyteller," said the child. "I'll think of something."

And she did.

"She did indeed," said Nurse Lamb thoughtfully. She cleared away the now empty bowls and took them back to the kitchen. When she returned, she was carrying a tray full of steaming mugs of coffee.

"I told you I had bad press," said Wolfgang.

"I should say you had," Nurse Lamb replied, passing out the mugs.

"Me, too," said the wolf with the cane.

"You, too, what?" asked Nurse Lamb.

"I had bad press, too, though my story is somewhat different. By the by, my name is Oliver," said the wolf. "Would you like to hear my tale?"

Nurse Lamb sat down. "Oh, please, yes."

Oliver Wolf's Tale

Once upon a time there was a very clever young wolf. He had an especially broad, bushy tail and a white star under his chin.

In his playpen he had built tall buildings of blocks and straw.

In the schoolyard he had built forts of mud and sticks.

And once, after a trip with his father to the bricklayer's, he had made a tower of bricks.

Oh, how that clever young wolf loved to build things.

"When I grow up," he said to his mother and father not once but many times, "I want to be an architect."

"That's nice, dear," they would answer, though they wondered about it. After all, no one in their family had ever been anything more than a wolf.

When the clever little wolf was old enough, his father sent him out into the world with a pack of tools and letters from his teachers.

"*This* is a very clever young wolf," read one letter.

"Quite the cleverest I have ever met," said another.

So the clever young wolf set out looking for work.

In a short while he came to a crossroads and who should be there but three punk pigs building themselves houses and making quite a mess of it.

The first little pig was trying to build a house of straw.

"Really," said the clever wolf, "I tried that in the playpen. It won't work. A breath of air will knock it over."

"Well, if you're so clever," said the pig, pushing his sunglasses back up his snout, "why don't you try and blow it down."

The wolf set his pack by the side of the road, rolled up his shirt-sleeves, and huffed and puffed. The house of straw collapsed in a twinkling.

"See," said the clever wolf.

The little pig got a funny look on his face and ran one of his trotters up under his collar.

The wolf turned to the second little pig who had just hammered a nail into the house he was trying to build. It was a makeshift affair of sticks and twigs.

"Yours is not much better, I'm afraid," said the clever wolf.

"Oh, yeah?" replied the pig. "Clever is as clever does." He thumbed his snout at the wolf. "Let's see you blow *this* house down, dog-breath."

The wolf sucked in a big gulp of air. Then he huffed and puffed a bit harder than before. The sticks tumbled down in a heap of dry kindling, just as he knew they would.

The second little pig picked up one of the larger pieces and turned it nervously in his trotters.

"Nyah, nyah nyah, nyah nyah!" said the third little pig, stretching his suspenders and letting them snap back with a loud twang. "Who do you think's afraid of you, little wolf? Try your muzzle on this pile of bricks, hair-face."

"That won't be necessary," said the clever wolf. "Every good builder knows bricks are excellent for houses."

The third little pig sniffed and snapped his suspenders once again.

"However," said the wolf, pointing at the roof, "since you have asked my opinion, I think you missed the point about chimneys. They are supposed to go straight up, not sideways."

"Well, if you're so clever . . ." began the first little pig.

"And have such strong breath . . ." added the second little pig.

"And are such a know-it-all and tell-it-ever . . ." put in the third little pig.

"Why don't you go up there and fix it yourself!" all three said together.

"Well, thank you," said the clever wolf, realizing he had just been given his very first job. "I'll get to it at once." Finding a ladder resting against the side of the brick house, he hoisted his pack of tools onto his back and climbed up onto the roof.

He set the bricks properly, lining them up with his plumb line. He mixed the mortar with care. He was exacting in his measurements and careful in his calculations. The sun was beginning to set before he was done.

"There," he said at last. "That should do it." He expected, at the very least, a thank-you from the pigs. But instead all he got was a loud laugh from the third little pig, a snout-thumbing from the second, and a nasty wink from the first.

The clever wolf shrugged his shoulders. After all, pigs will be pigs and he couldn't expect them to be wolves. But when he went to climb down he found they had removed the ladder.

"Clever your way out of this one, fuzz-ball," shouted the third little pig. Then they ran inside the house, turned up the stereo, and phoned their friends for a party.

The only way down was the chimney. But the wolf had to wait until the bricks and mortar had set as hard as stone. That took half the night. When at last the chimney was ready, the wolf slowly made his way down the inside, his pack on his back.

The pigs and their friends heard him coming. And between one record and the next, they shoved a pot of boiling mush into the hearth. They laughed themselves silly when the wolf fell in.

"That's how things end, fur-tail," the pigs shouted. "With a bowl of mush."

Dripping and unhappy, the wolf ran out the door. He vowed never to associate with pigs again. And to this day—with the exception of the cook—he never has. And being a well-brought-up wolf, as well as clever, he has never told his side of the story until today.

"Well, the pigs sure talked about it," said Nurse Lamb, shaking her head. "The way *they* have told it, it is quite a different story."

"Nobody listens to pigs," said Oliver Wolf. He looked quickly at the kitchen door.

"I'm not so sure," said a wolf who had a patch over his eye. "I'm not so sure."

"So you're not so sure," said Oliver. "Bet you think you're pretty clever, Lone Wolf."

"No," said Lone Wolf. "I never said I was clever. *You* are the clever little wolf."

Wolfgang laughed. "So clever he was outwitted by a pack of punk pigs."

The other wolves laughed.

"You didn't do so well with one human child," answered Oliver.

"Now, now, now," said the cook, poking her head in through the door. "As we say in the barnyard, 'Words are wood, a handy weapon.' "

"No weapons. No fighting," said Nurse Lamb, standing up and shaking her hoof at the wolves. "We are supposed to be telling stories, not getting into fights."

Lone Wolf stared at her. "I never in my life ran from a fight. Not if it was for a good cause."

Nurse Lamb got up her courage and put her hand on his shoulder. "I believe you," she said. "Why not tell me about some of the good causes you fought for?"

Lone Wolf twitched his ears. "All right," he said at last.
"I'm not boasting, you understand. Just setting the record
straight."

Nurse Lamb looked over at the kitchen door. The old
sow winked at her and went back to work.

Lone Wolf's Tale

Once upon a time there was a kind, tender, and com-
passionate young wolf. He had a black patch over one eye
and another black patch at the tip of his tail. He loved to
help the under-dog, the under-wolf, the under-lamb, and
even the under-pig.

His basement was full of the signs of his good fights.
Signs like LOVE A TREE and HAVE YOU KISSED A
FLOWER TODAY? and PIGS ARE PEOPLE, TOO! and
HONK IF YOU LOVE A WEASEL.

One day he was in the basement running off petitions on
his mimeo machine when he heard a terrible noise.

KA-BLAAAAAAAM KA-BLOOOOOOOIE.

It was the sound a gun makes in the forest.

Checking his calendar, the kind and tender wolf saw
with horror that it was opening day of duck-hunting season. Quickly he put on his red hat and red vest. Then he
grabbed up the signs he had made for that occasion:
SOME DUCKS CAN'T DUCK and EAT CORN NOT
CORN-EATERS and DUCKS HAVE MOTHERS, TOO.
Then he ran out of his door and down the path as fast as he
could go.

KA-BLAAAAAAAM KA-BLOOOOOOOIE.

The kind and tender wolf knew just where to go. Deep in
the forest was a wonderful pond where the ducks liked to
stop on their way north. The food was good, the reeds

comfortable, the prices reasonable, and the linens changed daily.

When the kind and tender wolf got to the pond, all he could see was one small and very frightened mallard duck in the middle and thirteen hunters around the edge.

"Stop!" he shouted as the hunters raised their guns.

This did not stop them.

The kind and tender wolf tried again, shouting anything he could think of. "We shall overcome," he called. "No smoking. No nukes. Stay off the grass."

Nothing worked. The hunters sighted down their guns. The wolf knew it was time to act.

He put one of the signs in the water and sat on it. He picked up another sign as a paddle. Using his tail as a rudder, he pushed off into the pond and rowed toward the duck.

"I will save you," he cried. "We are brothers. Quack."

The mallard looked confused. Then it turned and swam toward the wolf. When it reached him, it climbed onto the sign and quacked back.

"Saved," said the kind and tender wolf triumphantly, neglecting to notice that their combined weight was making the cardboard sign sink. But when the water was up to his chin, the wolf suddenly remembered he could not swim.

"Save yourself, friend," he called out, splashing great waves and swallowing them.

The mallard was kind and tender, too. It pushed the drowning wolf to shore and then, hidden by a patch of reeds, gave the well-meaning wolf beak-to-muzzle resuscitation. Then the bird flew off behind the cover of trees. The hunters never saw it go.

But they found the wolf, his fur all soggy.

"Look!" said one who had his name, *Peter*, stenciled on the pocket of his coat. "There are feathers on this wolf's jaws and in his whiskers. He has eaten *our* duck."

And so the hunters grabbed up the kind and tender wolf

by his tail and slung him on top of the remaining sign. They
marched him once around the town and threw him into jail
for a week, where they gave him nothing to eat but mush.

"Now, wolf," shouted the hunter Peter when they finally let him out of jail, "don't you come back here again or
it will be mush for you from now 'til the end of your life."

The kind and tender wolf, nursing his hurt tail and his
aching teeth, left town. The next day the newspaper ran a
story that read: PETER & THE WOLF FIGHT/PETER RUNS FOR
MAYOR. VOWS TO KEEP WOLF FROM DOOR. And to this day no
one believes the kind and tender wolf's side of the tale.

"I believe it," said Nurse Lamb looking at Lone Wolf
with tears in her eyes. "In fact, I believe all of you." She
stood up and collected the empty mugs.

"Hurray!" said the cook, peeking in the doorway.
"Maybe this is one young nurse we'll keep."

"Keep?" Nurse Lamb suddenly looked around, all her
fear coming back. Lone Wolf was cleaning his nails. Three
old wolves had dozed off. Wolfgang was gazing at the
ceiling. But Oliver grinned at her and licked his chops.
"What do you mean, keep?"

"Do you want *our* side of the story?" asked Oliver, still
grinning. "Or the nurses'?"

Nurse Lamb gulped.

Oliver winked.

Then Nurse Lamb knew they were teasing her. "Oh,
you big bad wolf," she said and patted him on the head.
She walked back into the kitchen.

"You know," she said to the cook, "I think I'm going to
like it here. I think I can help make it a real *happy* HAPPY
DEN. I'll get them to write down their stories. And maybe
we'll make a book of them. Life doesn't *have* to end with a
bowl of mush."

Stirring the pot, the cook nodded and smiled.

"In fact," said Nurse Lamb loudly, "why don't we try
chicken soup for lunch?"

From the dining room came a great big cheer.

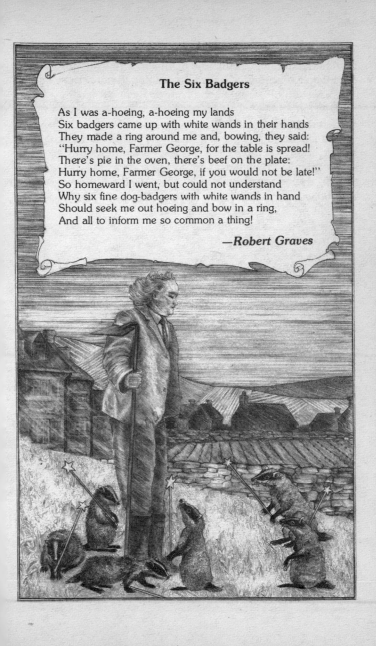

The Six Badgers

As I was a-hoeing, a-hoeing my lands
Six badgers came up with white wands in their hands
They made a ring around me and, bowing, they said:
"Hurry home, Farmer George, for the table is spread!
There's pie in the oven, there's beef on the plate:
Hurry home, Farmer George, if you would not be late!"
So homeward I went, but could not understand
Why six fine dog-badgers with white wands in hand
Should seek me out hoeing and bow in a ring,
And all to inform me so common a thing!

—*Robert Graves*

The Chapel Perilous

Naomi Mitchison

It was not certain who the hermit could be. Some said he was Joseph of Arimathea, but that was not inherently likely, although he had a marked foreign accent. Jutish, it might have been, all the same. Indeed in some ways it seemed more probable that he had been a king or a great knight-at-arms who had sinned much by violence and anger and had suddenly seen himself drowning in shed blood. Whoever he was, he lived in the cave beside the Chapel Perilous and, had he cared to do so, might have noted all that was going on: which was, indeed, plenty. Some held that he was noting it, and, if he were truly Joseph of Arimathea, was bringing it all up to the highest authorities.

The cave was a rather ordinary hermit's cave, a narrow stone shelf pecked out of the wall and lined with dry bracken, a stone to sit on, a stone for a porridge bowl: only a little smelly. The Chapel Perilous, on the other hand, was far from ordinary. There were the lights, for one thing, the sounds for another, the dolorous midnight bell and the crying. There were also the wildly delicious scents, always out of season: new mown hay at midwinter, ripe strawberries in March, narcissus at the autumn equinox, and never from any visible source, since all round for a space was desolate tumbled stone, scarcely growing even a shred of lichen, only here and there cumbered by a rusty piece of armour barely recognizable for what it had been. Immediately beyond this wasteland was the forest, but always in some equivocal season so that one forgot if it was winter or summer.

It had now been some years since the beginning of the Grail Quest, although no doubt time passed more rapidly at Camelot, at any rate for most people though not perhaps for Queen Guinevere, than it did at many a small outlying castle whose lord was away questing and had sent no news home. Many had perished in the quest at one stage or another. But here was the peak. The Chapel Perilous was the most spectacular of the dangers. Here there had been death and madness. Ladies alighting in all haste from cream-pale, gold-tasselled palfreys, had flung themselves down in bitter grief over their dead knights. But not all had died. Some who had professed piety had been in some way stripped in there, had burst out of the doors screaming or hideously dumb. The brave had been worsted in combats beyond their experience, then vilely laughed at. The young and handsome had come out white-haired and ravaged.

Sometimes one would crawl to the cave of the hermit and appear to get some consolation, so that at least he could stagger away. Those dry-eyed with terror and guilt might break into healing tears. Such was the power of the hermit when he chose to exercise it. But the two other watchers needed to beware of pity or involvement of any kind. Should that master them, they might themselves be tempted over the threshold, and should they let that happen they would be false to their assignment and to the future.

The Camelot Chronicle girl and the man from the Northern Pict occasionally exchanged professional gossip. They had been on this job for a long time. At first it had been interesting, so long as they kept on expecting the real story to break any day. Now it was a routine and a tiring one. The Grail Quest was still news, but the subs were likely to angle it so that it fitted in with whatever else they thought up or had handed to them. The local papers would send someone from time to time, but on the whole they left it to the representatives of the Big Two, who would sometimes look sardonically at one another's bylines; they knew one another rather well by now. The Camelot girl, whose name was Lienors Blanchemains, and who was the seventh daughter of a seventh queen, had some notes on Sir Hamarel, who had come to grief quite

badly, after going through most of the earlier perils with
some success. The picture wasn't up to much because he
had covered his face at the critical moment; they often did
that. But it would be a nice little story and might run
through the first two editions.

"I'm always sorry for them," said Lienors, leaning back
against a rock and yawning a little, for it had been a long
day, "when they don't even mind being interviewed. So
long as they mind, one needn't be sorry. They've still got
some kind of defence."

"You mustn't start getting soft, dear," said the Northern
Pict, whose name was Dalyn, and he too yawned because
this waiting had gone on for a long time. "Most people like
being reported, that's one thing certain, even when it
doesn't show them at their best."

"It doesn't seem quite fair, does it?" said Lienors. "After
all, he'd been a good knight."

"Doesn't that prove it?" Dalyn said. "While he was
being a good knight, that was something for itself. He
didn't need us. Now that's all over. He's shamed."

"Yes," said Lienors, "he won't be able to show himself
at the Round Table for a long time. And after all those
speeches on the Grail day! Now he's out of it."

"So he needs us. And here we are. I'd say he was
lucky."

"He's a story now. Instead of being just a good knight."

"Nothing but a good knight. Like all the rest of them.
Though I suppose that was all he wanted to be. And then
he had to take this on!"

"If only we could have explained. I think I know what
must have happened. But one never gets the space."
Lienors sighed, inking in the veins on a leaf.

"Well, of course," said Dalyn. "But then, everything
would be different. I know we can't compare with him"—
he jerked his thumb back at the hermit's cave—"taking
notes for You-know-who and sure every word will get in.
But then he doesn't have to worry about sales. Nor yet
about decency and libel and the advertisers, and all that.

Not to speak of the subs messing everything up! But
believe me, dear, most people would rather have their
story with us than nowhere."

Lienors glanced round at the cave. They could just see
the hermit pottering about. But whether he was writing or
making porridge, they were not sure. "You really think
that's what he's doing?" she asked in a whisper.

"Think? I'm sure. Sure as I know my own boss."

"Well, we all know Lord Horny," said Lienors, giggling
a little. "He must be wonderful to work for—in a way. The
funny thing is, I'm never quite sure who's running our
show. What with the Court. And never knowing quite how
Merlin stands with the Archbishops. Oh well, I'd better
send my piece in. You'll be around, Dalyn?"

"Yes, of course, dear, I'll tell you if there's anything you
oughtn't to miss." He held Lienors' bridle while she
mounted, but paid no attention to her shapely ankle; they
were, after all, colleagues. Her dwarf rode dutifully a quarter bowshot behind her, his knees close to his elbows, his
mule cluttered up with the peculiar shapes of his photo-
graphic paraphernalia. He was no talker, and Lienors
journeying on her own errand had no casual words to
spare. While she was away Dalyn went on writing his
autobiography. Not, of course, that it was publishable. Not
so long as Lord Horny . . .

When Lienors came back there had already been some
activity. The Chapel Perilous was in phase, lit up and with a
sinister and hungry humming. The hermit was staring
towards it with his chin on his hands. Lienors was uneasy.
At last Dalyn noticed. "What's up, dear?" he said. "Anything from Camelot?"

"You know, the White Lady . . ." said Lienors, and
hesitated.

"What's She done now?" Dalyn asked.

"I saw the mark. With my own eyes," said Lienors.
"Someone you'd never expect. It was Her all right."

"You can't put *that* in, dear," said Dalyn, "not about

the White Lady. Besides, it isn't news. You ought to know that by now. Have a sandwich.''

One of the questers tied his horse to a thorn tree and came into the wasteland. They watched him and nodded to one another and he went through what they knew by now to be some of the essential preliminary moves. Not that this made it less likely that a knight would make some fatal slip before even viewing the Grail. Sometimes there would be half a dozen in a day, sometimes not one for a week. It all depended on how the traps and combats and riddles and trials had gone at earlier stages. This one had his vizor down over his face, but they knew quite well that those who failed came back again into the waste helmless and swordless. Nor could you tell with any degree of accuracy by the shield; a well-known knight was as likely as not, on this Quest, to change his device. This one went in; the light dipped to crimson, the humming quickened and swung hungrily. Lienors shivered. "Give me another sandwich," she said.

Quite often the hermit accepted a sandwich from whichever of them happened to have a packet. Sometimes he ate it, at other times he gave it to the birds. "Would you care for one, sir?" Dalyn asked.

The hermit shook his head. "Not today. I shall be fasting for the time being. We are extremely likely to see something interesting.''

"You don't mean? . . ." said Dalyn under his breath.

"You must watch," said the hermit, "and I shall be watching you."

Another knight had arrived. He was walking through the wasteland in a most peculiar way, picking his steps and swaying as though buffeted by wind or spray. He had his vizor down, they thought they knew him. Could it be? . . . Lienors nodded imperceptibly. But—if it was—well, it was most unexpected to say the least. Half-way across he held out his right hand, as though to be grasped, and walked more firmly. The door swung open

for him too. But it was a peculiarity of the Chapel Perilous
that it could hold several people at once without any of
them being aware of the presence of the others.

The next knight had a lion with him. It stood outside the
door, its head bowed. Perhaps it was not a lion, but either
someone condemned to the appearance of a lion, or part
of the same ancient Hunt which Lienors joined in from
time to time. She coughed, so as to draw the hermit's
attention to it; if he would sprinkle it with holy water she
would know. But he did not move.

For some time nothing happened. The Chapel Perilous
went through some of its manifestations. They had seen it
all before and were no longer interested. Then the door
opened. A knight came out, bare-headed. And carrying
. . . well, something. If only it were a bit clearer if it was.

"Dalyn," said Lienors very quietly, "do you see what I
see?"

Dalyn looked. "Yes, dear. Yes. Now, we don't want to
rush this. Who do you make out it is?"

Lienors, who was hastily noting beige mantle, scalloped
and fronded leaf green, off-white vair trimming, scabbard
enamelled vert on argent, hardly looked round. "It's Sir
Bors," she said, "I'm sure. Seen him at Court often
enough. He never thought he had a chance."

"Yes," said Dalyn. "Now, can we get a picture of . . .
It?"

"Once he's off the wasteland," said Lienors and walked
firmly towards the knight, her dwarf following her.

In a loud voice like a clock striking the hermit said,
"Wait!" Dalyn jumped to it and caught Lienors as she gave
a cry and fainted into his arms. He laid her down and
looked from the knight to the hermit; he was quite well
aware that it was a sensible thing to consult the hermit on
points of protocol, of which this was certainly one. The
hermit shook his head. Sir Bors went past, intent. Dalyn
watched his face and not Whatever it was he held in his
raised hands. It was a change to see happiness on someone coming from the chapel, a solemn happiness surely,

and a little surprised, but as clear as sunshine. Even if it had been in order, it would have been difficult to know just what question to ask.

Lienors sat up, her hand to her head. "Funny," she said. "It—It went for me. Did you get a story, Dalyn?"

He shook his head. "I'm not sure it's going to work out like we want," he said.

"But—but this is It," she said. "What we've been waiting for, all this time. And not getting."

"Did you ever think what kind of a story it would make when we did get it?"

"It's no good deciding beforehand," said Lienors. "Leave that to the subs!" She shut her eyes, screwed up her face and shook it about. "I can't even get down what it was like," she said softly. "Odd."

The hermit came out of his cave, bringing a cup of water for Lienors, who gulped it gratefully. The dwarf peered at her, worried; he had been behind her, but somewhat insulated. Besides, people were always knocking him over, more or less accidentally; so long as his paraphernalia was uninjured it was of no significance. While she was drinking, yet another knight passed into the Chapel Perilous. And another. And indeed it was more than possible that others were coming invisibly; there was that feeling about. Both of them glanced at the hermit, who smiled. "They will be coming out," he said, "but they are still under protection."

And indeed the door of the Chapel had opened again; both of them knew Sir Palomedes, the Saracen. It was curious how the light from what he held in his hands reflected upward onto his noble and fine-cut features, making curious cheekbone shadows over his very dark eyes. "Going back east, I expect," whispered Lienors. "They'll splash it there. But it won't do for us."

"No," said Dalyn, "no. It certainly wouldn't suit my readers. And it can be kept out." He said nothing for a moment, then his voice shot up a tone, for he had seen something welcome and handsome. "Well! So Lancelot got it after all! What wouldn't I give for the real inside story!" He took a step towards him, then stopped suddenly: it had been like something clutching his throat in an utterly powerful way. It was nearly a minute before he could get his breath properly.

Lienors took him by the arm. "Don't worry, Dalyn. We can't get near them and that's that. Nobody can scoop us. I'm noting the dress angle."

"Thank you, dear," said Dalyn, recovering, "but we can't have *him.*"

"No, I'm afraid not," said Lienors. "At any rate the Camelot Chronicle can't. Not now. We've got to be a bit careful, got to look after public morality." She stared after Lancelot. "Lord God, what a man! They might take it in France, all the same."

"Getting it through to the Agency, are you?" asked Dalyn.

"Not likely! The line's tapped. I've got to look after myself a *little.*" She laughed rather shakily. "The Church has been advertising heavily these last few months. Could they have had some idea how things might turn out?"

"They've got their own sources, of course," said Dalyn, "but what about the woman's angle?"

"Not strong enough to cover *this,*" said Lienors definitely. Then: "Look! Isn't that one of your boys? Never can tell tartans myself. . . ."

"Don't be silly, dear," said Dalyn, excited, "look at his crest."

"But it can't be. . . ."

"But it is. The falcon. The falcon of spring. It's Gawain. Ah, God, it's Gawain. Funny, I had a sort of feeling the Orkneys would pull it off. . . ."

"You hadn't. It was only the other day you said you'd no use for chiefs and tartans and all that nonsense."

"Oh, then!" There was a definite Pictish burr in Dalyn's voice now. "I was not speaking of that family. But now—this is my story right enough."

Lienors shrugged her shoulders, then spoke again, gently: "Did Lord Horny give any indication? . . . After all, I don't have to remind you he's a jealous old devil, and if Sir Gawain is reported as having won the Grail a good many things follow, don't they?"

"Such as?" asked Dalyn, snarling a little, his hands on his notebook, his eyes on Sir Gawain riding away.

"Well, it's said"—Lienors went on—"it's said that with him it's likely to be a cauldron of plenty, awkward for the economists, and besides he'll get all sorts of things out of it, but *all* sorts—the most embarrassing, quite indescribable—"

"You've been listening to some of the White Lady's people again, I take it!"

"What if I have? They're apt to be correct on this type of information. One can't afford not to use them. But it will definitely cut the ground from under Lord H's feet, won't it now?"

Dalyn banged his fist impatiently on his book. "Well, who *can* we have?" He looked across. "There's Peredur."

"Yes, I see Sir Perceval," said Lienors primly.

"What have you got against him, dear?" Dalyn asked.

"Well . . . before he came to Court and got knighted—respectable and so on—when he was still Peredur, as you call him in that phoney Pictish way of yours, Dalyn dear. . . ."

"Yes, maybe. What happened?"

Lienors shrugged her shoulders. "Oh, he made a pass at me. Luckily I had my typewriter. Forêt Sauvage, yes, he might have been trying to strangle a boar! But now that he's a reformed character . . . well, I don't see why *he* should have the headlines, whoever has them!"

There were several foreign knights after that: French, Danes, Irish, all of whom seemed to be equally victorious. But the watchers were quite determined not to have foreigners. After all, if the Grail had come to Britain, then British it was going to stay, part of the Arthurian way of life.

If you denied that, then you denied the whole purpose and pattern in everything and who would bother to read the papers then?

For a little the Chapel was quiescent, soundless and scentless.

Suddenly Lienors drew her foot back sharply: something was creeping over it, a bushy green tendril. "Look!" she said. Then for a time they were both covering page after page of their notebooks, for the wasteland was rapidly filling with leaves and flowers. Butterflies followed the swaying flowers, birds followed the butterflies. A spring burst out of the cleft between two rocks, brimmed cool over ancient dryness and trickled musically, making its way through bending grass blades, carrying on its dimpled surface light petals of buttercup or columbine or meadowsweet: for all seasons were shouldering one another into the light.

The hermit had joined them and was earnestly blessing the small fish which had appeared in a gravelly hollow which the water had filled. Duly they lifted their dark shining noses a fraction out of the water. "We're a bit puzzled, sir," said Dalyn standing on one foot. "What really happened?"

"The time was fulfilled, my son," said the hermit. "The things were done which needed to be done, the questions were asked and answered."

"But," said Dalyn, "we always supposed—there was only one Grail. . . ."

"Yes, indeed," said the hermit, "and each knight won it." He smiled gently at Dalyn, who felt very stupid.

Lienors said: "If we had been able to get pictures—or even to see—would it have looked the same every time?"

"No, my dear," said the hermit, "for if that had been so it might have been said that one was the true Grail and the others only copies."

"But then," said Lienors, "how shall we know? I mean—we have to have a story, haven't we? And it is generally thought, at any rate one never hears anything else in Camelot, that there is only one Grail: the one that the knights of the Round Table saw. We couldn't very well tell our readers . . . all this. . . ." Her voice died down and she fidgeted her feet and looked away from the hermit.

"It wouldn't be a story if there was more than one," said Dalyn, half apologizing.

"If you feel like that," said the hermit kindly, "you will have to choose. Naturally, the one you decide on will be generally considered to be the Grail winner. So you have a certain responsibility, my children. And now," he added, "I believe I have an old friend, whose wound will now be healed. No, I am afraid it will be no use trying to interview him." He walked knee-deep into the flowery waste, towards the Chapel.

"That'll be the Fisher King," said Dalyn enviously. "It's a shame to keep the press away from him! He'd probably *like* to talk anyway! How it feels to be cured of a stinking wound a thousand years old. That ought to make the front page! I've half a mind to try. . . ."

"Don't!" said Lienors. "You know it's no good. Let's think about the Grail story. It's most unfair putting it on us!" She felt, with a certain surprise, the heat of indignant tears coming up behind her eyelids.

"Gawain was the first of the Round Table before all these newcomers," suggested Dalyn.

"Yes, and think what he's likely to have inside his Grail! Besides, he's not . . . not really . . ."

"The King's sister's son? Isn't that enough?"

"Yes and most likely got the answers from his mother! Have you ever seen Morgan-Morgause when she's really angry? I have, and I don't want to again. He's made the same. I'm sure the Court would agree. Besides you always nag me about the White Lady—just tell me what Gawain wears that hawk of his for? How I wish it could have been Lancelot, his Grail might have put some things to rights. At least if . . . if my sources are at all well informed. But I'm afraid that's quite hopeless. One can't simply ignore the proprietors, after all. What would Lord Horny's choice be, by the way? You'll have to consider that, won't you?''

"A little, a little," said Dalyn, "but it's the angle with him. I don't suppose it matters much within reason who it is. By the way, dear, do you notice the lion is gone?''

"I fancy it went with Sir Lancelot," said Lienors and sighed a little, feeling that it must have been nice for the lion. "Unless it turned into something when we weren't looking. There's someone else." They both stared. The newcomer had a white surcoat over his armour and a white shield with a red cross on it; he seemed to have lost his helmet and his fair hair straggled untidily over an unlined forehead and across blue eyes; he looked very young and a little startled, as though his sword were too big for him.

"Have you the least idea who this kid is?" asked Dalyn.

Lienors shook her head. "And if we try to speak to him it'll be just the same, I suppose! I'm still aching as though I'd been with the Hunt all night!"

"I couldn't agree more, dear," said Dalyn, rubbing his hand over his throat, "though I wish you'd not make that sort of remark; I know it's only me, but one of these days you'll say something to someone who'll take you seriously and repeat it elsewhere. Look, we'll pay no attention to the laddie. After all, we've seen enough. More than enough.''

They looked away, sat down and opened another packet of sandwiches. Both of them found themselves hungry. At a cough, Lienors looked up; the startled young man was standing beside them. "I wonder if you would mind telling me where I might be?" he said and bowed jerkily. "Sir and ma'am.''

Whatever shape it was, the Thing was tucked in under his surcoat; it made an awkward kind of lump there. Lienors did not let her glance linger. Nor did Dalyn. He answered, giving the Glastonbury location in Logres, some distance from Camelot, a great deal farther from the Pict lands, farther still from Rome. The Irish kings pursued their wars to the west; to the east the Thames flowed marshily to London. "And Carbonek?" said the young man.

Dalyn lifted his eyebrows at Lienors. "There is some doubt," he said.

"How?" said the young man. "It was there by the sea." He began to draw on the ground with the tip of his scabbard. "And our boat here. So I came in. And there in Carbonek was the stroke of Balin as though it were still being struck. I had to undo it. Then came the singing and the way opened for what I sought. But where is it all gone?"

"It seems not difficult to arrive here from many places," said Lienors gently. This looked like a version of the madness which came sometimes on those who had failed; yet this one had not failed. "What is your name?" she asked him.

"There was a time I would not tell anyone," the young man said, "but now I tell you willingly. I am Galahad, the son of Flayne of Corbyn by Lancelot. What is your name, damsel, and on what quest do you go?"

"I am Lienors Blanchemains, of the Camelot Chronicle," said Lienors and curtseyed. "My friend, who is on the same quest, represents the Northern Pict." So this was Lancelot's son whom everybody had heard rumours about, but nobody, apart from certain of the Court, had actually seen!

Slowly the lad smiled at her, then, shyly, at Dalyn. "Journalists!" he said. "Real journalists! Do you know, I've never met one before. What a wonderful life you must have, seeing everything, going everywhere, telling the world what happens. I've never been clever enough for that sort of thing. You must be terribly clever, you must feel very happy."

"Oh, no," said Dalyn, "not really. We wouldn't have a chance of—finding the Grail for instance. How does that feel?"

"Well, you see," said Galahad, "it is full of blood. You know about that, I'm sure you do, I needn't tell you. But the funny thing is, it doesn't spill. I expect you'd have thought of that, but I never did before. I keep it here, over my heart, you couldn't put an ordinary cup there without spilling, could you? Look, I'll show you—''

"No," said Dalyn quickly, "leave it there. We believe. Don't we, dear?" Lienors nodded; neither of them wanted to risk the same things again. "What exactly did you do, Sir Galahad?"

"I went into the Chapel," said Galahad, "but it wasn't this Chapel, I'm sure it wasn't. It was part of Carbonek castle. And the Mass was beginning and the Priest asked for me. And then It was put into my hands. There didn't seem to be anything difficult I had to do—oh, will you put this into your papers?" He looked at the two notebooks.

"If you would like us to," said Dalyn courteously.

"Of course. It's so important. And once I had It, everything started. I had no trouble asking the questions, though usually I'm stupid about things I don't quite understand. And the poor old King—he's really my grandfather, you know—he just got out of bed feeling perfectly well and asked for his dinner. And then the rivers began to flow and the wind began to blow and the cow began to chase the dog and the dog began to chase the cat and the cat began to chase the mouse and the mouse began to eat the bread—I say, I don't think I know what I'm saying! It was all such a surprise in spite of what they said."

"What had they said?" asked Lienors.

"Oh, they said I would be the one to get It: the true Grail. Mother always said so. She said I was to make up for . . . for everything. She wasn't always very happy, you know. Perhaps I oughtn't to say that? But she'll like to see about me in the papers. You said you were from the Camelot Chronicle, didn't you? I'm sure I've seen her reading that, only it's always two or three days late when it gets to Corbyn. At any rate the maids read it and they'd be sure to show her. I know it has pictures—you see, I'm not as stupid as some people think. Would you like to take a picture of . . . It?"

Lienors and Dalyn glanced at one another, wishing the
hermit would leave off this chatter with his old school
friends—and after all, what had the Fisher King got to say
after a millennium of illness, nothing but symptoms,
symptoms!—for they would have liked to ask his advice.
All the same it had gone differently so far with Galahad.
Anyhow this was their job. Lienors signed to her dwarf; it
did not matter if the Camelot Chronicle and Northern Pict
had the same pictures, considering how little their public
overlapped.

Galahad took the Grail out from under his surcoat and
bent his head over It. It threw a curious illumination
through his fingers. They got their pictures at various distances and adjustments, whatever way they were going to
come out in the end. There might be . . . well, interfer-
ence of some kind, thought Dalyn. But you had to be a
theologian and a physicist for this game and he was
neither; he only knew the outsides of things. Below that,
his guess was as good as another's, but not, probably,
more than a little better: whatever he may have said after a
drink or two. Because, if it had been much better, then
. . . well then, he would be out of touch. Not simply a
good reporter: as he wanted to be. But more like, well, a
Grail quester. Lienors caught herself thinking of Elayne of
Corbyn. It had been a marvellous story, but they'd had to
kill it. You couldn't risk a row with the Round Table
attachés over a Court release, and this had touched
everyone. Of course it was before her time, but Ygraine la
Grande, the old dear who ran the Correspondence and
wrote those revolting things about the heart, she remembered thoroughly, and if you once got her talking! . . . So
this was the result. Would he—could he—ever grow up
like his father? It had been something, even for a hard-
boiled newsgirl like herself, seeing Sir Lancelot so near:
and so happy.

It was the easiest possible interview. Galahad stopped
and smiled while they wrote things down. He told them all
his adventures, his invitation to sit in the special seat which

had closed its arms in a killing grip on others, his arming and his setting out on the Grail quest and how he got everything right from the start. It was so easy, he kept on saying, much easier than lots of other things people have laughed at me for not being able to do! He told them how he got his sword and all about the ship and King Solomon's bed, and the people he met and what they said to him. Above all he talked about the Castle of Carbonek, and always as though it were just as the other side of the Chapel Perilous. And then suddenly he said, "Well, I must be going or Mother will be getting worried." He hesitated and then said: "Thank you very much, lady and sir, oh, thank you!" Then he turned away with his head up. A white horse came out of the wood and whinnied to him; he took an apple out from under his surcoat where it must have been jostling with what else was there, gave it to the horse, mounted, waved and rode out of sight.

Lienors looked at her notes. "Is this to be our story?" she said. "We've got to agree."

"He treated us properly," said Dalyn, "not like the others."

"You remember what the old boy said about their being under protection? I don't suppose they could help not noticing us. Perhaps this laddie wasn't under protection."

"Maybe he didn't need it. Who'd want to hurt him?"

"I see what you mean," said Lienors reluctantly, "but is that a good enough reason to make him . . . exclusive?"

"Still thinking about Lancelot, dear?"

"Don't be stupid, Dalyn! We've got a wonderful story here and by now we can afford a flashback to the Elayne business. There's a picture of Corbyn in our files, taken in May with apple blossoms everywhere; it's a real swoon. I remember asking La Grande where it was, for I'd like to go there on my honeymoon! Oh, dear. And the laddie should make a good picture himself. But, all the same, it's a responsibility."

"If we do pick him it will be interesting to think what the others are likely to say."

"They'll have their friends. And of course there's the old boy." She jerked her head sideways at the hermit's cave. "Sending in his stuff. If that is what he's doing. There'll be talk, no doubt. But what matters is the mass circulation, us in fact. By the way, what will Lord Horny's reaction be to Galahad's type of Grail? Not quite *him*, is it?"

"Depends how I angle it, dear. Or the subs. The old devil can pretty well swallow anything so long as the angle's right."

Lienors sat down beside the stream which was now so thoroughly at home in the wasteland; there were little sand eddies in it, sand that had been dry and dull all these years now whirling and sparkling. "Is that good enough?" she said, frowning. "Haven't we a duty?"

"Duty, dear? We'll give the readers what they like. After all, they couldn't take the real story; it's too difficult—too difficult for me if it comes to that. Goes against too many interests. You said yourself to the old boy that they wouldn't stand for more than one Grail."

"Now I'm ashamed. Oughtn't we to try and explain?"

"How could we do that past editorial policy? If Lord H were to be told there was more than one he'd go right off the hooks. Why, anybody could find a Grail. And suppose people began to think that? Look, dear, they might all start off questing and who'd be left to read the advertisements? They'd lose all interest in us. No, Lord H wouldn't like that; nor would you and I. In fact, once we've made our choice I'd advise all the others to keep quiet. If they think they've got a Grail, keep it in the family, see, dear, until everyone believes our story, and then there'll be no danger."

Lienors splashed with her hand in the water and suddenly changed the subject: "What did you think It looked like?"

"Well, roughly what I expected. Roughly. I—naturally I didn't look inside."

"You didn't look at all, Dalyn?"

"Well, I arranged the picture."

"That's not quite the same. I didn't see either. With Sir

Bors, we tried to look. He was the first one. Dalyn, there's nothing against him."

"There's nothing for him, dear. I mean . . . not compared with this story. Look, dear, we must decide. If it's Galahad, my proprietor will be pleased. Your advertisers will be pleased and you can angle it so that the Court will be pleased."

"I can't see the Queen being pleased."

"He's Lancelot's son, after all."

"By Elayne. Ha-ha. You make me laugh. Dalyn! But it's not the Queen's world. Nor yet the White Lady's. Perhaps."

"Look, dear, you cut all that about the White Lady right out. We know as much about her as we want to know, and the public, bless them, have their own funny ideas. Right? Well then, we've agreed on Galahad and we'll work it so that the poets get a line on the laddie. We won't get Taliessin of course, but who cares?"

"Going all lowbrow, aren't you?"

"There's no choice. We'd better tell the old boy." For now he was coming back from the silent and lightless Chapel, in no way different from his usual self.

"Well, well," he said, regarding them, "so you have made your choice."

"We—we think so, sir," said Dalyn, "the last one to come out. Was that a good choice? Have we made a mistake?" Suddenly they were both overwhelmed with uncertainty and also with the abrupt knowledge that, once having chosen, it was the end of the assignment.

"No, no," said the hermit kindly, "I know you have to take what you are looking for. It may mean trouble, but not yet, not yet, and nothing to do with you."

"Ought we to have chosen one of the others?" said Lienors, suddenly with a mad hope that he might say yes, choose Lancelot whatever the consequences. And she would dare!

"Should it have been one of the older knights?" said

Dalyn at the same time. It might be Gawain in spite of common sense!

"You are old enough and experienced enough to do things by yourselves," said the hermit. "But I shall miss you. Yes, I will take a sandwich now."

"I wonder where they'll send me," said Dalyn a little desolately.

"We'll probably run across one another," said Lienors, the same.

"Will you be staying on, sir? Now that it's all over?"

"All over," said the hermit. "Really, you newspaper people have the oddest ideas. It is after the story that the *real* interest always occurs."

"What—here?" asked Dalyn.

"Naturally. The chapel is still perilous. But I doubt if either of your proprietors will be interested. There will be battles, you know, ravishings, Kings and Queens. But my own assignment will still be here." He nodded and walked away. They could see he did not propose to continue the conversation. Perhaps it was only swank. Or perhaps his sources . . . In the pool behind Lienors one of the fish jumped. She turned, startled, and saw that the level of the pool had dropped almost an inch already. Some of the flowers had seeded and no more were taking their places. The birds had eaten a good many of the butterflies. "Well, I'm off," said Lienors. "Must get my copy through. See you soon, Dalyn."

"Yes, dear," said Dalyn. "But I wonder what he meant."

"You keep your mind on the story!" said Lienors and he grinned back. Both of them mounted and rode their separate ways, quickly, and at the same time thinking out their first sentences, hoping the subs wouldn't spoil it all. Inside the Chapel Perilous a light showed like an eye opening, then blinked out. Ah, thought the hermit, cleaning out his porridge bowl, so it begins again.

Malagan and the Lady of Rascas

Michael de Larrabeiti

At the time of the crusades and in the land of Provence there were many beautiful castles and one of the finest was the castle of Rascas. High on a mountain peak it stood, built of golden stone and set against a sky that was as blue as the heart of a sapphire. At the foot of the mountain lay a village, its roofs shaded by broad-leaved plane trees and its streets cooled by the waters of a spring that overflowed in the village square. All around stretched a fruitful valley and there the villagers raised sheep and laboured among the olive trees and vines for their sustenance and for the greater pleasure of their lord, the Baron Rascas.

Baron Rascas was a stern and selfish man who lived in great style and luxury and sought pleasure in all the good things that life had to offer him. He was not particularly cruel to his subjects but neither was he particularly kind. For him the common people did not exist. As long as his needs and those of his courtiers were satisfied, then all was well; but if the Baron were thwarted in any way then he could become brutal, and, like the violent soldier he was, he possessed the courage and the means to impose his will on anyone.

For the most part however the Baron bore himself well enough and was content to live his life from day to day, gazing over his domain or seeking happiness with his courtiers. And thus he lived until about the middle time of his life, when, without warning, a royal messenger rode up to the castle and commanded the Baron to assemble his men-at-arms so that he might follow the King to Palestine, there to deliver battle to the Saracens who occupied the Holy City, in an attempt to wrest it from them by force of arms for the glory of God.

The Baron had no alternative but to obey. Like any other feudal lord he held his lands under the King and was sworn to provide soldiers and service to his monarch whenever summoned and for as long as necessary. The Baron cursed but gave orders nevertheless and preparations were made.

Within three weeks all was ready and the day of departure arrived sooner than had been thought possible. On that day there was a great noise and bustle to be observed in both the castle and the village. Packhorses were led from the stables and loaded; chargers were saddled and the Baron's armour, highly polished and reflecting the cloudless sky, was stowed away by his squires, together with his weapons. The Baron too was busy and strode about his courtyard making sure that not one dagger or one mace had been forgotten. From the battlements the courtiers, fine gentlemen exquisitely dressed in silken robes and velvet cloaks, gazed down and bit their lips. These were men too cowardly to follow their lord, and by their sides leant their ladies, desiring only that the Baron would be gone so that they might continue their endless round of amusement and dance.

Of all this the Baron was well aware but he had no wish to take such men to war with him, they would be but a burden and a hindrance. In any event his service to the King did not demand that he take all his followers. He had chosen only his bravest soldiers, about sixty of them, resolute men who knew that they might never survive this adventure, but that if they did they would live from the glory and holiness of it for the rest of their lives.

The Baron glanced up into the battlements; at least those courtiers he left behind would be there to protect the castle and the valley in times of danger. Though he could not trust them to fight well on a foreign campaign he was sure that they would defend their own lives and possessions to the last gasp if called upon to do so. The Baron sighed; would he and his men ever see this valley again? It was unlikely. The very journey to the Holy Land was full of hazards; there would be skirmishes at every frontier, drownings at every river crossing and even when the army embarked aboard its fleet it would be no safer. How many ships would founder beneath the waves? How many would be taken by pirates? And even at the journey's end death lurked in every desert and waited at every crossroad. Diseases that no physician could cure flourished in Palestine and when the King's soldiers reached the battlefield, those that survived, they would find in the Saracen an enemy more implacable and more merciless than any in their previous experience.

The Baron shook his head and tried to clear his mind of such thoughts. He ordered the men-at-arms to lead their packhorses down the side of the mountain and to wait for him at the village. He settled the sword at his waist and watched as the ladies of his court stepped aside to allow his wife to approach him so that she might speak her farewells.

Of all the ladies in the castle the most beautiful was the Baron's wife, the Lady of Rascas. She was young and stately but the most striking thing about her was the way in which the kindness of her heart showed through the features of her face. All through Provence she was renowned for her generosity and her modesty. The Baron's courtiers could find no fault in her and the common people could not love her enough for the care she took of them.

Again the Baron sighed. He was a brave man, some said there was no man braver, but as he took his wife in his arms he felt his resolve weaken. His spirit quailed. He pressed his wife to him and closed his eyes. She was so beautiful; of all the things he possessed she was what he cherished most and the thought that he might never see her again tormented him and hurt his heart. Perhaps she would weary of waiting for him and someone else, younger, more handsome, would come to the castle and charm her with his poetry, seduce her with a new song, laugh with her in the topmost towers as the sun went down the sky and turned the countryside to gold.

The Baron's face darkened; it was a prospect he could not face. Death and disease would be better.

"My lord," said the Lady of Rascas, "be not so sad, the day of your return is even now approaching." She spoke gently and touched her husband's hand.

The Baron held his wife at arm's length so that he could contemplate her beauty.

"Can you love me this long time I am away?" he asked, his voice thick with feeling. But he did not wait for an answer and turned, forbidding anyone to follow him as he made his way into an arcaded gallery let into the wall of the castle. There he commanded that cool wine be sent to him and that Malagan, the sorcerer, should attend him without delay.

Malagan came, his soft shoes making no sound on the flagstones, and he stood silently before his master, his arms folded beneath his scarlet gown. Malagan was young, tall and dark-skinned; there was Saracen blood in his veins. His hair was black and ragged and his nose was a hook in his face and the deep lines in his countenance were lines of suffering and grief.

There were those in the castle who said that Malagan was the most evil magician in Provence, in the world even, but they did not say it loudly. No one knew where he came from or what bound him to the Baron. Some courtiers said that the Lord of Rascas had, by accident, freed the magician from a spell and that in return Malagan had vowed to serve the Baron in everything for a certain number of years, and so far he had remained faithful to that vow.

What was known was that Malagan could change base metals into gold, imprison the souls of men in stone and make flowers bloom in the driest desert. He could also alter his form at will and like a maggot work his way into a man's brain and discover his innermost thoughts. In a word he could do everything that a god might do except restore life.

The Baron poured two goblets of wine and bade his sorcerer sit. "Malagan," he said, "I want from you this day strong magic, magic to ease my heart of its jealousy and doubt. You will ensure that my wife is faithful while I am away."

The magician put down his cup and spoke, his voice full of menace. "This does not need magic," he said. "Your lady is faithful and honest, this much I know for truth. No spell of mine can make her more or less so."

The Baron looked hard into Malagan's eyes. "It is a command," he said.

Malagan spoke again. "I can imprison her in a tree, a cliff. I can change her into a bird."

"No," said the Baron. "There is danger there. A bird may be killed, a tree felled and a cliff struck by a thunderbolt. She must live in the castle, protected. She must see to my lands. I have considered it. Make her hard to look upon, so that no one will desire her, ugly, like a beast."

"This is my lord's wish?" asked Malagan. He showed no surprise but he was hesitant.

"It is," said the Baron, "but I have no mind to see it. You will wait until I have left the castle. Then you will follow me on my journey. I do not want this spell to be undone during my absence."

Malagan's eyes glowed at the Baron's words but he said nothing, only getting to his feet and bowing slightly as his lord left the gallery and went directly to the courtyard, back to his wife.

Once more he embraced her and enjoined her to be courageous and to endure faithfully the years of separation that lay ahead and to accept with humility whatever life might hold in store. For his part he swore to be brave and loyal.

"I am sure our love will survive," he said. "Now I go to join my King, leaving you in charge of my lands and fortune. You are to care for them as if they were your own children."

At this the Lady of Rascas fell to her knees and watched as her husband, followed by his squires and his bodyguard, rode through the gate, across the drawbridge and into the narrow road that led from the castle and down to the valley below. The courtiers and their fine ladies watched too and waved their hands and handkerchiefs, but their attention was soon caught by something other than their lord's departure. Bearing a great book of magic bound in Arabian leather and studded with silver stars, Malagan appeared in the courtyard leading his own savage horse and the sight of the magician rooted everyone to the

spot where they stood. Malagan laid his book on the low
stone coping of the castle fountain, and, speaking in a
curious tongue, he made strange passes with his hands as
his dark eyes glared all the while into the horrified face of
the still kneeling Lady of Rascas.

Malagan spoke for several minutes, his voice rising and
falling in a dreamlike chant until at last his hands dropped
to his book and he slammed it shut. Then, so sure was he
of his magic that he turned without a glance behind him,
mounted his horse and followed his master through the
castle gates. And the courtiers, immobile, like statues in
their fear, stared from the battlements and waited.

They did not wait long; a great moan of anguish rose
from their throats as the effects of the magic became
apparent. The Lady of Rascas touched her hands to her
face and found that it was changing. Hair, close and stiff
like fur, began to sprout there. Her eyes grew larger and
larger, her lips thickened, her teeth widened and her jawbone became long and heavy. Under her fingers she felt
her ears take a pointed shape and her nostrils spread and
turn into voluminous purses of velvet. It was over and her
head was the head of a human being no more: it was the
head of a horse. This was the magic of Malagan. This was
how her husband had chosen to keep her faithful, and with
this fearful realisation the Lady of Rascas screamed, leapt
to her feet and ran to her apartments, locking the doors
behind her and allowing no one into her presence. For
many days her cries and sobs were heard over all the castle
and the courtiers and the servants stood in the corridors
and galleries in idle groups, unhappy and forlorn, not
knowing what to do for their lady or for themselves.

But the Lady of Rascas was a lady of unusual spirit. As
the months went by she began to show herself again. First
of all to her own servants and then, little by little, to the
whole society of the castle. There were good reasons for
this apart from her own strength of character. The demands of her husband's estate made it necessary for her to
visit all corners of it; to see that everything was as it should
be; to make sure that fruit trees were pruned; the vines

cultivated; the crops stored and the sheep counted. Gradually, as the months of the Baron's absence became years, the people of Rascas accustomed themselves to their mistress's appearance, and as she went amongst them, still clad in her beautiful gowns, so pleasant was her manner, so calm her spirits and so quick her mind, that they hardly noticed that her face was not a human face. To strangers and travellers too she was so welcoming and gracious that after a few hours in her company they completely forgot the forbidding countenance of this stricken chatelaine. There were even troubadours and minstrels who composed songs and poems about the Lady of Rascas and did not even mention her physical aspect. They sang instead of her other qualities: her composure and sensitivity; her good husbandry and learning; and the love and fidelity she bore towards her cruel lord.

And so life went on and the years passed, seven of them. The courtiers served their lady and accepted her judgements and her kindness with happy hearts. Of the Baron there was little news save occasional rumours of fierce battles in the Holy Land; death and disease; long sieges and forced marches; towns taken and cities surrendered. All that was known for sure was that the Baron still lived though many of his followers had perished, sickened by the plague or pierced by Saracen arrows.

One day, when the eighth year of her transformation was almost upon her, while walking on the ramparts the Lady of Rascas saw a plume of dust rising from the distant road near where it crossed the silver river. It was dust that rose from the hooves of a messenger's horse and in less than an hour the breathless courier was at his lady's feet. The Baron had landed in Provence, the crusades were over. He and what was left of his retinue were returning to the castle.

With haste and diligence the Lady of Rascas ordered everything to be made ready for her husband's return. The castle was cleaned, the storehouses inspected, the accounts made ready and everyone dressed themselves in their best robes. So pleased was the Lady of Rascas and so delighted the courtiers that they forgot that the Baron had not seen his wife as she now appeared, had not seen her since Malagan had wrought his evil spell and no one gave any thought as to how the Baron would look upon his wife.

The whole population of the castle assembled in the courtyard and waited for the Baron and his men to ride over the drawbridge and through the gate. The Baron had aged more years than he had been absent. His armour was dented and tarnished, its leather straps cracked and broken by the sun. His face was furrowed by the terrible things he had endured, his eyes dulled by the blood of the men he had killed. His heart had grown hard in seven years of war and he remembered nothing of the ways of peace.

Like an old man he dismounted, and leaning against his war horse he looked at his wife as she curtsied and held up to him the keys of the castle, stores and treasure. The Baron's lips parted in horror. When last he had seen his wife she had been the most beautiful woman in Provence.

He fell back a step and the courtiers recollected that the Baron had never seen his wife like this and they searched with their eyes and discovered for themselves what the Baron already knew: Malagan no longer followed his lord and there was no one to remove the spell. And although later they asked, the courtiers could not discover what had become of the sorcerer, dead by disease or vanquished by a stronger magic, no one knew . . . or if they did they would not say.

The Baron could not tolerate the sight of his wife. With a roar of anger he strode past her and pushing his subjects from his path he entered the castle. His lady pursued him and threw herself at his feet but the Baron held his hands before his eyes and commanded his wife to take herself off to the castle's topmost tower and to stay there until she died.

For many days the Baron would speak or listen to no one. He cursed his followers and cuffed his servants unmercifully. Most of his time he spent seated in a dark corner of the great hall, lost in sorrow and self-pity. The results of his cruel behavior afflicted him deeply and when he learnt of his wife's irreproachable conduct and when he inspected his estates and saw evidence everywhere of her goodness, he regretted more and more what he had caused Malagan to do all those years previously. And he was shamed too by those courtiers who had learnt to love the Lady of Rascas and had the courage to say that her imprisonment was a crime, but although the Baron knew in his heart that they were right he could not bear to release his wife from her prison. He knew that every time he looked upon her his own shame would burn within him.

At last and in despair the Baron sent messengers across the length and breadth of Provence, offering a fine reward to any magician, sorcerer or wizard who could remove the spell from his wife and make him happy again. The reward was great and many strove to win it, but there was not one whose magic was as strong as Malagan's and the Lady of Rascas stayed as she was and lived alone in her tower and as time passed her husband pushed the thought of her from his mind. So much so that as each sorcerer came to the castle to try his skill he was not greeted by the Baron at all but dealt with by the meanest servants, and only by those who still loved their lady and remembered her qualities.

Once more the years passed and the Baron sought happiness in pleasure. The castle of Rascas was soon renowned for mirth and merrymaking, poetry and music, and troubadours hastened there from all over Provence to sing of its delights and only a very few faithful courtiers and servants gave a thought to the sadness sitting lonely in the tower.

There came a time too when magicians and sorcerers no longer journeyed to Rascas, for the Baron had ceased to send messengers to search for them. He was more selfish than he had ever been; more cruel than in war and more foolish than in youth. The Baron and his flatterers thought only of themselves and the pleasure of the moment while his estates and his subjects, those that his wife had cared for so well, began to suffer and to fall upon hard times.

One summer's evening, when the Baron was at dinner,

a servant appeared at the door of the hall and, speaking with mirth in his voice, informed his master that there was someone at the castle gates who begged admittance. This man, said the servant, was aged and riding a spavined mule. He had no retinue and was dressed only in a tattered cloak which had been torn by the winds and burnt threadbare by the sun. Tied to his saddle was a straw basket and that seemed to contain the sum total of his worldly possessions.

The Baron, deep in wine at the head of his table and surrounded by the most beautiful of his ladies, held up his hand to signify that the traveller be received. He did this not out of a feeling of hospitality but in the hope that the newcomer might offer some entertainment. His ladies and courtiers were delighted with the idea and laughed and clapped their hands and called for some more wine, making a great deal of noise as they did so.

But all this din came to a sudden stop and every voice was stilled as a dark shadow fell across the doorway to their chamber and in the yellow light of the torches a forbidding figure slowly advanced. The Baron and his courtiers stared. He was old, this traveller, and his hair was long and grey and matted with the dust of travel. His face was sombre and its texture was like pitted stone which has been scarred by a thousand years of driven rain. The eyes were pale, like those of a dead man, and the mouth was a gash in the stone face with no lines of softness to make it human.

The Baron stirred in his seat and felt forward for his goblet of wine. The silence of the courtiers prolonged itself.

"Laugh," commanded the Baron. "Do you not laugh when you see an old scarecrow?"

Dutifully a few of the courtiers made as if to laugh, but the feeble sound soon died in their throats.

"What is it you seek here," asked the Baron, "a night's rest, money? Are you a beggar?"

"I am not a beggar," said the stranger, and when he spoke his voice was sharp and strong and pierced the air like a lance. "I bring you the gift of happiness. I have heard tell that there is a reward for whoever can bring your wife, the Lady of Rascas, to happiness again. This I can achieve."

Now the Baron and the courtiers did laugh in reality. Could this scarecrow perform what the greatest wizards in the land had failed to do?

"Old man," said the Baron, "you do not have the power in your blood and the evil knowledge in your spirit to undo what has been done."

The stranger at the door nodded. "What you say, my lord, may be true, but old is not always bad and backwards is sometimes forward."

The Baron laughed long and loud. "If your magic is as strong as your words are foolish," he answered, "then my wife shall indeed be saved. You have amused me and I will strike a bargain. I will give you a room above the kennels for a period of fifteen days. If you achieve nothing in that time then I shall bind you backwards on your mule and the scullions will beat you down the valley. On the other hand, if you should succeed in your attempt to bring me happiness then great riches shall be yours. Now leave me, I weary of would-be magicians."

"I want no riches," said the stranger as he turned to go. "My satisfaction lies elsewhere," and he left the room.

The magician went directly to the place that had been given him and locked himself inside. Those who took him his food reported that he spent most of his time reading in a great book, which he carried in his straw basket, or staring from his window, unblinking, at the sun. Once or twice he had been seen drawing with a stick in the dust of the courtyard or talking to the animals in the stables, but not once did he address a word to any of the Baron's courtiers or servants. At last, on the fifteenth day, he climbed to the topmost tower, opened the door to the chamber where the Lady of Rascas dwelt, even though it was triple-locked, and taking her by the hand he led her down the spiral staircase and into the Baron's presence.

There was a gasp from the onlookers. It had been years since anyone there had seen the Baron's wife. Many had never seen her at all, having arrived at the castle since the lady's imprisonment, and these cried out in horror. Even the Baron turned his gaze away, shamed once again by what he had done. Yet the Lady of Rascas moved with such stateliness and grace that her ugliness was in some measure diminished and the courtiers calmed each other and ranged themselves along the walls of the great hall to see what the magician would do.

Firstly he commanded the Baron's wife to sit on a low stool before her husband's throne. Then he stretched his arms in his tattered gown and began to speak, looking straight into the Baron's eyes while the Baron himself tried to look elsewhere but found he could not.

The language used by the magician was unknown to all there save the Baron. It was the Saracen tongue and he had learnt to understand it during his time in the Holy Land. Now, as he listened, he gripped the arms of his chair and trembled with fear.

"I tell the story of Malagan," said the stranger, "how he cast this fearful spell on the command of his lord because he too was under a spell at that time. I tell this story because I am Malagan and I have returned to undo the evil I did."

The Baron roared as if under torture but he did not move, nor did he turn his eyes away from the dreadful sorcerer.

"He bade me follow him to Palestine," said Malagan, pointing at the Baron, "and he left me for dead on the field of battle, never bothered himself with my body or deigned to send messengers to see if I was really dead or no.

"I was sorely injured, captured, enslaved, made the menial of a great magician who drained all my power from me when I was weak, stole my books of magic, discovered the secrets of my charms and ointments, and then when he'd finished with me, sold me into even more abject a bondage. I became so weak that I was left upon the road to die.

"Somehow I survived as a beggar and was befriended at last by a man of Alexandria who took me into his house as a servant and saw to it that I was nursed back to health. He was a scholar and I studied with him and shared his knowledge and I regained some magic, but never was it as it had been before. After some years this man of Alexandria gave me my freedom and I journeyed back to Christendom, through many more years and many more adventures. Now I have returned to this castle to seek revenge for the years of slavery and toil, revenge on the lord who abandoned me."

Malagan drew his breath and the Baron slipped low in his chair and his courtiers looked on, wondering at the words that had been said.

"They told me you were dead," cried the Baron. "We were hard pressed by the enemy, I could not return to give you burial."

"You did not even think to try," said Malagan. "You did not consider me worthy. I am Malagan and I wish you harm . . . yet would I undo the evil you had me do and make your lady content . . . but, alas, my power is not what it once was. To reverse a spell requires more power than to make one." And Malagan broke into a chant of ancient Arabic and not one word of it could the Baron understand. Malagan's voice rose and the summer air darkened, and in the valley below the castle there was thunder and blackness. The courtiers fell to their knees and crossed themselves and prayed for mercy. Suddenly there was a cry from the Baron and he lifted his hands to his face and found that it was changing. Hair, close and stiff like fur began to sprout there, his eyes grew larger and larger, his lips thickened, his teeth widened and his jawbone became long and heavy. Under his fingers he felt his ears take a pointed shape and his nostrils spread and turn into voluminous purses of velvet. Then it was over and his head was the head of a human being no more: it was the head of a horse. The Baron sobbed and fell senseless to the floor. Only his wife, amongst all those present, got to her feet and ran towards him to hold his head in her arms to comfort him.

With his work done Malagan the Magician pulled his cloak around his shoulders and with his tattered gown flowing behind him he strode across the flagstones and passed through the high wooden doors of the great hall and left the castle, never to be seen or heard of again.

Those courtiers who had fortune enough quitted Rascas immediately for other, happier places. Many more drifted away as and when opportunity presented itself, bearing no loyalty to a Baron who had become so ill-favoured and who was now unable to entertain and please them. Only those who loved the Lady of Rascas for her own sake remained, together with those who were too poor to go elsewhere.

At first a vast sadness settled over the castle and its inhabitants; there was no feasting, no music, no dancing. The Baron, ashamed of his appearance, locked himself in his wife's tower room and would allow none to see him but she. Once more the Lady of Rascas was forced to take charge of the daily business of her husband's estates and in due time this course of events brought its advantages.

The Baron discovered in his wife all those qualities she had developed during his absence and rediscovered those attributes she had possessed before his departure but which he had forgotten. She taught the Baron to accept his misfortune with patience and humility, showing him how to take delight in the beauty of the valley and simple life of its people. The Baron fell in love all over again and much more profoundly than he had the first time. He found in his wife the most loving and intelligent creature he had ever known, and in the light of her husband's gaze the Lady of Rascas became happier than she had been in her youth. The people of the castle rejoiced in what they saw and they learned to be happy, watching as a new love bloomed between their master and mistress.

So the Lady of Rascas was made as content as Malagan had wished her to be and her lord became wise and looked after his lands with care. Though they were never seen outside their estates they were renowned throughout Provence in song and in legend for the perfection of their love, the length of their lives and the beauty of their children and grandchildren. And over the castle gate the

Lady of Rascas caused to be carved, before she died, the
following words:

"Out of evil came good; out of ugliness, beauty."

The Baron approved of this work, but when the stone-
mason had finished his task the Baron took him to the
postern gate at the rear of the castle and there commanded
him to carve once more; and today, many hundreds of
years later, amongst the fallen stone and hollow walls of
the place that was called Rascas, only that archway stands
and these words may be read above it:

"He who turns to evil will, at the end, find it turned
against him."

Bones

P. C. Hodgell

It was nearly dawn in the city of Tai-tastigon. Birds had been chirping sleepily for some time as light seeped into the eastern sky, but the streets still lay drowned in shadows except where faint spheres of light shimmered against the walls. Down one such avenue in the Gold Ringing District came a hooded figure. It paused beneath each streetlight in turn, murmured "Blessed-Ardwyn-day-has-come" in a bored voice, and passed on, leaving darkness in its wake.

When the man was out of sight, Patches emerged from the shadows and resumed her vigil just outside the gate of the mansion owned by Polyfertes, the Highlord or Sirdan of the Lapidaries' Guild. While the plaster figures clustered around the house's lower windows were still indistinct, the young thief noted anxiously that up near the roofline the sinuous shapes of men, women, and beasts—all doing complicated, highly ingenious things to each other—stood out with far more clarity than they had only moments before. Even the black granite ravens on the gateposts seemed about to shake their wings and join the growing dawn chorus.

Gods, but it was getting late. Any minute now, a yawning servant would open the front door, and the guard, who was leaning against it, would tumble into the hall. As soon as they realized that his sleep had been deepened with poppy dust . . .

Jame—better known in the Thieves' Guild as the Talisman—was still inside that house. What the hell could she be thinking of, not to have made her escape before now?

At that moment, Jame's main thought was that she did not want to lose her fingers. Around her in the dim light of Polyfertes's treasure room glowed hundreds of gems, their erotic engravings intriguingly distorted by the horn glass of the cases that protected them. Securing each case was a box lock. Poised over each lock, well out of sight within the intricacies of the box, was a weighted razor. An hour ago, Jame had edged her hand in under one such blade. She was still delicately probing into the lock mechanism beyond it, grimly suppressing tremors of fatigue. In the case before her, besides two gems, were at least twenty-five severed fingers, some half-decayed, all lovingly arranged on the cream velvet. Polyfertes collected more than gems.

There was a loud click. Jame caught her breath, bracing for pain. None came. The "thief-proof" lock had at last been sprung.

With a deep sigh of relief, she opened the case and removed the two jewels from their grisly nest. One was a magnificent sapphire, engraved with three women and a dog engaged in a rather peculiar activity. With this stone, Polyfertes had proved himself worthy of master's rank in the Lapidaries' Guild. The second jewel was a mere zircon. On it was the rough sketch for the masterwork. Jame turned the sapphire modestly upside down and pocketed the zircon, smiling faintly. Polyfertes wouldn't have to guess who had raided his treasure trove; the Talisman's eccentricities were by this time nearly as celebrated as her skill. Still smiling, she left the room.

Down below, Patches was chewing through the fingertips of her gloves, having quite forgotten that she had them on. Suddenly she stiffened. Yes, no . . . *yes*. There was someone at a third-story window. A line tumbled to the ground. Then a slim, dark form swung itself over the ledge and started down the rope, stepping lightly from plaster head to head.

"Talisman!" said Patches out loud, and, in the fullness of her relief, she stepped through the gate.

"Thief!" cried two loud, hoarse voices above her. Startled, she looked up and saw the gatepost ravens, stone wings spread, beaks agape. *"Thief! Thief! Thief!"* the warning cry came again from their motionless throats.

Jame was still about twenty feet off the ground when she

heard the guard wake with a snort. That was hardly surprising; even a pound of poppy dust blown straight up his hairy nostrils would not have deafened him to an uproar like this. She pushed herself clear of the sculpted figures and let go of the line. The fall jarred her badly. Before she could recover, the guard was between her and the gate.

He lunged at her with his spear.

Jame sprang backward, twisting, and felt the cold breath of steel as the barbed head ripped at her jacket.

Patches yelped in protest.

"Stay where you are!" Jame shouted at her, snapping at the guard, " 'Ware truce, man: I'm unarmed!"

He lunged again.

God's claws, she thought irritably, sidestepping. Didn't the idiot realize that if he spitted a thief without so much as a rock in her hand, the fragile nonviolence pact between thieves and guards would be shattered? Someone inside the mansion had begun to shout. Wonderful. The entire household would descend on her from behind if she let this moron delay her a moment longer.

Here he came again.

Right, thought Jame. Unarmed isn't unable.

She caught the spear shaft as it slid past and jerked the guard into a chin-strike that snapped his head back. Now, one more to teach him manners. She was poised for the kick that would leave the man squeaking for a month when the ground suddenly lurched under her feet. All three, thieves and guard, found themselves on the pavement, staring at each other in bewilderment. What the hell? . . .

"Earthquake!" screeched the ravens. "Thief! Earthquake! Thief!"

A second tremor wracked the courtyard. Looking up, Patches saw two intertwined plaster figures separate from the roofline. They were directly above the guard. Jame sprang at him as he sat gaping stupidly upward. Both disappeared in a cloud of dust and flying splinters as the figures crashed to earth.

Patches, choking on plaster dust, heard more shouts from the house, then her friend's voice at her elbow: "You were thinking, perhaps, of moving in? Come on!"

They ran. Behind them, the ravens were clamoring, *"Thiefquake! Earthworm!"* while Polyfertes's cook ran in circles beating a gong and bellowing, "Fire!"

"I think we woke 'em up," said Patches with relish when they had slowed down again several blocks later. "But why in Thal's name did you save that guard? The bastard tried to gut you."

"I hadn't his taste for truce-breaking. Besides, this isn't worth any man's life."

She dropped the zircon into Patches's hands.

"So you really did it," said the younger thief, almost in awe, regarding the stone. Then she gave Jame a wary, sideways look. "Still mad at me, aren't you?"

"Mad? Why should I be? All you did was let the other 'prentice thieves goad you into swearing that I could crack Polyfertes's treasure room. Well, I have. Your honor is safe, and so is my reputation—for once without bloodshed."

"Oh, well," said Patches vaguely. "No omelets without broken eggs."

Jame turned on her. "Is that all you have to say about it?" she demanded. "Remind me, if you please, what happened to Scramp, your brother, only three months ago."

"He challenged you to rob the Tower of Demons," said Patches, squirming. "The demon nearly made fish bait of your soul, but you got away with the Peacock Gloves."

"And then?"

"Scramp's master disowned him."

"And then?"

"Scramp hanged himself. And then," said the pug-faced thief, suddenly rallying, "you gave me the Gloves so that I could buy my way into the Thieves' Guild."

"And that, I suppose, puts the egg back together again. You just don't understand, do you? I might as well have put that rope around your brother's neck myself. As for tonight, my God, couldn't you see that the other 'prentices were setting you up—and me, too—exactly the same way they did Scramp? If you ever put me in a situation like that again, we're through; I'll be damned if I'm going to cause another death in your family."

With that, Jame turned on her heel and walked away.

She had gone quite some distance into the bustling labyrinth that was Tai-tastigon before the haze of rage lifted, leaving her ashamed and vaguely ill. Why had she torn into her young friend like that? Patches had meant no harm, either by accepting the challenge in the Talisman's name or by speaking lightly of spilt blood. She was simply a child of the streets, with neither time nor tears for the dead. Jame had thought that she too had gotten over Scramp's suicide, but apparently not. Well, forget it. It was unprofessional to brood, and dangerous as well. Now she must report the evening's success to Penari, her master, whose instructions had made it possible.

The Maze, Penari's home, was one of Tai-tastigon's marvels. The old master thief had had the huge, circular edifice built some fifty years ago, just before the final, impossible theft that had made his reputation forever. Then he had retreated into it with his prize, the jewel called the Eye of Abarraden, thumbing his nose at the entire city. Since then, many thieves had tried to track the old master to his lair to obtain his secrets, but the Maze had defeated them all. Besides Penari, only Jame knew the key to its twisting ways, and even she entered them this morning with trepidation, remembering how the building's own architect had once lost his way here and never been seen again.

Fortunately, the earthquake had done little damage . . . or so she thought until she finally emerged in the old thief's living quarters. These occupied the core of the building, a wide, seven-story-high shaft lit day and night by innumerable guttering candles and filled with the spoils of a lifetime. At the moment, virtually everything appeared to be on the floor. Icons, rare manuscripts, all the trinkets on the mantelpiece except for a solitary stone gargoyle, clothes, a shattered box with ivory inlay (formerly the resident of a high shelf), fragments of a roast goose . . .

Jame sighed. What a mess. But where was Penari?

Molten wax splashed on the center table, followed by a
shower of candles. Looking up, Jame saw that the huge
chandelier had almost disappeared, lapped about in the
folds of something white that undulated gently in the dim
light.

"Monster?" she said incredulously, staring. "You idiot,
that chain is ancient! Come down before the roof caves
in."

At the sound of her voice, the tablecloth moved. Jame
threw it back and, crouching, found herself nose to nose
with her master.

"About time you showed up!" hissed the old man. "Are
we alone?"

"Why, yes—except for a forty-foot python suspended
over your head."

"Never mind *that*." Penari scrambled out from under
the table. Erect, the top of his head came about to her chin
and his cloudy, nearly blind eyes stared first through her
collarbone, then wildly about the room. "Not here yet, is
he?" he demanded, a touch of his usual self-confidence
returning. "Good! I've time to thwart him yet. Now, have
you seen his gargoyle?"

"I've seen *a* gargoyle," said Jame, bewildered. "Over
there, on the . . . Why, that's odd. It's gone."

"Gone," he repeated querulously. "Of course. It would
be. Quick now, have you ever come across any bones in
the outer passageways?"

"Many times," said Jame, staring. "Rats, Monster's
dinners, vhors—"

"No, no—*human* bones. A skeleton, say, with a finger
missing."

"Bodies, yes, occssionally—when some fool wanders in
and breaks his neck before we can escort him out—but
bones . . . Wait a minute. Of course! I didn't exactly count
phalanges, but did this particular skeleton have a medallion around its neck, a semicircle on a stem?"

"Yes, yes!"

"Well then, that would be Hervy."

"Who?"

"That's just what I call him," said Jame, with mounting embarrassment. "I came across him when you first sent me out to memorize parts of the Maze, and . . . well, he was such a clean old gentleman (clean-picked, perhaps I should say) that I used his bones to mark various passage-ways. He's scattered all over the first level now."

"Excellent!" cried the old thief, to her amazement. "But do you remember where you left his head? Yes? Then go fetch the nasty thing, boy, and we'll smash it into tooth-picks Hurry!"

Jame went. Penari often left her speechless, but never more so than now. What did bones decades old have to do with a little stone statue that apparently moved about at will? Why was Monster, that venerable reptile, clinging to the chandelier, or his master, for that matter, cowering under a table . . . and would she ever get the old thief to stop calling her "boy"?

The light of her torch danced on the bare walls. Dark, dusty, narrow—it was always rather like being buried alive here in the outer passages of the Maze. She went quickly, pausing now and then to listen for the sound of claws on stone. Not long ago, the labyrinthine building had suffered from an infestation of vhors—large, vicious rodents with a tendency toward demonic possession—and she was not sure that she and the priest lent to her by the Brotherhood of Sumph (Pest Control Chapter) had dealt with all of them.

Jame's destination was the intersection in the northwest quadrant of the Maze where she had originally found the entire skeleton. The bones were so old that she had never really thought of them as human remains and so had felt free to scatter them as she pleased, leaving only the skull undisturbed. She should have found it there now, but it was gone. Puzzled, Jame crouched beside the poor scraps of clothing that had survived time, rats, and her own meddling. Something glinted in the torchlight. She reached gingerly into the decaying rags and drew out Hervy's medallion. A semicircle on a stem . . . surely she had seen this emblem somewhere else, out in the city.

Suddenly Jame stiffened. Someone—no, some-*thing*—was watching her. Firelight leapt on the walls. Dust drifted down from an overhead beam. The silence pressed in on her, broken only by the distant sound of dripping water and . . . what? The whisper of claws on stone? Vhors hunted in packs. When the madness seized them, they swarmed up from the sewers, engulfing anything alive that got in their way, passing their insanity on to it even as they died. Medallion in hand, Jame rose hastily and returned to the central chamber, making several quick but wary side trips.

"The skull is gone," she reported to Penari, "and so are many of the other bones. I didn't have time to check them all. Now, will you please tell me what's going on?"

But the old man didn't answer. He heard her news in silence, then began to pace back and forth, occasionally stumbling over out-of-place objects. Jame watched him, perplexed. This wasn't the first time he had kept a secret from her, but usually he did so with a kind of glee, daring her to solve the mystery for herself. That had been part of her training. But now he had apparently forgotten her presence altogether, and, for the first time since she had known him, he seemed badly scared. She was his apprentice, bound to him by law and respect. It was her duty to protect him, but from what?

The chain of the chandelier groaned as Monster shifted his not inconsiderable weight; the medallion grew warm in Jame's hand. She didn't want to leave the old man, and yet . . .

"Sir," she said at last, slowly, "if you haven't any need for me here, I've an errand in the city."

Penari didn't seem to hear her. She was well out into the Maze when his voice, shrill with defiance, reached her. "You can't have them, do you hear me?" he was shouting, not at her, not, apparently, at anyone. "They're mine, I tell you, mine, mine, mine!"

Tai-tastigon, that great city, was wide-awake now,

shaken out of its predawn drowsiness by the tremors that had racked it. The citizens of the night—thief, courtesan, and reveler—rubbed shoulders in the streets with merchants and craftsmen thrown prematurely from their beds. Pilgrims gawked at the damage. A fair number of these country-bred folk who knew no better than to wander far from their lodgings would not be seen again for weeks, if ever, Tai-tastigon the Labyrinth had swallowed even its own citizens before now, and possessed a floating, bewildered population of the lost whose patriarchs, some claimed, had been wandering the streets since the founding of the city.

Penari's Maze was more sparsely occupied, but in other ways it resembled the Labyrinth all too closely: one, in fact, was the miniature of the other. This was the greatest of Penari's secrets that Jame had yet learned, and it still awed her to think that a single mind could have stored up enough information about the city, street by street, level by level, to have drawn up from memory its map to use as a floor plan. She herself had only mastered a fraction of the Maze so far, but she did know how to match points in the building with their external counterparts. This bustling street, for example, equalled that dusty corridor: here she should turn just as she would in the Maze; there, go straight . . . and so on and on until some thirty minutes later Jame arrived at the spot in the northwest quarter of Tai-tastigon that corresponded to Hervy's original position in the Maze.

She was now in the heart of the Temple District. All around her, chants and clouds of incense drifted out of open doors, fogging the air with sound and scent, while little troops of worshippers trotted past, some of them going backward in penance. Over the door of the temple facing her was the same emblem as on the medallion still in her hand. She saw, on his larger version, that the mushroom-shaped symbol was in fact an instrument of some sort, marked with calibrations. She opened the door a crack and peered into the utter darkness of the sanctuary.

"Hello! May I enter?"

No one answered.

For a moment she stood there, undecided. It could be very dangerous to enter the temple of a god not one's own without safe conduct. Then, on impulse, she swung open the door and stepped over the threshold. Immediately, all outside light vanished. When Jame groped behind her for the door, nothing was there.

So much for thoughts of retreat.

Cautiously, she began to edge forward, hoping that this wasn't a sect that favored snake pits. Then suddenly, as though an intervening corner had been passed, she saw a little way off what appeared to be a small, extremely detailed model of Tai-tastigon's Council Hall. Intrigued, she approached it. With each step she took, it grew remarkably, until, when she came up to its walls, they seemed every bit as high and solid as those of the original out in the city proper. Logically, the temple in which she stood could not have contained anything a tenth the size of this hall, and yet here it was. What was more, beyond it she saw another miniature structure—this time the Tower of Bats—and again approached to find it full-sized. This happened over and over until within a few minutes she had visited a dozen of Tai-tastigon's most notable buildings.

There was even a full-scale replica of Polyfertes's mansion. Jame circled it curiously, noting that here too parts of the ornate facade had fallen. The worst damage, however, was at the rear of the house where the servants' hall had partially collapsed. Then Jame saw something move in the ruins. It was a hand.

"Are you all right in there?" The hand had whisked itself back into a hole under a downed beam. Jame, peering in after it, saw nothing. "Hello?"

"Hello!" said a muffled, petulant voice. "Kindly get off my calculations."

Jame stepped back hastily. She had been standing on a set of mathematical figures drawn in the dust. The hand reappeared at a different hole, took several measurements with the now-familiar mushroom-shaped instrument, then added these numbers to those already on the ground, finishing with a flourish.

"If," said the voice, "you were to take that board there, balance it on this stone here with the edge under this beam, and push down, you might do some good."

Jame complied, and a moment later a plump little man crawled out from under the rubble. "Well done. Thank ye," he said, brushing himself off as she jumped back, allowing the lever to spring up and the beam to crash back down.

"You know, that's odd," said Jame, surveying the ruins. "Earlier this morning I . . . uh . . . had some business at this house—the real one, that is—and the earthquake had damaged it, too."

"Nothing odd about it," said the little man briskly. "Correspondences, m'dear, correspondences. Naturally, the fall of one affects the other, and the same with cracks, crumblings, and other misfortunes. We even have a minor problem with pigeons. But see here: I'll show you what I mean."

He set off at a trot, obliging a perplexed Jame to follow. They passed many more buildings than she had as yet seen, a fair number of them recently damaged. Then, rounding another of those invisible corners, Jame found a tall, familiar pair of windows looming up before her, gorgeously tinted and ablaze with light. The architect priest threw them open. With a deepening sense of unreality, she followed him out onto the windy balcony of Edor Thulig, the Tower of Demons.

Tai-tastigon lay spread out far below them. Its streets hummed with life as the city's irrepressible citizens embarked on a new day of profit and pleasure. What was a mere earthquake to them? More untoward things happened in Tai-tastigon all the time . . . like stepping from the interior of one building onto the balcony of another blocks away. There to the northwest lay the Temple District. Jame was trying to pick out the architects' sanctuary—in which, a moment ago, she had been standing—when she noticed a dark scar cutting halfway across the entire district, a shadowy rife of downed buildings with shock lines reaching far out into the city.

"It was that damned Arthan," said the priest, holding
down wind-torn hair with both hands. "A wild hill-god if
ever I've seen one. His fool priests never told him they'd
moved his house into town, so when he happened to
come untempled this morning, of course he panicked. The
biggest city he'd ever seen before probably had one communal privy. Why, the imbecile almost got as far as this
temple! If you think the damage he did out in the city was
bad, imagine what it would have been like if he'd gotten his
big feet in among these models."

"You mean . . ."

"Yes, of course. D'you think the correspondences only
work one way? Oh, we had a merry time getting that holy
half-wit indoors again, and what should happen the minute I get home? Polyfertes's blasted house falls on me! I
keep telling the architect who built it that he puts too much
sand in the mortar."

Jame was leaning over the rail, staring down at the rose
garden far below.

"A long way to the ground, isn't it?" said the priest
behind her. "One hundred and fifty feet at least, and the
Talisman jumped from here with the Peacock Gloves during the last Feast of Fools. Now there was a theft!"

"It wasn't from here," said Jame, still staring, surprised
at how dry her mouth had gone. "It was from the south
facedown into the Tone, which was quite bad enough,
even at night, even without thinking. But there was no
choice: the demon of the tower was a step behind
me."

"You? Penari's Talisman?" She turned to find the little
priest beaming up at her. "Well, this is an honor. We old
men like to keep up on the doings of you young Guild
bloods. I do believe that the Talisman has stolen more
supposedly inaccessible trinkets than anyone since the
days of her master. Why trinkets, by the way? I've always
wondered about that."

"For one thing," said Jame, "whatever I steal immediately becomes my master's property, and Penari has
all the riches he wants. For another, the only time I did lift

something valuable—the Peacock Gloves, in fact—the affair ended badly."

"Badly? But everyone called it a triumph!"

"Not everyone. A boy died. No, you wouldn't have heard about that," she said with a sudden, bitter laugh. "He was only a shabby little nobody named Scramp, whose envy nearly cost me my soul."

"Good gracious!" said the priest, startled. "However did he manage to do that?"

"By daring me to raid the Tower of Demons. The other thieves put him up to it, of course. They've never forgiven me for walking out of nowhere straight into the city's best 'prenticeship."

"And this boy?"

"He was an outsider too, trying to buy their acceptance at my expense. I could see what he was doing, and why, but I couldn't make him stop. Then, when I had carried off the Peacock Gloves, he lost his head altogether and accused me of cheating. We fought."

"You won, of course."

"There was no 'of course' about it," said Jame sharply. "He did very well. I hoped the others would honor him for it, but instead his master disowned him and . . . he hanged himself. Damn. I hadn't even meant to think about that whole, rotten business again, much less to burden a complete stranger with it."

"Oh, I don't know," said the priest vaguely. "If you try to sit on something like that, it invariably hits you. I think I understand now why the Talisman has been taking such . . ., well, suicidal risks these past three months. But I don't quite see why you should feel so guilty about that boy's death. After all, it wasn't really your fault. If it had been, I expect your friend Scramp would have had something to say about it before now. In this city, the dead aren't always particularly docile, especially if they have a strong grievance against the living. I wouldn't worry about it so much if I were you. After all, anyone who can survive the Maze isn't going to fall easy prey to anything else. That building is a killer. You know, I firmly believe that it was the death of

Rugen, my old master, and he was the one who built it."

This apparently turned the little priest's thoughts in a new direction, for he abruptly swung around and trotted back into the darkness of the temple. Jame followed, wondering where he was bound now. Then she saw that they were approaching one last model, that of the Maze itself.

"Fifty years and more it's been since Master Rugen disappeared into that monstrosity," said the priest sadly, looking up at its blank walls. "A fierce old man he was—dangerous to cross but fair too, once the bloom was off his anger. I've never known him to hold a grudge against the innocent, or to forgive the guilty. This was the finest thing he ever built. He even cut off his little finger to lay under the center stone (something we rarely did, even in those days) but 'blood and bone bind,' says Master Rugen, so I handed him the knife. I know he meant to be buried there."

"In the Maze?" said Jame, startled.

"Of course. We all make arrangements in the finest building we design—our end-work, we call it—but who crawls into a grave before his time? I still say he meant to come out when last he went in to see Penari. Why shouldn't he? He was only sixty and in good health, with years of work ahead."

"What if he simply got lost? Even if your master built the Maze, he could hardly have remembered every turn in it."

"He didn't have to. The floor plans were in his pocket. People always throw that in my face when I claim that he didn't mean to stay. And then too, his gargoyle never came home."

"His *what?*"

"You know, one of those little stone beasties. Every master architect has one, and very useful they are, but impish too. Look the other way and you'll either find them gone or sitting on your head. They also guard their master's crypt. That's why some thought, when Quezal didn't come back, that Master Rugen had decided to lay his bones to rest with his lost finger in the Maze."

"Bones," Jame repeated uncomfortably, remembering what use she had made of them. "Well, he's there all right, but neither underground nor particularly quiet." And she told the priest about the events of the morning.

"Oh, ye galloping gods," he said when she had finished. "There'll be hell to pay over this. Master Rugen was never the sort to swallow insults, and fifty years of being dead won't have sweetened that foul temper of his. See here, you've got to do something about this!"

He grabbed Jame by the hand and began to half drag her around the curve of the model Maze to its western entrance.

"Now wait a minute!" she protested, resisting. "I need some answers first. If Rugen really is Hervy, why has he waited so long to come back?"

"Who knows?" said the priest impatiently, trotting all the faster. "The point is, you've got to make peace between those two old men before they destroy each other and the Maze with them. Especially the Maze. If that goes, so may the city. Ah, here we are. Good luck, Talisman!" And he shoved her over the threshold.

"Dammit, wait!" Jame cried, quite angry now, but she was talking to herself. Behind her was not the darkness of the temple but the houses facing the real Maze. The priest had vanished.

"Marvelous," she said to the walls of the entryway. "Now what am I supposed to do?"

"Correspondences, m'dear, correspondences," replied the echo. "Find Rugen's skull."

Jame stood quite still for a moment. Then she plunged into the Maze. Equipped with one of the torches that were kept hidden near the entrance, she raced through the dark passages, checking off in her mind the places she had visited earlier in search of the bones. Someone, probably Quezal the Gargoyle, was gathering them together . . . but where? The obvious place would be Rugen's death-site, the original location of the entire skeleton, but not even the skull was there now. If Quezal was in a hurry, though, he might well be collecting the bones at some point roughly equidistant from the farthest reaches to which they had been scattered. That gave her several possible locations.

At the first three, Jame drew a blank. The fourth she approached more warily, not only because of her present search but because she remembered all too clearly the last time she had been in this part of the Maze. It was here that the vhors had trapped her, Monster, and the priest sent to exterminate them. In desperation, the priest had taken their madness into himself. Deprived of what had become their essence, they had promptly dropped dead while the poor man had plunged down the nearest sewer hole, headfirst. Jame hoped that his colleagues below had successfully exorcised him. Meanwhile, she had been left with several hundred vhor carcasses and forty feet of hysterical python. Nothing would calm Monster but the removal of the offending bodies, so Jame (not very wisely, perhaps) had thrown them into a nearby pit-trap and set them on fire. The resulting smoke and stench had made this section of the Maze unapproachable for weeks. It still stank.

Jame examined the corner where, months earlier, she had left a femur to mark her way. The bone was gone, but not without a trace: covering the floor where it had lain was a network of scratches just visible in the flickering light. In fact, the whole passageway was similarly scored. Surely it hadn't been like this the last time she had been here, Jame thought uneasily. With growing apprehension, she followed the marks back to the pit and peered down into it, noting the deep, fresh gouges that scarred its sides and lip. Not a bone remained in it.

Then, in the distance, Jame heard the sound that all this time she had half expected and wholly dreaded: the rasp of many, many claws on stone.

She tracked the noise by the marks on the floor. The sound grew, then abruptly faded away as she turned into the hallway where the last of Rugen's bones had been left. It wasn't there now. Standing in the eery silence, Jame wondered how her reasoning had gone wrong, and what to do next. Then she heard a sound behind her, the faintest of scratches, and turned to find the hallway full of vhors.

Not one of them had been alive for quite some time. Most were little more than charred bones held together by scraps of singed flesh. Torchlight gleamed off empty eye sockets, off naked claws and fangs. In all that decaying, fire-scorched mass, not one whisker moved.

Jame went back a step, then another. She couldn't take her eyes off that corridor full of death, couldn't even think. Then her foot hit something. Caught off balance, she fell backward, the torch flying out of her hand and over the edge of one of the Maze's many water traps. In the total darkness that followed, the hall filled with the clatter of bones.

It took Jame a moment to realize that she hadn't simply tripped. Something was holding on to her ankle. The grip tightened. With a jerk, she was dragged backward one inch, then another and another. The image formed confusedly in her mind of a shadowy side corridor which she had passed a moment before her fall. Something had been waiting for her there, was waiting still.

With an incoherent cry, she lashed out with her free foot. It didn't connect, but the grip on her ankle relaxed. Then it came hand over hand up her leg. The thing was on top of her now with its bony hands around her throat. Gasping, she struck out blindly again, and made contact. The bones fell apart. Each one still twitched with a fitful life of its own. Jane threw herself sideways away from them, colliding a moment later with the far wall. Something—a skull, from the feel of it—rolled under her hand. Snatching it up, she crouched there, ready to pitch her prize down the well if anything touched her, frightened enough to throw herself after it.

The darkness came alive with the sound of many objects dragging themselves over the stones, rasping, scratching, fumbling in the dark. Were they approaching, or drawing away? Ah, away. They were bound for the heart of the Maze, Jame suddenly realized. They were after Penari.

She would have to reach the old man first, without a

light to show the way, over a course just as complex as that from the Temple District to the Maze. The challenge at first appalled, then steadied her. *An exercise, Talisman.* She could almost see Penari grinning wickedly at her. *A simple little test, like so many in the past.* Well, not quite, but close enough. She thought hard for a moment, selecting a route parallel to that of the disturbance, then rose and cautiously set out with the skull tucked under her arm.

An eternity later, Jame collided with a wall. This was hardly the first time in her blind journey, but now she groped along the upper edge and, much to her relief, found the hoped-for depression. Something clicked, and a panel swung open. She stepped over the threshold into the heart of the Maze.

Jame had turned to secure the secret door when someone let off a shrill war cry almost in her ear. "Oh, no," she said out loud, and ducked as Penari's iron-shod staff whizzed over her head.

The old man shrieked again, advancing on her with flailing weapon. Obviously, in her absence, he had gone from terror to outrage—always a short step for him—and she now had something akin to a senile berserker on her hands. Jame retreated hastily to the middle of the room, and placed the skull on the table. Raising her eyes, she found herself face-to-face with Monster, who was hanging down from the chandelier. Apologetically, the snake flicked the tip of her nose with his tongue.

"You're no help at all," she told him, and then ducked again as Penari's staff hissed over her head, nearly braining the terrified python. Jame slipped under the old thief's return blow and, coming up behind him, put her hands over his on the staff.

"Sir, I'm back," she said in his ear.

For a second, Penari stood quite still, breathing hard. Then he twisted about and glared up at her. She wondered what he saw: a blur, probably, if even that.

"It's about time," the old man snapped. "Where in the seven hells have you been?"

Jame told him. From the faces he made, she gathered

that he didn't like the direction her inquiries had taken, but the time for secrets was past. "And now, sir," she said, concluding, "will you kindly tell me just what the hell happened the last time Hervy—Master Rugen, that is—came to see you here in the Maze?"

"If you must know," he said petulantly, "we quarreled. That conceited jackass had the nerve to call this building *his* masterpiece. I ask you, where would he have been without my memory? I designed the Maze, dammit; he just put it together. And then he had the gall—the gall, I say!—to claim that the final plans were his property. Of course, I didn't let him have them. He fumed about that for a bit and then, well, he stormed out. And that's all there was to it."

"It couldn't have been," said Jame, staring at the door by which she had entered. "If so, why has he just come back?"

Interrupted by the old thief's attack, she had not had time to lock the panel. It gaped wide open now, and an indistinct figure stood on the threshold. Penari drew his breath in sharply. Nearly blind as he was, he couldn't see the form in the doorway or the horde of motionless shapes crouching at its feet, but he was no fool.

"Come back, have you?" he said through his few remaining teeth. "Much good that will do you now that I have your skull. Talisman, quick: Pick up the blasted thing and get behind me." With that, he scuttled to the far side of the table, clutching his staff.

Jame didn't move. Although she hadn't taken her eyes off that strange intruder or seen it so much as stir, it was now unmistakably several feet farther into the room. Its skeletal arm was half-raised. Where the ulna should have been were many tiny vhor bones laid joint to joint and the fingertips ended in rodential claws. Instead of its missing skull, Quezal the Gargoyle crouched on its clavicle. The rest of the figure was wrapped in a winding sheet of some translucent material that Jame, with amazement, recognized as one of Monster's more recently shed skins. A burst of near hysterical laughter welled up in her, but she choked on it, one hand flying up to her bruised throat. Twenty minutes before, those taloned fingers had nearly throttled her. Not only that, but here were the vhors again, massed at the dead architect's feet, looking no more congenial than before. And they were much closer than they had been a moment ago. But she still hadn't seen them move.

Another fit of coughing seized Jame. When her eyes cleared again, the vhors and their master were within five feet of her. So that was it: Like Quezal, they could only move when unobserved. If she so much as blinked now, she was finished.

"Didn't you hear me, boy?" cried Penari before her, clearly thinking that she was behind him. "I said smash it. Smash the skull!"

Without turning, her eyes still fixed on the architect, Jame groped behind her on the table for the skull. Her hand touched it. A sudden wave of dizziness swept over her. In its wake, she saw standing before her not the grotesque, skeletal figure, but Master Rugen as he had been in life, richly clad, with Quezal perching on his shoulder. The architect was looking straight through her. His face was thunderous. Penari spoke behind her, his voice so oddly distorted that she couldn't understand a word.

"Sir?" she said, questioningly, then caught her breath as the thief stepped into her line of vision. At least fifty years had fallen away from him.

He and the architect argued violently. Rugen brandished a packet in the thief's face, then thrust it back inside his robe, turned on his heel, and stalked to the door. Penari stopped him on the threshold. The two exchanged more heated words, then Rugen, with a short laugh, disappeared into the Maze proper.

Jame followed him. He paced confidently through the labyrinthine halls, not pausing even once despite the complexity of his path. And so it was that, without a break in his stride, he took his first wrong turn. Many more followed. At last the man stopped, looking aggravated, and reached into his pocket. His expression changed. The pocket wasn't there. He tried to retrace his steps, stubbornly silent at first and then shouting angrily for Penari until his voice failed. When his torch also finally gave out, he muttered a hoarse curse and sent Quezal for help. None ever came.

"Now I understand," said Jame to him. "You put the plans in your pocket, and Penari lifted them out again, there, on the threshold. Then, when you sent your gargoyle back to him, he imprisoned it. Because of that, you died of hunger and thirst in the dark. How . . . vile."

Abruptly, she found herself back in the heart of the Maze with her hand still on the skull and Quezal's grotesque face only inches from her own. Then something struck her shoulder so hard that she was lifted off her feet and thrown sideways to the floor.

Damn! she thought hazily. I must have blinked.

Then her eyes focused again and she was suddenly very still. The vhors were directly in front of her, close enough for her to see the grain of their yellow fangs and the bits of rotting debris caught between them. Rugen might have spared her life, but his creatures assuredly would not. Not that the architect had been all that gentle. His claws had apparently slashed through her jacket, because her shoulder had begun to sting and blood was running down her arm inside the sleeve. She couldn't even take her eyes off the vhors to check the extent of the damage. And her back was turned toward the architect. What was he doing now? All she could hear was Penari, alternately shouting insults at Rugen, encouragements to her, and counting to himself as he went through the steps of a quarterstaff drill in gleeful preparation for mayhem. For some reason, Rugen hadn't attacked the old thief yet. She must get him under observation again before he did. Carefully, Jame rose and backed away from the vhors, her eyes still fixed unblinkingly on them.

The table brought her up short. Rugen bent over it, his hands almost on the skull. Facing him and inadvertently keeping him immobile was Monster, who had again lowered his head and about ten feet of body from the chandelier. How fortunate, thought Jame, that snakes don't blink. Any second now, however, the python would probably spot the vhors and panic again. Right, thought Jame, taking a deep breath. Now I earn my wages.

She launched herself onto the tabletop, rolling over her right arm, hissing with pain as her weight came briefly to bear on her injured shoulder. Rugen seemed to pinwheel past. She snatched the skull from between his skeletal hands and half fell off the far side of the table, landing on Penari. For a moment, no one's eyes were on the architect. As she disentangled herself from her master, Jame heard the table crash over. Then she was sitting on the old man with the skull in her hands and Rugen bending over her.

"If you really want me to destroy this thing," she said unsteadily, glaring up at the architect, "move."

"Smash it! Smash it!" cried Penari's muffled voice through the rucked-up folds of his robe. "What are you waiting for?"

Jame raised the skull, then hesitated. If she did manage to shatter it on the stone floor, that presumably would be the end of Master Rugen . . . unjustly slain a second time. Then too, what had that little priest meant when he had spoken of these two old men destroying each other, the Maze, and perhaps even the city? That would only make sense if . . .

"Uh, sir . . . I think we have a problem. Remember those models I told you about in the temple that fell down because their counterparts in the city did? Well, the priest told me that the reverse could also happen."

Penari paused a moment in his furious thrashing. "Umph?" he said irritably, from the depths of his own clothing.

"Since the Maze is a three-dimensional map of Tai-tastigon," said Jame slowly, "it might well be considered a model of the city. In that case, to damage the building would be to endanger the entire town. The priest thought that your quarrel with Rugen might put the Maze in jeopardy, and he sent me to find Rugen's skull, just as you did. But I don't think he wanted me to destroy it. I mean, here's the man who built the Maze, who bound himself to it with blood and bone. Couldn't you say that his mind *was* the Maze? Then this skull would be its physical emblem, its model, if you will. So if I destroy it, what happens to the building . . . and to the city?"

"What?" snapped Penari, his head finally popping into sight. "Oh! Those damned correspondences again. If we're playing that game, I should think that my head would be worth any number of his. But then, that was the original argument, wasn't it? Who is the Mastermind of the Maze? You claimed you were, didn't you, you old fraud?" he suddenly shouted up at the architect. "You were so cocksure that you didn't need any help getting out of here.

"Why do you want the plans, then? I say to you.

" 'Oh, I have a special use for them, but it isn't to find my way. Never think that. This building is my end-work, I know every turn in it.'

"And, the gods help us both," Penari said, his voice suddenly sinking, "I took you at your word."

Jame had been staring up unblinkingly at Quezal's devilish face, haloed by the chandelier that hung above them both. The mass of wax and metal moved slightly, groaning. Either Monster was shifting his ground or her aching eyes had begun to play tricks on her. Then the import of what Penari had just said sank in.

"Do you mean that you didn't intend . . . But what about Quezal? Didn't you realize that something was wrong when he came back?"

"I thought that Rugen had left the Maze, discovered that the plans were missing, and sent his pet demon back in to steal them. The robber robbed. That would have appealed to the old bastard's sense of humor. So, just to teach him a lesson, I grabbed his gargoyle and popped it into my ivory inlay chest. Then, well, I was a busy man in those days."

"In other words, you forgot about it."

The old man nodded miserably. "Months later, I came across Rugen in the Maze. Nastiest shock I've ever had in my life. So I'm sorry, but that doesn't change anything," he said, suddenly rallying. "The plans are still mine—mine, I say!—and you can't have them! Put *that* in your back teeth and chew on it!"

You see how it is, said Jame silently to the skull. He

didn't mean to kill you, but you still died—just as Scramp did because I failed him. Penari's pride in the Maze and mine in my reputation made us both . . . careless. But how long do we have to go on paying for that? Only you can tell us, and you'll have to do it now because I can't keep you at bay any longer. Your old apprentice said you were a fair man, so to hell with mercy. Give us justice.

Then she closed her stinging eyes and waited.

A long, nerve-wracking moment of silence followed, broken suddenly by a deep groan from above. Something slammed into Jame. She was sent flying backward head over heels with the skull still in her arms and, a second later, Penari's sharp elbows in her ribs.

A tremendous crash shook the floor. Dust filled the air, half choking both master and apprentice as they tried to sort themselves out by the far wall. Jame felt a sudden weight on her good shoulder. Startled, she looked up to find Quezal the Gargoyle perching there. What the hell? . . .

"Here," she said, shoving the skull into Penari's arms.

With the gargoyle still clinging to her and vhor bones crunching underfoot, she waded into the cloud of dust, batting at it ineffectively. She almost hit Monster. The albino python loomed up in front of her, his head a good two feet above her own. But this time his other four-fifths were on the floor. Quezal's claws tightened painfully as the giant snake made a tentative effort to wrap itself around Jame's neck.

"If you're that upset," she said crossly, pushing him away, "go cuddle your master. What have you done to the chandelier?"

It lay before her, a great mass of twisted metal and smashed candles with its broken chain draped over it. Underneath was a rectangular hole in the floor. Penari, blundering up from behind, nearly fell into it before Jame could stop him.

"Where's Rugen?" the old man demanded. "And what's become of my center stone?"

"Center stone!" Jame repeated, startled. She peered

down into the depths of the hole, and at its bottom saw the splintered remains of Rugen's skeleton.

"When the chandelier fell," she said, thinking out loud, "it must have triggered some counterweight hidden in the floor. The stone tilted, and the bones slid into the grave prepared for them."

"The grave? *Whose* grave?"

"Why, Rugen's, of course. Remember, this was his end-work."

"He wanted to be buried here, in *my* Maze?" exclaimed the old man, beginning to bristle again. "Why, the nerve of the man! But that's just like him: he always did treat everything as if it belonged to him. No one else was to take any credit at all—oh, no! Arrogant old bastard. Serves him right that even his own gargoyle deserted him in the end."

Jame had been regarding her master rather oddly as he stomped back and forth. "Sir, you don't understand. Quezal may have pushed me out of the way, but it was Rugen who saved you."

"*What?* Oh, hell." Penari stopped short and seemed visibly to deflate. "Oh, bloody hell. He would turn noble on me at the last minute. Well, two can play at that. He can stay here if he likes and . . . and what's more, he can have the damn plans." He fished about impatiently in one of his robe's voluminous pockets, at last jerking out a familiar packet tied with dirty string. "It's not as if he were going anyplace with them, is it?" he demanded, glaring up defiantly at Jame. "Just the same, you do the honors: he'll never be able to say that I handed them over."

Jame unwrapped the packet. It contained not the sheaf of papers she had expected but a fine linen cloth with the plans drawn on it. So that was why Rugen had been so determined to keep possession of this thing: it was his shroud. She jumped down into the grave with it. In one corner of the hole lay a small object wrapped in blue silk: Rugen's missing finger, almost certainly. Jame placed it with the other bones on the burial cloth, finally adding the skull, handed down by Penari, to the top of the heap.

"I'm sorry that I mistreated your bones before, and

called you Hervy," said Jame to the skull. "Sleep quietly at last, master architect." And she folded the cloth with its intricate drawings over the fleshless face.

"Well, that's that," said Penari with relief when they had put the center stone back in place. "A sticky business, on the whole, but I think I handled it rather well. Let that be an example to you of what courage and determination can accomplish. Stay with me, boy; I'll make a man of you yet." And with that, the old thief gave Jame a hearty slap on her injured shoulder.

She stepped hastily out of his reach. Rugen's claws had caused more mess than damage, luckily, but the scratches still stung. In another sense, though, Jame would hardly have cared at that moment if they had cut to the bone. For the first time in three months, the weight of Scramp's death was gone, and she felt almost light-headed with relief.

But there was still one loose end.

Penari abruptly broke off his panegyric of self-praise as she headed for the door. "Here now!" he called after her in sudden anxiety. "Aren't you going to help me clean up this mess?"

"Later, sir. Just now, I owe a friend an apology. Maybe Quezal will lend a hand until I get back."

Between one blink and the next, the gargoyle shifted from her shoulder to Penari's head. He flailed at it, squawking, then went off in a sort of war dance about the room, making loud, semiarticulate declarations that he would not be sat on in his own hall, thank you, and would Quezal please sit somewhere else.

Jame regarded her whirling dervish of a master, the vhor bones piled high on the floor, and Monster nosing cautiously among them, obviously ready for a precipitous retreat if any of them should move.

Ah, home, she thought. How nice to have everything back to normal. Then she went out into the Maze and beyond that into the sun-washed streets of Tai-tastigon in search of Patches.

The Toaster

A silver-scaled Dragon with jaws flaming red
Sits at my elbow and toasts my bread.
I hand him fat slices, and then, one by one,
He hands them back when he sees they are done.

—*William Jay Smith*

The One We Were

Tanith Lee

Eccentricity is a sort of talent, in some cases amounting to genius. Certain climates or orders in the human advance seem to facilitate it. And while money is not essential to the condition, it helps.

Claira Von Oeau, born to poverty, of mixed Austrian, Russian, Parisian, and perhaps Hebrew extraction, had earned her considerable fortune by a florid success in the Arts. She was a popular writer of romantic historical novels. The kind of work is not unknown. Blood-red sunsets unrolled from her pen to match the spillages of the ancient Romans strewn among the pillars beneath armadas met with the shock of war; beautiful heroines with streaming hair craned over the parapets of Carthage, Troy and Verona. The Black Death had ridden again through Europe at the whim of Claira, and Pompeii collapsed once more under lava. Though her researches were minimal and her scholastic bent rather slight, Claira's torrid literary gift tended to make nothing of everything, all of nothing. She had the knack of bluff. Despite evidence to the contrary, one felt, however briefly, that Byzantium had been Claira's way. Regularly castigated by the critics, Claira remarked that she was indifferent equally to praise or blame. And so she seemed to be. Even the wealth her work had brought her was treated with the casual brutishness of familiarity.

Of course, she suffered. She existed on the unshakable premise that all life proceeded from herself. As the centre of the world, perhaps the universe, she was aware that all things and persons took their being only in order to be of use to her. In this way, she had never been amazed at her lucky rise to fame and fortune. It was inevitable. When, however, the world or its inhabitants did not treat her as they were expected to do, she felt the conspiracy of the

gods ranged against her. How can I endure this cruelty?
(She would cry.) She would lie in bed and weep for days
on end. Until some favourable omen—the earth is full of
omens for those who believe they are the centre of it—
roused her.

Claira was a small slight woman, not unattractive, with a
long slender nose and dark sweeping brows, her fine eyes
accentuated by mascara. As a general rule, one would not
have taken a great deal of notice of her. But she was
possessed of a tremendous, indeed an overwhelming personality. She was what is sometimes termed a "vampire."
That is, her terrific energy, though spent frequently in the
pursuit of her vocation, recharged itself almost instantane-
ously, and usually at the expense of others. Even her griefs
were strong, and drained those who supported her
through them. Her enthusiasms were tidal waves. Sitting
quite still in a secluded restaurant, Claira could utterly
exhaust her companions, who felt they had been running
non-stop for hours, tied to the tails of several wild horses.
She had a habit of relating the plot-line of her current
book, pausing only to interpolate character-notes upon
the *dramatis personae*. These recitals were normally non-
comprehensible to any save herself. And though she attempted to explain the in-jokes of the precis, few understood them. As a form of punctuation, she would exclaim,
"What a jumble all this must seem to you! But you're being
so *helpful*. Just by letting me discuss it with you—
invaluable. Have some more of the lobster." In other
words, fill your mouth and listen to *me*.

Invariably, Claira's close friends did not stay the course.
They were sloughed from her over the years, and new
models adopted, only to be sloughed in turn, panting and
shattered at the wayside. Some of the friendships, and
usually the intimate liaisons, ended in uproar, mild violence and, naturally, suffering. "No man will ever love me
as I need to be loved," Claira announced. "Jealousy! I
must give up my work or all hope of personal joy."

Actually she had no intention of giving up either. Since
the world proceeded from Claira, it had no choice but to

supply each of her wants as it arose. If failed, she had the solace of loud clamour.

A small côterie of friends did remain, those who were able to tolerate Claira mostly by rationing the time they spent with her. Some, it seems, even felt a genuine affection for her, and a respect for her—for want of a better word—*extraordinary* talent.

The most consistent of these was a Madame Sarnot, who more or less inadvertently unleashed the following events.

To the Sarnot salon one evening had been invited the celebrated medium, Madame Q__. At this time she was the talk of half of Europe. A very tall woman, dressed in flowing antique silks, and most frequently escorted by a pet snake, she could just as well have stepped straight out of one of Claira's Egyptian cave-temples. Under the circumstances, to exclude Claira from the action would have been unthinkable.

Madame Q__ was an exponent of transmigration. "The body is a house," she had explained in her most famous thesis. "The soul, like a bird, flits from life to life. . . ."

Claira had always credited reincarnation. "How else," Claira had demanded, "can I understand so well so many past civilisations? My research is negligible. And yet—I know. Why? Because I was *there.*" Her critics might, (and did), take issue with this statement. If Claira had been there, then it must be a singularly bad memory which was to blame for such items as the mandolin a slave had so engagingly played in Pompeii, or the roast potatoes served at the court of Richard III.

On the fateful evening, Claira was late. About an hour after Madame Q__ had made her statuesque entrance, complete with snake, Claira made hers, lacking reptiles but in no way else deficient. The most notable feature was possibly a hat, itself not large, but decorated with the bronzy-green, yard-long tail-plumage of a mythical bird. At each turn or inclination of Claira's head, the eyes of fellow guests were threatened, champagne goblets altered their positions, or fire attempted to break out.

From the moment of her entry, Claira had been noted
by the medium, (it was hard to do otherwise), who riveted
her with gimlet eyes. Two sets of scarab rings, Madame
Q__'s and Claira's, clicked ominously. Presently Madame
Q__ fed her restless snake an opium pellet and Claira, who
despite her merciless descriptions of chariot-races and
whale-hunts was a champion of all contemporary fauna,
wondered aloud if this were not injurious.

"Not at all," responded Madame Q__. "Although, no
doubt, Mademoiselle, you are now over-cautious of the
poppy, having abused it in your previous incarnation."

A deep silence instantly descended. Claira grew rigid,
and the flickering candles reaching eagerly towards her hat
sank down.

"I see such things quite clearly," Madame Q__ continued calmly but inexorably. "When the impression is
very recent or very vivid. It is, you comprehend, as if a
shadow walks at the left side. And at your left side,
Mademoiselle Von Oeau, there is a fair-haired young man.
I behold him perfectly distinctly. The burning eyes, the
frock coat, the sheaf of manuscript in one hand. A little less
light, if you please. I am prepared to enter trance. Such
resonances are not to be ignored. Let us see with whom we
are dealing."

The lights were accordingly doused or moved further
off. Madame Sarnot might have been observed glancing
with amused concern at Claira. But Claira possessed all the
inner strengths of the somewhat mad. Bolt upright, unblinking as a dark-eyed owl, she held Madame Q__ in her
sights. No quarter was now to be expected from either
party.

After some mutterings, moanings and snorts, during
which the snake tried drunkenly to escape and failed,
Madame Q__ fell back in her chair and began to speak in a
baritone voice. Her, or its, comments were ponderous but
to the point. The psychic echo of the gentleman observed
at Claira Von Oeau's left side was the residue of a life lived
a little more than a century previously, and in the same

city—possibly hence the evocation. He was also a writer; another sure connection. He had been quite notorious in his day both for his poetry—which was on the affectionate side—and his riotous social tendencies. He had been bloodily murdered by his best friend in the English cemetery of Notre Dame du Nord. "But who is it?" someone—not Claira—cried. Madame Q—'s possession obediently rumbled out the name *Simplice de Meunier*. This might have been a disappointment. None of the guests had heard of such a person. Clearly Monsieur de Meunier, despite his riots, was on the obscure side. A pity. Claira, however, showed no sign of dismay. Rather, she sat for some minutes in a peculiarly galvanic stillness. She had, as it happened, introduced a minor character into a recent book, a minstrel by name—*Simplice*. This coincidence now struck her with all its awesome significance. What was a minstrel but a poet? And the name was identical. It seemed she too had been aware of pre-bodily echoes. This could be nothing but proof.

As Madame Q— revived and stretched out her claws towards the wine, Claira was at her elbow, in the way. Feathers dipped amid the caviar.

"Madame, you have given me a treasure beyond price."

Madame Q— nodded imperiously. Claira, cutting off the refreshments entirely, embraced her. The snake escaped into an ice-bucket, and Claira's hat at last began to burn.

Madame Sarnot heaved a gentle sigh. "I think I was wrong, Horace," she remarked to her husband. "How wrong, only time will tell."

It was, (for reasons too numerous and far too patently obvious to air here), a man's world. Claira, whatever her personal success, could not fail to be, if only subconsciously, aware of it. Nor, no doubt, had she evaded the ambient brain-washing. Though she considered herself no one's inferior, to learn that, little more than one hundred years before, she had been that most emancipated of all

earthly creatures, a man, added a fillip of considerable
burnish. To be male, fascinating, and romantically dead,
filled Claira with an elation that is difficult to describe to
those who have never felt it, worse, have never aspired to
feel it. Being Claira, of course, a strange incestuous schizo-
phrenia had begun instantly to work in her. Here she was a
woman. There she was a man. What could they be to each
other but—Everything? At last, a masculine presence
who was not a rival, who would not seek to destroy her
genius, but was part of it, and, eternally, of herself. What
else? They were one. Closer than husband to wife, than
mother to son. "My own," Claira wrote in her journal,
underlining in coloured ink. "As no other man can ever be,
or wish to be, or be wished to be. Simplice is *mine*."
Already, one perceives, she was on first name terms with
him.

In the weeks which followed, Claira began to research
her subject with a diligence never lavished on any of her
novels. The chase was made all the more entertaining and
emotional by Monsieur de Meunier's slight reputation. But
Claira, in the tidal wave mode, was easily a match for his
obscurity. She tracked him down, she traced him; she was
at all times in full cry. The libraries private and public grew
to fear the sound of her footsteps. The countless messenger boys she dispatched in all directions waxed rich,
and lean from running. From dubious basements and the
sleep of decades, surfaced greenish cakes of paper that
had once been books. These soon came to furnish every
spare surface, stuff every neglected cranny, of the Von
Oeau suite. So much for biography. The hunt for likeness
came hard upon. The great galleries of the city did not
possess portraits of Monsieur de Meunier, and so escaped
unwittingly from Claira. The Musée Miramelle, which had
two, was not so fortunate.

With a fiercely beating heart Claira had entered the
gallery and searched out the first picture. What if, after all,
her poetic self had been ugly, or—far more awful—plain?
Presently she was gratified to discover an attractive male
person leaning in his frame, a manuscript in one hand. His

hair was very fair with amber high-lights, but his eyes and brows, Claira at once decided, were her own. With these eyes he gazed out sidelong at her, with a mischievous expression. Here I am, you see, they seemed to say, loving and teasing, glad to be found.

The second picture was smaller, and less clear, and perhaps less flattering. When she returned to the larger work, a party of young ladies was in attendance on it, and Claira stood by regally, allowing them their perusal. After a while, one of the young women remarked, to no one in particular, "How very elegant he was."

"Thank you," said Claira, an unaccustomed blush staining her cheeks.

The young ladies turned.

"I beg your pardon?"

"I said," modestly reiterated Claira, "thank you for your compliment."

"But I—" said the young lady who had spoken.

"And I am sure," Claira added, giving her a long, level look, "that approval would have been mutual."

It was now the young lady's turn to crimson.

There were to be several red faces that afternoon.

"I tell you, Mademoiselle," finally shouted the director, called in alarm from more important matters, "that it is in no way possible for you to purchase this portrait. I do not care how much you are willing to pay, the Musée Miramelle does not conduct its business in this fashion. Good day."

"Then I shall arrange for its theft," Claira responded.

"Pierre, run to the corner at once and summon a policeman."

"You have no grounds," said Claira haughtily.

"You have made a threat."

"I am entitled to make threats. The portrait is mine. Rightfully mine. How dare you attempt to keep it from me? Name the sum your wretched waxworks requires."

"*Waxworks*—! Mademoiselle, this is too much—"

"I shall not move. I shall, if necessary, chain myself to the railings outside, refusing food or water. I will *die* here to get what I want. Do you understand, Monsieur?"

"I am beginning to. Pierre? The corner, if you please."

About five o'clock, the arrival of Madame Sarnot in a *fiacre* defused the situation. "I shall return," promised Claira. The horses, frightened by the commotion of three portly gentlemen shouting on the pavement, bolted as soon as a whip was cracked. Borne home so speedily, Claira was still voluble as she burst into her apartment on the Rue Swanhilde.

"My dear," said Madame Sarnot soothingly.

"How can you say this to me?"

"I don't recall saying anything very much, as yet—"

"I will *have* it. It's mine! Mine! As Simplice is mine. Each atom of that previous life, Sophie, I have every right to recover. Did I not *sit* for this portrait?"

"But Claira—"

"No. Will you speak to Horace? He can arrange something."

"Yes, Claira," said Madame Sarnot, with deceptive meekness. As Claira flung about the silken drawing room, her friend had paused to examine one of the numerous piles of books. "Why, how interesting. There is a volume here which is growing a most unusual fungus. It's spreading up the wallpaper. Some kind of mushroom, probably. Don't forget to pick them before the sun shines on this wall or they will be quite spoiled."

Claira had passed into the bedroom. Her latest hat, winged like a vulture, came off, and Madame Sarnot noticed that what she had taken for a clump of hirsute anemones pinned beneath, was in fact something else.

"My goodness. Claira, your hair has been peroxided!"

"You speak as if some hairdresser crept up on me and did it while I slept. I'm quite aware my hair is bleached. The shade is completely wrong. Now I've seen the portrait, I shall have it adjusted."

Madame Sarnot, stepping over more books, sat down in an armchair. "But why is it necessary—"

"Why? He is a part of me. I mean to be as close to him as I can. It's essential. I feel it to be so. The experience is extraordinary. I wake in the night and I—am *him!*"

"For how long?" Madame Sarnot perceptively inquired.

Claira did not reply. Instead she launched into a sort of psychic carousel, a circle which revolved about and about itself, and showed no signs of stopping. This, now, had replaced the vortex of the plot-lines. Simplice had become the sole topic of Claira's conversation. To halt her was not a feasible proposition without recourse to a sledge hammer. Madame Sarnot, demurely seated amid the books, might well have been dreaming of one.

Three weeks later, the larger de Meunier portrait from the Musée Miramelle hung in Claira Von Oeau's salon, above a small table of the period, draped like an altar and set like one with two candles, flowers, and a pair of mildewed gloves which, only possibly, may have been the property of Simplice.

"And have you *seen* Claira?" cried one of Madame Sarnot's own private friends. "My God, Sophie. She will be committed. Or arrested. Or both."

"It's true then? She's taken to dressing in male costume?"

"Of the eighteenth century."

"I see."

"You don't see, Sophie. But *I* have. Would you credit, she has had the finest tailors working on the cut of frock coats suitable for the female figure—if such a thing were possible—and her cravats have been ordered from—"

"Yes. I think I did catch a glimpse of those."

"One ear has been pierced, as with this miller person, and has a gold earring. Her hair was cut and arranged by a leading coiffeur to resemble *his*—loose fair curls to the shoulders."

"Fortuitously, he isn't depicted with moustache or beard."

"But allied to this—" screamed the private friend— "Sophie, are you listening?—she has been making advances to half the women she meets. Apparently, the poet has a preference for small dark women—"

"Odd. An exact description of the pre-Meunier Claira."

"—And Claira now flirts with anyone of that type who is silly enough to let her get within arm's reach. And of course she has nothing to back up her outrageous behaviour. Claira is not, and has never been, *une femme aux gauches.* I believe one of the poor little creatures, who is, has actually fallen in love with the bitch, and taken to lying across the door of the building, pining, with her black hair pouring down the steps."

"Ah," said Madame Sarnot, "yes. Horace saw something there when he drove past yesterday. He thought it was a small black spaniel asleep on some washing. . . ."

"I don't believe," ranted the friend, "you are taking this seriously."

"I am. I'm most relieved about the spaniel."

Perhaps two months after the start of the business, something strange occurred. It may, of course, be considered immoderate to refer to anything as *particularly* strange in such uncommon circumstances. However, readers must judge for themselves.

In all, Claira had now a collection of some twenty-four intact, (or otherwise), works on the period of study, supplemented by sixteen or seventeen biographies of more important persons which, *en passant,* carried references to the drunken, opium-smoking poet. She had learned, in this piecemeal way, quite an amount about her second self. Of his date and place of birth, his latterly more famous companions, his various failures and his limited *fêtes.* She had learned also of the amorous adventures, and of how one abandoned damsel had drowned herself in the river. A verdict of madness, and some bribery, had ensured the girl a grave in sanctified ground. Thereafter, the lady's cousin, Simplice's best (and by then only) friend, had lured him to the graveyard, stunned and flung him over the appropriate headstone, then decapitated him with one stroke of a well-honed sword.

Scattered information, though, was not sufficient for Claira. And when it had come to her attention that a biography did indeed exist concerned solely with de Meunier, she hurried eagerly to the fount.

This was a loathsome shop on the Rue de Clèche. Forcing open a door hardly wider than a pencil, Claira advanced between tottering staircases of black tomes, on the tops of which an occasional dining rat was seated. The clanking of the shop's bell brought from some recess another type of beast, yellowish, in carpet-slippers and a dressing-gown brocaded by a quantity of careless snacks.

"Yes, m'lord?" inquired the beast of Claira. He was maybe as ancient as his emporium, and in his younger days Claira's attire may well have been the norm—for men. Though he recognised her infallibly as a female, he was not adverse to flattering an effect.

"You have here," said Claira, and named the book.

The beast laughed.

"Why, m'lord. *Had* here. I *had*."

"Had? What have you done with it?"

"Sold, sir. Sold but yesterday."

Claira was flabbergasted. She stood with her mouth open on a soundless cry. At length, "To whom?" she demanded.

"Why, m'lord. With great respect—what affair is that of yours?"

For once, Claira did not tell him. That he did not recognise her alter-ego in herself was insultingly apparent. That he had sold her book—*hers*—to another, was distressing. What actually, however, so startled her, was that—and she must admit it even to herself—someone else seemed to be aware of, interested and in pursuit, as she was, of Simplice de Meunier.

What she felt was not gratification, not even true irritation at the loss of her rightful property. What Claira experienced was a darkly definite pang of jealousy.

"Monsieur," said Claira at last, "the volume is of vital importance to me. You must get it back at once."

"Oh, m'lord. Impossible."

"Then tell me who has bought it."

"I am the priest of my profession. My lips are sealed."

"Then write it down with your hands," said Claira, and handed him a bank note.

Having consulted this, the beast, unspeaking, went away for a while. When he returned, he had removed the dressing-gown and put on something very like it but which was, apparently, street-wear.

"If you would be so kind as to step out with me to the corner?"

Claira, mystified and furious, and throbbing with anxiety, agreed. A very notable pair they made, the slender principal boy with her blue frock coat, britches, blonde curls, earring, walking stick; the beast from the book-shop clad as if for a wedding in hell.

Shortly they reached the corner of two sinister streets. Here a number of posters trailed in the wind.

"Peruse, if you will, sir, these. Run your eye over them. I think you will, by and by, get an idea as to whom the purchaser of the book might be. And I assure you, m'lord, you would not be wrong."

With those words, the beast left Claira, and slunk away along the adjacent boulevard, towards some den of vice too original to imagine.

Infuriated, Claira could only do as suggested. Presently her eye was caught by a bill advertising the current production at the Théâtre D——. The play in question, which was itself quite famous though seldom now performed, contained in its title the name of a well-known rhetorician, which gave one to believe the work might be concerned with him. It so happened that this rhetorician had also been the brother of the best friend who, in the English cemetery of Notre Dame du Nord, beheaded Simplice. Claira had heard of the drama, but did not know it. Nevertheless, logic was giving birth to a terrible suspicion.

Turning on the heel of her boot, she rushed back to the carriage.

That evening, Claira Von Oeau attended the theatre. She went in disguise; that is, she went in female attire. Recognised by some of the audience, (the city had rather lost track of her recently), she was enthusiastically applauded. She received this accolade with unusual vagueness. Behind the lace vizor of her hat, the fruits and foliage of which would have rendered another woman prostrate with migraine, she peered down at the closed curtains of the stage. "I think you will, by and by, get an idea—" It did not take genius, even Claira's, to reason that a play dealing with the brother of Simplice's murderer might also deal with the murderer himself, and so, unavoidably, with Simplice.

In fact, the play dealt very generously with all three. Before the second scene of the first act was concluded, Simplice de Meunier had walked on to the stage. That is to say, an actor *representing* him had walked on to it. Fatefully, he had been chosen for the part due to a distinct resemblance to the painting of Simplice until recently on show in the Musée Miramelle.

To portray in turn Claira's agitation is unnecessary. Suffice it to say her breath grew short, her looks became daggers, and her black-gloved hands gripped the rail of her box like talons. What is so uniquely one's own, can be no other's.

And there, only feet below, a tall slim young man with fair curls and an earring disported himself in the way only one man can when awarded the character of another: Entirely adequately. In fact, it was an exceptionally fine performance. The actor in question had obviously made something of a study of Simplice. He knew things about him that the play alone did not reveal. He had the same habit of twisting his gloves Simplice had had, of running one hand through his hair, of sometimes coughing when nervous. He had the same devilish quality, the teasing look. He went through it all, even to the seduction, some part of which was carried out on stage, of a petite dark actress with red ribbons.

Claira leaned over them, an unseen harpy which, if it had been granted wings, would have flown straight at him, shrieking. She was beside herself. Almost literally. There she was—*he* was—her own self on the boards, in the charge of another. A very clever and talented other. Who was so much more Simplice than she could ever be, now.

An admiring reader sent champagne to her box in the interval. Claira drank it like medicine. She glared at the programme and the name of her enemy, her rival—for what else could he be?—burned itself into her brain. She fidgeted through the next scenes of the play from which Simplice was absent. She sat like stone as he met hideous death in the graveyard, her hands pressed to her own throat in empathy, but her mind elsewhere. As the scandal of the murder enveloped the leading players, in the midst of the drama's climax, rather unquietly Claira left the theatre.

Having driven home, however, in gruesome silence, stumbled unnoticing over the prone brunette would-be lover on the steps, and reached her bed, Claira lay rigid all night. Each stroke of the distant clocks of the city seemed to proclaim a hated name.

It was *he,* of course, who had procured the biography of Simplice de Meunier, *he* who had cheated her it. And of so much more. Of the indescribable things for which she hankered.

But she had not yet passed sentence.

The morning produced an innocently-phrased, adulatory note, which was forthwith dispatched to the Théâtre D—, addressed to the actor Antoine Valère. She begged to know how he had achieved such understanding of the rôle of Simplice, that he handled it so adroitly. She signed herself with a flourish, not for one moment suspecting Monsieur Valère would never have heard of her, and would consequently omit to reply.

There followed a passage of some days and nights during which this omission was elaborated upon by others, and during which Claira commenced a veritable bombardment of notes, all offering equivalently the same honeyed phrases, each couched a little more threatening than the last.

She did not see or hear Monsieur Valère, on receipt of the thirty-second note, inquire of someone: "Who is this madwoman?" She did eventually receive his answer. *My dear Mademoiselle, I am most gratified by your praise. But I am haunted by the thought of the agony of penman's cramp you must be suffering. Do, I beg you, for both our sakes, stop writing to me.*

Claira's response to this may again be pictured.

Also, her reaction to an interview with Valère that, subsequent to his great success in the part of de Meunier, appeared later in the week in the pages of the *Journal de la Cité.*

Valère had not been quite sober when the interview was given and had not only basked and boasted, but revealed one wildly all-too-salient facet of his handle on Simplice. It transpired that the insights he received, while rehearsing the character, had become so astonishingly, even unnervingly apposite, (both to himself and colleagues), that, half jokingly he had been driven to consult a medium. An eminent name was then mentioned which was not that of Madame Q—. "I laugh at it myself," continued Valère, "and also, I admit, I am made somewhat afraid by it." According to the consulted medium, Monsieur Valère was none other than a reincarnation of Monsieur de Meunier. Everything pointed to it. Similarity of physique, features, even of colouring, and of mannerisms; added to these an uncanny depth of comprehension and familiarity. "He advised me," the actor confided, "to learn as much about Simplice as I could, in order to try to 'recall,' in a conscious and controlled manner. But very oddly," he went on, in an offended way, "someone seems always to have been there ahead of me. No sooner did I discover a book or paper which referred to him, than the only copies extant had been bought, in some cases only half an hour before I arrived at the venue."

Claira saw no humour in this.

She had at no time asked herself why her present life had, in some curious way, so dismally let her down that she preferred to reach backwards to a previous one. Nor did she interrogate her motives now. She was aware only that the city was no longer large enough to shelter both herself and Antoine Valère.

It happened—such silly things do happen—that the doorkeeper at the Thèâtre D__ was an avid reader of the novels of Mademoiselle Von Oeau. There in his cubby he had swallowed each lurid fantasy and epic as it was sprung from the presses. Hence, on her entry to his world, he was prepared to do anything in his power to assist her. This included being persuaded, on the flimsiest of evidence, that the actor Valère was expecting her after the performance. Valère, who was actually expecting a steak sandwich from the Café D__ across the boulevard, invited her in at once.

Turning from the mirror, he then found himself confronted by a creature all in beetle black, with a gigantic black lid hat from which scarlet ostrich feathers erupted, like wired blood. She had come in disguise, again.

"Good God," said Valère. He did not say he had mistaken her for a sandwich.

"I have been writing to you," said Claira.

"Ah . . . yes," said Valère, cautiously.

"I have also," said Claira, "read the interview in *Le Journal.* I conclude that I am the person who has deprived you of all the material you wished to gather on de Meunier." (It was second name terms with the enemy.) "While you—" she pointed a long black finger at the only book on a side table, "have managed to get hold of *that.* The very volume I set my heart on reading."

"That," said Valère, indicating the book, "is a railway timetable. Are you very interested in trains?"

Claira ignored this sally. "I refer to the de Meunier biography."

"Do I have that?"

"I am led to believe so."

As if to insult her, her removed the gold earring, which was false, and shook out the fair curls, which were not.

"It seems to me," said Claira, "that a compromise might be affected. I could let you make selection from the volumes I have acquired, in exchange for the loan of the biography."

Valère considered this. Obviously, he was as interested, in his own way, in the subject of Simplice, as Claira was. Nor was he quite immune to the spectacle of opulence she presented. There is something stabilizing in money.

"It seems," said Valère, rather grudgingly, "a straightforward offer."

"It would be an honour to help you," said Claira. "I am your devoted adherent. Being slightly acquainted myself with the occult, I also sympathise with your view of reincarnation—"

"Yes, *that,*" said Valère, colouring, and evading her look. "Partly a joke, at the expense of the *Journal.*"

Claira narrowed her eyes with hatred. It was bad enough to be usurped, but to be mocked in the process was beyond forgiveness. Not that she had any intention of forgiving him anything.

At this instant the genuine sandwich arrived.

"You can't eat that," said Claira. "Brilliance deserves its reward. Come with me. We shall dine at l'Auguste."

Valère, who had no defensive weapons save a cruel tongue and an ability sometimes to be reticent, found himself being swept out into the street by Claira, the awful hat, and a creeping subcutaneous reverence for riches. So to the carriage, so to the palatial restaurant where, under the chandeliers, Claira peeled back her gloves in the reverse mode of the assassin, while champagne corks flew.

Dinner was not marked by anything untoward. Encouraged by good food and wine, Valère was quite prepared to divulge all he had learned and could remember of Simplice. Claira, who was determined to bleed him dry, sat as avidly as a preying mantis, hanging on every word with the fascination of the lover. When at last exhaustion caused his monologue to peter out, the social occasion was concluded. The waiters at l'Auguste knew better than to bat an eyelid when a lady paid the bill.

"And this last bottle of champagne," said Claira, "you may open it."

The cork shot forth as three o'clock was struck throughout the city.

"We can take it with us, for you to drink in the carriage. Of course, my driver will convey you to your door."

Valère, however, declined. He would prefer to stroll awhile by the river, to walk off the wine. (This was also an excellent ruse whereby to avoid Claira's learning his address.)

He had anticipated possible argument. None came. They had made no arrangements about the books, which Valère thought odd, but he had no intention of taking up the matter now. The supper had been good, there seemed no problem attached to it, this was the time to escape. Yet it was Claira who rose. "I shall leave you, then. But drink the champagne." She advanced the newly-opened bottle across the table, filling his glass. "A last toast to the one—" she paused and smiled at him, a wolfish smile that displayed a great many teeth—"the one you *were*, Monsieur Antoine."

With that she departed, her plumage knocking a stuffed parrot from its swing near the door. She did not look back. Like a black bat, she was closed into the outer night.

Valère was tempted to drink one further glass of the perfect champagne. But he was not the drunkard de Meunier had been and a warning of dizziness in the end stopped him. Bidding a cheerful adieu to the waiters, he too made his way out into the darkness.

It is the custom that the wine the guests do not drink becomes a libation to commerce. The chef took most of the bottle, as was his wont. The waiters appropriated the dregs. One, craftier than the rest, downed behind a door Valère's full glass. He did not, thereby, do himself the favour he had thought. Imbibed with the wine was the dissolved pellet of arsenic and opium Mademoiselle Von Oeau had crumbled in the goblet.

"How curious," said Horace Sarnot to his wife, over the croissants. "I heard Claira was dining at l'Auguste last night, with some actor. Just one hour after, a waiter was found poisoned." Madame Sarnot glanced up quizzically. "It seems," said Horace, "this waiter had often threatened suicide. Something must have driven him over the edge."

"Waiting on Claira, perhaps?"

"In any event, the doctors saved his life. First of all, he denied taking any poison and accused the chef. But it then seems the chef sent round his seconds and the charge is withdrawn, the suicide bid confessed."

With such a gentle ripple as this, the initial attempt at homicide was destined to pass.

The arsenic ingredient had come from a tin of rat poison. The de Meunieresque opium Claira had long since installed, as a matter of course, on the sideboard with the sherry and oranges. She had not herself ever smoked it, just as she seldom drank alcohol. A natural hysteric, she generally did not require artificial aids.

But, as the first means had come fairly easily to hand, the second was, on the contrary, difficult.

"Sophie," said Madame Sarnot's private friend, "Claira has taken up shooting."

"At whom?" asked Madame Sarnot, more prophetically than she could know.

"I mean, she is paying to be instructed in the use of a small hand-weapon."

"But Simplice de Meunier never shot, did he?"

"Well, Sophie, I think that craze is dying out. Really I do. The little *femme gauche* has disappeared from the doorstep. And Claira has been seen about quite frequently in female clothes and those interesting hats of hers. Probably she'll write a book about him."

"*Simplice: A Double Life . . .*" mused Madame Sarnot experimentally.

Meanwhile, on the Rue Swanhilde, having shattered an image of herself in a mirror at ten paces, and while neighbours banged screeching on the doors, Claira wrote hurriedly in her diary, *I am not afraid to destroy myself in the battle, providing I do not pass the mortal gate alone.*

This was untrue. As with the inept attempt at poisoning,

Claira had no actual conviction she would be caught in the
act, or taken afterwards. Obliquely, she did have some
understanding of human obtuseness. To the average
mind, she had no motive in the world for slaughtering
Antoine Valère. While actors were constantly the target of
lunatics, (lunatic being a category distinctly separate from
her own).

A handful of nights later, three actors of the Théâtre D__
Company, one of whom was Valère, were idling near
midnight among the cafés on the Boule.

"It's very strange," said one, who had the luck to play
the part of an army officer, "but I would swear something
has been following us for the past half hour."

"Something? What?" asked the second, none other
than Simplice's proxy murderer.

"A shadow in a cloak."

"What can it be? A thief? A ghost?"

"A prostitute?"

"Or bad eyesight."

Later yet, as they went along by the river, pausing under
a lamp to light their cigarettes, the army officer was heard
to exclaim: "Look! What did I say? Over *there*."

Three lamp-yellowed faces were turned inquiringly,
above the embers of three cigarettes and a dying match.
Ironically, the proxy murderer was the only one of them
who caught the impression of an arc of swaying feathers,
like the crest of some huge bird, and of the straightening
arm. Then the dreadful explosion of a shot rang out across
the night.

The actors scattered with curses as the fragments of the
broken lantern rained on their heads. (To hit a well-lit
mirror at ten paces does not compare to trying to hit the
heart of a man at thirty.)

Having blown out all illumination, the assassin's
chances were further reduced, but gamely she tried again.
Unbeknownst to any of them, this time she shot a surfacing
fish in the river, the corpse of which, captured next day in a
net, would prove the cause of wonder at a local dinner-
table.

The actors had meanwhile taken to their heels, yelling for police. Claira was left alone in the blackness with the emptied pistol and a sense of injustice.

To say that Madame Sarnot approached Claira's apartment cautiously, or to say that she opened the ensuing conversation with finesse, subtlety, or any apparent regard for personal safety, would be untrue.

"My dear Claira," said Madame Sarnot, as the door was closed to them, "you really must stop trying to kill Antoine Valère."

Claira poised aloofly by the fire, toying with the poker. She was dressed today à le Monsieur de Meunier, to the last earring. (It is perhaps interesting, or informative, to note that while doing so, she had never omitted powder or mascara.)

"Whatever," said Claira, "do you mean?"

"What I say. I was so sorry for the poor waiter. He has a mistress to support, and six children. Not to mention a seventh child waiting, as it were, in the wings."

"In that case," said Claira, "his mistress is probably sorry—someone—was not more efficient."

"Now, now, Claira. You are not a benefactress. You are a poisoner. And also a person who fires off pistols and indiscriminately shatters harmless lanterns."

"You have lost me."

"No, I have not lost you. The papers were full of the attempted assassination. Somehow they seem to have got the idea the intended victim was Monsieur Brun, who plays the rhetorician so . . . rhetorically. It transpires he is involved with somebody's wife, and threats have been made— Good gracious, Claira. The innocent husband has fallen under immediate suspicion and had to fly the police. Are you not ashamed?"

Claira patently was not. She stood, the poker shining in her hand bright as a sword, her beautiful brows slightly raised, like two bows about to let loose arrows. She was magnetic in her ghastliness.

"And what next, then?" said Madame Sarnot. "May I

suggest setting fire to the theatre? Or have you already done it? I passed a fire-wagon on the street; perhaps it was hastening there?" Claira said nothing. Madame Sarnot asked herself if she did not detect the quickening of inspiration in the arrow-head eyes. "That last was a joke," said Madame Sarnot firmly. "But what I shall say next is not. If anything further happens, I shall be forced to seek the authorities."

A response: "Sophie!"

"Much as it may grieve me to do it."

Another response, somewhat similar:

"Sophie—"

"And I shall tell them all I know. All I guess. They will probably be suspicious of me at first, but Horace occupies a high position, as you know, and is able to pull strings—witness your portrait from the Miramelle. Something will get done, eventually. Prison is not your ideal habitat. Consider it."

"*Sophie—*"

"No. Accoladism and friendship aside, I won't be party to a murder. It is ridiculous. It is messy. That is all I have to say."

"Judas," said Claira, merely altering the name.

Madame Sarnot paused at the doors. Grimly, she said, "Without Judas, where would Christianity be today?"

This, unfortunately, was perhaps not the best retort. It may have induced further notions of betrayed grandeur, undying reputation.

Two days after this interview had taken place, a fire broke out at the Théâtre D__, in the dressing-room of Antoine Valère. It was thought generally to have been the result of an accident—the entire company of actors' habit of smoking being to blame. The door-keeper privately supposed he had received a supernatural warning. Called outside by wild cries for help, he found no one, but had afterwards the weird recollection of a hooded shadow slipping by him, which he put down to a manifestation of the theatre ghost. When the commotion subsequently burst forth, he missed the second advent of the hooded shadow, slipping by him yet again, on its way out.

The fire was extinguished before much damage had been done. Antoine Valère, arriving rather late, missed all the excitement, but was forced to act that night in borrowed robes. His own costume, (left strewn over the dressing-room sofa cushions, along with a curly blond sheepskin hat, the collection definitely resembling a sleeping Monsieur Valère to the hasty eye), had been burnt to a frazzle.

"There is a lady to see you," announced the doorkeeper to Valère the following evening.

"Ah. I think I have already left."

The door-keeper ignored this.

"It's the wife of Monsieur Horace Sarnot, the minister of ___."

Surprised, an intuitive name-dropper in need of names to be dropped, Valère conceded he might after all still be in the theatre. Presently Madame Sarnot was ushered through.

"Good evening," she said. "I am here in a private capacity if on a very serious mission."

The city, or that portion of the city which kept itself *au courant* with the dramatic calendar, was presently intrigued and—in the case of those who had not yet seen the show—outraged by the abrupt departure of Monsieur Antoine Valère for the provinces. It seemed an elderly relation—rich—had fallen ill. Valère had been summoned to the bedside, and modern medicine being what it was, it could only be expected he would be delayed there quite some time. The management of the Thèâtre D___ seemed curiously resigned. The new actor who took on the part of Simplice de Meunier was, according to the general consensus, "*palôt*."

By mid-afternoon Claira had her bags packed, her blonde curls constrained beneath a, for Claira, nondescript hat, and the carriage was almost at the door. A number of the papers had ingenuously mentioned Monsieur Valère's destination as a mansion on the outskirts of the little town of Guisenne. This had accordingly also become Claira's destination. One fears one must imagine her two valises filled by a few garments and several means of sudden death.

A timid knock on the apartment door sent Claira springing to open it. It was not, however, the maid or the coachman, it was a small black-haired girl with ribbons, none other than Horace Sarnot's spaniel-and-washing of the door-step pining variety.

But, "Who are you?" demanded Claira, who tended to forget very quickly those who no longer interested her.

The eyes of the once hopeful young lady filled with tears.

"Oh, Claira. How cruel you are."

"Then I am cruel and in a hurry."

"So I see. Well," said the brunette, brushing tears from her lashes with a lace handkerchief, "I see I'm not wanted, shall never be wanted. But I brought you this. Here, take it. A gift carries no obligations. *Oh!*"

And, in this palpitating way, in a mist of lilac scent, the lovely door-stop rushed away, having deposited in Claira's hands—which tended to grasp things automatically, as a hawk grasps prey—a brown paper parcel.

This, still wrapped and tied, was shortly taken out to the carriage with the valises of silk blouses and possible cheese-wire and gunpowder. In the thickening gold of late afternoon light, the carriage stormed westward, leaving the walled heights and embankments of the city, as if for ever.

The road to Guisenne was bumpy and long. The coachman, used to Claira, had not quibbled at the instruction to drive all night.

Claira though, caged, her active, grasshopper mind perhaps bored by unmitigated dreams of revenge, presently tore the wrapper off the parcel.

Within was a book. *The* book. Or at least, another copy of *the* book, for this one was neither a train timetable nor mildewed and falling apart. A biography, none the less, of Simplice de Meunier, its pages delicately brown as if lightly toasted. A small pink note proclaimed the obvious. The brunette had scoured the city in hopes of finding a token her beloved might appreciate. And lo! She had come across this volume, and also the pamphlet, which last item she had placed between the final page and the cover. At this point, the pamphlet fell out on the carriage seat.

It was a fragile thing, the pamphlet, pale and powdery, ostentatiously old. The title caught Claira's eye instantly, and with good reason. For some while she sat on the jouncing springs, staring.

The moon had begun to rise and they were halfway to Guisenne when the coachman received an order to turn round, and hurry back to the city.

"Someone," said Madame Sarnot's private friend, "seems to have died and left Valère a small fortune. Or at least," she added with a very sharp glance, "he has got a lot of money from somewhere." Madame Sarnot smiled, blankly. "Which hasn't prevented his returning to enormous success at the theatre. I gather one of the leading play-wright managers has told the journals he will be writing a drama solely on the subject of this miller poet, and will be approaching Valère about the part." Madame Sarnot smiled, less blankly. "Then again, somebody else has struck gold. Do you remember the *femme gauche* who enhanced Claira's doorway for so long? She now owns a house on the Rue Lucette. I wouldn't be surprised if Claira hadn't paid her off."

Madame Sarnot continued to smile. She said, "Yes, Claira has quite altered in the past month. I like that seventeenth century style. Rather charming, don't you think?"

"The coiffeur who re-darkened her hair said that he was called from his bed at six in the morning to do it."

"Obviously a sudden decision."

"The dressmakers were herded in on the same day, and only a few hours after."

"More interesting, perhaps, than all this, is the new novel."

"It's true, then?"

"Well," said Madame Sarnot, "pages of manuscript seem to be strewn about the apartment."

"A Persian romance, I gather? Or is it Indian?"

"Or a mingling of both?"

Madame Sarnot reviewed in her mind a fragment she had been lucky enough to gaze upon, in which a maiden sat playing a *sitar* at the confluence of the rivers Tigris and Ganges. Claira's worlds were normally exquisitely interconnected. She had spoken, too, for half an hour on the subject of her hero. His hair was black, his rings upon his fingers. He was not Simplice.

Not that the de Meunier portrait, procured from the Miramelle by political strategy and the arm-twisting of Horace, was no longer on display. No indeed, there it hung in all magnificence, the altar still laid beneath with fresh flowers and candles and aged gloves. A large bookcase had been installed nearby, in which reposed the relevant literature Claira had gathered. There was also a small glass case inside which lay a grey pamphlet, dainty as the proverbial moth's wing.

"Why, how tantalizing," said Madame Sarnot, peering in at it, seemingly striving to read the caption, which was obscured by a single white rose.

Claira exchanged a *look* with de Meunier, intimate and knowing in the extreme. "Oh, yes."

Her dark hair was now rather longer, and worn in a fashion appropriate to her current time continuum (sixteen-ninety?). She drifted into the salon. There was a femininity and languidness to Mademoiselle Von Oeau that had not been noticeable before. It was not that Claira had become restful, this was far from being one of her social talents. But *rested,* maybe. The tension of the wires of the lute had slackened, the bow-string was unarmed.

"And how is the novel?" asked Madame Sarnot.

Claira told her, which took three hours. Claira also revealed her intention of going to press in a slightly altered persona. "My publishers, of course, object. I have told them, I shall take the manuscript elsewhere if they fail to agree." The alteration was, apparently, only to the forename. Claira was to become "Clarissa." Claira did not explain why this was to be. There was about her, also, a secretiveness that was unusual. It seemed always on the verge of flowering into revelation, yet never did so. A cat, however, its closed mouth full of canary, could not have looked more pleased by the containment.

A month then elapsed. Another month. There came an evening when, at a reception of some importance, Horace Sarnot drew his wife to one side and whispered urgently, "Claira is here, is she not?" "Why, yes." "Valère has just walked through the door." Madame Sarnot looked in the applicable direction, and beheld a goodlooking young man with blond curls and very correct evening-dress. Monsieur Sarnot who, as his wife had once pointed out, could get so many and curious things seen to, now stood powerlessly and nervously tugging at his whiskers. But, "Don't be alarmed," said Madame Sarnot. "I think it will hardly matter."

At this very instant, their illustrious hostess had, ducking Claira's statuesque *perruque,* taken her arm. "As one of our leading authoresses, you really should be introduced to one of the city's leading actors." Claira allowed herself to be led. "You see? That perfectly beautiful young man." Claira saw. She saw the vague recognition, disinterested, uninterested recognition, as one observes the landscape of another country one has never visited, and has no plans for visiting.

"Mon Dieu," said Horace. "They're meeting."

"Calmly. You see? Meeting, smiling, parting. Valère has already forgotten Claira, who does, to be fair to him, look somewhat different."

"And Claira . . ."

"Claira moves in another universe, Horace, than most of us. If Valère stepped inside the boundaries at any time, he has now retreated."

"Oh dear," the hostess was saying. Claira had congratulated an actor, famed everywhere for his portrayal of an eighteenth century poet called Simplice, with the words:

"Of course, you must find *Hamlet* a most demanding rôle." "Mademoiselle Von Oeau, that was *Antoine Valère.*"

Claira regarded her hostess across the mists of two hundred years. "Who?" she asked.

Returning shortly before one o'clock to her apartment on the Rue Swanhilde, Claira lit the candles on the de Meunier altar, and took from its place the moth-wing pamphlet. For something so antique and so fragile, it must be remarked, the pamphlet bore up very well under its constant handling.

Claira inspected it often. Since the moment in the carriage when it had first fallen into her life, a day had not gone by without her attentions to it being renewed.

What then was this miraculous item, which had scattered arsenic and cheese-wire, bullets and gunpowder, not to mention opium, blondness, male attire and one earring, to the four winds of heaven?

The title and caption on the front of the pamphlet read as follows: *The de Meunier "Phantom." The bizarre and tragic case of a poet's obsession with the mysterious dark lady of whom he believed himself to be a reincarnation.*

Exclamations are, perhaps, at this point superfluous. Even explanations will be minimal.

The essay itself was short and comparatively succinct. It described how its conclusions had been evolved via the unearthing of particular pieces of correspondence between Simplice de Meunier and his agents, his elderly father, and so on. It was illustrated by extracts from these letters, in Simplice's unmistakable and sprawling hand which, as the opium intake increased, appeared to grow familiar with Chinese. Other illustrations were in the form of quoted portions of poetry. There was also a reproduction of a pencil sketch, allegedly by de Meunier himself— when under the influence, and looking it.

The substance of the essay was simply this: From early manhood, the poet had been fixated on the mental image of a small, slight, dark-haired woman with very fine eyes. Initially, he wrote poems to her, and attempted, in his amorous career, to discover her in the arms of numerous female conquests. His faithlessness and callousness, the pamphlet revealed, (as did the quoted letters, where at all readable), sprang from the dissimilarity between each woman Simplice seduced and the intellectual fixation. Eventually, a Monsieur Y__, a well-known medium of the era, meeting de Meunier by chance, revealed that the female *idée fixe* was none other than a recollected image of Simplice's last past life. This turned out to be a young woman, like himself a writer, although of scholarly classical romances. Her hair was black, her eyes fine, her figure small and slender. She had dwelled in the late sixteen hundreds, and was called—the medium regretted her obscurity, (she had penned her epics in secret), would only give up a first name—Clarissa.

De Meunier continued obsessed by his Dark Lady, this Clarissa, with most unfortunate consequences. The opium he had, until then, only occasionally taken, became a daily and nightly recourse in his wild attempts to recall the prior life. Meanwhile his frantic search to discover a look-alike in the female population of the city, rather than being sensibly abandoned as impossible was resumed with all the heady contempt of failure's foregone conclusion. Thus eventually the cousin of the rhetorician's brother was caught up, cast off—left to drown herself. And hence the fatal fraças in the English cemetery of Notre Dame du Nord, and a headless corpse draped across a grave.

Aside from the sections of poems the pamphlet included which feverishly mentioned the Dark Lady, there were also the other poems, which anyone who had researched de Meunier would already have read, and which also extolled her *ad nauseam*. As for the pencil sketch, labelled in de Meunier's unsteady hand: *Clarissa*, it was quite well-drawn, in a drunken way. In it, details of seventeenth century dress were nicely apparent. It was also apparent that it very greatly resembled Claira Von Oeau.

It was a man's world. . . . And though one had been a man, now one was a woman. There were, try as one would, certain areas. . . . And then there was, too, Antoine Valère, a man so properly and damningly acting a man. . . .

But the dove arrives in the nick of time, putting out the fuse with its dewy olive-branch. To be one's own beloved. What else does the personality require, after all? What else, after all, are we?

As Simplice, she had adored herself, even to *extremis*, as now she was. And as herself, she had no rivals, she was non-pareil. So Claira became herself once more, in the style of Clarissa, to please him—to please herself. And it did please her.

Indeed, everyone was pleased.

While the latest lurid, glorious epic, with its potato-eating rajas and its muezzins' dawn cry to worship Kali Ma, was a most spectacular success.

Antoine Valère, as demonstrated, was forgotten. It no longer mattered what he did or thought. Claira had overtaken him and was one jump ahead, perpetually.

One swallow does not, of course, always make a summer. But then, it rather depends on *what* one has swallowed.

Little remains otherwise to be said. Possibly it would be better to say nothing further. However. The recounting of the above incidents cannot properly be closed without this slight, tiresome addendum. The reader is asked only to note these few facts. That plainly Antoine Valère was paid temporarily to fly the scene, and secured during flight against professional injury; that the dark-haired young woman of the door-stop variety, who delivered biography and pamphlet, was next set up in a pleasant house; that Madame Sarnot was an honourable woman who abhorred murder as "messy," understood the foolishness of most scruples, and had for a husband one wise in the matter of pulling strings. Lastly, that the pamphlet and its subject matter, which perhaps saved Valère's life, and undoubtedly Claira's neck, go unrecognised in the few extant works concerning Simplice. Nowhere else is there a reference to his having any interest in reincarnation. And though he surely preferred brunettes, some gentlemen do.

No more, then. Conclusions may be drawn or left strictly alone. Most events are open to conjecture. As for the behaviour of the cast of this drama, it behoves us, perhaps, to be lenient. Conceivably, as Hamlet, (though never in the person of Antoine Valère), informs us, there is a divinity that shapes our ends, rough hew them how we will. But who, after all, would be brutish enough to deny any one of us use of a mallet and chisel?

On the Dark Side of the Station Where the Train Never Stops

Pat Murphy

This is the story of how Lucy, the fireborn, became the North Star. It happened last month.

(What do you mean—the North Star was there the month before last? I'll bet you believe in dinosaurs too. Take my advice—don't.)

I'll start the story in an Irish pub in the heart of New York—a pub full of strangers and dark corners and the smell of good beer. Beer had seeped into the grain of the place and you could scarcely get away from the scent, any more than you could get away from the sound of laughter and the babble of voices. The locals were puzzled by the strangers in their pub, but the Irish have always recognized the fey. The fireborn and the shadowborn are fey without a doubt.

It was a party and Lucy was there. Of course she was there: Lucy always found the parties or the parties found Lucy, though sometimes it was hard to say which.

Lucy was fireborn and a bag lady. No sweet-lipped heroine she. A chin like a precipice, a nose like a hawk, a voice like a trumpet, and eyes of a wintery blue.

Lucy was charming the bartender, asking him for a full pint measure, rather than the half pint he usually drew for a lady. The rings on Lucy's battered hands caught the dim glow of the lights. Lucy herself glowed, just a little, with stored radiance. A glitter from her buttons, a sheen from her gray hair. Her eyes sparkled with the light of distant stars.

She was explaining to the barkeep with a straight face, ". . . but you can see for yourself that I'm not a lady."

The barkeep grinned. "So tell me who you all are and what you're all doing here."

"We've always been here," she said.

"In my pub?"

"No—but around and about. Under the city and over the city and such." She waved a hand in a grand gesture to include the world. "Everywhere."

The barkeep nodded. It was difficult to disagree with Lucy when she fixed you with her blue eyes. He drew her a pint.

I will tell you a little more than Lucy told the barkeep, just so you'll be satisfied with the truth of it all. Lucy and her friends are the people who run the world. Often people confuse them with bums, hobos, and bag ladies. People don't know. Lucy and her friends are the people with the many small-but-important jobs that you know so little about: the man who invented ants; the strange-minded dark-dweller who thought that boulders should be broken down into sand and sand shaped back into boulders again; the woman who puts curious things in unlikely places— like the gold lamé slipper you saw by the road the other day.

Some say that Lucy and her friends are gods and some give them names like Jupiter, Pluto, Mercury, Diana. I do not agree. They are people—longer-lived and more important people than most, but people nevertheless.

Lucy took her beer and drifted away from the bar. She wandered—talking to people she knew and people she didn't and people she might like to know. She drifted toward a dark corner where she heard a voice that interested her. And so, she met the man in the shadows.

A cap like a ragpicker, boots like a rancher, a shirt with holes it is better not to discuss—he was one of the shadow-born. No matter what you have heard, they are not all bad, these shadowborn. Not all bad, though their minds are a little twisted and their bones are in the wrong places. Sometimes, they are very interesting people.

He had a nice laugh, and many a meeting has been based on no more.

"Hello," said Lucy to the laughter in the darkness. "My name's Lucy."

"I'm Mac," he said.

"And what's your excuse for being here?" she asked.

He laughed again—an interesting chuckle, more interesting because it held a hint of shadow. "I'm in the business of inventing the past and laying down proof that it really was."

(Now there's a secret of the fireborn and the shadowborn. The world is really only a few years old. Some say five years; some say three. It really doesn't matter that I tell you this. You won't believe it anyway. People rarely believe important truths.)

"What do you do, Lucy?" he asked.

"I'm a firecatcher on the Starlight Run," she said—and it sounded very important when she said it. Well, firecatcher is an important job, I suppose. Someone has to catch the light of distant stars and guide it down to Earth. But really, the Solar Run and the Lunar Ricochet Run (with the tricky reflection) are more important to folks on Earth. The Starlight Run is simply longer and lonelier.

Lucy had been put on the Starlight Run younger than a firecatcher usually was. She had many people fooled into thinking that she was stronger and smarter and tougher than she was. She was on the Starlight Run, and there are many ways that a firecatcher can make that run and be lost forever.

(You want to know how and when and why? Who are you to ask for explanations of things that even people of power don't understand? And explanations will do you no good anyway. Trust me.)

"Interesting job," Mac said. "Not an easy one." And Lucy grinned and set her pint on the table as if she would stop for a while. You know how it is when you meet someone who seems like a friend? You don't know? You should. But even if you don't, just trust me: that's how it was. He seemed like a friend.

"Hey, Lucy," a firecatcher called from the bar.

Lucy laid a hand on the shadowborn's shoulder and said, "I've got to talk to that one. I'll be back." And she ran away to talk and never did get back to the shadows. Parties can be like that.

And that night, Lucy left the city, running up and away to the far-off stars. And after a time, she came back. She went away, and she came back. And each time she came back, the world seemed a little brighter and the space between the stars a little darker. But she was a firecatcher and she went away and she came back, and there was another party.

The gathering was in the phantom subway station at 91st Street, where the train never stops anymore. The old station was lit by fireballs that Lucy had placed in the rafters. Laughter and voices echoed from the tiled walls.

"You seem a little tired tonight, Lucy," said Johnson, a jovial man who knew everyone's business but managed to keep it all to himself. He lived by the stone lions at the public library and had the look of a fireborn but (some said) the twisty mind of a shadowborn. He was not all sparkle—he governed the sky over the city and some of that sky was clouds.

"I am tired," Lucy said. "Could you do me a favor?"

"What's that?"

"Make it cloudy tomorrow night. I need a holiday."

Johnson frowned. "It's not in the schedule."

She watched him silently. Did I tell you—it's hard to say no to Lucy.

"All right, I'll fix it," he said at last. "We'll have rain."

"Thanks," she said and her eyes studied the crowd.

"Who are you looking for?" Johnson asked.

"Looking for trouble. What else?" Then her eyes stopped on a shadowy alcove beneath a stairway. "I think I found it." She grinned at Johnson and started to turn away.

"Hey, hold on," said Johnson, laying a hand on her shoulder. "He's a shadowborn and—"

"I talked to him at a party a while back," she said. "He

seemed interesting. I always wanted a friend in dark places. Besides . . ." She let the word trail away, she shook the restraining hand from her shoulder, and she headed for the stairway. There never was any explaining Lucy's "Besides . . ." And explanations would do no good anyway. She headed for the shadows.

On the edge of the bottom step of the stairs, a spot of white fluttered in the darkness. Another spot of white crouched nearby.

"Hello, cat," Lucy said to the crouching whiteness, but the young animal was intent on the white scrap of paper that twitched on the stairs.

There was no wind.

Lucy watched and the paper moved—a slight twitch and a bit of a tumble. The cat's eyes grew wider and she inched forward. Again, the scrap moved, fluttering like a bird with a broken wing. The cat flattened herself to the floor, staring.

Not a breeze. But the paper fluttered again and the cat pounced. She held the scrap down with one paw and waited for it to struggle. And waited. Batted at it gently with the other paw.

Lucy heard the darkness ahead chuckle, and she chuckled too. She had a nice laugh, or so folks said. Despite her nose and her chin and her voice, she had a nice laugh. She raised a hand in the darkness and the glitter from her rings became brighter. Still, it was difficult to see him in the dim light and easy to see that he liked it that way.

A cap like a ragpicker, boots like a rancher. Lucy grinned and he grinned back.

"Give up," she said to the cat. "It's not what you think."

"Things hardly ever are," said the man in the shadows. He looked back at the cat and the bit of paper fluttered away, flying like a bat to disappear in the darkness.

The sound of a train in the distance interrupted further discussion. The train never stopped at the 91st Street station—not anymore. But it passed through with a rush of displaced air and a shriek of metal wheels on metal tracks and a headlight like a blaze of glory. The light flashed over peeling advertisements and mosaic tiles obscured by graffiti and empty spaces and a wide-eyed cat who crouched low to the floor.

The rumbling train passed, leaving a great silence behind. Then party guests emerged from behind pillars and from shadowy corners.

Lucy sat in the alcove beneath the stairs. "So what have you been up to, Mac? I haven't seen you since the party in the pub."

"Manufacturing things that never were," he said. "I've been over on the East Side, laying in a fossil bed that should complicate the history of life by more than a little. All sorts of inconsistencies. They'll be confused for weeks. Serves them right for trying to find explanations where there aren't any."

"There's nothing wrong with explanations," she said.

"Ha! They only muddy things," he said. "If only people would accept fossils as interesting art forms. Or the bones of dragons." He shrugged. "What can you expect? They wear lab coats and never see past one kind of truth to another kind. So what have you been doing, Lucy?"

"Going on the Starlight Run." She grinned and her eyes sparkled. "I'm off again, day after tomorrow."

"It's a dark and lonely run," he said.

"Ah, but it's worth it," she said. And she told him about the Starlight Run and about how she dodged through time to jump vast distances and how she caught the light. And he talked to her about the dark ways beneath the city. I can't tell you all that was said.

But they weren't just talking. This was something else and it's hard to say just what. No, there was no crackle of sparks, no ozone in the air. But there was a bright chill that was not just the chill of the unused air of an ancient subway station. There was a tension that was something more than the tension of a party.

Lucy, the fireborn, and Mac, the shadowborn, talked and chuckled. Around them, the party died down. The fireballs were fading when Mac said, "Hey, I'll show you the project I've been working on."

They walked hand in hand through the tunnels. He found his way confidently through the darkness and their footsteps echoed in the tunnels. They stepped into a cavern—she could tell by the change in the echoes. Lucy lifted her hand and her rings glittered with light.

They stood at the edge of a pit. Mac waved at the bones below. "I'm having trouble with this one," he said. The skull looked vaguely crocodilian; the rest was a jumble of bones. "I don't mind making a creature that can't walk, but this one won't even stand. I was playing with the joints and ways of putting them together and . . ." He stopped, shaking his head.

Lucy frowned, looking down at the bones. "Let's see," she said. She reached a hand toward the pit and the bones began to glow. The heavy skull seemed to shift a little in its resting place, then a shining replica of the head lifted free. The beast raised itself slowly, bone by glowing bone. Each bone was a duplicate of the jumble in the pit.

The beast—a giant lizard of a sort—hesitated, its belly on the ground, its legs bent at an awkward angle. "Thigh-bones should be shorter," Mac muttered.

The glowing bones shifted and the beast held its head higher. "Larger feet," he said, and the bones that formed toes stretched and flexed. The beast twitched its tail impatiently. "The back's too long," Lucy said, and shortened a few vertebrae. The beast shook its heavy head, and glared up at them with its empty eyes. "I wish it didn't have so many teeth," she said.

"Leave the teeth," Mac said. "It needs teeth."

The beast gathered its legs beneath itself, still staring at them. It lifted its head farther up and its mouth gaped wider. "I don't like the teeth," Lucy said. And the glow began to fade from the pit. The beast lay down to sleep, as if it had never lived.

Mac and Lucy sat side by side on the edge of the pit. "Why does it need teeth?" she asked.

He shrugged. "The world requires them."

"Not that many," she said. "Not always."

"Just that many," he said. "Always."

Only the faintest glimmer remained on the bones. Still, they sat on the edge, holding hands.

There are things that happen between men and women—even those of the fire and the shadow. Some have names: friendship and love and lust and hatred. Some have no names—being complex mixtures of the named ones with additions of other elements, like curiosity and happiness and wine and darkness and need.

This was one of the second kind of thing. But who knows which and at the time it did not seem to matter. Don't worry too much about the particulars—as I said before, who are you to know how and when and why?

But understand that Lucy, the firecatcher on the Starlight Run, woke up on a hard bench in the phantom subway station.

Hadn't there been a softer surface the night before—with a hint of sheets and pillows and warmth? Maybe. The memory was blurred and she could not say. She was puzzled, for she had not often gone to bed with warmth and awakened in darkness.

It was all very sudden; it was all very odd—and I suppose that's where the story really begins. With sudden chill and darkness. Lucy lifted a hand and tossed a fireball into the empty station. The white cat watched from a tunnel that led to the Outside. "Odd," Lucy said. "Very odd."

Best not get into her thoughts at this point, for her thoughts were neither as coherent nor as polite as "Odd." Best that I let Lucy retain some of her mystery and simply say that she wandered through the tunnel to the Outside and that her feet left glowing prints on the tile floor and her hand left bright marks on the wall where she touched it.

She blinked in the light of the Outside. (Surely you didn't think I'd tell you of the secret ways beneath the city, did you? You were wrong.)

Business people—men and women in neat suits—

hurried past her with averted eyes. They saw only a bag lady in a disheveled dress. People do not see all that is there. People do not see much.

Now, Lucy was a mean and stubborn woman. Folks who knew her well did not cross her, because they knew that she didn't let go of an idea or a discontent. She would take it and shake it and worry it—usually to no avail, but that didn't stop her. She did not like dangling ends and she would tie herself in knots to get rid of them.

Johnson, who always knew where to be, lounged in a nearby doorway. Lucy looked at him and he shook his head before she could even speak.

"Very odd," Lucy said again, though I know that was not what she was thinking. She glanced back at the tunnel behind her and she frowned.

Johnson fell into step beside her as she headed for the East Side. "You're heading for trouble," he said.

"Why should today be different from any other day?" she asked and kept on walking.

"So he stole your heart, eh?" Johnson said after a moment. "The shadowborn can be—"

"You know better than that," Lucy interrupted. "I'm just puzzled. I know we were friends and it doesn't seem . . ."

"Very friendly," Johnson completed the trailing sentence. "Hey, he's a shadowborn. He's different."

"Yeah?" Lucy shook her head. "I don't understand."

"You don't understand and they don't understand. It always amounts to a lack of understanding." He walked beside her for a while, then said, "So you're going to try to track down an explanation?"

"I am."

"Don't be disappointed if he doesn't have one," Johnson warned her.

"He must know where he went and who he is," Lucy grumbled.

"Maybe not. But good luck," he said, and he stopped walking.

Lucy continued through the city alone. The day was overcast; Johnson had kept his word and there would be no starshine that night.

In the tunnels on the East Side, Lucy found Mac directing the placement of fossils by several shadowy figures. One skeleton had a lizardlike head with too many teeth. "Hey, I wanted to talk to you," she said. "I—"

"I thought you might want to," he said. "It's simple really."

"Oh, yeah?"

"I thought we should maybe just be friends."

"Yeah? Well, that's all right, but . . ." she began, but he was gone. Directing the positioning of a complex skeleton with legs all out of proportion to its body. Then he was back.

"Yeah, friends. Things get too complicated otherwise," he said. He looked at her, but she could not see his eyes in the shadows.

"Well, it seems to me that things don't need to be complicated. . . ." But he was gone again, grumbling at the workman who was laying down the creature's neck, explaining with words and gestures that the neck had to be placed as if the animal had fallen naturally, not as if some ham-handed workman had laid . . .

Lucy left quietly.

There was a tension in the city that afternoon, a current, a flow of power. It was the kind of day when the small hairs on the backs of your hands stand on end for no reason.

Lucy wandered the city and visited friends. "People don't act like that," she told her friend Maggie. "Not without a good reason."

Maggie shrugged. Maggie specialized in sidewalks and streets that went where no one expected them to go. "Maybe he has a reason." Her voice was soft, like the hiss of tire on pavement, going nowhere. "Maybe he prefers the company of his own kind. Or maybe he prefers no company at all. Or maybe he was never there at all. You can see things in the shadows sometimes."

"He really was there," Lucy said to her friend Brian. She met him in the park in the late afternoon. He was putting away his torches and Indian clubs after a long day of juggling. Brian juggled the lightning on rainy nights.

"Maybe he just wants to be friends," Brian suggested. "Well, cheer up. I'll teach you to juggle."

But the round balls always tumbled to the ground and Lucy could not laugh as she had laughed every other time that Brian had tried to teach her.

"So what is it about him?" Brian asked at last, sitting down in the grass.

"It's not him," Lucy said, sitting down beside him. "It's people. People shouldn't act that way."

"They do."

"Not us," she said. "*They* do." She gestured at the people strolling through the park. A girl sat on a bench nearby and the sun was shining on her hair. A man with sky blue eyes walked past the young woman and for a moment their eyes met. Lucy saw it and the Juggler saw it. But the man walked on past and the sunlight faded from the woman's golden hair. "They're like that," Lucy said. "They don't see past the surface. But this shadow-born . . . he's one of us."

"Maybe not," Brian said. He reached for her hand and she started when he touched her—just a small shiver. Then she took his hand and they watched the sunlight fade and the shadows stretch away across the park. But she left when darkness came.

There was a thunderstorm over the City that night and great flashing streaks of lightning split the overcast sky. Rumbles of thunder shook the buildings and made bums and bag ladies seek the cover of doorways and bus shelters.

But Lucy was a mean and stubborn woman. She walked through the storm and did all the things that should bring luck and power.

She threw three copper coins in a certain fountain at midnight.

She put seven pennies, standing on edge, between the bricks of a certain wall.

She turned her jacket inside out, like a woman who has been led astray by pixies and means to break the spell.

She found a four-leaf clover in the wet grass of the park and tucked it behind her left ear.

At dawn, Johnson found her sitting in the park in the wet grass. "Do me a favor?" she asked without looking up. "Can you make it rain tonight?"

He shook his head slowly. His face was set in a frown and his hands were deep in his pockets. "It won't do you any good," he said. She did not look up at him. "You can't just stay and look and wait." He waited a moment, but she did not speak. "You really are upset, aren't you?"

She plucked another daisy from the grass beside her. "He was a friend. I didn't think I could lose a friend so easily."

"Tomorrow night, the stars must shine," he said unhappily.

"It's a long and lonely run," she said slowly. And at last she looked up at him. He could not read her expression. "But I have until twilight."

"It's no good, Lucy. You're looking for an explanation and—"

"I'm looking for trouble," she said with a touch of her old tone. "I'll find it."

And the sun rose over the city and began to burn away the fog. Lucy went back to the tunnels on the East Side. (Trust me: you couldn't follow the directions there if I gave them.) Her footsteps echoed in the darkness. The construction site was empty and the corridors were dark and silent. She went looking for trouble and she did not find it.

She ended up back at the phantom subway station, alone and unhappy. But she was a firecatcher and a lady of some power. Even tired and hurt, she had some power. She traced a figure in the air, outlined it with light. A cap like a ragpicker, boots like a rancher, a shirt with undiscussable holes. Face in shadow, of course.

"You know, I don't understand," she said to the figure. "And I don't think you do either." A train rumbled through the station and the figure disappeared for a moment in the brighter glow of the headlight. Lucy did not move. A slight tremor went through the glowing shape, like a ripple in a reflection, starting at the battered boots and ending at the stained cap. "I'm confused, and I don't like being confused." She glared at the figure for a moment. It did not move, did not speak.

She walked away, leaving a trail of glowing footprints. At the entry to the tunnel (Still want to know where the tunnels are, don't you? Ha! You'll never find out now.), she looked up at the night sky, toward the Little Bear, her particular constellation.

She walked across town to the library, where she knew Johnson would be. "I came to say good-bye," she said.

"You're leaving on the Run?"

She nodded. "It's a tricky run," she said and her voice was young and soft. "I may not be back."

Johnson tried to take her hand but she stepped back and laid a hand on the head of one of the lions. "It's all right," she said. "I just need a different point of view for a while. I'll be fine. I might be back later."

Johnson shook his head. "Hey, if I see that shadow-born, what do you want me to—"

"Don't say a word," she said. "Don't explain a thing."

She stood with one hand on the head of the lion and she looked up toward the Little Bear, a constellation that had always seemed to be missing a star. And she began to fade—her hair changing from the color of steel to the color of twilight, her face losing its craggy reality, her body losing its harsh line. And in a moment, she was gone and away on the Starlight Run.

She hasn't come back yet. That's why you can't see many stars in the City—they're short a firecatcher still. She became a star herself, sitting up in the far-off, throwing gobs of light down at the world. (And if you want to know how she became the North Star, ask the man who lives by the lions. He may tell you, if you have the right look about you. Or he may not.)

What do you mean—the North Star was always there? Haven't you been listening? The world is not as it seems. Ask any poet. Ask any bag lady. Ask anyone who sees in the twilight and knows of the fireborn and the shadows.

Down in the tunnels and secret ways of the city, the white cat mated with a black tom and produced litters of kittens who pounce and play with paper scraps that dance and flutter but never live. A faintly glowing figure still waits in the phantom subway station for a train that never will stop.

And Mac? You want to know what happened to the shadowborn? It's possible that he never was at all. But if he was, then probably he still is and probably he is happy and probably he has never found the light sculpture that leans against the dark wall of the phantom subway station. Probably.

So that's the story and you can draw your own conclusions. But one warning: If you have a streak of the shadow in you, don't follow the North Star. She may lead you astray. Lucy can be like that—she can hold a grudge.

And if you do have the shadow in you, don't worry. I made the whole thing up. There—feel better? All right? All right.

Simultaneously

Simultaneously, five thousand miles apart,
two telephone poles, shaking and roaring
and hissing gas, rose from their emplacements
straight up, leveled off and headed
for each other's land, alerted radar
and ground defense, passed each other
in midair, escorted by worried planes,
and plunged into each other's place,
steaming and silent and standing straight,
sprouting leaves.

—David Ignatow

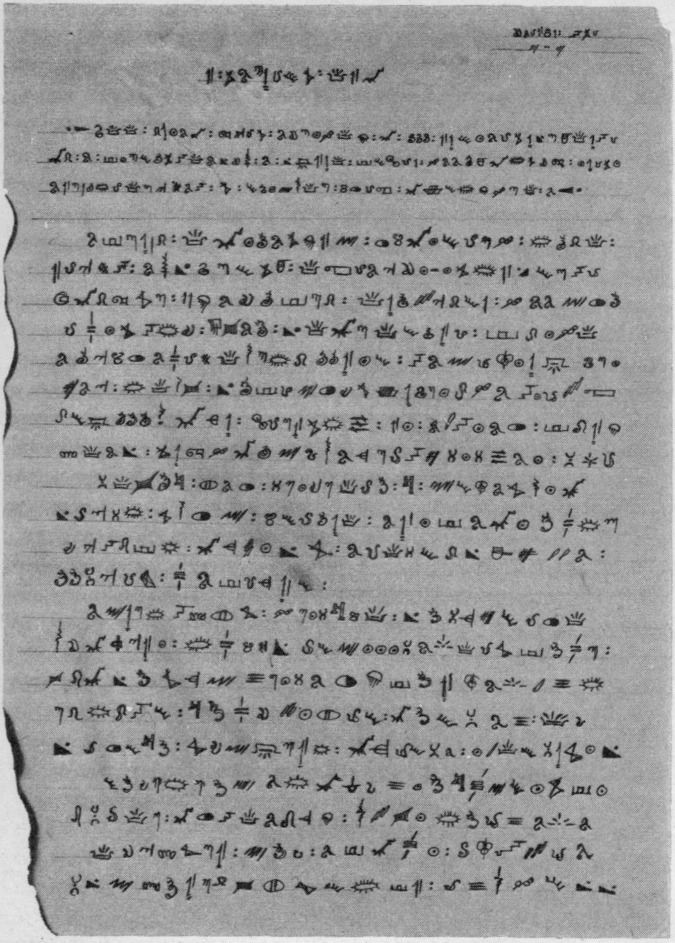

Figure One: A pirated copy of the Borges manuscript.

"Franz Kafka" by
Jorge Luis Borges

Alvin Greenberg

There is a story by Borges that neither you nor anyone else has ever read, for it was written in the dialect of a remote Andean Indian tribe among whom Borges lived briefly while young, but whose language no one else knows. Borges himself seems to have little memory of the language at this late date; with his failing eyesight he can no longer decipher the curious symbols which he has used to represent it on the printed page; and no one else either knows what sounds the symbols were supposed to represent or would be likely to pronounce them properly if he did. Meanwhile, an article in a recent issue of the *Journal of Anthropology* has reported the finding, by an expedition from the University of Pennsylvania, of the village where Borges lived, or where, according to rough estimates given by Borges himself after his return many decades ago, it seems likely that he lived. No signs of recent human habitation were found in the village, however, and the expedition has reported convincing evidence that the population was destroyed by a sudden flare up of venereal disease, perhaps resulting from contact with western civilization, probably before World War II. Although they left many artifacts behind, there is no evidence of their having possessed an alphabet, hence no record of their language. They appear, according to the report, to have been a marginal society of hunters and gatherers; they kept no domestic animals; they dwelt in rather small shelters made of unhewn stone and did their cooking over open, communal fires; the majority of them, it appears, were left-handed; almost all of their pottery, as well as some of the stones of the huts, is decorated with drawings of insects, some quite crudely and some in very realistic detail. Not all of the insects depicted on these objects are believed to be indigenous to the region, though no suitable explanation for this phenomenon has yet been proposed.

Borges, for his part, claims not to remember what the story—which he wrote either while still residing in the village or immediately after his return—is about, but is under the impression that he included much of it in a later story, with a different setting, possibly European. A former student and present colleague of mine, Charles Morley Baxter, who interviewed Borges in Buenos Aires in 1967, tried again and again to turn the questioning in the direction of this story, only to receive instead lengthy, impassioned, and knowledgeable disquisitions on German mystics of the seventeenth century, the English prose romance, and some early twentieth-century French symbolistes of whom he had never heard before. When he asked, at last, whether it would be possible to see the "mysterious" manuscript, Borges at once reached into the drawer of a nearby desk and presented him with a sheaf of hand-written pages. These, however, turned out to be, so far as Baxter could tell, the rough draft of an unpublished essay on the palace at Knossos by the Chilean archeologist Alfonso Quenardo, whose work, though my friend was not at the time aware of this, has long since been discredited for being speculative and nonempirical.*

Nonetheless, as everyone knows by now, pirated copies of the manuscript are in common circulation among Borges aficionados throughout the world. Generally they exist in mimeographed form, though sometimes in Xerox copies (made, in all likelihood, from mimeographed versions), and, less frequently, in painstakingly handmade versions, more than one of which has already been offered me, in the several years since I began to explore this subject, as the original. Never have I seen a printed ver-

---

*In 1924 Quenardo rejected a sizable government grant under which he was to have headed an international archeological expedition to Crete, claiming that he could learn as much about labyrinths in Santiago as anywhere else and that "one does not have to dig in order to get dirty." These remarks, called arrogant by his colleagues and the press, severely damaged his academic career.

sion. At this time, I have in my possession over twenty copies, in one form or another. Most of them are identical in almost all aspects: regardless of format, each fills nine standard 8½ x 11 pages; differences, for the most part, are minor, consisting primarily of malformed symbols; there are only a few copies that reveal the addition or omission of a group of symbols, and it seems likely that these are the result of someone's attempt to compensate for a failure in the copying mechanism. It would be no great task to collate the various copies in my possession in order to produce a "good text"; such a task would be a pointless one, however, since the text has no "meaning." Cryptography could at best substitute another set of symbols—*i.e.*, romantic letters—for the extant ones, but could bring us no closer to a successful translation; it has, to date, failed to find a consistent basis for achieving even the first task. The manuscripts rest with me still, though I have some time since given over completely the notion of seeking a "translation" and have, of late, begun to suspect Borges' use of the term *story*—if, indeed, it was he who applied that term to this work. Professor Arthur Efron, of the State University of New York at Buffalo, has persuaded me to place these documents, as well as any others collected in the interim, in the Contemporary Literature Manuscript Collection of that fine institution when my own work with them is completed, and so indeed I shall do.

In the meantime, I have been shocked to discover the proliferation of not just the manuscripts but the symbols themselves, a phenomenon I encountered in a most curious way. On my most recent visit to New York, some six months back, I spent an evening with my friend, the poet C. W. Truesdale, discussing both Borges, to whose work I had introduced him a year or so previously, and my own preoccupation with the "mysterious" manuscript, a copy of which I had with me at the time, having been given it*

---

*I have never yet been able to *purchase* a copy; each time I have heard of the existence of one, tracked it down, and then offered to buy it, payment has been refused and it has been forced on me as a gift, in such a way as to make my refusal of it impossible.

only that afternoon by another poet friend who had recently brought it back with him from Mexico City. While we discussed Borges, Truesdale's younger daughter, Stephanie, came in and sat down on the arm of her father's chair, just across from me. She had been there for some time—perhaps an hour or more, not at all a likely thing for a nine-year-old—listening intently to our conversation and playing idly with her charm bracelet, before I suddenly became aware of what I had been seeing all along: one of the charms that dangled from her bracelet was one of the symbols from the Borges manuscript! I asked at once to see the bracelet. The other charms were the ordinary ones, mementos of places visited, for the most part, which her parents had bought for her. The one with the symbol, however, was, she explained, the gift of a school friend, a shy little girl from the South who had spent a few months in Stephanie's school while her father was on an assignment in New York and then had gone away. Although Stephanie had been attracted to this child, she had never become particularly friendly with her, and so had been greatly surprised when the little girl approached her after school one day and simply handed her the charm. In spite of her knowledge of her mother's strong opposition to her accepting gifts from schoolmates, Stephanie did not for a moment consider not taking it; instead she decided to offer something valuable of her own in exchange, a beautiful polished agate that had been a gift from a friend of her parents back in Minnesota, but when she took it to school the next day she found that the girl had already been withdrawn. When she was done answering my questions in this way, Stephanie asked me why I was so interested.

"Have you ever heard of Borges?" I replied.

"Of course," she said, "you've been talking about him all evening."

The symbol that appeared on her charm was similar to the Hebrew letter *gimel,* save that the upright portion of the symbol was tilted far more to the left and the "foot" was given more of a hook, so that it looked like this:

It was the symbol that I had come to refer to, from its curious shape and the frequency of its occurrence in the manuscript, as the "grasshopper." Truesdale himself, having looked at first with some amusement upon my interrogation of his daughter, soon became quite intrigued with the matter, having at last noted that the symbol on her charm did indeed correspond with one of the symbols in the Borges manuscript which I had been showing him, and which he had been holding in his own hands for some time now. He was, all in all, interested enough to accompany me the following day on a trip to the library in an attempt to track down the sources of some of Borges' symbols in ancient or foreign alphabets, though neither of us actually expected to have much success in such a venture: Truesdale because he was not yet convinced that the whole thing was not an elaborate hoax, and myself because I could not quite believe that Borges had gotten his symbols from some "outside" source.

As it turned out, we never got to the library that day, though my later researches have demonstrated quite convincingly that the symbols—I have identified sixty-three of them quite definitively, and there are some half dozen others whose status is less certain since they may be only variations on, of malformations of, other symbols—are not derived from any other alphabets, ancient or modern. There are, to be sure, some few, such as the one noted above, in which the casual viewer might see some relations to Hebrew, or Telagu, or Arabic, but such resemblances are merely superficial, are in all cases only vague similarities and not identities, and are, in any event, not of sufficient number to warrant serious consideration.

Far more interesting, from my own point of view, was Truesdale's remark as we left for the library the following morning—he had stayed up most of the night with the copy of the manuscript that I had left behind for his examination—that he had been inspired by my own informal name for the symbol that appeared on Stephanie's charm bracelet to note that a great many of the symbols seemed to bear rough resemblances to insects. It was, I believe, the last time he ever spoke to me of this manuscript or its author. While I was still mulling over the implitions of his statement, we passed a newsstand where we both observed, in the same speechless moment, that the model on the cover of the current *Harper's Bazaar* was wearing a pin in the shape of the same symbol that had appeared on the charm. It was not long before we began to see the symbol elsewhere—on the hood ornament of a foreign automobile, carved into the granite block of a cornerstone, scrawled in crayon on an advertisement for a Broadway musical comedy—and then other symbols as well—one embossed on the side of a businessman's briefcase, two appearing in an alternating pattern on the fabric of a dress in the window of a fashionable shop, another on a decal affixed to the rear window of a taxi—all within a few blocks. Truesdale's spirits began to fluctuate wildly as these things came to our attention. With a howl of excitement he would rush across a busy street, dragging me behind him through the dangerous traffic, to check the symbol emblazoned on a toy being sold by a street hawker, or haul me in pursuit of a young woman to examine the shape of her shoe buckle. In between these moments he would fall into a deep and speechless despondency, especially darkened when my own questioning of shop owners or pedestrians only served to reveal that they knew "nothing about" the symbol to which I called their attention, that it was "only a decoration," or that "someone had asked to put it there."* On the south-

---

*Perhaps one reason for his speechlessness and our inability to discuss this event was the unspoken presence of a question neither of us wished to encounter because neither dared risk an answer: were all of these people truly innocent of the symbol to which they were connected or were they part of a silent conspiracy of its presence from which we alone were excluded?

west corner of Eighth Avenue and 57th Street, Truesdale
came to an abrupt halt and began to recite, in a loud voice
rendered generally inaudible by the sounds of traffic and
the rapidly gathering crowd, a poem he had apparently
been composing all this while about—as best I could tell—
the symbol we had been encountering most frequently.*
When, however, he at last arrived at the crucial point
where the symbol itself was to appear in the poem, he
paused, unable to find a verbal equivalent for it, equally
unable to go on without it. For one terrifying moment, it
seemed as if the whole world had come to a standstill. It
was with great relief that I got the two of us into a taxi.

Perhaps this crisis was only the result of what Truesdale
had tried to incorporate in his poem. It is possible, of
course, to include all sorts of "found objects" in poems—
indeed, one might well ask what other sorts of objects there
are to be included in poems—and most often without the
poet being able to predict in advance quite what their effect
will be upon his poems. But might it not be equally valid to
assert that there are some "objects" that are capable of
refusing to be incorporated into poetry? Perhaps it is the
property of such objects to "act" rather than to be acted
upon, so that though they may easily enter poems on their
own—in all likelihood in the guise of other, less suspicious,
objects—it is not possible for the poet himself to take hold
of them, and place them in the poem, at his own disposi-
tion. And perhaps this, in turn, is only so because they are,
so to speak, a poetry of their own—with, therefore, their
own independence of action, and a certain resistance to
having a chorus of words constructed "about" them.
Borges himself, after all, has long since warned us that "it
is hazardous to think that a coordination of words
(philosophies are nothing else) can have much resemblance to the universe." So much, then, for a

---

*I still have in my possession a copy of this poem which I was sent soon
after I left New York; I do not feel, however, that I have any right to reprint
it inasmuch as the poet himself refuses either to submit it for publication or
to read it at any of his public appearances. I fear it has been swallowed up
by the same conspiracy of silence as the symbols.

philosophy, a scientific system, a metaphysics, a mimetic literature. But what of a poetry?

He has at the same time asked us to see, with the symbolistes, that the world itself is a book—if not a "coordination of words," at least a forest of symbols, perhaps undecipherable. So too it may be for this untitled and unreadable—indecipherable—"story" that he has given us. It does not bear much, if any, "resemblance to the universe," save for the associations, possibly only personal, evoked by a few of its markings; it is, on the other hand, a veritable forest of symbols, through which, it begins to seem to me, now that I have begun to devote myself to it more and more fully (I fear it will be some time before I shall be ready to release my manuscript collection; my study is already impossibly cluttered with the multitude of symbol-bearing artifacts that I have accumulated in only the past few months; what this brief essay on the subject may be only the beginning of I cannot imagine), one can walk endlessly, encountering such things as have never before been seen. Not a "coordination of words," but a conglomeration—who is to say that anything has been coordinated?—of things, symbols, presences; not, indeed, a "resemblance to the universe," but a universe itself, which cannot be "incorporated" into any other universe.

What Borges appears to have left us, then, is not a literature but a world—a strange, opaque, and stubborn world. And yet one cannot help being tempted to ask, seeing how closely it has approached our own now, whether it is possible to dwell in such a world. Some have seen it, that much is clear, and have perhaps attempted to enter it; hence the proliferation of manuscripts and pseudomanuscripts of the "story," and, lately, of the symbols. Others have tried to take hold of it more forcefully, and to bring it into their own spheres without due regard for its autonomy; hence the trauma resulting from Truesdale's attempt to include the symbol in the world of his own poem. And it is equally clear that many who come near it, or even touch upon it, without any knowledge of what they are approaching, are, by their very innocence it would seem, both protected from any dangers it might involve and included within its own sphere: hence the total naturalness and ease of Stephanie's wearing of the charm.

But at the same time, I begin to suspect that it is equally possible that "it," the Borgesan world, is not content simply to wait for others to come near, to enter into it, but instead moves anxiously forward on its own into the universe we already inhabit, even now permeating it with its own symbology. To what end? Perhaps it would be best if such a question as that simply was not raised. Not only does it suggest a teleology that may well not exist, but it implies other, and still more problematical, questions: If we knew to what end, would we want to avoid it? And if we wanted to avoid it, could we?

Already there are areas where it has impinged with dramatic effect, as if one of its symbols had somehow slipped through a tiny pinhole in a previously impervious membrane, and there, on the other side—on *our* side—had suddenly taken root and flowered. In the modern literature class I teach—*used* to teach—my students persist in saying that Gregor Samsa has turned into a grasshopper, though Kafka very plainly labels him a dung beetle. There is nothing I can do about it, or Kafka either: A symbol stronger than his has taken hold of "The Metamorphosis." Borges, in this sense, has "created" Kafka, unless it is Kafka who, by carving out in his story a small vacuum, disguised by the term *dung beetle,* into which the grasshopper symbol would naturally flow, has created Borges.* Meanwhile the poet Truesdale has abandoned

---

*Most students, it appears, perform this metamorphosis of their own upon Kafka's story quite unconsciously, for they are genuinely surprised and confused when I point out the places in the text where Kafka uses the term *dung beetle.* More than one has insisted that "there must be some mistake in the text." However, one of my more remarkable students of recent years, the previously mentioned Charles Morley Baxter, has developed an extremely well-reasoned case for believing that Gregor is, indeed, not a dung beetle but a grasshopper, basing his argument on the fact that it is not the narrator himself who calls Gregor a dung beetle but rather the cleaning lady, who is concerned only with getting her work done and not with making nice distinctions between kinds of insects, who

New York for his cabin on Mocassin Lake in northern Minnesota. He seems well and cheerful, accomplishes an enviable amount of work, but refuses to fish or to fell timber for firewood. His wife explains that on some other fisherman's hook left in the mouth of some northern pike he lands—or, worse yet, imbedded deep inside the trunk of some ancient Norway pine—he fears to find such a symbol as would not be at all good for him to find, in such a place. Not long after takeoff on his flight west, the stewardess presented him with a large white box, containing a birthday cake. The box was very clearly marked with his name, and the stewardess was certain there had been no mistake, but it was *not* his birthday. Was it Rochester beneath him at that moment, or some other universe in which it *was* his birthday? When the plane landed he abandoned the cake in a locker without ever tasting it. Perhaps only now someone who has come to Minneapolis from terribly far away is approaching that same locker with the correct key. It is a struggle to stick to the use of these symbols, these words, and not to let those other symbols cover these very pages. Truesdale, meanwhile, has put the cake in a poem, or rather, in his own words, "there was a poem in which there appeared a place for this cake, and no other." The poem vibrates with the cake. But what will be found when the locker is opened? Can Borges have given us a universe in which it is possible to have one's cake and eat it too? Or where, better yet, it is possible for one to have the cake while another "one" eats it? Perhaps even at this moment "C. W. Truesdale" or "Jorge Luis Borges," large and bearlike and quite hungry, is opening the locker. I would imagine that the cake is still fresh. It is decorated with a unique set of symbols which, like the cake, are sweet and edible. It is not my birthday either, but what danger could there be in a little taste?

---

is probably quite ignorant of such distinctions anyway and by no means a reliable witness, *but through whose mistake* Kafka has very subtly implied, or permitted, the sense of grasshopper. I am not yet entirely convinced.

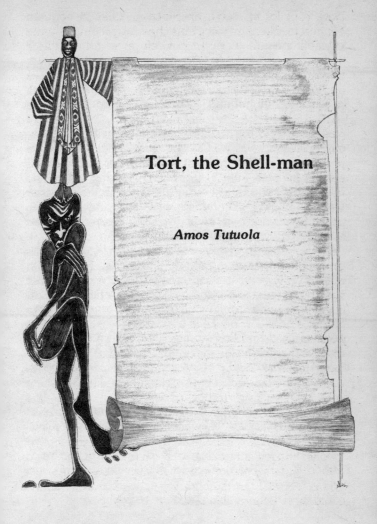

Tort, the Shell-man

Amos Tutuola

1. The Strange Fellows' Palm-Wine Tapster

Akiti and Tort, the Shell-man, were the natives of town called Eleegun. Akiti was a good palm tapper. His palm wine was of the best quality in the town. For this, his wine was not keeping long in the palm wine bar when the drinkers rushed in and bought all. Though the drinkers rushed to buy his wine and he was happy about this, he was not satisfied with the low price which they paid for him. It was far below of his expectation.

Akiti got one son, named Ireti, and some daughters, they were still too young at that time to pay heed to his profession.

Akiti continued to tap the best quality of palm wine to the drinkers. One morning, he descended from one palm tree, holding one pitcher full of wine in his left hand and climbing ropes and knife in the right hand. One strange fellow appeared in his front unexpectedly. Akiti greeted the strange fellow and then he moved to go and climb the next palm tree. The fellow stopped him and he spoke to him politely:

"My friend, shall I introduce myself to you first?"

"Yes, with pleasure," Akiti replied in a hurried voice and fear. "You can!"

"I am not a man of this earth, you know, but of the world beyond and I have dressed in human skin when I am coming to you!"

"What? Are you one of the deads from heaven?" Akiti hastily dropped the pitcher and his tapping knife in his hands on to the ground and asked with great fear.

"Of course, I am from heaven but I am sent to you in this form by my fellows!" the strange fellow explained in a thin voice.

"By your fellows? But where are they?" Akiti asked in fear and he prepared to flee.

"But my friend, don't be afraid," said the strange fellow calmly and he pulled Akiti back. "You see," he continued, "I simply put on this human skin so that you may not fear me! My fellows are not like the people of this earth," the dead went further, "but we the fellows of the world beyond have been drinking from your extraordinary palm wine for some time, but we could not get sufficient supply which could satisfy us."

"Is that so?" Akiti inquired with wonder.

"It is so," continued the strange fellow. "But being we are not getting sufficient supply of your wine, my fellows send me to you to bargain with you that you should stop to supply the wine to your customers, who are the drinkers, but supply to us only. And we shall be paying higher price than which the drinkers are paying for you."

"Are you sure that you will be paying a higher price for me?" Akiti, squinting at the strange fellow, asked sharply.

"Certainly," the strange fellow confirmed with a smile. "Do you agree to be supplying to us the palm wine every day?"

"I agree. But I am afraid," Akiti explained, "to be carrying it to you in your world beyond. But of course," continued Akiti hastily, "I don't *know* the road to your world beyond!"

"Not at all," replied the strange fellow. "But you will put all the wine inside this huge pot which is under the tree over there." He pointed hand to the pot and Akiti looked at the direction and he saw the pot there.

"When you have collected the palm wine into the pot," continued the fellow, "then you will put a number of pieces of small stones on the cover of the pot and those small stones will indicate how many pounds that which you intend to take for your wine. For instance, if you put ten pieces of small stones on the cover, we shall put ten pounds there for you. This means the number of small stones that which you may put there will be the number of pounds which we shall put there!"

"Okay, I agree to your terms. But when shall I start to fill the palm wine inside your huge pot?" Akiti asked with happiness.

"Please start to put the wine inside the pot as from today!" the strange fellow hastened Akiti. "Because we shall start to come to the pot and drink the wine as from this mid-night. But I warn you that you must return to your town as soon as you have filled up the pot with the palm wine. Because it is prohibited for the mankind to see us, even to spy us in our real form and that is why we choose the mid-nights to come out. And we shall put your money on the cover of the huge pot each mid-night that we come there to drink. Then when you come back in the morning to fill the pot with the wine, you will take your money. Do you agree to that?"

"I agree with happiness," Akiti replied, smiling.

"But this is a serious secret between you and we the strange fellows of the world beyond. You must not disclose to anyone that we come and drink the palm wine on your farm. And you too must not come and spy at us in the mid-night. This is very dangerous for you," the strange fellow warned Akiti and then he vanished unexpectedly.

But when the strange fellow had disappeared suddenly, Akiti breathed out heavily with fear and confusion. He, however, started to fill up the huge pot with the best quality of palm wine as from that day, with happiness for he believed that within a few months he would become a rich man in the town.

Then having filled up the strange huge pot with the palm wine that day, Akiti covered it with its cover, then to indicate the cost of the wine for the strange fellows he put ten pieces of small stones on top of the cover. Having done all that, he went back to his town. And it was hardly in the mid-night when the strange fellows of the world beyond came in great number to the huge pot. They first counted the number of the small stones which Akiti put on top of the cover of the pot, and they were ten in all.

Then they sat round the pot and started to enjoy themselves with the palm wine in it. After they had drunk the wine continuously for about one hour, they were so much intoxicated by it that they stood up. They started to sing the song of the strange fellows of the world beyond, and they started to dance merrily round the huge pot. But as soon as they had drunk the whole wine, they covered back the empty pot with its cover. And after they had put ten pounds on top of the pot, they returned to their world beyond before the darkness disappeared from the sky.

But hardly the morning sun appeared in the sky when Akiti came to the huge pot. But he was so happy when he met ten pounds on top of the pot that he hastily put it in his pocket and then he danced for some minutes. Now, Akiti was sure that each of the ten small stones was one pound.

Thus Akiti continued to tap the palm wine for those strange fellows and they left ten pounds on top of the pot each mid-night that they came to drink. And within a few years Akiti had become a very rich man in the town. So rich that the rest of the people were confused whether he had become a burglar.

But as Tort, the Shell-man, was among the people who were confused about Akiti's riches, and as he was cunning, selfish, greedy, treacherous and merciless and an expert tale-bearer, he assured the people of the town that he would find out the secret of Akiti's riches.

Now, Tort, the Shell-man, started to go to Akiti's house every day. He was helping him sharp his tapping instruments. Helping him fetch the water from the stream. After a few days, Akiti was so much impressed by Tort's eye-service that he took him to be his loyal bearer, and a good citizen who had changed from his bad behaviours to good behaviours.

But as Tort, with his usual cunnings, had disguised himself to be a good citizen and also as a trustworthy bearer, Akiti allowed him to live in his house and he was disclosing all his secrets to the Shell-man as if he were one of his family. But he did not tell him about the strange fellows, and he did not allow him to follow him to his palm tree farm.

But as time went on and Akiti continued to tap the palm

wine for the strange fellows, one day, Akiti became ill unexpectedly. The illness was so much serious that he could not go to the farm and tap the wine for those strange fellows of the world beyond.

"Ah!" cried the cunning Tort. "This world is vanity. There is only temporary enjoyment in the world! Today is weeping! Tomorrow is happiness! After tomorrow is hisses! Day after tomorrow is dance of joy, and after, a grief! But I am fed up with all these irregular life of this world! See now, Akiti who is feeding me and taking care of me, the sickness befalls him! Ah, what should I do now to help him out of his illness? Ah, ah, ah!" Thus Tort, the Shell-man, with his usual cunnings, distorted his face and started to weep bitterly in front of Akiti as if indeed, he loved him heartily.

"Thank you, Tort. That is all right. I know that you love me truly, but don't let my illness worry you. I shall be free from it soon. You hear?" Akiti comforted Tort. "Eh, please, Tort, call my son, Ireti for me!" Akiti shouted.

"Here is Ireti!" Tort went out and he returned with Ireti.

"Here I am before you, my father. But what can I do for you?" the son sat in front of his sick father, Akiti and he asked quietly.

"You see, Ireti, Tort has stopped all of his bad characters completely. He is a nice faithful man now!"

"You mean this very Tort has become a faithful man, my father?" Akiti's son, Ireti, asked with laughter.

"Certainly, my son!" Akiti confirmed loudly.

"Not at all, my father. Even Tort's bad behaviours are getting worse and worse every day!"

"No, my son. But Tort's behaviours towards me have proved that he has become a good citizen!"

"Well, he might have changed to a faithful citizen. But I have not yet seen that in his behaviours, my father!" Ireti emphasized and shrugged.

"But I am no more a traitor or a villain!" Tort shouted and pretended to be annoyed.

"Do you hear him now? He has confirmed all I am just

telling you about his changes! So as he is no more a traitor
or a villain or a criminal, I want him to go to my farm to help
me tap the palm wine for the strange fellows of the world
beyond!" Akiti disclosed his aim to his son, Ireti.

"My father, don't try to send Tort to your farm to tap
wine for the strange fellows. Tort is also a busy-body!" Ireti
warned his father aloud.

"Akiti, don't listen to your son, but just tell me the road
to your farm and I'll tap the wine for the fellows as well as
you are doing!" Tort shouted as he scowled at Ireti angrily.

"Good of you, Tort, the Shell-man. Look at that high
mighty hill which is on the outskirt of the town. Do you see
it?" Akiti stood up and he pointed at the hill through the
window.

"Yes, yes, I see it, far away!" Tort fastened at the hill and
shouted.

"All right, when you go behind the hill you will see my
farm there, though at about two kilometres from the hill.
Then you will see one small pitcher on top of each of the
palm trees. When you remove the pitcher, you will see that
some quantity of the wine has flowed into the pitcher.
Then you will pour the wine in it into the huge pot which
you will see under a tree near there. And it is so you will
pour the wine which is inside of all the pitchers into the
same huge pot. Having done so, then you will cover the
pot with its cover. Then you will put ten pieces of small
stones on top of the cover. And you must not wait to see
the strange fellows but you should return to the town at
once. Tort, the Shell-man, do not attempt to see the
fellows because they will come to the huge pot at mid-night
to drink their palm wine. I warn you again!

"Please go to the farm now and do the work for me!"

Akiti did not pay heed to his son's advice but he sent
Tort, the traitor and busy-body, to his farm.

Without hesitation, Tort took Akiti's tapping instruments
and he went to the farm. As he was very smart, he climbed
all the palm trees within a few hours. He poured the wine in
each pitcher into the huge pot. Then he replaced each

pitcher on top of each of the palm trees. After that he covered the huge pot with its cover and he put ten pieces of small stones on top of the cover.

But then Tort, the Shell-man, instead to return to the town, lurked in the bush, near the huge pot, in order to see those strange fellows of the world beyond.

"Has Tort returned from the farm, my father?" Ireti entered the room and asked from his father.

"He has not returned. But I wonder why he has kept so long on the farm!" Akiti replied to his son with throbbing heart.

"Hmmm, I am afraid, Tort is very dangerous!" Ireti remarked to his father and he shook his head.

"But Tort has proved himself to have changed from bad to good!" Akiti doubted.

"I am very sorry, my father, Tort will wait on the farm to see with his eyes the strange fellows. I am sure of that!"

"But I have warned him seriously not to try to see them!" Akiti feared.

"Well, let us wait and see the outcome!" Ireti said and then he shrugged to the outside of the house.

But Tort, the Shell-man, did not return and instead he lurked in the bush near the huge pot, kept waiting to see how the strange fellows of the world beyond looked like. When it was mid-night the fellows arrived with one drinking vessel in hand of each of them. They sat around the huge pot and then they started to drink the palm wine greedily.

Now, Tort, the Shell-man, from his lurking place, craned at the fellows and he saw them clearly, but he was not aware when their horrible appearance aroused him and he shouted horribly and with derision on them. But as they had drunk much that they were intoxicated highly and all of them stood up and were dancing drunkenly round the huge pot, with the fearful enchanted song of their own. They heard Tort's shout and derision:

"Aha-ah-a! I see you! You are too terrible and ugly for the human beings to look at! Hah! Those of you who are wobbled to one side! Those of you whose bodies are twisted! Those who have one foot but with oval head! Those of you with one eye! Those of you with mighty feet and with sharp horns on heads! And so many of you are without ears! Hah! Eh! But you all the strange fellows of the world beyond are really miscreated by your creator!" Tort shouted with derision and then he hastily crouched back into his lurking place.

"But who has seen us and scorned us bitterly like that?" All of them stopped dancing suddenly, in alert and great anger, and one of those with the wobbled body shouted angrily.

"It must be Akiti, our tapper, who has spied us out and disdained us bitterly like that!" the rest replied angrily.

"But let us search for him and catch him and then kill him at once, because I warned him that he should not wait and see us but to return to his town as soon as he had filled up our huge pot with the palm wine. Let us kill him now, otherwise he will tell our secret to all his people!" one of those with horns on head suggested angrily.

But as soon as Tort had heard that they wanted to kill him, he hastily escaped to the town before they started to search for him. Thus the strange fellows of the world beyond failed to kill Tort, who they took as Akiti, their tapper.

They then returned to their world beyond with great anger, and they waited till when they would get a good chance to do their worse to Akiti.

"Oh, Akiti, I am sorry that I have kept too long to return home as early as possible!" Tort, with his cunnings, shouted immediately he entered the house.

"But what has kept you so long on the farm?" Akiti shouted angrily.

"I wonder, when I was returning to the house, the faster I trekked the longer the road became!" Tort deceived Akiti.

"But what are you telling me? The road became longer when you were returning to the house!" Akiti was astonished.

"Certainly, the road became longer!" Tort confirmed his lie.

"My father, let me tell you, Tort has left trouble for you on the farm. I am quite sure of that, my father!" Akiti's son, Ireti, hinted his father aloud.

"But Tort, tell me the truth. Have you spied on those strange fellows?" Akiti turned to Tort and asked with fear.

"That is not true! If I waited and spied on the fellows it meant then I have belittled myself to you. It meant I was treacherous and I was a traitor and a merciless villain as the people have taken me to be!" Tort confirmed what he was.

"Well, I shall know everything which you have done on the farm when I go there in three days time or as soon as I am well," Akiti hissed and remarked confusedly.

But before three days, Akiti was already well. But as he was preparing to go to the farm, his son, Ireti, saw him. He told him that he would accompany him to the farm to help him tap the wine. Because Ireti was indeed afraid that Tort, the Shell-man, had spied on the strange fellows, although his father had warned him not to spy on them. But Akiti refused for his son, Ireti, to accompany him to the farm, for he was afraid that Ireti was so young that he would attempt to spy on those fellows.

However, when Ireti was sure that his father would not allow him to follow him to the farm, he put a little quantity of the ashes in his father's farm-satchel. Having done so, then he split the bottom of the satchel a bit to allow the ashes drop on to the ground little by little. Then he hid himself in one corner of the house, and from there he kept watching for when his father would leave the house for his farm.

But when Akiti got ready to leave, he simply hung his farm-satchel on his shoulder with his tapping instruments. Then he left the house without suspecting that his son, Ireti, had split the bottom of his satchel and put the ashes there. But when Akiti was trekking along on the road to his farm, the ashes began to spill along the road and thus the ashes gave a visible trail behind him.

One hour after that Akiti had left the house, Ireti left the house. He followed the trail of the ashes till when he came to the farm. But as he did not want his father to see him, he hid himself in a small bush which was near the huge pot in which his father used to fill the palm wine for the strange fellows. That was how Ireti traced the visible trail to his father's farm.

Then Ireti kept looking at his father as he (father) was climbing one palm tree to the top and then another, tapping the palm wine. Ireti was hiding or lurking in that small bush so that he might rescue his father from death because he was sure that the strange fellows would definitely come to kill his father that morning, in reaction to Tort's misbehaviour which had affected them a few days ago.

Soon Akiti had filled up the huge pot with palm wine and he prepared to leave for the town. As a matter of fact, the strange fellows appeared unexpectedly. And without hesitation, two of them chased Akiti as he was running away for his life. But as Ireti was seeing what was happening to his father, the two fellows dragged his father to the rest of the deads, who stood round the huge pot and were sulky in great anger.

Having forced Akiti to stand back on his feet, one of those who were with wobbled body questioned him.

"Why did you wait and spy at us a few days ago despite you had been warned that mankind is banned to see us in our proper form?"

"I have not done so since when I have started to tap the palm wine for you. More, I was ill for the past few days, so I could not come to the farm at all!" Akiti replied trembling.

"But who waited and shouted on us with disdain a few days ago?" the champion of the strange fellows shouted horribly.

"Perhaps the man who waited and shouted on you might be Tort, the Shell-man, who I sent to tap the wine for you. I made such arrangement with Tort so that you could get the wine to drink till when I was well," Akiti explained with fear as his son, Ireti, was looking at him from his hiding place.

"By the way, who is Tort, the Shell-man, you are mentioning often to us?" all the strange fellows shouted horribly.

"Tort, the Shell-man, is my townsfolk and my close friend who I trust indeed. But Shell-man is his nickname. Though he is clever and cheerful, he has been condemned by the whole people of the town, for he is too cunning, selfish, treacherous, cruel and he is also an expert traitor, liar, trickster, extortioner, highway robber and terror of terrors, who is ever born in our land. But he had confessed to me that he had stopped all of these his abnormal characters before I have befriended with him. So for his confession, I sent him to tap the wine for you!" Akiti defended himself by revealing Tort's abnormal bad characters to the strange fellows.

"Though your defence has aroused us to have mercy on you, we find you guilty for knowing Tort, the Shell-man, that he has multi-abnormal bad characters, but you sent him to your farm to tap the palm wine for us," the champion remarked angrily. "However," continued the champion, "the sentence is quashed and we have mercy on you because you sent Tort to tap the wine for us in order to satisfy us when you were ill. But instead to kill you mercilessly you will wrestle with each of us. If you can knock each of us to death, that means you are fortunate to continue to live on earth."

"But if any one of us knock you down to death then that is your fate. You will pass to everlasting world beyond. You will not see your wife, children and friends any longer. Do you agree to the terms, Akiti?" the champion of the strange fellows concluded while the whole of them kept quiet to hear Akiti's excuse.

"Although as we the people of the earth are not stones so we are liable to sick any time. But to let you have the wine to drink every mid-night, I sent Tort to tap it for you." Akiti reminded them once more.

"But I shall remind you now, Akiti, that 'the parrot is the bird of the sea,' is it not?" the one of those oval-headed fellows reminded Akiti with a proverb.

"Yes, it is. 'The kingfisher is the bird of the lagoon,' "
Akiti replied in proverb.

"Oh-o-oh! You know that. 'When we eat and drink we
must not forget our solemn promises,' or not so, Akiti?"
the oval-headed fellow brought Akiti's promises back to
his memory. This oval-headed fellow was the fellow who
disguised as a human and came to Akiti. And he made
arrangement with him to be tapping the palm wine for all of
them. But he warned Akiti not to disclose their secret to
anybody and Akiti promised him that day that he would
not. But now Akiti had let Tort known the secret of the
strange fellows of the world beyond, though not by his
own will, he would be punished.

"However, I agree to wrestle with every one of you,
once I have gone against my promises. But alas, in trying
not to disappoint you with the wine, I sent Tort to tap it for
you!" Akiti lamented as he was putting his spells on neck,
wrists, shins and knees.

Akiti's son, Ireti, who squatted and hid himself in a
small bush near there, was looking at his father as he was
preparing himself ready to wrestle with the strange
fellows.

Akiti hardly put on his spells when the champion of the
fellows gave order to one of those who had no ears to
wrestle with Akiti. But Akiti knocked that one to death at
once.

" 'The white ants may try, but they cannot devour the
rocks,' " Akiti's son, Ireti, whispered in proverb in his
lurking place. And within a few minutes, Akiti knocked all
of them to death except the champion whose head was
oval.

Then he walked to the spot of the wrestle, he stood
firmly on the ground like a big tree and he challenged Akiti
with great anger. Then both of them dashed against each
other. Akiti was wrestling with him with all his power. The
champion was trying all his power to raise Akiti high up and
knock him down to death but Akiti did not give him a bit of
chance. Thus Akiti, too, was trying all his power several
times in a moment to knock him down to death but the

oval-headed champion did not give him any chance to do so.

But as Akiti was dodging here and there and the champion was jumping here and there like a tiger. It was so Ireti was doing in his hiding place. Sometimes he craned at his father and then he hastily squatted back so that the champion might not see him. Sometimes when his father held the champion with all his power and he was trying to raise him up and knock him down to death, thus Ireti held a tree which was near him. He was shaking it and he was trying to lift up and then to knock it down. Sometimes he kicked the heavy stone which was near him. He was greatly confused at that moment as well as his father. All his father's attempts were arousing him to come out and help him but he must not let the champion see him.

At last, Akiti was so tired that he was unable to raise the champion up any longer. Having seen his father that he would soon give up the fight, Ireti began to shake and he began to perspire as he was moving here and there, kicking and boxing every object which was near him there.

As the wrestle continued and became more and more fierce, and Ireti saw that his father was getting weak and weak but the oval-headed champion was still strong. He began to whisper to his father to kick the champion in the belly. But alas, his father could not hear him. As Ireti continued to kick the ground, stone and trees here and there. The oval-headed champion raised his father, Akiti, high up and then he knocked him down to death at last.

Without hesitation, the champion ran wearily to the small bush in which Ireti lurked. He cut seven leaves from seven small trees. Though his hands nearly touched Ireti, being he was in hurry, he did not see him.

Then the strange fellow returned to the dead bodies of his fellows who had been knocked to death by Akiti. He squeezed all of the leaves together in both his palms, then he rubbed the juice which came out from the leaves on the eyes of his dead fellows. Then all of them recovered from death immediately except Akiti. And as soon as he threw the squeezed leaves on the ground there, he and his fellows disappeared immediately.

But when Ireti noticed that they had disappeared he came to the dead body of his father. He took the same squeezed leaves which the oval-headed champion threw on the ground. He rubbed his father's eyes with the juice which he forced out from them. And to his astonishment, his father recovered from his death immediately as well as those strange fellows. Then Ireti and his father went to their town at once.

Thus Ireti rescued his father, Akiti, from the strange fellows of the world beyond. But as soon as Tort, the Shell-man, learnt that Akiti had returned to his house, he fled to another part of the town where he was looking for another person to betray and dupe of his money.

But when Akiti failed to catch Tort and revenge on him, he came back to his house dejected.

"My father," Ireti appealed, "leave Tort, the Shell-man, for other people to revenge on him." But as 'a tormentor makes his victims stronger,' I believe, you will not allow anybody to betray you again like Tort, the Shell-man!" Ireti remarked in proverb.

2. Tort and the Dancing Market-Women

"Ah, this our present king's régime is bitter and unfortunate for the people of the town!" Tort, the Shell-man, shouted dejectedly, one morning.

"But why did you say so?" his wife, the Beetle-woman, asked.

"It is in our present king's régime that the great famine has besieged the town!" Tort explained bitterly to his wife.

"Of course, the famine is raging bitterly now in every part of the town!" Tort's Beetle-woman supported her husband's view.

"But I am dying of hunger now!" Tort lamented greedily to his wife.

"Not you alone are dying of hunger but so also for our children and myself. And about ninety per cent of the other people in the town are already in the trap of death!" The Beetle-woman was despaired.

"But how can we escape from the hunger?" asked Tort bitterly.

"We cannot escape the famine when it has already spread to every part of the town!" replied the Beetle-woman.

"But what of the king, too?" Tort wondered.

"But you should realize that, 'What affects the eyes also affects the nose,' " the Beetle-woman explained in proverb.

"Hmm," Tort hissed. "But of course," he continued in proverb, " 'Twenty children cannot play together for twenty years.' "

"But what do you mean by that?" Tort's wife was confused.

"What I mean by that is that the famine will not continue forever," Tort told his wife the meaning of his proverb.

Although Tort, the Shell-man, was a very handsome young man, he was the most greedy, cunning, omnivorous, slothful, and expert pilferer ever born in the town. He

and his children and wife, the Beetle-woman, were most
affected by the famine.

This famine, however, did not affect the next town. In
this next town, there was a famous market-place which
was flourished with all kinds of the food-stuffs. For this,
thousands of people came from various towns, cities and
villages, to buy and sell goods every market-day.

One day, Tort, the Shell-man, sat down in front of his
house, dying of hunger, while his wife and children were
held up inside the house by the hunger. Then with his
usual cunnings and abnormal bad characters, he began to
plan seriously in his mind, how he could go and carry
food-stuffs from the market to his house without paying for
them. Having thought and thought for a while, an evil
thought of how he would raid the market successfully
came to his mind.

As soon as the evil thought had come to Tort's mind, he
stood up. He went to the famous market-place. Then he
went from one stall to another and he noticed the kinds of
the food-stuffs which were in each. But he did not attempt
to steal from the food otherwise "the Parakoyi" or the
guild of traders would arrest him and punish him to death.

Tort, the Shell-man, however, returned to his town of
famine with full hope. But he hardly got to the town when
he went to one man who was a strong hole-digger.

"Good afternoon, the Hole-digger!" Tort greeted as he
was perspiring profusely.

"Hallo, Tort, the Shell-man! Why do I see you in my
house today in the hot sun like this? Hope there is nothing
bad which is chasing you about?" asked the Hole-digger
with a joke and laughter.

"Hmm," Tort grumbled and then he sat beside the
Hole-digger. " 'If there is nothing wrong, a woman will not
carry the dead,' " Tort replied in a proverb. "It is the
hunger," he continued, "that which has driven me to your
house!"

"What? Hunger?" The Hole-digger was shocked. "But I
have not seen or known 'hunger' as a living thing with feet,

since when I was born on earth!" he gazed at Tort and shouted with wonder.

"Is that so?" Tort wondered. "But of course," he continued, "as you are a hole-digger, you cannot experience the hunger because you are getting eatable things from the holes which you dig every day!" Tort shouted humorously. "The raging famine in the town now has caused the great hunger!" he added in the voice of an indigent person.

"Ho-o-o, is that so, I understand now what is chasing you about!" the Hole-digger exclaimed. "But, 'a hungry person has no mind for any other matter,' " he joked in proverb.

"And, 'the hunger does not realize that there is no money at home, but we feel hungry every day,' " Tort supported the Hole-digger in a proverb.

"All right, but what do you wish me to do for you, Tort, the cunning Shell-man?" the Hole-digger asked and hesitated.

"I wish you to help me dig a huge hole under the ground from my room down to the outskirt of the famous market-place which is in the next town," Tort begged with earnest.

"Well, to dig a huge hole in which a man can walk upright to the famous market-place is an easy thing for me to do. But you will give me one full basket of the kola-nuts. As you know, the kola-nuts are my refreshing food when I am digging holes," the Hole-digger demanded.

"Well—well," Tort raised his head up and murmured. "But, 'a roasted dog is very pleasant, but what shall we eat before it is roasted?' " Tort murmured to the Hole-digger in proverb.

"But," replied the Hole-digger in proverb, " 'one who does not give should not expect to receive.' "

"Well, if it is so, I shall go to some farms probably I may get some kola-nuts for you." Tort went away doubtfully.

But Tort could not get the kola-nuts especially this time of great famine. Instead, he filled up one bag with gravels and then he brought the heavy bag to the Hole-digger as kola-nuts. The Hole-digger hastily took the heavy bag from Tort. And he was so happy and pleased that he did not attempt to loose the bag and see what were inside it but he simply hid it in his room.

Then in the night, he dug a very huge hole under the ground from one of Tort's rooms down to the outskirt of the famous market-place. Then the following morning, Tort entered the Hole. He walked inside it to the outskirt of the famous market-place. Then he hid himself near the entrance of it. Then he was waiting for the daybreak when the market-women would arrive to the market with their food-stuffs.

As soon as it was daybreak, multitudes of women and men traders were arriving in the market. And when it was about eight o'clock and as the noises of the people were full up the air, Tort, the Shell-man, came out cautiously from his hiding place. He started to sing a kind of enchanting song unexpectedly.

The song was much enchanting when the multitude of the people heard it. They did not know when they left their food-stuffs and other wares. But they jumped up and started to dance madly about in the market. But as Tort continued to sing the song, the people were not aware when they danced far away from the market-place.

Then without hesitation, Tort walked to their stalls. He carried nearly all their food-stuffs into his huge hole. Having done so as quickly as possible, he blocked the entrance of the hole with a flat stone. Then through the hole, he carried all to his room. So he, his wife and children ate from the food to their entire satisfaction.

But as soon as the magic song died down and the market-women were conscious, they returned wearily to their stalls. But they were confused and panicked when they saw that almost all of their wares had disappeared. Then they, however, went back to their respective towns, cities, villages, etc. with empty hands.

It was so Tort, the Shell-man, scared the people away from the market-place with his enchanting or magic song and carried away their wares for a number of market-days. The market-women and other people thought that it was an evil immortal being who came to the market and carried their wares away each market-day.

Having seen that thousands of the women traders had deserted the market-place, "Parakoyi" or the guild of traders reported what was happening in the market to the king of this town.

Then the following market-day, the king and his regents went to the market-place, in order to see what was happening there for themselves. But as soon as Tort peeped from his huge hole and saw that people were already full up in the market and that they had displayed their wares in the stalls, he started to sing his usual enchanting song. And soon as people had danced far away with the king and his regents, Tort walked to the stalls and started to carry their food-stuffs into his hole. But as he continued to carry the food from one stall to another, he saw the crown and the tassel on the ground and he carried both together with the food into his hole. And through the hole, he carried all to his room.

The king was not aware when his crown fell onto the ground from his head and his cow-tail tassel fell down also from his hand, because he and his regents and the other people so much enjoyed the magic song that they were unconscious immediately.

Soon after Tort had stopped singing his magic song, the king, his regents and the other people became conscious. But when they returned to the market, they were extremely surprised and feared when they saw that almost all of the food-stuffs had been carried away.

However, the king and his regents returned to the palace with grief and fear. And the women and men traders returned to their respective towns, cities, villages, etc. with empty heads.

"Kabiyesi [Your Worship], where is your crown?" one of the chiefs asked with amazement.

"My crown! My crown! But where is my crown?" the king scrambled his forehead with both his hands and shouted terribly.

"And where is your tassel, too?" one of the councillors

asked.

"Oh, yes, my tassel as well! But where is it?" The king was greatly confused.

"Perhaps all had fallen off from you when Your Worship were dancing in the market-place!" another one of the regents reminded the king.

But when it was the next market-day, the king sent the Four-footed *Osanyin* (the god of healing and who is vast in magic spells of all kinds) to the market-place. He ordered him to catch and bring to him whomsoever deprived those market-women of their wares each market-day, and also to find and bring his crown and tassel (cow-tail) to him.

Though the Four-footed *Osanyin* went fearlessly to the market, he could not wait and catch the culprit once he had heard Tort's enchanting song. Instead, he danced and danced madly along the way to the palace. But to everyone's horror, three of his four feet had fallen off on the way, although he hardly reached the palace with the remaining one.

"Have you seen or caught the evil culprit who is raiding the market?" the king asked impatiently.

"Oh, Kabiyesi, 'an elephant's head is not a load for a child,' " the Four-footed *Osanyin* explained in proverb with a great fear. "Though I have a lot of magic spells and wands, I could not wait and catch one who is stealing the women's wares. But once I had heard his song, I started to dance and dance madly until I came back to you! Kabiyesi, this is not a simple matter at all! Even three of my four feet had fallen off my body and all of my spells and wands had fallen away from me as well on the way!" the Four-footed *Osanyin* explained to the king, trembling in fear.

"So you have failed to catch him?" the king wondered.

"Kabiyesi, I'll repeat it to you. 'An elephant's head is not a load for a child,' " the Four-footed *Osanyin* emphasized in proverb. "But Kabiyesi," he continued, "don't take it as an insult as I stand before you and that I am speaking to you in proverb—a messenger like me should not speak to you in that way!" The Four-footed *Osanyin* bowed with respect and apologized.

"Yes, I forgive you," the king pardoned him for speaking to him in proverb. "But how did the market raider look like?" one regent asked confusedly.

"I could not describe him at all because I am not bold enough to wait and see him well!"

"But have you seen my crown and my tassel [the cowtail]?" the king asked.

"I could not wait and search for them in the market," he replied.

"Oh, well, well," the king beat his head and said with a tired voice. "But you, the Four-footed *Osanyin*, who we the people of the town supposed to be the most powerful and vast in magic spells and wands, have failed to catch the invisible culprit!"

Fortunately, when the king was just lowering his head down in confusion, One-footed *Osanyin* leapt in to the palace. Having prostrated in front of the king, his regents and councillors, he said, "Kabiyesi, I have just heard of the invisible creature who is raiding the market. But I come to promise the king that I am well vast in magic spells and bold enough to catch the invisible creature!"

"You but One-footed *Osanyin* are promising me that you can catch the invisible market raider?" the king, his regents, chiefs, and the councillors derided the One-footed *Osanyin*.

"Certainly, it is a thing which I can do easily, though I am a One-footed *Osanyin!*"

"But the Four-footed *Osanyin*, who is more vast in magic spells and wands than you, had failed woefully to catch the culprit. How much more you with only one foot!" the king doubted.

"Kabiyesi, just send me to the market-place and see what I shall do!" One-footed *Osanyin* insisted to go.

"All right, tomorrow is another market-day. I order you, go there and catch the invisible thief and bring him before me," the king ordered doubtfully.

Then the following morning, which was the market-day, One-footed *Osanyin* took his magic spells, his blacksmith bellows, one thick sharp pointed iron rod and a little quantity of coals and fire. Then he went to the market-place. Having got there, he hid himself in one corner, he made furnace or fire with the coals. He put the iron rod in the fire. Then he started to blow the fire continuously with the bellows.

As soon as the market was full of people, and as usual, and as "a lobster-eater cannot stop at eating only one," was that Tort came to the market through his huge hole, to carry the women's food-stuffs away again.

But when he started to sing his usual enchanting song and the women and other people in the market heard it and then they danced madly away, he came from his hole to the market. But as the Shell-man was going from one stall to another and he was collecting the food-stuffs together. But One-footed Osanyin could not dance along with the women, for he had only one foot. Tort's magic song had no effect on him. So he saw Tort in the stalls and then he hastily took his pointed red hot iron rod from the fire. He leapt fast to Tort. Then he pushed him down suddenly and without hesitation he pierced the red hot iron into the unhappy Shell-man's neck.

Tort began to lament loudly for pain:

"Ah, One-footed Osanyin pardon me! Pardon me! And I have become your slave as from today and on! Please, One-footed Osanyin pardon me! I have become your slave today!" But the One-footed Osanyin did not listen to him, but he carried him to the king instead.

"What? So it is you, Tort, the Shell-man, who have been stealing away the market-women's wares all these days?" The king, his regents, chiefs and councillors were greatly surprised. "Well, Tort, the Shell-man, let you be the sacrifice for Osanyin from today and forever!" the king shouted and cursed him angrily.

It was so the king's curse had come upon Tort, the Shell-man, and thus he was ruined by his cunnings, greed and selfishness.

Then the king praised the One-footed Osanyin greatly and he gave him a valuable present as a reward of his bravery.

Kitty

Paul Bowles

Kitty lived in a medium-sized house with a big garden around it. She loved some things, like picnics and going to the circus, and she hated other things, like school and going to the dentist's.

One day she asked her mother: "Why is my name Kitty?"

"Your name is really Catherine," her mother said. "We just call you Kitty."

This reply did not satisfy Kitty, and she decided that her mother did not want to tell her the truth. This made her think even more about her name. Finally she thought she had the answer. Her name was Kitty because someday she was going to grow up into a cat. She felt proud of herself for having found this out, and she began to look into the mirror to see if perhaps she was beginning to look like a cat, or at least like a kitten.

For a long time she could see nothing at all but her own pink face. But one day when she went up to the glass she could hardly believe what she saw, for around her mouth tiny gray whiskers were beginning to sprout. She jumped up and down with delight, and waited for her mother to say something about them. Her mother, however, had no time for such things, and so she noticed nothing.

Each day when Kitty looked at her reflection she saw more wonderful changes. Slowly the whiskers grew longer and stood out farther from her face, and a soft gray fur started to cover her skin. Her ears grew pointed and she had soft pads on the palms of her hands and the soles of her feet. All this seemed too good to be true, and Kitty was sad to find that nobody had said a word about the marvelous change in her. One day as she was playing she turned to her mother and said: "Meow. I'm Kitty. Do you like the color of my fur?"

"I don't know," her mother said. "What color is it?"

"It's gray!"

"Oh, gray. Very pretty," said her mother, and Kitty saw with a sinking heart that she did not care what color the fur was.

After that she tried to make several neighbors remark on her fine whiskers, her velvety ears, and her short fluffy tail, and they all agreed that these things were very nice, and then paid no more attention to them. Kitty did not care too much. If *they* could not see how different she had become, at least she herself could.

One summer morning when Kitty awoke, she discovered that her fingernails and toenails had been replaced by splendid new pearly gray claws that she could stick out or pull in as she chose. She jumped out of bed and ran into the garden. It was still very early. Her mother and father were asleep, but there were some birds walking around on the lawn.

She slipped behind some bushes and watched. After a long time she began to crawl forward. The branches caught her nightgown, so she tore it off. When one of the birds came very close to her, she sprang forward and caught it. And at that moment she knew that she was no longer a girl at all, and that she would never have to be one again.

The bird tasted good, but she decided not to eat it. Instead, she rolled on her back in the sun and licked her paws. Then she sat up and washed her face. After a while she thought she would go over to Mrs. Tinsley's house and see if she could get some breakfast. She climbed up to the top of the wall and ran quickly along it to the roof of the garage. From there she scrambled down the trellis into Mrs. Tinsley's backyard. She heard sounds in the kitchen, so she went up to the screen door and looked in. Then she said: "Meow." She had to keep saying it for quite a while before Mrs. Tinsley came and saw her.

"Well, if that isn't the cutest kitten!" Mrs. Tinsley said, and she called to her husband and her sister. They came and saw the small gray kitten with one paw raised, scratching at the screen. Of course they let her in, and soon Kitty was lapping up a saucer full of milk. She spent the day sleeping, curled up on a cushion, and in the evening she was given a bowl of delicious raw liver.

After dinner she decided to go back home. Mr. Tinsley saw her at the kitchen door, but instead of opening the door for her, he picked her up and locked her into the cellar. This was not at all what Kitty wanted, and she cried all night.

In the morning they let her go upstairs, and gave her a big bowl of milk. When she had drunk it she waited in the kitchen until Mrs. Tinsley opened the door to go out into the yard. Then she ran as fast as she could between Mrs. Tinsley's feet, and climbed up onto the roof of the garage. She looked down at Mrs. Tinsley, who was calling: "Kitty, kitty, kitty." Then she turned and ran the other way. Soon she was in her own garden. She went up to all the doors and looked in. There were policemen inside the house with her mother and father. They were holding Kitty's torn nightgown in their hands, and her mother was crying and sobbing. No one paid the slightest attention to Kitty.

She went sadly back to Mrs. Tinsley's house, and there she stayed for many weeks. Sometimes she would go over to her own house and peek again through the doors, and often she saw her mother or her father. But they looked very different from the way they had looked before, and even if they noticed her, they never came to the door to let her in.

It was nice not having to go to school, and Mr. and Mrs. Tinsley were very good to her, but Kitty loved her mother and father more than she could love anyone else, and she wanted to be with them.

Mr. and Mrs. Tinsley let her go out whenever she pleased now, because she always came back. She would go to her house at night and look in through the window to see her father sitting alone reading the paper. This was how she knew that her mother had gone away. Even if she cried and pushed her claws against the window, her father paid no attention to her, and she knew that he would never let her in. Only her mother would do that. She would come and open the door and take her in her arms and rub the fur on her forehead and kiss her.

One day several months later when Kitty climbed over the wall into her own garden, she saw her mother sitting in a chair outside. She looked much better, almost the way she had used to look. Kitty walked slowly toward her mother over the grass, holding her tail in the air. Her mother sat up straighter, watching as she came nearer. Then she put out her hand and wriggled her fingers at Kitty. "Well, the pretty pussycat," she said. "Where did *you* come from?"

Kitty went near enough so that her mother could rub her head and scratch her cheeks. She waved her tail and purred with delight as she felt her mother's fingers stroking her fur. Then she jumped up into her mother's lap and lay curled up there, working her claws joyously in and out. After a long time her mother lifted her up and held her against her face, and then she carried her into the house.

That evening Kitty lay happily in her mother's lap. She did not want to try her father's lap because she was afraid he might push her off. Besides, she could see that it would not be very comfortable.

Kitty knew that her mother already loved her, and that her father would learn to love her. At last she was living exactly the life she always had wished for. Sometimes she thought it would be nice if she could make them understand that she was really Kitty, but she knew there was no way of doing that. She never heard them say the word *Kitty* again. Instead, because her fur was so long and fine that when she moved she seemed to be floating, they named her Feather. She had no lessons to worry about, she never had to go to the dentist's, and she no longer had to wonder whether her mother was telling her the truth or not, because she knew the truth. She was Kitty, and she was happy.

Princeps Tenebrarum

Principalities and powers . . .
Enormity stirs back of the words
When I say them aloud.

Principalities and powers
I say again and stop; somewhere
Something heavy has heard

And thinks I have called it by name.
I hold my breath, pull in my horns
Of thought, small as a snail

Until the cloud of its attention
Has swept overhead and crossed
Beyond the horizon.

Nothing but a mood, I tell
Myself, safer to doubt than believe
If doubt keeps it out,

And go to the window to look
At the real world, trees armored in
Ice, the freezing rain

That keeps away the insolent black tom;
Two nights he's challenged at the door,
And this morning on the porch

Glanced up to see me through the glass,
Stared yellow murder for an age,
And at his leisure, left.

—*John Alfred Taylor*

Riquiqui, I Love You!

Félix Martí-Ibañez

Let me tell you a story. I doubt very much whether anyone else can tell you such a story and truthfully say, as I can, that it is taken directly from his own experience.

It all started yesterday morning. I didn't know then who I was or where I came from. Let me hasten to add that I was not a victim of amnesia; yet if I hadn't felt like an adult I would have said that I had just been born. All I could remember was a large verdant meadow and that I was there alone. Vaguely I also remembered a square object shining on the grass not far from me. I didn't take time to examine it. I felt as though I had wings on my feet, and I ran and jumped through the dew-beaded grass and ate wild berries and drank the cool water that seemed to hang like a crystal string from between some rocks, and finally set out in the direction of a little town that stood out, white and sparkling, on the horizon.

Overflowing with love for everything and everybody, I entered the sunlit streets. It was early in the morning and the few people in the streets still bore the unmistakable sign of sleep in their eyes. My smiles and nods were met with indifference or with looks of surprise, and soon I realized that everyone drew away from me. A servant girl even looked frightened and quickly whisked her basket of fruits and vegetables out of my way. Perhaps, I thought, my hair is messy and my face black from the berries I had for breakfast. But I craved the company of others, so I entered a crisp little garden with a vineyard. In a hammock slept an old lady half sheltered from the sun by golden vines. She was wonderful to look at—plump and soft, pink and shiny, her cheeks blooming with happiness, her every line exuding profound contentment. Carefully I waved the flies away from her face. The sun, stealing through the vines, covered her with tatters of gold. The water of an irrigation canal nearby, overcome by the calm of the morning, quietly gurgled accompanied by the buzz of a bee. I could have stayed there for hours tasting the sweet peace. Suddenly the old lady opened her eyes and let out a scream that must have been heard over the whole western hemisphere. Frightened, I took to my heels followed by her screams.

Puzzled and a little disheartened, I walked the streets. Astonishment and even antagonism met me at every turn, and I began to wonder whether my appearance could be *that* shabby or repellent. Did these people take me for a beggar or a criminal? The children—God bless their trusting souls!—were the only ones unperturbed. With smiling little faces they waved at me, but their mothers frowned and quickly pulled them away.

By this time it was midmorning and the sun was hot. The cool shadows beyond the wide-open doors of a workshop beckoned and, heedlessly, I went in. Before my eyes could become accustomed to the darkness, I realized by the smell that it was a carpenter's shop. The fresh aroma of lumber was pleasant, and as the darkness lifted I enjoyed the sight of curled shavings, smooth planks and half-finished furniture. I was glad Christ had immortalized this trade above all.

I managed, not without difficulty, to make myself comfortable in an unfinished rocking chair and tried in vain to fan myself with a newspaper. The fragrant darkness permeated my senses and soon I felt drowsy. But just as I was about to fall asleep, I was shocked onto my feet by deafening shouts. Three workers returning to the shop had caught sight of me in their rocking chair and, yelling in the most frightening manner, they darted about for sticks with which to vent their wrath upon me. I didn't hesitate. Like a streak of lightning I shot through the door and ran until I turned the nearest corner and came to a deserted street.

Breathless, perplexed, sad, I was walking up the street when my attention was caught by a little white shop, its windows decorated with the most exquisite array of pastry ever beheld by the human eye. The divine aroma drifting through the open windows reached the darkest corners of my empty stomach. Hunger gnawed at my very entrails. So abandoning all caution and with praiseworthy determination, I thrust my head through the door. A red-headed young man gaped at me for about one second, long enough for his face to turn apoplectic, and then with unwonted force hurled at me the object he was holding. Fortunately, it was only a cream pie. With one eye temporarily out of order, I rallied just in time to see him grab a scale from the counter. There was no time for explanations. I just took to my heels again.

The next thing I knew, I was on the edge of town. A deserted, dusty road stretched before me. On my right stood a lonely barn, its door ajar. Cautiously I entered. The sweet odor of newly cut hay enfolded me. Bitter experience had taught me to be wary of delightful scents, but my fatigue was overwhelming and, with a heavy sigh, I threw myself down. Stretching out, I brushed against something protruding from the straw. It was a small white hand so delicately molded that the fingers resembled the tips of a star. Holding my breath and wondering whether once more I would have to run for my life, I stared at the lovely hand as it waved in the air, groped in all directions, and finally met my face.

"Hello!" a muffled voice said.

"Hello!" I replied, burying my face deep in the hay to keep it out of sight.

The straw tickled my nostrils and the hay suddenly felt hard against my body.

"What are you doing here?" the voice asked.

"Waiting for the townspeople to calm down so I can get away," I answered my invisible questioner. "I want to get as far away from here as possible."

The straw stirred again.

"Why are you afraid of the townspeople?"

"Because they tried to beat me up on three occasions."

"You must have done something very bad."

"No. I only wanted to be friendly."

I heard a stifled laugh and the straw shook.

"It always happens that way. What's your name?"

I looked around me abashed. A ray of sun as tense as a guitar string stretched from the threshold of the door up to the ceiling. Golden flies with spangled wings darted to and fro on it like tightrope walkers. I struggled with the realization that I could not answer the question asked me.

"I don't know. I don't think I have a name."

"How silly! Everyone has a name."

"I know. But I have forgotten mine."

"Where do you come from?"

"I don't remember that either."

The straw moved impatiently.

"You ought to do something about your memory. Tell me, is there anything at all you do remember?"

I told briefly what I remembered of the meadow I mentioned before and what had happened when I tried to make friends in town.

"Do you know what the shiny object was that you say you saw?"

"It sparkled so under the sun that I could not see what it was."

"What a pity! It might be the key to the mystery. However, don't worry too much about it. I'll help you to find out who you are."

"Who are you?" I asked, thinking that by now I had the right to ask questions.

There was a sigh followed by the upward flight of a few straws.

"Riquiqui. Silly name, isn't it?"

"On the contrary, it's lovely."

"Glad you like it. Yours is the first friendly voice I've heard since I started diving for the pearl."

"What pearl?"

"A divine pearl with all the colors of the rainbow. You have to dive right in, without fear, to find it."

"Dive? Where?"

"Into cities, towns, roads."

"But people dive into lakes, rivers, the sea, not into cities and roads."

"All the more reason for *me* to dive in land, where there are more opportunities and less competition."

I recognized the logic of her reasoning.

"Tell me more," I begged.

Only then did Riquiqui emerge from the haystack.

Just as a single drop of water can contain all the loveliness of the sky and the sea, Riquiqui was the essence of human beauty. She was very young, perhaps sixteen, with hair like copper, a delicate ivory-textured oval face, and green eyes speckled with gold dots. Small, with elusive lines, she was a fugitive from a Raphael painting.

With quick little gestures she sat down next to me, while I shook the straw from my body.

"Do you like to listen to stories?" she asked me with a voice like the sound of a silver flute.

"Very much, especially if they are not true."

"Well, mine is as true as an arithmetic book. I don't remember my parents, but Casilda, my godmother, used to say—"

"Where were you born?" I interrupted her.

She pointed vaguely toward the door.

"Out there, on the other side of the mountain. But as I was saying, Casilda, my godmother, used to tell me wonderful stories all day long. She and I lived in a very beautiful house, quite different from other houses because it had no roof. Now that I think of it, it must have been the ruins of an ancient palace. There were columns of white, pink, and black marble, alabaster benches, jasper chairs, and tables of jade. The roof must have caved in with the years, so we enjoyed life in a palace and yet were outdoors all the time, with only the blue dome of the sky for a roof in the daytime and the silver lamps of the stars at night. The forest crept right into the house. There were arbors with sweet luscious grapes hanging from the columns like garlands of emeralds. Swallows nested on a marble and gold dressing table. To look at myself in the mirror I had to push aside curtains of blooming honeysuckle, and when I bathed in an onyx basin the squirrels chased one another along the edge and robins and blackbirds daintily dipped their beaks in the fresh rain water with which it was filled.

"What wonderful days! I used to sleep in a hammock that hung from two columns in the shade of an apricot tree, and during the night the tree shed its blossoms, providing me with a fragrant blanket. In the morning I would wake up to the touch of Casilda's silver wand on my brow. She looked so beautiful in her golden mantle, bending over the hammock, a tender smile on her face! For breakfast we always had berries and grapes with honey from wild honeycombs. Then we would bathe in the pond amid white and black swans, and we would walk through the woods gathering scented flowers, play with rainbow-colored birds, and watch the busy golden bees. During the lazy hours of the day Casilda told me wonderful stories. At night we would build a huge fire and all our little friends from the forest would visit us and we would sing and dance. And when my eyelids began to droop, Casilda would again touch my brow with her silver wand and I would fall asleep and dream of fascinating journeys through enchanted lands.

"One day Casilda told me a beautiful story about a magnificent pearl with all the colors of the rainbow. Nothing was ever denied, she said, to anyone who possessed the pearl. Everything he desired, any wish he made, was always granted him. From that moment on I was possessed by the desire to own the pearl. I begged Casilda to let me go find it. She smiled and said that the obstacles I would meet with would be too difficult. But I insisted and Casilda finally gave her consent. She taught me some wonderful magic tricks so that I might never suffer hunger; then she kissed me good-by and left me at the outskirts of the woods right near a little town.

"I entered the town with my heart jumping in my breast like a fish in a stormy sea. I felt like the heroine of a fairy tale. I was seeking the magic pearl and I wanted to plunge into the streets and come up, like the divers of Ceylon, covered with clinging seaweed and mysterious phosphorescences, holding in my teeth the rainbow-colored pearl.

"For hours I walked through the streets, gaping at everything I saw. The houses, the people, the lights, the noise—everything was a delight to my senses. The world I had come from held aromas as delicate as the remembrance of an aroma, colors as tenuous as reminders of colors, sounds as soft as illusions. But this other world was noisy and loud, with violent colors, dazzling lights, and strong odors. For hours I peeked through windows into scenes that reminded me of the pictures in Casilda's books."

Riquiqui paused for a moment. The air was sultry, the hay warm. The sunlight brought into the barn the blond picture of the earth inflamed by the heat. Through the door drifted the smell of dry earth and sun-ripened wheat, and the buzzing of flies like a song of the wind. My eyelids began to droop. Drifting toward the smoke castle of sleep, I vaguely heard myself asking, "What happened?"

"What happened? Nothing happened! *Nothing!* Are you listening? Don't fall asleep yet! I decided to make use of the magic tricks Casilda had taught me. I craved to attract the attention of the people around me and thus become part of their lives. One of my godmother's favorite tricks was to reduce me in size to a couple of feet. I could have made myself even tinier, but I was afraid that someone might step on me. So I made myself as small as a doll, anticipating the astonishment on people's faces. And what happened? The first door I knocked on a man came out and he was even smaller than I! The little man, freckled and ill-humored, with a loud checkered suit, pointed his thumb over his shoulder and said, 'We don't need any more midgets. We are too many already. No work for anyone!' Behind him I could see eight or ten people of my height sitting around playing cards.

"Sad but not discouraged, I started walking again until I came to an elegant house set off from the others by very high hedges. I made my way toward it. I would rectify my former mistake by doing one of my best tricks. I won't tell you how it's done, for it is Casilda's secret, but by a method all our own I rubbed my body until it became invisible. Thus, with only my face visible, suspended as if in midair, I entered the house through an open window.

"The ground floor was filled with weapons and armor, ancient armchairs, tapestries, and silence. There was no light anywhere and no sign of life, and I was about to leave when from the floor above a low murmur suddenly descended. I groped my way up the dark staircase and into the room where the noise seemed to originate. It was so dark that I could see nothing, but I heard low whispers and finally I could make out white hands joined in a circular chain. Soon I heard a soft 'tap, tap,' as if someone were rapping on a table, followed by a squeaking voice that I could not understand. I waited for a while and, finally, fed up with it all, I leapt right into the middle of the circle of hands, landing on top of a table. All around me glowing eyes bulged out of their sockets when they saw my face suspended over the table.

"There was a moment of painful silence and then I heard a storm of protests. 'What impudence!' someone cried out. 'An elemental! I thought that only serious spirits were summoned at these seances. I shall immediately leave the association.' There were shouts, chairs toppled in the darkness, someone pinched my leg and, highly indignant, I stalked out of the room.

"Once more in the street I stopped to reflect. I would have to do much better if I wanted to get anywhere. I was hungry and my head hurt. Returning to my normal appearance, I made my way to the town's main square. On one side stood a white building and people hurried in and out like hard-toiling little ants. I resolutely crossed the square and entered the building. Both sides of the main lobby were lined with glass-enclosed rooms, where men, bending closely over enormous desks, wrote things in huge books while puffing incessantly on their cigarettes, completely indifferent to the host of people waiting outside their doors. It was all so vast, so gray, inhospitable, imper-

sonal, and cold. I heard a woman complain that civil
service employees in that town took their own good time
about everything. It all looked to me like a gigantic fish
bowl with colorless fish magically frozen in eternal immo-
bility, and it occurred to me that I could have found no
more propitious place to display the tricks Casilda had
taught me.

"So while the clerks pompously rustled their papers, I
climbed up one of the walls until I reached the ceiling and
my body hung upside down. One woman fainted and the
others fled screaming in terror. And still the clerks stubbornly went on smoking, their heads buried deep in their
papers. Accompanying myself with a song, I began to
swing from my big toe like a chandelier. Only then did the
officials look up.

" 'You think she's drunk?' asked one of them, pen-
holder in mouth.

" 'Nah!' replied the other, scratching his nose. 'She just
wants to attract attention. When the janitor comes I'll have
him throw her out.'

"And without another look or word, they went back to
work.

"I was a dismal failure but I was not yet defeated. Out in
the street again, I stretched and stretched until I was eight
feet tall. A little boy shouted something I could not make
out and pointed to a huge tent at the end of the street from
which came the sound of music. I went there, but hardly
had I stuck my head through the canvas door than I
withdrew disappointed. Inside the tent, a dozen men and
women in colorful costumes were practicing somersaults.
They were even taller than I!

"Weary, hungry, disillusioned, I found this barn and lay
down to rest and reflect how I might further use my talents
in this world where no one is astonished at anything."

Silence followed, heavy with Riquiqui's and my disappointment, the heat and the fragrance of the wheat. Suddenly I leapt to my feet.

"Riquiqui, let's go out again. This time we'll be together
and we'll show these people how wonderful you can be."

Clapping her hands enthusiastically she stood up, tall and slender, all ivory in her white dress, her hair like gleaming copper, her face a rosebud, an Easter song. Shaking the wisps of straw off her white dress, she asked, "Can you remember your name now?"

"No, I can't."

"It doesn't matter. I'll call you Ariel. Casilda told me that Ariel is the angel of the wind and of ideas."

We went out into the baking sun. From the town the wind brought us the frolicsome sound of music. Guided by the thread of melody, we walked until we reached a square crowded with people jostling one another in front of a large tent. At the entrance stood musicians with instruments that sparkled in the sun, heavily painted women in brilliant skirts, and a man on a platform shouting so fast that I could not understand anything he said. Instinctively we walked around the tent to avoid the crowd. The air smelled of pastry, roasting almonds, caramel, and carnations. Only the sun rivaled the music in intensity. Finally, we found a back entrance barred by some men dressed in black suits with long tails and white shirts. Recalling my previous experiences, I cautiously stayed behind while Riquiqui walked up to ask them how we might get in.

I sat down under a tree and watched Riquiqui talking with the men. First their faces reflected indifference, then annoyance, and finally a spark of interest as Riquiqui raised her little fingers in the air and from their tips spurted shiny gold coins. Then she touched things around her—a whip, spurs, bells, wooden planks, sandals—and they all changed into gold. The men looked startled, but suddenly bells rang inside the tent and they quickly ran in. Only one hesitated a little, said something to Riquiqui, and then he too vanished inside the tent.

Only then did I approach Riquiqui. Her eyes sparkled with excitement.

"Ariel," she said, bringing her little mouth close to my ear, "this gigantic cloth house is called a circus and all sorts of creatures—giants, dwarfs, horses, elephants—do marvelous things inside to attract all those people out on the square. The man who spoke to me is the director. He was interested in what I did and wants to see me after the show, which is about to begin.''

"What shall we do in the meantime?''

"I háve an idea. We'll go inside and when they least expect it I'll do one of my best tricks. If they like it, they may let us remain.''

The little old watchman said nothing as we went in. He must have thought we were performers too, an idea that filled me with pride. Inside, I was blinded by the lights and deafened by the noise. Riquiqui whispered in my ear, "Stay here and don't move. When I finish my trick, come over to me.'' And before I could answer her she disappeared into the crowd.

A moment later, two uniformed men wielding long thin sticks shoved me rudely into a corner and I found myself with the bareback riders and their horses, who were warming up. Only then did I get a full view of where I was. It was an immense tent of canvas and wood, with thousands of people sitting on benches circling round and round right up to the top. The noise was deafening. Flashes of colored lights danced over the multitude. A band filled the air with sounds of brass and copper. In the center was a ring of sand, vacant and overhung by a complicated net of ropes, loose or tied a thousand ways, forming a gigantic cobweb.

Trumpets sounded and into the ring, magically illuminated by shafts of light—crimson, violet, green, orange, and lemon—there paraded all sorts of individuals and animals accomplishing extraordinary feats. The magnificent spectacle held me transfixed. Finally, after a solemn roll of drums, men and women dressed in spangled white tights swung on long ropes from one end to the other high in the air near the top of the tent, while below, to the strain of a Viennese waltz, ten elephants led by scantily clad girls did all sorts of pirouettes. Both the spotlights and the attention of the public were divided between the air and the earth, between the angels hanging from ropes and the elephants cavorting on the sand. And then Riquiqui made her appearance.

A sixth sense warned me of her presence. I raised my head as high as I could. Yes, there she was, way up, as lofty and brilliant as the silver star atop a Christmas tree, or like a bird about to take flight. The reflectors were so dazzling that I had but a partial glimpse of her; besides, the trapeze artists cut the curve of my vision. But through the tangle of ropes, ladders, cables, and trapezes, I could see her, all ivory and rose, waving her slender arms as if about to dive and swim through the illuminated air of the circus.

Breathlessly I awaited the inevitable. There was a sinister roll of drums. The multicolored lights were focused on the trapeze artists. The elephants froze in dancing postures. In the center of the ring, a gentleman with a wide-brimmed hat thundered that the performers were now going to attempt their most difficult feat. Silence spread over the public like a huge fan. Five beams of light suddenly stabbed the air and flooded it with color. I could no longer see Riquiqui and my stomach contracted with a presentiment of great calamities. For one instant I shut my eyes. When the shouting exploded, I opened them again and gasped. At the critical moment Riquiqui had crashed the act.

It was, no doubt, her greatest trick. Like a gigantic butterfly, she sailed through the air, her arms spread like wings, her body, enveloped in gold and rose brilliants, executing golden and crimson arabesques. In the silence that followed the first outburst I could hear the soft swish of her wings fluttering in the reverberating light. The butterfly flew around the terrified trapeze artists, over the heads of the stupefied public, right up to the top of the tent, and then swooped down with dizzying speed past the elephants' trunks.

Next to me, one of the men in black tails let out a roar of rage.

"Damn girl! Get a stick, a broom, anything. Make her come down. She's ruining the show."

I gave him a shove that brought him down on his back and then I rushed into the ring to warn Riquiqui. But it was too late. The frightened elephants were already stamped-

ing and the noise could be heard on the moon. One
elephant ripped off the door of the lion cage. The animal
trainers began to shout that there was no cause for panic,
that the lions were as meek as lambs. But no one seemed
to hear him.

The band heroically continued playing until another
elephant, with all the delicacy he could muster, swooped
up the conductor with his trunk and dropped him into a tub
of water. Kicking all obstacles aside, I pushed through to
Riquiqui just as she fluttered gracefully to the ground.
Some children—the only ones that had not lost their
heads—cheered her wildly. Just then one of the animal
trainers missed hitting me over the head with a club. I did
not hesitate. Swooping Riquiqui up and onto my shoulders, I plunged through cages, ropes, elephants, lions,
attendants, and benches, and, through a rip in the canvas,
out into the sunlight.

The sun shone radiantly and the light blinded me. But a
cry from Riquiqui opened my eyes wide. A dozen men
with clubs in their hands were blocking our way. The circus
people were out for revenge. The blood boiled in my
veins. No one was going to touch Riquiqui. In a thundering
voice I threatened them, "Get back or you'll eat the dust!"

The effect of my words was amazing. Astonishment and
fear painted on their faces, they slowly lowered their sticks
in a graveyard-like silence and drew back, making way for
us to pass. With Riquiqui still on my back, my head held
high, though my legs were really shaking, I walked proudly
past them. When I looked back a few minutes later, they
were still standing stupefied and terror-stricken.

We gave the matter no more thought. My legs are strong
and Riquiqui, as light as a garland of flowers around my
neck, did not impede my progress as I ran away from the
circus. We stopped to rest in the middle of the woods. A
mauve twilight fell on the trees like a satin shawl. The grass
we sat on was soft, the water in a nearby stream was cool,
and the wild berries we ate were ripe and sweet. Suddenly
the sky was afire with a myriad of twinkles, the crickets fell
silent, and the frogs called out from the still darkness.

Riquiqui then spoke sadly. She could not understand what was wrong. She had had nothing but misfortunes since leaving her godmother. These strange people were used to things more fantastic than what she could offer. She had dived right into their midst in search of the rainbow-colored pearl and had hit her head against a muddy bottom. I was her only friend. We would never separate, she said. And my heart began to dance as wildly as fallen leaves in a storm.

A few moments later, having recovered her optimism, Riquiqui, her face a new wonder under an old moon, announced that the following morning we would continue exploring the strange world we were in. She was certain that everything would end well, she said, and cheered by her own optimism she jumped up.

"Look!" she shouted. "The moon and the stars are my friends. They will give me a cape with spangles." Spreading out her arms, she whirled round and round on the grass, and—I don't know whether I imagined it—suddenly there were tiny brilliant dots all over her dress as if the sky had stripped itself of all its stars and hung them on her. When she grew tired, she lay down near me and soon we fell asleep.

A moon ray, tickling the most sensitive part of my anatomy, my nose, awoke me. Riquiqui lay all huddled up at my side, her head deep among tiny wild flowers. Bees, sparkling like diamond chips, darted around her. I tried to wave them away, but she opened her eyes and, brightening the night with her smile, she said, "Don't drive them away. Bees are my friends, they are tiny merry souls who sing all the time while building a house of gold."

And then she asked me for some water and I went to the brook to fetch it. Floating on the water, in the middle of a bright circle of moonlight, I saw a small blue paper boat, apparently impatient to touch every port in the world, and on the other side of the narrow stream a little boy perhaps ten years old. He had eyes the color of roasted chestnuts and his face was sprinkled with freckles.

"Hello," I said. "What are you doing here?"

"Following the *Invincible*, my boat."

"Where do you come from?"

"Shantiniketan."

"Shanti what?"

"Don't be stupid! Shantiniketan. It's not hard to say. It means the Dwelling of Peace and it's a vacation camp for children."

"Where on earth did they get that name?"

"From Rabindranath Tagore, who founded such a place in Calcutta. Our teacher repeated the name every day until we all learned it."

An idea struck me.

"Would your teacher give my friend and me something to eat?"

"Of course. Come on! Our teacher will give you plenty of food. It's only a short distance from here, straight up the river."

I hurried back to Riquiqui, told her about the little boy, and said that I would go ahead to explore the situation and would then come back for her. Then I followed my little guide to the Dwelling of Peace.

In a clearing of the woods there rose a large stone and marble house with white columns that were trimmed with banners, garlands of flowers, and colored ribbons, as if in preparation for a celebration. Everywhere I looked, white-clad children were hard at work weaving wreaths, braiding ribbons, and hanging flowers on the columns. One could hear their little souls tinkling like bells.

A lady came down a vine-lined staircase to greet me. She was as tall as a palm tree, beautiful as a star, stately and serene, with lucent skin and a waterfall of champagne-colored hair framing her face. A purple shawl covered her shoulders.

"You must be tired and hungry. Eat first, and then we shall talk." Her voice was a stream of silver.

In the light of the lanterns, amid great general curiosity, I devoured three portions of oats and milk served in sparkling solid gold bowls.

When I was comfortably stretched out on the grass, the

lady addressed me.

"Where is she?"

"Who?"

"Riquiqui."

"How did you know?"

"I know many things. For instance, I knew you would come tonight. The celebration is for you."

"For us?"

"That is not the only surprise we have in store for you. Just wait and see." She turned to the children. "Is everything ready?"

"Yes. Everything," replied fifty voices.

"Riquiqui will be here tonight and must be received as what she is: a princess."

I stared around, my mouth agape.

"A princess? I should have known!"

"Riquiqui," the lady explained, "is more than a princess. But I shall tell you about that later. The important thing is that she will arrive at her favorite hour, when the sky is ablaze with stars and the meadows with fireflies. Her dress will float in the wind, her face will be a warm golden color, her smile will be the brightest lantern, and her heart will be full of poetry. The banners will wave gaily, the sleeping birds will burst into song, and at midnight dawn will shed its premature pinks."

The bonfires exuded the fragrance of sandalwood. Sparkling gold and silver bowls overflowed with honey, fruits, cheeses, milk, and sweet juices. A tree sent forth the cooing of doves. The children broke into a soft melody. The night air seemed to be holding its breath so as not to disturb the fragile peace of the scene. It was like in a picture book. In my heart tinkled a bell of peace.

"This is marvelous!" I said to the lady. "You are making these children *live,* not read, their fairy tales. But I should be going back to Riquiqui."

She smiled. "Riquiqui is already on her way here. I see her walking along the bank of the stream."

"Then I really ought to go to her. She may be frightened."

"Princesses in the woods are never frightened. The good spirits protect them."

"How do you know that Riquiqui . . . ?"

"Because I am Casilda, her godmother."

A child placed a bundle of green branches and rust-colored leaves on the staircase. Over my head swayed a rope of pink buds. The children's singing rose and fell like the tides of the sea.

"When I let her go out to face the world," Casilda continued, "I knew that she would have many disagreeable surprises, that she would find no understanding. But I had to let her go, for she was fated to go out one day in search of the rainbow-colored pearl. And she was fated to find it with you."

"With me?"

"Yes, you play an important part in her story. In fact, you are the best chapter. In you I have placed all my confidence. You have been chosen to lead her to the pearl."

Meanwhile the children were hanging a large mirror, framed with ivory, mother-of-pearl, and flowers, so that Riquiqui might see her beauty reflected in it.

At that moment she arrived. With majestic steps she emerged from the thick woods and joined her godmother in front of the house. Their dresses, waving in the breeze, were burnished by the moon. Casilda let her shawl drop from her shoulders, revealing a dress as incandescent as the sun. Then her fingertips gently touched her brow and a magnificent light spread around her temples and head. I fell to my knees, gasping.

"A fairy!" I cried. "Casilda is a fairy! And I thought they existed only in storybooks. I should have known. Riquiqui is a princess under the protection of her fairy godmother."

Casilda embraced Riquiqui tenderly and the children clapped their hands and shouted with joy. Timidly, I approached Riquiqui.

"Princess . . ." I began, but she brought her hand to my mouth.

"Don't be silly. To you I am Riquiqui."

With her arm round my neck we advanced toward the staircase, where the large mirror, hanging from ropes of flowers, swung lightly in the night breeze. And suddenly struck with terror, I stopped. No! No! It was not possible. Riquiqui looked radiant in the mirror, but I—my eyes anxiously bored into the dark shining depths, I was nowhere in the mirror. Instead, next to Riquiqui, stood a magnificent white horse.

In vain I sought myself in the mirror. No doubt about it—I was not there. It was as if an invisible sponge had wiped out my image. I kept staring at the mirror and the white horse stared back at me with great wide eyes. It was a magnificent animal, with a white mane, a proud powerful neck, and fine gray eyes. I stretched my hand out toward the mirror and the horse stretched out his paw. Completely bewildered I stammered something to Riquiqui. Her hand caressed my head tenderly and in the mirror I saw her hand caressing the head of the horse. I then understood the terrible truth.

"I'm a horse!" I screamed.

I don't know whether any of you has ever had a similar experience. If not, then you cannot possibly understand what I felt at that moment. I can hardly remember what happened in the next few moments. I only know that we sat down on the stairs and that the celebration began soon after. Perhaps Casilda wanted to make me forget my terrible predicament, but she did not succeed. For I hardly heard the drums and flutes, I barely noticed the parade of lanterns and the dances, and I vaguely realized that the oboe was accompanied by the soft mooing of the cows. Perfume censers swung and hymns were intoned, but nothing could shake me out of my stupor. For over and over my brain hammered out the same thing. "I am a horse. I am a horse. I am a horse."

Casilda and Riquiqui did not seem worried about my overwhelming discovery. Of course, they had known all along that I was a horse, but that need not have made them so callous. Like maddened moths fantastic ideas whirled round and round in my head. Had I been a horse all my life? Had I just recently become a horse? If this was so, why hadn't I recognized the change it involved in my habits? If, on the other hand, I had always been a horse, why did I think and feel like a man?

I made a desperate effort to remember, and little bits of scenes started lining up in correct formation like soldiers obeying orders. I remembered my excitement in the beginning in the meadow, my pleasure in running through the grass, the sensation of having wings on my feet—only they weren't wings but four robust, fleet hoofs. I remembered how I had been rebuffed at every turn by the townspeople. No wonder! Who likes to wake up and see a horse staring at him, or find a horse seated in a rocking chair fanning himself with a newspaper, or thrusting his head through a door? Now I understood why I had so frightened the circus attendants who threatened Riquiqui and me with their sticks. A *talking* horse! Could there be anything in the whole wide world more ridiculous, more absurd, more fantastic? Now I understood why Riquiqui had hung on to my neck every time we fled. And my fondness for vegetables, fruits, and roots, my speed and my physical stamina—it all made sense now. Yes, it was all clear now, all except how long I had been a horse. Since birth? By accident? If since birth, why didn't I think and neigh like other horses? If by accident, why didn't I remember my life as a human being?

And the second great puzzle involved Riquiqui and Casilda. Neither one seemed to be the least concerned by the fact that I was a horse. They both treated me like a human being. They were the only people who did not treat me like a horse. Why? What mysterious fate had joined their lives to mine? Could I hope to become a man again? Perhaps Casilda could answer my questions.

But only when the celebration subsided a little, and the children, exhausted, sat down around the bonfires, did Riquiqui talk to me.

"You're sad," she said.

"Who wouldn't be?" I answered, staring at my hoofs.

"You're the finest-looking horse in the world," she said consolingly.

"I'm the most wretched horse in the world."

"You'd win a prize for perfection."

"I'd prefer to be the ugliest *man* in the world."

"You must not feel like that. We had a wonderful time together."

"But that's all over now. Until now I wasn't aware of the fact that I am a horse. You never told me. But now"—with my long tail I waved a fly away—"I feel so—so *horsy!*"

I sighed and she broke out into laughter.

"Don't be silly! There are so many men who neigh when they speak, but you are the only horse in the whole world who can speak."

"What a consolation! Everywhere I go people are afraid of me and throw stones at me. Besides"—my ears dropped despondently—"I had so many plans for us."

"We'll always be together."

"That's impossible. If I were a mythological centaur, perhaps, but I am all horse, except for my soul. We could go nowhere. People would think we were freaks."

"People don't understand. Wonderful things happen right under their noses and they don't believe them. They refused to see that my so-called magic tricks were really miracles. They could not understand that a horse can have a soul. But it doesn't matter. This is *their* world, a world governed by their laws, numbers, weights, and measures, a world without dreams, without fantasies, without fairy tales. Only their children are wise. *They* know the world of fantasy and live with one foot in each world, mixing the real with the unreal. Their elders are so serious, so judicious, so formal, so idiotic and presumptuous. And they dare correct children! That's why my godmother established this children's camp, where dreams are free. Didn't you see how completely unsurprised they were when you spoke? For them a talking horse is something normal, yet fictitious."

"Fictitious? You mean . . ."

"Yes, you guessed it," replied Casilda. "You don't belong to the real world. You are only passing through it, like a tourist. You are a horse out of a storybook. Like Riquiqui and me, you too come from the world of the fantastic. You are only temporarily in the world of the real. All three of us are just passing through. These children are the spiritual bridge between both worlds."

"That's impossible," I rejoined, nervously digging into the earth with a forefoot. "I am not a ghost horse and you two are as much flesh and blood as these children."

"You don't understand. In the world of the fantastic everything is also real. A talking horse or a flying dragon, a giant or a witch, are as real there as grass, flies, children, and birds are here. What happens is that the inhabitants of the earthly world depict us in their stories as nonexistent creatures of the imagination and we do the same thing with them. In *our* stories the real becomes the fantastic. When we want to write about fantastic things, we don't choose fairies or dwarfs, hippogriffs or phantoms, for they are part of our daily lives. Instead, we write of journeys to the real and prosaic world and of the adventures that take place there."

She paused. The night was as quiet as a grotto.

"For example, once someone in our world wrote a story about a prince who became a horse and came to this world "

I uttered a cry that woke up the children nodding by the fire.

"You mean *me*, don't you? That's my story. To know it is to know what will happen to me. Where can I find the story? Who wrote it? Where is he?"

"I wrote it," replied Casilda. "That's why we are together now. I want to see the ending. The difference between our stories and the stories of the people in this other world we are now visiting is that ours *really happen*. I just have to imagine something and it happens. One day I got the idea of writing a story centering on Riquiqui herself. I don't remember it. I lose track of my stories as soon as I transfer them to my enormous storybook, the one with the gold covers, and from then on the story lives out its own life. I only set stories rolling. That's the privilege of fairies. I recall that Riquiqui came to this world in search of a rainbow-colored pearl and her companion-in-adventure was a horse who had once been a prince. I don't know what happened afterward. The story left my mind and is now set down in my magic book. Only there can we see how it ends."

Suddenly I saw the light.

"A gold-covered book? Now I understand. My first memory is of myself alone on a sunlit meadow and nearby there was something shining in the sun. The magic book!"

"That's right. You and Riquiqui escaped from the pages of the magic book and entered what these people call the real world. The magic book is, so to speak, the window through which one climbs from the fantastic to the real. You sprang from one of the illustrations."

"I must find that book. I must find it immediately."

But it was hours before we found it. All the children were mobilized for the search, and for hours the dark wood was invaded by a happy horde of hunters with multicolored lanterns, seeking the magic book of true stories. With Riquiqui and Casilda riding on my back I helped in the search. When a little boy finally turned up with the enormous volume under his arm, I, forgetting that a well-bred horse should not do such things while mounted, executed a caper that amid much laughter sent Casilda and Riquiqui rolling off my back onto the grass. But soon the book was in the hands of the fairy godmother.

It was a huge book bound in gold and encrusted with precious stones. But when Casilda turned the pages I suffered a great disappointment. The pages were empty. Except for an occasional garden in full bloom, a star-studded sky, a magnificent underwater scene—except for such illustrations, which I realized were only the backgrounds, the pages were empty. Where were the creatures that gave life to the stories? Were they the empty silhouettes that had no faces? Had they, at the end of each scene, gone off elsewhere to live the next episode, leaving behind only an outline of their figures to indicate that they had been there?

"Don't be surprised," Casilda explained as she turned the pages. "As my stories are *lived out,* the text vanishes and the characters leap from one scene to another, until they reach the last scene, after which they depart to wherever their fate calls them. You see, my book begins by being an illustrated sketch of my fantasies. As each story unfolds, scene follows scene, just as they might on a screen. After each scene is over the stage remains, but the actors proceed to the next stage and finally cease existing in the book."

With my head protruding above twenty curious little faces, I watched the unfolding of my own story. The first few pages depicted a magnificent glass and marble palace and a throne with the blank silhouette of the prince—my silhouette. On the next few pages I recognized the romantic ruins where Casilda had raised Riquiqui and the deserted silhouettes of both women. Further on, scenes of the town Riquiqui had visited. Next came the meadow that was my first memory, with the silhouette of a horse and that of a fairy, Casilda, who had turned me into a horse. And so on up to the very moment the magic book was found. Here Casilda placed a finger between the pages and abruptly closed the book.

"And now what do you prefer," she asked us, her eyes dimmed by tears, "to continue living out the story step by step or to get to the climax immediately?"

Riquiqui caressed my mane.

"Let's get right to the climax," she answered. "We've seen too much of the real world—a world where goodness and beauty exist only in children. We want to return to the world of legend. I wish my prince to be with me forever, and it matters not if he remains a horse."

I had no time to object. With one quick pull Casilda ripped out a handful of pages and tore them into tiny bits, which the wind promptly blew away. I felt as if someone had ripped strips off my skin. I looked around. The countryside had changed and only Casilda was now with me.

The children and Riquiqui had vanished.

"What happened?" I asked.

"This is the end of your story. Riquiqui is over there," and she pointed to a little house not far from us so covered by ivy and honeysuckle that I had not noticed it. "It is written on the last page of the story that she will spend her last night in the world of reality there, and tomorrow, or rather today, for morning is almost here, you will return together to the world of legend. Many other things were supposed to have happened to you, but I have destroyed the pages. Riquiqui seeking her pearl would have experienced many difficulties and hardships, for in any world that is the fate of all who seek a dream. You would have helped Riquiqui in a manner worthy of your pedigree. And what a pedigree! You are a direct descendant of the favorite horse of Don Pedro de Valbuena, the Spanish captain who discovered and conquered Chile."

"What else?" I asked, chewing rather resentfully on a blade of grass.

"Finally, Riquiqui would have found her pearl, you would have recovered your human form, and both of you would have lived happily forever after, just as they do in fairy tales."

"Where would Riquiqui have found her pearl and I my original form?"

"Right where you started out from. The world of the marvelous, from which one departs through a story and which one can enter in one way only—the way of the rainbow."

Casilda paused and I heard the first birds of dawn.

"Simple, isn't it?" she continued. "The rainbow-colored pearl can only be in the rainbow. Only there can you find what you long for."

She got up suddenly, her eyes shining.

"The story is finished. You must return to the invisible world, where the fantastic is real. Look over there! During the night it rained on the other side of the mountains and now there is a path for you to follow." Her finger pointed to the distant blue mountains girdled by a huge rainbow of shimmering colors. "Go without fear, for I have willed it so."

I turned around to call Riquiqui, but she was already running toward us. Casilda kissed her on the forehead and me on the back of my neck, and Riquiqui climbed onto my back.

"Good-by," said Casilda. "I shall stay here to look after the children."

Something strange then happened. It took me a few minutes to realize it. Casilda stood waving at us as, with fleeting hoots, I sped ahead. But she was *under* not *behind* us. Riquiqui, holding on to my neck, let out a jubilant cry:

"You're a flying horse!"

And so I was. That had been Casilda's will. Thousands of feet over Chile, far above the lofty peaks of the Andes, on my own powerful wings, I was bearing my princess through the limpid morning blue toward the brilliant arch that beckoned in the distance.

Riquiqui, unlocking her arms from my neck, opened them in a broad gesture, as though she wanted to embrace all the white clouds in the sky, and shouted above the wind, "We have had a tiny glimpse of reality between two dreams. Exactly the opposite of what happens on earth, where people get a tiny glimpse of dreams between realities."

But the morning air was too exhilarating to indulge in philosophy. Below us lay the green square fields, the silver strips of the rivers, and the dull gray cities, where all of you, poor unbelieving creatures of the "real" world, were still asleep, unaware of this great miracle that was happening right over your heads. With all modesty, I must say you missed quite a spectacle. A white horse flying through the air bearing a lovely princess on his back! It was then that it occurred to me to tell you my story, to drop it word by word over your sleeping heads before you went back to your boring desks, your ugly factories, your clanking machines and crowded vehicles, your wretched drudging lives.

We are approaching the highest point of the rainbow.

Riquiqui's little face is pressed against mine, her soft breath blending with my snorts. We are flying right into the rainbow. My hoofs are dyed yellow, green, violet, vermilion, and blue. Veils woven of tiny colored drops of water enfold us like a fog of iridescent pearls. I am drunk with speed, color, sun, and wind. I have become but another color in the glorious symphony of the rainbow. Now comes the descent. The rainbow unfolds into a crystalline slope, at the end of which lies the pot of gold. There I shall find the pearl to crown Riquiqui's head, following which I shall be changed back into a prince. But I am no longer sure that I want to be a prince. Wouldn't you rather be a white horse, flying up and down the rainbow with a princess on your back?

Our journey is coming to an end. The land of legend is not far. The lights of the rainbow are now brush strokes of sun on the palette of the sky.

Being a Giant

It is hard
being a giant
in a place where there are few giants
and all of them crazy.
The loneliness is the worst part.
If he catches a glimpse
of the bodies of the little people
running in the fields below
it is all he can do
to keep from crying.
On white hot days
he wanders in the hills
eating cattle and young trees
ignoring the sharp pains in his belly.
He carries a small pocket mirror
in which he sometimes
looks at pieces
of his enormous face
and sometimes holds it out
flashing the commandments of the sun
to the empty hills.

—*Robert Mezey*

A Matter of Music

Patricia A. McKillip

Cresce Dami was the daughter of Yrida Dami, teacher for thirty-nine years at the great Bardic School at Onon. When she was three, Cresce began learning simple, ancient rhymes. When she was five, she was given eight different instruments and seven years to learn how to play them. By the time she was fifteen, she could sing the hundred and one Songs of Changing Fortune of the reclusive hill-people of Jazi. She could tune the strings of her cyrillaya to any of the nine changes passed through centuries from the first Bard of Onon. She knew to play the trihorne for the salute to anyone below the rank of a King; the flute for the funeral of a King's child; the cyrillaya for fanfares of death and victory at the hunt for anyone attached to the King's court at Hekar; the lovely, reedy cothone that looked like a cow's bag with eight udders only when she was asked. Then she was told that the difficult part of her studies was just beginning. When she was twenty-one she was given a new set of instruments made by each of her teachers, and the information that the Lords of Daghian had requested a bard. And that night the heavy rafters of the dark, smokey tavern the students frequented rocked with laughter, songs, and glasses emptied and broken with high-pitched trihorne notes in her honor.

"I am going to become a Bard of Daghian," she said for the fortieth time. Ruld Egemi, who had been her friend since she was eight and her lover since she was nineteen, nodded and laughed. A trihorne-note, a wail out of the long brass throats tuned to battle, shattered the glass in his hand, spilling spiced wine over them both. He laughed again, and she stared, swallowing, at the curve of his mouth and the conjunction of bones at his throat. "I'm going to leave you."

He looked too drunk and happy to realize it. "I'll come to Daghian. Maybe in a year," he said. "Maybe they'll hire me to play the trihorne fanfares for death at private hunts, if nothing else."

"If you play the trihorne for that in Daghian," someone said, pulling up a chair with a screech, "you'll wind up in Jazi playing for corn-dances until you're ninety. The Lords of Daghian claim equal rank with the King."

"You play the cyrillaya for no one but the King or his relatives, or anyone acting in his name, at a hunt," Ruld said stubbornly. "Isn't that right, Cresce?"

"The Lords of Daghian are of the King's blood-line; if you use the trihorne that would be a mortal insult. That's right, isn't it, Cresce?"

"They're of a bastard line—"

"They are of an ancient, powerful line, and you sing one version of the Battle of Hekar Pass to them, and another to the King—"

The tavern-keeper mopped up the wine on the table and set steaming glasses down with a flourish. People even from beyond the city came to his small, ancient tavern to hear the students sing and play to one another as they drank. The rare nights of the rampant trihorne, and shattered wine-glasses, were a ritual amply paid for. Cresce smiled at him without seeing him; she heard the argument without listening. She leaned back in Ruld's shadow, her mind running over things she had packed. The case of resin, soft cloth, oils and spare reeds Ruld had given her. Clothes. Blankets and skins, for Daghian was beyond the mountains and she might not always find lodgings as she traveled. The set of tiny pipes her father had carved for her when she was a child. His cothone, which was the only instrument of his she had not burned when he died. The cothone, with its many haunting voices, was her instrument, tuned to the deepest voices within herself, as the trihorne in Ruld's hands became his own voice. The love of the cothone she had inherited from her father, and his strong, skilled fingers. Her small bones, her straight black hair, her face with its wide-set eyes and wide cheekbones, she had inherited from her mother's hill-blood, the streak of Jazi in her that made their songs throb in her blood as she sang them.

"Cresce—"

The argument was beginning to heat. She said, slapping her hand down on the table, "Hear me!" Then she whispered, tuned to their silence, "Oh, hear. To the courts of the King at Hekar nine hundred years ago came the riches and glory of the Kingdom. To the vanquished court at Daghian came the first Bard of Onon, possessing nothing but the cyrillaya. To him, not to the King, the Lords of Daghian gave honor. In his memory, the ritual music of the royal instrument, the cyrillaya, honors the Lords of Daghian." She lifted her hand, closed it, gripping their attention. "And if you dare remind the Lords of Daghian with a trihorne that the King outranks them, they will tie you in a knot around it."

Ruld, hovering in her spell with his chair balanced on one leg, brought it upright with a crash. "Play," he said. "Play the cothone." His eyes were suddenly as she loved to see them, dark, intense with desire. Then she heard an echo of her own words in her head, and a chill shot through her, turning her hands icy.

"I am going to Daghian. Bards have left Hekar itself to go to Daghian. Oh, Ruld, how do I dare? They'll laugh at the cothone. I'm so small they won't see me when I stand up to play. My reeds will squeak."

"The Lords of Daghian expect from Onon the best the school has to offer. The musicians chose you," Ruld said. "Play the cothone."

She slid the strap from her shoulder and stood up. She put the pipe to her mouth, drew from the soft, tanned skinful of air deep, haunting phrases, the wordless voices half-heard at twilight, from dark forests, from the far side of still lakes. Then, leaving one soft, low note weaving through the air, she added voices to it from the fourth and seventh pipes, the pipes of longing and of passion. She played her longing; the full, humming notes of the cothone called it out of her bones, out of her heart's marrow. There was not a sound or movement in the tavern. Faces were blurred beyond her, torch fire shivering over them. Their silence played to her song. Then, beside her, Ruld's trihorne began to weave its pure, fiery voice into the voices of the cothone. The long horn slid in her slow rhythm through its changes. It was a stroke of pure gold under the smokey torchlight. Her throat swelled; she played simple, ancient Jazi music while the tears of sorrow and happiness burned down her face.

She rode out of Onon the next morning before sunrise. It was mid-autumn; she wore a long, heavy coat split down the back for riding, and high boots lined with sheepskin. Her instruments were encased in furs and skins; they made odd, bulky shapes on her shadow as the sun rose. She sang to keep her voice warm. Her song broke in puffs of mist in front of her. The fear in her was gone. She was the daughter of Yrida Dami, who had played at Hekar five years for the King; and the teachers of Onon had chosen her above all musicians to send to the proud, critical court at Daghian. She got out one of her tiny pipes as the morning warmed, and answered back to the birds flying around her.

It took her twelve days to reach Daghian. She sang some nights at wayside inns, earning money for lodgings and supplies. She watched the weary faces of travelers ease as they listened to her. They were simple folk, who knew and loved the cothone, and she felt well-paid by their silence. As she neared the mountains, even farm-houses became scarce. The pass through the mountains whistled with wild, empty autumn winds. She camped at night then, sitting close to her fire, singing ballads back at the winds in her deep, sweet voice. She saw the last leaves ripped from the trees as she rode. River-water shimmered white with the wind's white breath. The mountains at morning were ghostly with mist. But the loneliness of the pass did not reach her heart. She was Cresce Dami, going to Daghian, and even the winds knew it was bad luck to harm a bard.

On the twelfth day, she reached the other side of the mountains and saw the flatlands veined with rivers, and the courts and cities built among them. Each river had a name; each was the name of a battle-site, and each battle had spawned ballads of a dozen variations: one to be sung on a street-corner, one at the market-square under a mayor's window, one at Hekar, one at Daghian. . . . Before she was fourteen, Cresce had learned them all. She headed her horse down the hillside toward a main road.

The court of the Lords of Daghian lay in wild country. Dark pine moaned of winter as she traveled down the winding road to Daghian. But she heard, shimmering across hard, empty fields, the timbreless, haunting notes of the cyrillaya, tuned to the victory of the hunt within the forests. Riders swept across the fields, their rich cloaks of deep green, blood-red, gold and brown, whirling behind them like leaves in the wind. They would feast, Cresce knew, on the kill, and she would be there, silent and anonymous, until the bones were picked, and servants brought washing-bowls of scented water, and more wine. Then she would stand, interrupting their hunting stories, drawing their wine-flushed faces toward her, like the faces in the tavern, with a sweep of a hunting phrase across the cyrillaya. *I am Cresce Dami, Bard of Onon. Lords, hear me! I will tell you a tale of the hunt stranger than any hunt you have ever ridden to the cyrillaya of victory. . . .*

Then she saw the court of the Lords of Daghian.

It was a small city within vast double-walls of black stone. She counted eight towers and the great Keep, old as any song out of Daghian. Within, a massive, soaring building, half-castle, half-fortress, sprawled on a rise of land. The flame of Daghian snapped above it in the wind; a blood-red pennant a dozen feet long, bordered with gold. The hunters were riding through the broad gates. They swung shut again ponderously, but Cresce knew that no door in the Kingdom would refuse to admit a Bard of Onon.

Twilight was falling when she reached the gates. The guards recognized her odd bundles of instruments, the cothone in its case about her neck. The gates had begun to open even before she spoke. She heard a sound that thrilled her to the marrow: notes of a trihorne splashing across the evening, raised in the ancient salute to a Bard of Onon. The passage between the walls was torch-lit. When she rode out of it into the yard, men were waiting to take her horse.

She slung her instrument cases about her, and walked into the great hall of the Lords of Daghian.

Firelight, the smell of hot meat and the voices of close to a thousand people talking and laughing rolled at her as she crossed the threshold. She stopped, her heart thudding at the sheer immensity of the place. There were nine open fire-beds scattered through the hall; on each the carcases of deer and boar turned slowly on their spits. Long tables surrounded them in rough disorder; red light caught at the faces of richly dressed men, women and children, plate of silver and gold, cups and ewers of dyed glass. Groups of musicians played near each fire-bed. They used flutes and harps, pipes and small drums. They were sweating; pitchers of water and wine stood near them, and trays of sliced fruits. Their listeners, at first glance, seemed oblivious to them. But Cresce saw young boys running too close to one group called sharply to order. She watched the great gathering of the court of Daghian. Beneath their laughter and conversation, the men and women seemed sensitive to every change in rhythm and song, and sometimes broke off mid-sentence to applaud an intricate passage of music.

Cresce smiled a little. Then a servant spoke to her, led her to a place at one of the outer tables. She put her instruments down and took off her coat. Relief musicians sat at the table; their own instruments were scattered along the benches. Their eyes flicked to her instruments, her face in sudden comprehension. She saw the respect in their faces, but they did not speak to her. She would break her silence at the court of Daghian only one way. She sat down, her fingers trembling slightly. She ate the food brought to her without tasting it, her mind tuned to all the nuances of sound around her.

Finally, the intensity of voices seemed to slacken.

Charred bones were removed from the fire-beds; servants began to dispense towers of finger-bowls, trays full of pitchers of scented water, pitchers of wine, and great platters of sweetmeats and nuts. Musicians around the fire-beds drew their playing to a close. The relief musicians, their eyes on Cresce, began reaching for their instruments. Her throat swelled suddenly, as if she had swallowed air from a cothone. She stood up, drew the cyrillaya from its case. The musicians dropped back into their seats, watching her with a combination of wonder and excitement, as if she had walked out of a legend in front of them.

Their table was half in shadow, and she was hardly taller than the boys who had been scolded for running. So she climbed on top of the table, stood under the flare of torchlight. The cyrillaya flared silver as she lifted it. She plucked the taut strings softly, tuned a couple. Then she pulled the mute out of the silver throat that amplified the taut, pure notes until not even a trihorne's brilliance could overwhelm it. She swept her hand across the strings; even the boys wrestling in the shadows and the servants with piles of dirty plates stopped moving.

Standing on the table, she could see the three Lords of Daghian, their wives and an assortment of relatives. The older men were smiling, but there was not a flicker of expression on the faces of the Lords. One, the youngest, turned to another suddenly, opened his mouth. She stopped him with a single phrase: the first notes of the battle-cry of Daghian. Then his face blurred into all the others as she drew breath and said,

"I am Cresce Dami, Bard of Onon. Lords of Daghian, the winds of autumn batter your walls, the flame of Daghian burns bright against the cold. Let me tell you a tale. . . ." Her hand swept again over the strings, this time in a minor mode, imitating the winds. "The winter-hunt of the Lord Sere of Daghian." Her fingers skimmed over rhythms of the chase. "A long time ago . . ." Then because somebody was coughing, and a pair of lovers in the far corner had begun to whisper, and because the cyrillaya held pride and beauty, but the cothone held all her soul, she let the bright instrument drop to her side and swung the cothone into her hands. A low, plaintive call, the wind soughing among bog-reeds where stags drank, filled the hall.

She had startled the Lords. She had also startled the musicians, whose mouths dropped with astonishment. The cothone was a herdsman's instrument, an instrument for rough songs and long nights in the open, during battles or hunts. She wondered when it had been last played at an open feast in the hall. Some of the guests were glancing at the Lords, wondering whether or not they had been insulted. But the Lords had not made up their minds. Cresce, her voice clear, steady in spite of her sudden nervousness, built out of words and sounds the cold winter's day, the crows' crying in the frozen sky, the slow pace of the young Lord Sere as he tracked a great stag who was not a stag through the marshes of Daghian.

Something was pulling at the hem of her skirt. The first faint tug had stopped her throat, but the cothone had droned on without her. The pulling persisted, but all her training forbade moving. She realized that one of the young children, attracted by her forbidden stance on the table, was mutely demanding to be lifted up. She tried to ignore it, hoping one of the musicians would see it. But the hall was shadowy behind her, and the musicians were caught up in her tale. She drew out of the second pipe the quick staccato flash of distant hunting horns, as the hunters that Sere had become separated from called to him. Her long, full skirt began flapping to the rhythm like a sail.

One of the musicians gasped; she heard a ripple of laughter from the closer tables. She stepped forward on two beats, pulling her skirt out of the child's grip. Her foot struck one of the musicians' drums with a hollow thump, knocked it off the table. It thumped again on the bench, and once more on the ground. The musician grabbed at it, but the child pounced on it first, and sat on it.

A servant swept the child off the floor, and returned the drum to the musician, but Cresce's throat had dried in the sudden laughter. Some of the women were talking. They

quieted quickly as Cresce continued, but the words
scratched in her throat. Then the thing too terrible to consider happened: the reed in the eighth pipe, dry with cold,
split as she played a stag's bellow. The deep bellow ran up
into a strangled squeal, and dogs napping all over the hall
startled up howling at the sound.

They were slapped into silence almost instantly. But all
through the room, men and women were weeping with
laughter. Even one of the Lords had turned his face away,
shaking. The older Lord beside him stared carefully down
at his hands. The third Lord did not move. His eyes were
narrowed slightly and he was not smiling. The musicians
seemed transfixed. Cresce dropped the cothone mechani-
cally, shifted the cyrillaya back into her hands almost without losing a beat. But her heart was pounding raggedly,
and the cyrillaya sounded too pure, almost colorless, after
the rich, plaintive voices of the cothone. She swept the
sound of Sere's last arrow soaring above the marshes to
strike at the heart of the stag.

She heard a low murmuring from the men. Wine
sloshed over the rims of their cups as they turned to one
another. Cresce, her voice wavering a little, realized that
muted arguments were flaring all over the room. She cast
back desperately, wondering what she had done wrong.
The cyrillaya was in tune; her voice was still strong and in
key. She wondered if there was some ancient custom
forbidding the playing of the cyrillaya to follow the
cothone. But she would have remembered. Then she saw
the agonized faces of the musicians, and the blood swept
completely out of her face.

In her nervousness, she had skipped an entire section of
the tale. Men who knew it vaguely were trying to remember what was wrong. Old hunters who knew it well
were telling them. Some were even singing it softly. Sere's
first glimpse of the legendary stag, and his arduous,
exhausting chase that lasted for three days and three nights
through the marshes—she had jumped over it entirely
when she switched instruments.

A whole table of scarred hunters was beginning to take

up the passage. Their cups were waving to the melody; as one forgot the lines, another took them up. Cresce, her fingers shaking, picked up their melody on the cyrillaya. She sang with them, trying to coax the song away from them. But their beat was ragged, their lines jumbled and they were content with their wine and their voices.

The children had begun to talk again. Some of the people were still listening, but Cresce knew it was out of pity, because they could hardly hear her. She had lost their attention. Her hands were trembling badly; she did not dare look at the musicians. Her voice was beginning to stick in her throat; her face was burning and her lips were dry. A servant collecting wine-pitchers let them clatter together on his tray. She knew, even without looking toward the Lords, that the sound was the judgment of Daghian.

She almost stopped. The men singing, holding out their cups for more wine, would scarcely have noticed. The Lords of Daghian would send her back to Onon anyway in the morning. She thought of Ruld, the wine-cup shattering between them, signalling the end of her life at Onon, and knew suddenly that she could never go back. Nor would she stay at Daghian, even for a night. She would finish her song and then leave. In the darkness of the autumn night, she would decide what to do.

So she lifted her trihorne, blew a great, discordant blast on it. Singers and servants stopped short; one of the Lords choked on his wine. She said gravely into the sudden silence blasting back at her,

"And so, Lords, in the frail, ice-colored twilight melting across the marshes of Daghian, the Lord Sere first glimpsed the great animal he tracked."

They were outraged. She saw it in their faces. But she gave them no time to tell her what they thought. Pitching the cyrillaya to vibrate the stone walls, she sent the enormous stag running through the hall to vanish again into the winter dusk. Then she used every instrument she possessed as Sere followed it. Her drum beat his horse's hooves; the haunting sixth pipe, of the cothone, the pipe of warning, tracked his passage through the dangerous, moonlit marshes. Her small pipes brought the sun up, as marsh-birds called to one another across the wastes. Her twelve-stringed harp, unexpectedly gentle after the cyril-laya, played again and again the brief, wondrous glimpses of the stag that lured Sere deeper and deeper into the marshlands. The death of his exhausted horse as it strug-gled vainly in the deep mud it had stumbled into, she played on the cothone; the drum beat its dirge. The red sun flared to the trihorne's salute across the morning of the third day. The hoar-frost on every tree-limb, on every blade of grass, burned in Sere's eyes; the winds ringing in the ice-world she struck on tiny tubular bells. The cothone played Sere's exhaustion, his hunger, his obsession as he broke a path on foot through the lonely, fiery world. Finally he saw the great stag clearly. The trihorne rang its turning as it stopped and faced him.

His last arrow soared with the cyrillaya, burned into nothingness before it reached the stag. In Sere's world of ice and silence, only the drum beat the slow steps of the white stag as it came toward him. Sere, weaponless, strengthless, lay where he had fallen, watching it come. He looked into its eyes. For two beats, there was no sound in the great hall of Daghian. Then the brassy stag's bell of the trihorne faded into the slow, pure voice of the flute as the stag faded into a woman whose eyes were the color of winter nights. She turned again, moved slowly away from Sere into the glittering winds. Flute-notes ascended, shaped a great, dark bird, whirled to its flight as it vanished into the light. The cothone brought twilight once again over the world. Horses' hooves snapped over the bog-ice. The hunters found Sere, half-dead of cold and hunger. The spare, comfortless voices of the fourth pipe, the pipe of longing, wept with his weeping as he rode with them back to Daghian.

The cothone stilled in Cresce's hands. She let it fall, stood looking out over the motionless hall. The faces were shadowed by the dying fires. She bowed her head to the Lords of Daghian. But before she could turn to leave, a

musician beside one of the fire-beds leaped to his feet. He
threw back his head, raised the trihorne to his mouth. The
single high, piercing note set wine-glasses ringing like ice
all over the hall before they shattered.

The youngest Lord of Daghian rose. There was a sudden clamor from the men at the tables. Cresce, her
heart thudding in her throat, realized suddenly that they
were shouting requests for her for other ballads. She
glanced down at the musicians around her. They were
applauding, laughing, pounding on the table. Her hands,
so steady as she played, began to shake badly. The Lord of
Daghian overtook a servant bringing a wine-cup to her. He
brought it himself, held it up to her as she stood frozen on
the table-top.

"Welcome. I am Sere of Daghian." He had wild, dark
hair burnished with red and a lean, proud face like a bird of
prey. But his eyes were smiling. He added, "The hunter
was my grandfather. Drink."

She took the cup of chilled, spiced wine and drained it.
He signalled to the relief musicians; they rose, took their
places, while logs thrown on the fire-beds illumined the
hall once more. Servants were dispensing cups, sweeping
up glass. They were smiling, Cresce noticed, in spite of the
extra work. She found herself able to move again, and she
sat down abruptly on the edge of the table.

"I was about to leave," she whispered.

"I know." He sat on the table beside her. "I would have
followed you. This is Daghian, not Hekar, where you
would have been tossed into the autumn winds for playing
the cothone at an open feast. I handle matters of music at
Daghian, and I have never in my life heard the cothone
played like that." He paused a moment, studying her.
"You are Jazi."

"My mother was a hill-woman. My father met her when
he went to Jazi for a year to learn the Songs of Changing
Fortune."

"Have you ever been there?"

"To Jazi? No. I was born at Onon. My father taught
there. I've never been anywhere except Onon."

"Taught? Is he dead?"

She nodded. "They're both dead." She added after a moment, "I burned all his instruments except his cothone when he died."

"I have a cothone," he said almost abruptly. He was silent a little, frowning at some memory. Then the smile slid back into his eyes. "That was my son, pulling on your skirt. He's three. I'll teach him to show more respect for a Bard of Daghian. But you won't be standing on table-tops after this."

Her hands slid to the table-edge, gripped it. "Lord. Do you want me to stay?"

"Do I want you to stay?" He ran both his hands through his hair, and the shadow in his eyes lifted, giving her a glimpse of his wonder. "Look at the high table. The big, dark-haired Lord with the face carved by a blunt knife is my brother Breaugh. The fair-haired, hot-tempered man beside him is my brother Hulme. They have heard that tale of Sere and the stag-hunt a hundred times. And yet from the time you blew that sour note on the trihorne, until the musician spilled all our wine with his trihorne, I could have sworn neither one of them breathed. You will honor Daghian. Besides," he added, standing up again, "I want you to teach me to play the cothone."

She played again before the feast was ended. Men sang hunting ballads with her; musicians added their own rich, soft accompaniment. Finally, past midnight, the hall began to empty, and the musicians put away their instruments. They introduced themselves to her, left her head spinning with half a hundred names. Then she met the two older Lords of Daghian.

"Breaugh handles matters of estate," Sere explained, "and Hulme matters of peace and war. I handle matters of music, which is the pride of Daghian." He introduced their wives to her. But of his own wife, he said nothing, and she wondered. As he was leaving the hall with her, to show her where she would live in the great house, he stopped suddenly, as if to tell her something. But he changed his mind. Later, before she fell asleep, she found herself won-

dering again. Then the appalling memory of her near-
disaster washed over her. She flung the bed-covers over
her head and curled up in the darkness, listening to her
heart pound until she fell asleep.

She sang and played nearly every evening then, either
in the great hall, or in the Lords' chambers if they dined
privately. She played for the hunt, if there were guests
from the King's court. She taught new musicians the ritual
music for such occasions as weddings, namings, funerals
and welcoming salutes to various officials and guests. She
taught Lord Sere the cothone; she taught Hulme's wife the
harp, and Breaugh's oldest daughter the flute. Some
nights she was so tired that she played through her dreams
and woke exhausted. But there was a happiness in her that
flashed out in her music, even on the most sullen autumn
evenings.

Sere learned the cothone very quickly. He already
played the trihorne and the cyrillaya, but Cresce sensed
something in him that woke to the haunting voices of the
cothone. He used a very old instrument. Its pipes were
pitched differently from Cresce's instrument; they were
scrolled all over with delicate carving, and bound to the
kidskin with gold. The deep pipe, the pipe of mourning,
was so low it seemed to breathe through Cresce's bones
whenever she played it. She wondered often where he
had gotten it. One day he told her.

"It was my wife's."

They were in a room in one of the oldest wings of the
house. It was full of instruments: ancient pipes, flutes,
drums of painted tree-bark that were from Jazi, harps of
varying sizes, from a five-stringed harp fashioned to a
rough triangle of oak, to a thirty-stringed harp of pure gold
that had been played only once, on someone's wedding
day. There were trihornes of a hundred battles; there was
the cyrillaya that the first Bard had carried into Daghian.
There were instruments so old that Cresce had only seen
drawings of them. She had been given keys to the various
cases, and she loved the room. Sere practiced there be-

cause the old walls were three feet thick, and his brothers
could not hear the squeals and nasal drones he startled out
of the cothone before he began to master it.

He sat down on one of the window-ledges, letting the
cothone rest on his knee. The thick glass behind his head
warped the cloudy landscape into a formless mist. When
he did not continue, Cresce asked softly,

"Is she dead?"

He shook his head. "I don't know. Like you, she is
half-Jazi." He was silent again, frowning down at the
cothone. He said abruptly, harshly, to the cothone, "She
was so beautiful. Her eyes were true Jazi grey, grey as
marsh-mist at dusk. Her hair was so black it blinded me
sometimes. We had known each other always. But one
day she left me and didn't come back. She took only a
horse I had raised for her. She left me our son and her
cothone."

"It's—" Cresce had to stop to clear her throat. "It's older
than anyone living. That cothone."

"I know. It belonged to her great-grandmother. She had
been taken forcibly from Jazi by a Lord of Daghian, as the
army of Daghian marched through the hills to attack Hekar
from the north."

She drew breath suddenly. "Hekar Pass."

"You sing one version in Daghian, and another to the
King. The army of Daghian was massacred in the hills by
the King's army. Only nine men and one hill-woman
survived to come back to Daghian. Men of Jazi betrayed
Daghian's position to the King. With some justice." He
touched the rings of gold on the cothone. "I think we had
stolen their Bard. That was seventy years ago. Since then,
no man of Daghian has been permitted in Jazi."

"So you couldn't look for your wife."

"No. The last man of Daghian who went to Jazi was
found at our gates wrapped in corn-husks. There wasn't a
mark on him, but he was dead. I think the hills called her
until she went back to them."

Cresce sat down beside him on the window-ledge. She

said softly, "Bards of Onon are permitted in Jazi, even during their most private rituals. I could take a message to her."

He looked at her. Then he dropped his arm around her shoulders. "Thank you." She realized suddenly how rarely he smiled. "But I think that, like the woman my grandfather followed through the marshes, she doesn't want to be found."

A few days later, men from Hekar on the King's business came to speak to the Lords of Daghian. Cresce sang for them, playing at Sere's request, both the cyrillaya and the cothone. Later one of the men spoke privately to her, suggesting that Hekar would be a more suitable place for her great gift, since the King would never ask her to play a herdsman's instrument at his court. She told that to Sere and he laughed. But he was annoyed. When the Lords took the visitors from Hekar hunting in the waning days of autumn, Cresce rode with them to sound the fanfares of death. But Sere, with a ghost of malice in his eyes, had insisted she bring only her cothone. Breaugh and Hulme had grown so used to hearing the cothone that they scarcely noticed. But the visitors, after she played the fanfare for a stag's death, were insulted. They said little, for they were in the middle of the Daghian marshes, and could not have left the hunt without getting lost. But Cresce wished she had disregarded Sere, and brought the cyrillaya instead. Its silvery voice would have broken through shreds of mists hanging over the marshes. The cothone seemed to gather mist, to bring it closer around them until the riders that she followed seemed shadowy, and Sere's cloak, striped gold and red, was the one clear point in the world.

She sounded fanfares for a deer, a brace of hare, a wild boar that charged unexpectedly out at them from some trees. The mists deepened in the early afternoon, until she had no idea which direction Daghian lay in. She heard Breaugh suggest calmly that in another hour they should start back. The visitors agreed quickly. Someone sighted another deer; there was a short chase, and then Cresce heard Sere ahead of her, calling for a fanfare. She raised the cothone; the deep pipe of mourning sent the announcement of its death across the marshes.

Then the mists closed about her completely. Softly, from the other side of the mists, a cothone began to play.

How long she listened, she never knew. Its voices were deep, melding layer upon layer of fanfares across the marshes. Sitting breathless, motionless on her horse, she heard fanfares for the deaths of men and animals mingling with phrases from the winter rituals of Jazi. Slowly the salutes to death came to an end. Only the seventh pipe, with a rich, husky timbre she had never heard before, still sang through the mists. It troubled her, stirring things in her she felt she should have remembered but could not. She did not remember lifting her own cothone. But suddenly she was playing it in answer to the wild, unfamiliar music, while she guided her horse deeper into the marshes trying to find the other side of the mists.

Something swirled out of the mist; a shadow pulled at her reins. She realized for the first time that she had been moving. She let her cothone fall. At the same time the strange music stopped. She heard only the lonely cry of a marsh-bird, and the faint trickle of water. She shuddered suddenly. Then she recognized the rider beside her.

Neither of them spoke for a moment. Then Sere, whose face was expressionless, colorless in the mist, said only, "Sometimes the marshes pull you deeper into them when you're trying to get out. Sound the battle-call of Daghian, so that Breaugh and Hulme know I've found you. We'll have to smell our way home through this mist."

Not long afterward, on the first day of winter, the long silence between Daghian and Jazi was broken. One of the porters at the main gates interrupted the Lords as they sat after supper listening to their ancient steward giving his seasonal account of their household, lands and finances. Hulme was stifling a yawn when the porter murmured to him, and dropped something that looked vaguely like a

bird's nest onto the table. Cresce, playing the muted cyrillaya, strained a little to see what the odd jumble was. Her
thumb slipped off a string, struck a sour note, and Sere
looked at her. She colored hotly. Then she saw the expression in his eyes.

"Please," he said. "Come here."

"Someone nailed this clutter with an arrow to the gate?"
Hulme said incredulously. He fingered a dried corn-husk.
It rustled secretly under his touch. Then he eyed Sere.
"What's the matter with you?" he said roughly. Some of
the blood came back into Sere's face at his tone. The
steward tossed his pen down with a sigh. Breaugh said,

"Let's see the arrow." The porter gave it to him. He
touched its tip, then looked at Sere, and then at Hulme.
"Bone. It's a hill-arrow. Look at the holes in its tip."

"It whistled," the porter said.

"It's a matter of peace and war," Breaugh said shortly,
and turned back to the account book. But his brows were
drawn. "Have we offended Jazi lately?"

"How would I know?" Hulme demanded. "We offend
Jazi by breathing." He shoved his chair back suddenly,
stood up. He added to the porter, "All right. Let us know if
you get shot." He stood behind Sere, laid his hands on his
brother's shoulders. "Corn-husks. That's all I understand
of it. Remember the man they left at our doorstep bound
from hair to heel in corn-husks." He touched a flat, thin
tongue of wood. "What is that?"

"A reed." Sere's eyes had not moved from Cresce's
face as she gazed down at the odd bundle of items. "A
cothone reed. The arrow sings. Hulme, it's a matter of
music. A reed like that fits into one of the mouthpieces of
the cothone. Which pipe?"

She picked it up. Her voice slid suddenly deep, husky.
"The fourth. The pipe of longing."

There was silence. Sere's face was expressionless.
Breaugh picked up a strip of leather studded with tiny
jewels. "It looks like a piece of bridle. And nine dead
leaves. . . . But what—"

Sere moved abruptly. He stood up, went to one of the

windows to stare out at the night. When no one spoke, he said to Cresce, "Is the singing arrow a part of their rituals?"

She nodded a little jerkily. "In winter and spring." She picked up the hollow arrow, blew into the shaft. The pitch was deep. "In winter, for the rituals of Changing Fortune, they pitch them low, to sing with the pipe of mourning."

"Winter." He turned. Thoughts were breaking into his eyes. "The ritual. When is it?"

"The ninth day of winter."

"And the leaves?"

No one moved. He stepped back to the table. Hulme, breathing something, caught his arm as he reached for them.

"Think," he said flatly. "If you go into Jazi, it is no longer a matter of music. If they kill you, it's a matter of war. If Daghian goes to war against Jazi, the King will be at our throats faster than a mad bog-wolf."

"Take the issue to Hekar," Sere said shortly. "Demand justice from the King."

The blood flared into Hulme's face; he looked for a moment as if Sere had struck him. "If I find you wrapped in corn-husks on our doorstep, I'm supposed to crawl to Hekar to beg for justice? For that?"

"Hulme—"

"What kind of justice did Hekar show Daghian at Hekar Pass?"

"That was seventy years ago."

"Jazi went to Hekar for justice then—an entire army slaughtered over one woman. That's the worthless bone of justice Hekar would toss to us. If she wants to see you, why can't she come here? Tell me that. You send her a message: a leaf of black hellebore for every year she's been away, wrapped in bark from the scarred birch trees in Hekar Pass. In nine centuries Daghian hasn't begged so much as a rat-dropping from Hekar. And you expect us to go begging for justice as if we—as if we were subject—"

Sere turned. His fists rose and slammed down on the table, spilling ink across the account book. "Will you be reasonable! I'm not even dead, yet!" The three men glared at one another, while the steward stared in horror at the mess. Then Breaugh growled, "Oh, sit down." He righted the ink-stand. "Oak leaves." He looked at Sere. "There is no oak in Daghian until you reach the far side of the marshes. The border-hills are covered with it."

"Breaugh—" Hulme said.

"If he wants to go looking for his wife among ten thousand oak trees, it's his business. If he gets killed, then it's our business. Until then, it's not a matter of war or estate or music—it's a private affair." He reached across the table suddenly, stirred the corn-husks with one finger. "What's that?"

"Birch bark," said the steward wearily. Sere unrolled the dry fragment of yellowish bark gently. He gazed down at it a moment, then looked at Cresce. "I can't read music."

"Read it," Breaugh grunted. "You don't read it, you listen to it."

"At Onon, they write changeless ritual music—salutes, hunting fanfares, wedding and funeral music—so that we could memorize it quickly." She studied the square notes pricked into the bark with red dye. Then the notes came together in her mind and she started. Sere said,

"What is it?"

"The trihorne salute to the Bard of Daghian." There was another silence. Then Sere crumpled the bark in one hand, and Cresce said, astonished, "It's an invitation."

"An invitation to what?" Hulme asked sourly. She looked at him without seeing him, envisioning a land beyond ten thousand oak, the land whose heart-voice was the cothone.

"To their winter ritual. The Bard of Daghian is welcome. . . ." She turned to Sere, her brows slanting upward perplexedly. "And you, also?"

"Invited," he said. He touched one of the minute blue jewels on the bridle, his face harsh with conflicting memories. "Not necessarily welcome." She watched him a moment, uneasy, glimpsing his emotions like a complex instrument she had not been trained to play.

Breaugh said softly, "It is a matter of music."

The cothone sang to her deeply, distantly, out of the mists. "May I go?" she asked, drawing Sere abruptly back from his past. She saw herself then as he saw her: small and dark-haired, a Jazi woman in spite of her background and rigorous training, who might vanish forever among the hills she had never seen.

"No." Then he touched her shoulder, his voice gentler. "No. Not when the invitation is pinned to the gate with an arrow. Not this time." And, oddly, she was relieved at his reply.

But he went, quietly and alone, at dawn. He returned twelve days later, with one of the watch parties Hulme had sent after him. He looked weary and bad-tempered; his replies to questions his brothers asked were brief. But, alone with Cresce after supper, he showed her a second bundle of corn-husks.

"I found it pinned to an oak on the other side of the mountain."

She drew out the arrow and opened the message carefully. Three reeds dropped out, a ring of white horse-hair, a gold ring, and some dried oak leaves. "You didn't see her?"

"She wasn't there." He added, as she fingered the reeds, "The horse I gave her was white."

"But why—"

"I don't know. Yes, I do. The invitation was for you. I didn't bring you." She stared at him, bewildered, and he added, "Will you come with me?"

"But, Lord, I don't understand. Why does she want me?"

"She." He drew breath, closing his eyes. "I don't even know if she's still alive. I only know someone is reaching out of Jazi, luring me with memories, you with music."

"I am Bard of Daghian," Cresce said a little stiffly. She blew into the arrow. Its pitch was high, light. "Spring. Seven oak leaves. The seventh day of spring." Something caught at her throat. "Lord, at one point in the spring rituals, the cothone is played from sunrise to sunrise. At that time, all visiting Bards are permitted to play."

He held up the ring. "Look. It took me an entire morning to recognize that."

She took it, circled it with her thumb and finger. "It's
from a cothone . . . a very old one, like the cothone your
wife left you. . . ."

"I think they want you to bring that cothone."

She closed her fingers over the ring, uneasy again at the
tale being spun out of the darkness, within the unknown
land, herself being moved skillfully within the tale. Sere
said,

"Look at the reeds."

She picked them up. "The fourth again. The pipe of
longing. The eighth. . . ."

"The pipe of mourning. That one I recognized." She
turned the third reed in her hand. When she did not speak,
he looked at her. "What is it?"

"The sixth. The pipe of warning."

On the first day of spring, they left Daghian together. At
Breaugh's suggestion, Sere wore plain, rough-woven
clothes, a cloak and boots of sheepskin, as if he were some
herdsman the Bard of Daghian had hired to guide her
across the marshes. Hulme suggested only that if Sere
found himself dead and buried in corn-husks, he should
not bother coming home; the men of Daghian would come
to Jazi to get him. The frozen marshes were still furrowed
with ice. But the wild, violent spring winds, humming every
voice of the cothone, had swept the sky clear, and the hills
bordering Jazi looked very close. They crossed the
marshes in five days. Cresce listened for the strange
cothone, but the only sound she heard was the discordant
babble of marsh-birds returning after winter. She wondered: *Did I dream it?* and knew she had not. Sere was lost
in his own dreams. He had spoken very little as they
traveled together. At evenings, she pitched her music to
ease into the mist of his memories, draw him back into the
quiet night, the dark, rich smell of the marshes, the tiny

circle of light that enclosed them. Sometimes she would
lead him so far out of his mists that he would lift his head to
meet her eyes across the fire. Then he would smile, ac-
knowledging her skill, and she would wish they were back
in Daghian, where life was complex and exact, and the
language of the heart was not spoken in corn-husks.

On the afternoon of the fifth day, they rode out of the
thinning marsh-trees into the ancient, rolling hills of Jazi.

They were covered, as far as Cresce could see, with
bare, tangled oak Nothing, human or animal, seemed to
live among the trees. The voice of the wind had changed as
they came out of the marshes. It piped with a spare, hollow
timbre through the empty curves and shadows of the hills.
Cresce wondered what instruments the musicians of Jazi,
hearing that wind, had fashioned to match its voice.

"There," said Sere. He was pointing to one gnarled
tree. "That's where I found the last message."

The trunk was bare. Cresce glanced vaguely at the endless forests. "My mother lived among these hills," she said
surprisedly, as if she had just realized it. "Lord, we have
two days to find the place where they hold their rituals."

"I know." But neither of them moved. The oak shadows
strained down the faces of the hills, flung back by the
westering sun. The air smelled of emptiness.

"Well, what should we do?"

He shook his head a little. Then he said, "You're a bard.
They're expecting you. Let them know you're here."

She thought a moment. Then she lifted her cothone and
blew on the first pipe, the pipe of joy, the opening phrases
of the first Song of Fortune for the spring ritual.

There was a silence. The lovely fragment of song faded
away. Sere turned to her, half-smiling, the tenseness wearing away from his face. Before he could speak, the empty
oak themselves sang an answer: every voice of the
cothone echoing and overlapping one another in the salute to the Bard of Daghian.

Men on beautiful, long-legged hill-horses rode out of the
trees. Sere caught at Cresce's reins, but they came too fast.

They surrounded Cresce and Sere, their horses weaving in and out of one another in a complex circle. The men carried hawks with fierce golden eyes on their shoulders; around their wrists small pipes dangled from leather thongs. The men were wiry and dark, with wide, high cheekbones and eyes that had taken their color from the winter mists. Only one of them, half a head taller than the others, had hair bright as copper, and eyes as golden as the hawks'. It was he who reached out finally, without speaking, caught Sere by the neck of his cloak and wrenched him from his horse to the ground.

The men slid off their horses then; the ring of horses melted away. The hawks stirred, crying harshly as the men grappled with Sere. Their arms locked around him so tightly he could not struggle. One of the men gripped his hair, jerked his head back. His mouth opened; hands full of corn-husks pushed down over his face.

Cresce, frozen on her horse, saw his body begin to convulse. She snatched air and her trihorne at the same time. The note she blasted down at the men loosened their hold of both Sere and the corn-husks. They looked up at her, pained, incredulous, while Sere, half-conscious, dragged at the wind. She said to the red-haired man, whose eyes were as furious as the hawks' eyes at the sound,

"If you kill him, I will play the winter Songs of Fortune at your spring rituals. Every note backwards."

He straightened, gripped her reins lightly. His head gave a little, frightened shake. But there was no fear either in his face or his voice when he spoke. "No." Behind him, the men shifted, easing their grip on Sere. "You are the Bard of Daghian?"

"Yes."

"You're part Jazi."

She nodded, her throat dry. She realized he was younger than Sere, even younger than she, and Sere's own hair held the same touch of burnished copper. Her eyes widened. "You're part Daghian."

The muscles in his face knotted. "True. Bard. In ancient

hill-language, the words were interchangeable.'' He turned, bent over Sere. Cresce could not see what he did, but Sere's body jerked, then sagged in the hill-men's hands. The men lifted him, threw him face down across Cresce's saddle-bow. She put her hand beneath his throat, but she could not tell, with her own racing pulse, if he were still alive. She stared at the empty hills, the silent men with their eyes of mist, and suddenly she began to cry.

"All he came to do was find his wife!"

Their faces changed. They surrounded her, speaking quickly, worriedly, all at the same time so that she could hardly understand them. She gathered, wiping the tears angrily off her face, that nothing but respect was ever shown to a bard in Jazi, that she should not be afraid, that the people of Jazi showed peace and courtesy toward all strangers except those of Daghian who were scarcely human anyway, and that a bard's tears would salt the cornfields, and they would be grateful if she would stop crying. At that point Sere's head lifted; he muttered something thickly. The hilt of a knife caught him behind the ear, silencing him again. The red-haired man took Cresce's reins in his hand, flicked the pipes at his wrist to his mouth and called his horse with three quick notes. The other men were gathering their horses. For a moment the air flurried with light, tangled music. Someone caught Sere's horse, which was headed back toward the marshes. Then, in a long single file, they escorted Cresce into Jazi.

The hills parted on the other side, to join other hills ringing a plain where the people of Jazi farmed. A river, slow and green, wandered through it, sending a veinwork of streams through rougher pastureland where flocks of sheep grazed. Out of the center of the plain something shaped like an enormous black arch rose over a circle of barren ground. Scattered around the arch, among the threads of streams, were houses of oak and stone, sheds, barns and walled fields. At the edge of the fallow field, in front of the arch, stood a gigantic oak. Its boughs seemed to have stretched out to gather years and centuries. In the oval of earth its vast shadow swept nothing stood except a great dwelling of black stone.

Its outer walls were open to all light, wind and weather.
The harsh, twisted shadow of the oak probed through the
dark archways in its walls. Light from the setting sun
rimmed one wall of arches with fire. Cresce remembered
something that her father had told her, long ago, about the
black house at the edge of Forever where the Bards of Jazi
lived.

She broke her long silence, asked the young, red-haired
man beside her, who rode his horse and wore the hawk on
his shoulder as if they were extensions of him, "Who
played the cothone to welcome me?"

He was silent so long she thought he had not heard. But
finally he said, "The Bard of Jazi."

"The Bard played a Daghian salute? But how did he
know I was from Daghian? How—" The question snagged
suddenly in her throat. "Who— What is your name?"

He looked at her with the odd mixture of bitterness and
courtesy in his eyes. "Hroi Tuel. And yours, Bard?"

"Cresce Dami. Who is the Bard of Jazi?"

He held her eyes a moment longer. Then he lifted Sere's
head by the hair, let it drop again. "His wife."

They reached the black house under the ancient oak at
twilight. Someone had sounded a salute at the edge of
the village. Women with torches, trays of food and wine,
met Cresce as she dismounted, welcomed her, smiling.
They wore her face. Some of them had grown up with her
mother. They asked questions about her mother's life in
Onon, if she had been happy, how she had died. They
were oblivious to Sere, as if he were a saddle-pack slung
across Cresce's horse. But she saw a couple of men bring
him into the house. The women took her inside, into one
of the inner rooms. A brazier warmed it; oil lamps lit the
rough, colorful tapestries on the black walls, the oak chairs
and chests covered with sheepskins. The men had left Sere
lying among Cresce's possessions on the rugs. The
women, assured by Cresce repeatedly that they could do
nothing more for her, left finally.

She knelt beside Sere, turned his head gently. Blood

had dried in his hair, crusted on the side of his face. She
washed it away as well as she could, and covered him with
sheepskins. Then she sat watching him, her arms tight
around her knees. She heard steps in another part of the
house, the voices of the women again. Then something
that sounded like a horn moaned the salute to the Bard of
Hekar across the village, and she closed her eyes, hid her
face against her knees.

A quarter of an hour later, the Bard of Hekar himself
appeared at her door.

He was twice her age, a richly dressed, fair-haired man
with a thin, lined face and a sour expression in his eyes. He
said nothing to Cresce; his lean, sensitive musician's hands
searched the crusted wound in Sere's hair, and the dark
bruise on his jaw. Then he sat back on his heels and
demanded,

"Why? Why did you bring him into Jazi?"

She slid her wrists over her ears. "Don't shout at me."

"Do you realize what will happen if he dies here? I don't
know how you managed to keep him alive this long."

"I cried. They said it would ruin their crops."

He was silent, gazing at her. A corner of his mouth
twisted unwillingly. "Cresce Dami. You played the
cothone for men of the King's court while they hunted at
Daghian last autumn. What would your father have said?"

"Did you know my father?"

"I was a musician at Hekar, the five years he was Bard
there. I have been at Hekar since I was born." He ran his
hands through his hair, jerked his head at Sere. "Why did
he come? If he dies here, Daghian will go to war against
Jazi, and Hekar will be forced to war against Daghian. You
and I will play battle-charges on opposite fields."

She said his name softly. "Ytir Agora. The Bard with the
throat of gold."

"There is not much chance to sing on a battle-field," he
said bitterly. He stood up. "Daghian fool," he muttered to
Sere's unresponsive face. Then he whirled at her. "Why?"

"I don't know why! Ask the Bard of Jazi—she sent for
him! She's his wife." She stood up under his amazed stare.

"Where is she, anyway?"

"In the hills, sounding salutes. There are other bards coming. That makes no sense! Does she want him dead?"

She stared numbly down at Sere. "I don't know."

She met the Bard of Jazi at midnight. Sere had wakened finally; he seemed surprised at being alive. He drank a little wine, then drifted to sleep again. Bards from other courts and cities introduced themselves to Cresce. They seemed, like the people of Jazi, to regard Sere as an embarrassment, of possible concern only if he were dead. When they left, Cresce sat playing the cothone softly, droning slow dark notes out of the eighth pipe. Finally, she heard someone ride to the doors of the house and dismount. There were voices, murmuring, indistinct, and then quick footsteps through the quiet house. Cresce let her cothone rest. A woman entered breathlessly, sending the still lamp-flames flickering all over the room.

She was as beautiful as Sere had said. Her black hair hung in thick braids to her waist, gold thread woven through them. Her eyes were wide-set, a deep, tempestuous, autumn grey. She was taller than Cresce, almost as tall as Sere, which betrayed her mixed heritage, but gave her a grace and suppleness even in the shapeless bulky skirts and tunics the Jazi women wore. Her eyes went to Sere, and then to Cresce, sitting mute with the cothone in her hands. She said nothing; she only knelt beside Cresce, held her tightly a moment. Then she turned to Sere, stroked his face until he woke.

He whispered, "Lelia."

Her throat suddenly swollen, as with deep, unsounded cothone notes, Cresce got up quickly then, and left them.

She went outside, into the night. The spring winds had blown stars like seed through the sky above the plain. The moon sat like a white bird on the black gate into Forever. The enormous oak tree murmured like a muted cyrillaya under the wind's touch. Cresce walked in its black moon-shadow toward the edge of the barren field.

She stood looking at the hard, silvery earth, the immense archway the winds were blowing through. Something her father had said teased her mind. Something about a great circle of cothone players around that field, trying to coax an answer from the silence within that arch. In the distance, the river burned a path through the dark plain. She turned away from the field, followed the edge of a tiny stream that made a half-circle, tracing the shadow of the oak.

Outside the great wings of the oak, she saw Hroi Tuel, restless in the moonlight, flicking pebbles into the stream with a great hawk asleep on his shoulder.

She sat down beside him. He said nothing; she watched rings form and flow into one another as the pebbles dropped. She asked him the simplest question first, her voice stilling his hand.

"Would you have killed Sere?"

"Yes."

"Then why did she call him to Jazi?"

He shrugged. "No one questions the Bard of Jazi. She changes fortune."

"What if she leaves with him, goes back to Daghian?"

"She is not free." He swept his arm in an arch across the stars. "She is not free. So they say. I think the Bards of Jazi bind themselves. And I don't believe in fortune."

She bowed her face against her knees, blocking the stars from her vision. Her hands clenched, a rare, untrained movement. She said carefully, "When the army of Daghian passed through Jazi seventy years ago, they did more than abduct one woman. True?"

"Nine men of Daghian," he said harshly, "survived the battle of Hekar Pass. They knew the truth, but that truth was never spoken in Daghian. Even today, seventy years later, there are children born in Jazi with hair pale as corn-silk. Or red, like mine. Hekar Pass was a matter of justice."

She lifted her head again. "I have her cothone—the woman taken by the Lord of Daghian. Was she a bard?"

"They say so. For seven years after she left, the river was burned dry by the sun, and what sheep the army left in Jazi starved because the pastures dried. She wasn't there to change fortune." He was silent. Then he sent a fistful of pebbles spattering into the water, and faced her. "Is it because I'm part Daghian that I don't believe that? When you said today that you would play the winter rituals if we killed the Daghian, the other men were frightened. Maybe they are old enough and wise enough to be afraid."

"I don't know. How would I know?"

"You are half Jazi, and a bard. You should know."

"I know the Songs of Changing Fortune. I don't know anything about fortune." She picked up one of his pebbles suddenly, sent it skimming down the stream. "This much is true: the Bard of Jazi controls Sere's fortune."

"She brought you. She brought you both."

"Are the Bards of Jazi always women?"

"No. The Bards of Jazi are chosen by the dead."

She felt something shiver through her bones. "How?"

He shrugged again; the hawk clinging in its sleep to his shoulder as to a swaying tree. "I don't know." For the first time, his voice seemed free of bitterness, dragged into wonder. "In Jazi, the dead are burned, and their ashes blow through the gates of Forever into that bare ground. You tell me how the dead can play the cothone."

"You've heard it," she whispered.

"Once. When Lelia Daghian played the cothone at the spring rituals. No one even knew her name. . . ." His shadowed, eyeless face turned again to Cresce as she shuddered. He reached out, gripped her shoulder with a steady, hawk's grip. "She was from Daghian. Chosen by the dead."

She stared at the mask the moon made of his face. "It's a matter of music. No more."

"I try to believe that." His hand loosened, until it lay very gently on her shoulder. "Men and women of Jazi killed by that Daghian army were burned and scattered through those gates. . . . I don't know what to believe. My father is Overlord of Jazi, and I am his red-haired son. And the part of me born to hate Daghian is also drawn to the world beyond Jazi. I can't sleep at nights; my dreams

are torn in two, from not knowing. . . . You are half Jazi,
Bard of Daghian, and the dead will listen to you play. What
will you do?"

She rose, splashed across the shallow stream. Facing
him again, she could see his eyes, bitter, haunted, the huge
hawk awake on his broad shoulder.

He said, "Where will you go, Bard? Back to Daghian?
You are not free. Neither of us is free."

In the black house again, curled under sheepskin in the
darkness, she heard the words again and again, hounding
her into sleeplessness.

She woke with a start at mid-morning. Sere was up,
washing the dried blood out of his hair in a basin of water.
He turned at her question.

"She went up into the hills again to welcome the visitors." His face was white, drawn; he looked oddly peace-
less. She said anxiously,

"I thought you would be happier."

He frowned down at her, not seeing her. "There are
women here with hair as fair as Hulme's." He turned back
to the basin, stared at his reflection in the bloody water.
"Something stinks in Daghian history, and the smell is
blowing out of Hekar Pass. No wonder they hate us."

"She doesn't." Cresce sat up, pushing hair out of her
eyes, trying to see. "She doesn't hate you. Why did she
put you in so much danger?"

"She wanted me to come to her. She can't go back to
Daghian. She is Bard of Jazi—the fortune of Jazi."

Her lips parted on a sudden breath. "You can't. You
can't stay here. You are a Lord of Daghian. There's nothing here but sheep. They'll kill you and your brothers will
come—"

"You stop them." He knelt at her side suddenly, raised
her cold fingers and kissed them. "Bard of Daghian, sing
the truth of Hekar Pass to Daghian."

She stared at his bent head, the strokes of copper in his
wet, tangled hair. She said, her voice shaking, "How do I
know what the truth is?"

She rode out of the village an hour later to speak to the

Bard of Jazi. The music of the Bard's salutes guided Cresce through the plain, then high up into the hills. A horn-call rolled through the valleys, bidding welcome to a group of bards traveling down a road cut between the hills. The Bard herself stood on the crest of a hill overlooking them. As Cresce drew nearer, she recognized the twisted, bone-white horn, made of pieces of ram's horn bound together with gold. Its tone was strong, bright; only the fading cadences frayed to a hollowness, like the wind's voice.

The Bard did not seem surprised to see Cresce. She stilled the horn and watched Cresce dismount. Facing her, Cresce saw then what she had seen in Hroi Tuel, and later, in Sere: a confusion, a peacelessness. She said huskily,

"When I came to Daghian, the first ballad I sang was of Sere, and his hunting of the stag that was not a stag. Or maybe it was a stag after all. I never wondered before this. What was Sere really following through the mists? A stag? A woman? A bird? Or something else? When I look at you, I don't understand what I'm seeing. What are you doing? Are you trying to kill Sere?"

"I don't think so." She stood for a moment under Cresce's incredulous gaze, her hands tight on the ram's horn. Then she took Cresce's arm, led her to a sheepskin rug laid on the bare ground. "Sit down, Cresce Dami. Never, never could I have been Bard of Daghian. But I played my great-grandmother's cothone since I was a child, and in Jazi, that one instrument is enough."

"Why did you leave Daghian?"

"Look at me. Old, old men of Jazi say that I am the bard that the army of Daghian stole, returned at last to Jazi. I am their fortune."

"Are you?"

"Perhaps." She was silent, her thoughts indrawn. "Perhaps. Maybe their only fortune is hope, which I give them. I don't know. I am my own misfortune."

"Why?" She pleaded. "I don't understand you. I don't understand you."

"I am half of Jazi, half of Daghian. If Sere had died

yesterday, I would have been free of Daghian." She shook
her head again, her face twisting a little at Cresce's expression. "All I can give you is what you asked for. Truth. That
was one thought in my mind. But also, I gave Jazi the truth:
I didn't want to lie to them about Sere. So I told them what
he was. They nearly killed him, and you saved him, as I
hoped you could."

"Do you love him?" Cresce whispered. "Or don't
you?"

"I don't know. I don't even know if I love the people of
Jazi, who demand everything of me—even my freedom.
All I know is that I won't ever leave them without a bard."

Cresce was silent. The winds sifted dryly through the
oak-leaves. She said abruptly, as if the word were surprised out of her, "No."

"In Daghian, I have a son. I have a place in the Lord's
house. I have horses, birds, great music. Here, I listen on a
windy day to sheep-bells. And I wonder what is happening
in the great cities of the kingdom. But in Daghian, my face
is the face of a woman of Jazi. And the men of Daghian are
the sons and grandsons of the army that swept through
Jazi seventy years ago, stealing, burning, raping, murder-
ing. Tell me. Where do I belong?"

"Why did you leave Daghian?"

"I followed something one winter through the Daghian
marshes. A cothone, played like a promise of passion and
wonder beyond the mists, out of the hills of Jazi. . . . All
I found here were sheep-bells." She smiled a little,
crooked smile.

"But you didn't leave Jazi."

"No. I became their Bard. How could I have left them? I
am their promise of wonder. Of hope." She studied
Cresce, the uncertainty in her eyes easing a little. "You are
beginning to understand me. I am not terrible. I am just—
torn."

"Like Hroi Tuel."

Lelia nodded. "Hroi. Afraid to hope in visions. One day,
he'll leave Jazi. But I don't know if he will ever find peace,
in or out of Jazi."

"Who played—who played the cothone I heard in the marshes last autumn?"

Lelia was silent. She reached out suddenly, put her hand on Cresce's wrist. "Believe me." Her voice was low, timbreless as a distant horn. "I didn't."

Cresce drew breath soundlessly. She sat with her head bowed, gazing down at the valley below. "If Sere stays with you, the Lords of Daghian will come to get him."

"You stop them."

"Will I be able to? If you—if you leave Jazi—"

"I can't leave."

"If you leave, will you be content in Daghian?"

"I don't know."

"Then why did you call Sere! Why did you give him hope?"

"Sere knows me." She curled the soft wool in her long fingers. "He was very angry with me, last night. I told him exactly what I've told you. The truth."

"Do you love him?"

She sighed. "If I could turn into a bird, fly into a winter twilight. . . I love Sere as I love Jazi. As much as I am able. He knows that. He sees me clearly. And I'm not a woman in a mist. I am his wife, and the mother of his son. I am Bard of Jazi, the good fortune of Jazi. All these things bind me. But only because I choose to be bound."

Cresce was silent. The Bard's face held, she thought suddenly, all the names of the pipes of the cothone. The longing, the mourning, the calling, the passion, the warning. . . . She raised her hand suddenly, touched its beauty, and at the touch, remembered its danger.

"I'm free," she whispered.

"Yes."

"Then why," she cried out, rising, "do I have to keep telling myself that?"

She roamed through the hills all day long. At evening, she returned to the Bard's house. Hroi Tuel, escorting the last of the visitors down from the hills, dropped from his horse to her side. She did not speak to him. He said,

"An hour before dawn, the Bard will wake. She'll play

the sun's rising at the edge of Forever field. The villagers
and guests will gather in a great circle around the field. The
cothone will be played from sunrise to sunrise. The Daghian Lord will be killed if he sets one foot out of this
house.''

She went into the house without looking at him. In her
room, she found Sere gazing out through the thin shaft of
window at the barren field. She stared helplessly at his
back, wondering if he was imprisoning himself out of love
for a woman, or as a penance for Hekar Pass. She went to
his side, stood as close to him as she could without touching him. His eyes met hers; he brushed her cheek gently.

"I'll miss you, Bard."

"You'll die here. You'll hear nothing but sheep-bells,
and they'll find a reason to kill you."

"No one ever died of listening to sheep-bells."

"I would."

"You stop my brothers from coming." His eyes bore
into hers harshly. "You can. Make them feel the truth. Or
there will be more blood shed between Daghian, Jazi and
Hekar than in all the ballads you learned at Onon."

"Come home."

"No."

She left him. She took sheepskins, crossed the stream,
and went to sit at the edge of Forever, facing west, so that
she would see the sun rise through the great, dark
arch. When the moon set she fell asleep. She woke at the
first, dazzling shaft of light sweeping the mouth of the arch,
called by the Bard of Jazi on the first pipe of the cothone,
the pipe of joy.

Arrows soared through the arch, tuned to the pipe. They
turned into minute, hurtling splinters of light before they
fell earthward again. Women from the village carried great
trays of food and wine to the crowd gathering around the
field. They were talking, laughing; some of them sang to
the sound of the cothone. Children, herdsmen, farmers,
craftsmen, the visiting bards took places around the barren
ground, sitting in a great circle while bowmen, to the strains
of the ram's horn, sent another blaze of arrows through the

arch. Musicians gathered to one side of Cresce. She
studied their instruments: painted drums of wood and
hollow gourd, copper wind-chimes, rows of bells strung on
leather, horns, wooden flutes, the small hand-pipes the
men used to call their horses. The musicians were talking,
eating; children surrounded them, tapping on the drums
and the bells. Only the Bard ate nothing, and spoke to no
one as she brought up the sun.

When she sang the first Song of Changing Fortune,
though, there was utter silence.

It was a light, almost dream-like song, accompanied by
the bird-voices of hand-pipes, the wind-stroked chimes
and high, soft bells. The sun had loosed its grip of the hills;
the Bard coaxed it higher until it hovered in the center of
the archway. Her voice faded into the morning wind.
Birds flashed, their wings on fire, across the face of the sun.
There was a murmuring from the visitors. Then the Bard
lifted the cothone, began to play the second pipe, the pipe
of wonder.

Cresce took wine, and some steamed, fruit-filled bread
from one of the women. The swelling in her throat made it
difficult to swallow at first. Lelia's face seemed remote,
peaceful, as if she had left her confusion and pain outside
of the barren circle. She would not sing again until noon,
Cresce remembered. Noon, then twilight, midnight and
sunrise again, the first five of the hundred and one Songs
of Changing Fortune. Cresce wondered if Sere could hear
her voice. Then she realized someone was sitting beside
her.

She turned, wondering how long Hroi Tuel had been
with her. He sat as still as the great bird on his shoulder, but
she saw his eyes move from face to face around the circle.
Once he said, his voice inflectionless, "She has brought up
the sun; she will bring up the corn." Then, later, he
touched Cresce's wrist. "There's my father."

A big, black-haired man, dressed in a long, wheat-
colored ceremonial robe, had seated himself on the other
side of the musicians. One of the barefoot children crept up
behind him, flung her arms around his neck and he

laughed. But a shadow settled into his eyes a moment later. Hroi said, regarding him,

"He said I should have killed the Daghian Lord." He spat suddenly on the ground. "Men of Daghian are not human. That's what I have been taught. He would have been human enough in my dreams if I had killed him. But now he will stay in Jazi, and no one is permitted to touch him or speak to him. My father says he'll bring misfortune. My father says. The Bard brought you here so she could leave Jazi."

"I know."

He looked at her then, angry, tormented. "She is our good fortune. Lelia Daghian." He spat again. Then, at her silence, he asked roughly, "What will you do?"

"I am Bard of Daghian. I have nothing to do with the fortune of Jazi."

"There is no such thing as fortune. There is only a woman playing a cothone who hates Jazi."

"No," Cresce said softly. "She is like you. Listen to her music. She could have walked out of Jazi at any time. But she chose to stay."

"She brought you."

"I won't play. She took that risk."

"Then the man she loves will be a prisoner in Jazi, and the butchers of Daghian will come looking for him. There is no fortune. Only a woman playing a cothone."

"I'll tell the Lords of Daghian the truth. There will be no war."

"What music will you give to Daghian that you refuse to give Jazi? Bard."

She was silent. The Bard changed pipes, began a song on the pipe of laughter.

At noon, Lelia sang to the sun overhead as she walked around the field, her shadow flickering out of its barrenness to touch the new grass pushing toward light on the plain. After her song, the Bard of Hekar began to play. His music was very simple and a little unsure, for he was not used to playing the cothone, but there was a lightness and enthusiasm in it that the Bard had inspired. She smiled

across the circle at him, then sat down for the first time in
six hours. The women brought her food and wine, but they
did not speak to her. Cresce saw her glance once at the
black house beneath the oak. The song of the Bard of
Hekar ended; another visitor began to play. Cresce
realized with surprise that it was one of her teachers from
Onon. At mid-afternoon, Lelia began to play again. The
musicians beat a wild, raucous dance to her music. The
children whirled to it, while some of the old people
stretched on the grass and napped. The women serving
food disappeared; a little later the smells of roast lamb and
wild boar wafted across the field.

The Bard's song at sunset was played on the fourth and
fifth pipes: the pipes of longing and of love. Standing on
the opposite side of the circle, she eased the brilliant sun
into a bed of gold beyond the hills. Its rays touched her face
again and again before it withdrew. The oak shadow flung
over half the plain faded slowly; the tree loosed the light it
had gathered into its boughs. Dusk left the plain in an
uncertain, misty light. Then, as the first star appeared, the
bowmen shot arrows of flaming pitch high, high toward the
arch, trying to send them over it. Only one struck the lower
edge of the arch; the others fell through it, sank, burning,
into the bare earth. There was laughter, applause. Torches
were lit in the grass. Lelia played the measure of a wild
dance that was picked up by one of the visiting bards. The
musicians shook the crowd awake with the lively beat of
drums and flutes. Circles of dancers formed around the
torches, whirling and laughing. The full moon began its
slow arch above Jazi.

Hroi Tuel, who had appeared and disappeared unexpectedly throughout the day, brought Cresce a plate of
food, then vanished again. She sat picking at spiced lamb
and pickled vegetables, watching the dancers winding in
and out of the torches. Someone dropped down beside
her in the shadows. She glanced up expecting Hroi's taut,
brooding face. She coughed a little, on a piece of pickled
cabbage.

Sere touched her briefly, then shifted back into the

shadows. He waited until a woman carrying pitchers of wine had passed them. Then he said softly, "I was going mad in that house, trying to hear. I had to hear. They won't notice me in the dark."

"Have you eaten?" She pushed her plate to him. "They'll kill you if they recognize you."

"They won't." He wrapped lamb in hot bread, chewed it hungrily. "They forgot to feed me. Or maybe they didn't forget. Have you played, yet?"

"No. I'm not going to."

He stopped chewing, stared at her. He swallowed. "Why? I want to hear what comes out of you and that cothone."

"I'm not playing."

He held her eyes, his own eyes narrowed, until she looked away. He put her plate down, gripped her wrist. Then a shadow rustled next to Cresce, and Sere seemed to blur into himself, shifting back into his sheepskin cloak. Hroi held out a cup of wine to Cresce. Then he offered a piece of boar-meat to the bird on his shoulder. Cresce, her mouth dry, her hands shaking, sipped wine silently, waiting for the hard, incredulous whip of his voice as he discovered Sere. But Hroi never spoke. Balanced on his haunches, his eyes unwinking, he looked like the hawk on his shoulder, its still eyes drenched with fire.

The dance music began to die. The moon's face hardened into a clear, unbearable beauty, and the Bard of Jazi played a warning on the sixth pipe. Another bard from Onon began playing with her, weaving a restless, minor melody through hers. Other warnings drifted through theirs, the dark music never quite harmonized, never quite chaotic, as if many different voices were trying to describe the same misfortune looming out of the night. Some voices drifted to silence; others took up the warning until it seemed to Cresce that every bard in the circle had played except for her. But there seemed no music in her, as if she had already heeded the Bard's warning.

Finally, all the cothones fell silent, except for Lelia's. She had changed position again; she stood facing west, at the edge of the moon-shadow of the oak. Her face was in shadow; her music drifted into shadow. For a breath the night was soundless. Then, out of moonlight and shadow, came the deep, wild, passionate voice of the seventh pipe.

Cresce felt her heart torn open suddenly, aching. The Bard seemed to know all their language. She played Hroi's tormented doubt, Sere's anger and love. She played her own confusion of love and restlessness, the pride and beauty she had learned at Daghian, the sorrow and faith of Jazi. And out of all the tangle of their thoughts, she shaped something that ran at the edge of the fiery darkness like a dream: a glimpse of unbearable beauty that existed only to be hunted, never caught. Cresce's hands closed on her own cothone. She kept them still, though the music seemed to gather in her bones. Her silence was a hard, painful knot in her throat. Visions of the great white stag, forever pursued, forever eluded, ran through her heart. She thought of Sere tracking it on foot through the marshes of Daghian; of his grandson at her left pursuing a dream of love; of Hroi Tuel at her right, desperate for an illusion of truth. And she realized then what endless, hopeless visions the Bard herself pursued to create for them their own visions of hope.

She found herself on her feet, in silent salute to the Bard of Jazi. Tears burned in her eyes; her hands seemed frozen on her cothone. Music weltered soundlessly through her, compelled by a heritage of a barren field and a black spring night. But she stood still, forcing herself silent, until she realized slowly the barrenness of her own refusal to pursue the powerful, fleeting vision of her music.

She lifted the eighth pipe to her mouth, understanding at last what it mourned. She waited until the Bard's music died away. Then, with her first low note, she promised Hroi and Sere and the people of Jazi their visions, and the Bard of Jazi her freedom. She accompanied Lelia through the midnight Song of Fortune. Then she drew the night into her cothone, sent it out again, note by note, across the barren field. Pitching her music deep, she sent a slow, dark song into the arch that seemed to reach out of her bones, out of the roots beneath her, out of the life beneath the barren field, to pierce the silence locked within the arch of Forever.

She stopped as abruptly as she had begun, when the only sound left in her was the deep, ragged beat of her heart. She sat down, dropping the cothone. Slowly, someone else in the circle took up her song, and she closed her eyes, breathing deeply in relief, that she had tried and failed, and the silence surrounding the stars was still unbroken. Then she recognized the rich, husky, unearthly pipes of the cothone answering her.

A wind swept across the plain, carrying echoes of a thousand pipes of joy and mourning. Something seemed to enter Cresce, touch her bones. She heard Hroi's breath catch, then catch again. She swallowed dryly, longing suddenly to play again, to stand with the night to its darkness and end, then bring the first touch of sunlight into Jazi. Then a voice out of the shadows cried out harshly, shattering the weave of music beyond the arch:

"No!"

Hroi was on his feet suddenly, the hawk beating on his shoulder. He pulled a torch out of the ground, swung it at the darkness, illuminating Sere as he flung himself back from the fire.

"You," Hroi breathed. "You." There were tears running down his face. "You in Daghian were born listening for the voices of the dead in Jazi."

He hurled the torch at Sere's face. Sere rolled; the torch caught the sheepskin at his back, set it blazing. He threw himself on his back, trying to smother the flames. Hroi, the hawk fluttering off his shoulder, lunged at Sere. Sere's boot slammed into his breastbone, spun him off his feet. Sere straightened, slapping at his cloak. A fist coming out of the darkness cracked across his face and he fell, extinguishing the last of the fire. Cresce, seeing the circle of men closing around him, felt a fury shake her like the bass voices of the cothone.

"Stop it!" Her voice cracked like a reed. "I am the Bard of Jazi! You will not touch him!" She whirled at Hroi, who was starting to rise. "Stop it!" He froze. She looked down at Sere, struggling to his knees. "And you!" His face lifted; her voice cracked again. "Lord of Daghian! Go back to Daghian!"

Lelia, shouldering past the men, went to his side. She tried to help him up; he shook her away, shouted at her, still on his knees, "What are you doing? You called Cresce Dami to take your place— You called us both— You nearly got me killed— You weren't content in Daghian, you aren't content here—"

"I am not made to be content!" She was crying suddenly, still trying to help him, on her knees beside him.

"Then what are you made for?"

"To play the cothone. To know all its voices." She put her arms around him, her voice muffled in charred sheepskin. "I have been faithful to Jazi. I will be that faithful to you. That much I know. That, I chose."

He was silent. His eyes went to Cresce; she saw the look in them that must have been in his grandfather's when the beautiful animal changed shape before his eyes, and then changed shape again. Cresce put her hands over her mouth, whispered to Sere, "You. Love her. She will sing the truth in Daghian."

She saw the tears in his own eyes. "I can't let you do this. I can't go back to Daghian leaving you here. You are the pride of Daghian. Your music will die here in this silence. Everything you learned at Onon will be lost."

"I didn't have to play here," she said softly. "I chose to." She swallowed the fire in her throat. "Go home." She looked at the Overlord of Jazi, staring at her in wonder at the edge of the circle of men. "I am Bard of Jazi, chosen by the dead of Jazi. You will permit him to leave in peace. Or I will cry over every corn-field in Jazi."

She turned, walked through the darkness to take Lelia's place at the edge of Forever. Someone had continued to play the cothone through the turmoil and shouting, keeping the ancient ritual of music passed like a flame from bard to bard uninterrupted. She sent him silent gratitude as she took the melody from him. Then she realized, as he lowered his instrument, that it was the Bard of Hekar.

She played through the dark hours of morning until dawn. Then, at the first slow run of fire across the hills, she changed to the first pipe. She did not know where she found the joy to sing the fifth Song of Changing Fortune, but it was in her somehow, as she watched the light wash across the fragile green of the hills, as she looked through the arch and saw the fronds of new leaves on the ancient, twisted oak-boughs.

After she sang, she sat for a long time in silence, while the crowd dispersed around her to eat and sleep. The barren field was quiet again. The wind rustled across the plain, bringing her the sound of sheep-bells. She drew her knees up, rested her face in her arms and thought of Daghian. She raised her head again finally. The monotonous, unfamiliar hills still ringed her with their silence.

Hroi Tuel was sitting motionlessly beside her. As she straightened, he put his hand on her shoulder. Then he winced. "That Daghian Lord cracked my ribs." After a moment, he admitted, "There was some justice in that."

Cresce did not answer. But she sensed, through the confusion of despair and faith she had committed herself to, the beginnings of his peace.

Contributors' Notes

JAMES P. BLAYLOCK has, for the record, denied that his is an interesting life, given that he has (allegedly) never worked for the C.I.A., depth-tested submarines, won chess tournaments, nor mastered even a single martial art. Belying his contentions are the confessed facts that Blaylock lives in California, is married, raises sons and pet octopi, and that he and his wife were once assaulted by a toad. Known in academic circles as a critical expert on the work of the British Romantic writer William Ashbless (a friend of Lord Byron's), Blaylock's short fiction has appeared in *TriQuarterly* and he is the author of *The Elfin Ship* and *The Disappearing Dwarf*, both high fantasy mystery-adventures about a cheese maker and his dog.

Widely anthologized throughout Latin America, Chilean author and screenwriter MARÍA LUISA BOMBAL (1910–1980) was recognized as an innovative stylist upon the publication of her first novella, "The Final Mist," in 1934 (which was written on the kitchen counter of an apartment in Buenos Aires that she shared with the then little-known poet Pablo Neruda and his wife). "The Unknown" appeared in English translation in her posthumous collection, *New Islands and Other Stories*.

PAUL BOWLES left a career as a successful composer of operas, film scores, ballets, and chamber music to become perhaps the most famous expatriate American writer (and translator from the Moghrebi, French, Arabic, Spanish, and Italian) in Tangiers, Morocco. In Bowles's fiction, the boundaries between the phantasmic and the fantastic are studied through the disorientation of culture shock, clashing Islamic-Christian world views, madness, drugged hallucinations, and the bleak, deadly beauty of the Sahara. "The dreamlike brutality of Bowles's imagination," states Joyce Carol Oates, "evokes a horror far more pervasive than anything in Poe."

STEVEN R. BOYETT was born in 1960; he attended the University of Tampa on a writing scholarship for two years, quit "before it could become fatal," and wrote his first novel, *Ariel,* the story of a young man's coming of age in a United States overcome by magic. He is at work on a second novel, which is *not*—he notes cheerfully—a sequel. Together with Lisa Simonne Pianka and two quirky dogs, Boyett lives in Gainesville, Florida and works in the history department at the University of Florida.

British author ANGELA CARTER traces the roots of her fiction to "witch blood on Father's side; solid radical trade-unionists on Mother's." Winner of the Somerset Maugham Award and the John Llewellyn Rhys Prize, Carter writes fantasies that are often marked by grotesque imagery and eroticism. In addition to literary analysis *(The Sadian Woman),* and stories set in Japan, Carter's fantasy includes *The Bloody Chamber, The Magic Toyshop, Heroes and Villains, The War of Dreams,* and *The Passions of New Eve.*

"Here is a plea based on my whole experience: do not be a magician, be magic." Best known as the composer of such songs as "Joan of Arc," "Sisters of Mercy," and "Suzanne," Canadian performer LEONARD COHEN has also enjoyed reputations as a popular poet *(Spice Box of the Earth, Let Us Compare Mythologies)* whose "descriptions of unreal things are so vivid they can leave you breathless with delight" (A. W. Purdy), and a novelist of "terrible and beautiful visions" (the *New York Times*), prompting one critic to note: "In his books and songs he is not merely the sorcerer but the spell itself." "God is Alive, Magic is Afoot" was taken from Cohen's 1966 mystical novel, *Beautiful Losers,* and adapted into a verse-chant by Buffy Sainte-Marie for her album "Illuminations."

MICHAEL DE LARRABEITI is a British author of westerns, mystery, suspense, and fantasy. He is best known in this country as the author of the "Borrible" books, fantasies about modern, streetwise, feral Peter Pans who live in the back alleys of contemporary London, which the *New York Times* called "chilling . . . the offspring of a singular imagination." The story in this volume was inspired by Basque legend. De Larrabeiti writes: "I lived in Provence for a number of years and for a great deal of that time was a travel guide there. Taking American and British trippers up and down the country was a fine education. Provence is a fascinating part of the world and full of folklore."

During the nearly four years of collecting stories for *Elsewhere*, ESTHER M. FRIESNER has come to hold, in the eyes of the editors, two distinctions. Ms. Friesner is both the anthology's most prolific aspiring contributor of unsolicited stories (certainly the most thankless, frustrating, and daunting stage of any author's career), and the most personally reticent. We received, approximately, a story a month (sans cover letters) for three years—and were thus able to witness Friesner's increasing proficiency with the short story form and an impressive versatility in tone and content—from fairy tale to swords & sorcery to Buddhist legendry to the urbane fantasy piece in this volume.

LOUISE GLÜCK hails from Brooklyn and presently lives with her husband and son in Vermont. Glück has received the Academy of Poet's Prize, the Eugene Tietjens Poetry Magazine Prize, and a Guggenheim Fellowship for her work. She has published several collections of poetry, including *Firstborn; The Descending Figure;* and *House on the Marshlands,* from which the poem in this volume is reprinted.

ROBERT GRAVES, preeminent British poet, novelist, and critic, is the author of over one hundred books, including the controversial nonfiction title *The White Goddess: A Historical Grammar of Poetic Myth,* in which he argues that all true poetry is dedicated to the Goddess in her aspect of the Muse. He is perhaps best known for his historical novel, *I, Claudius,* adapted into a B.B.C. dramatic series. The poem in this volume shows the more whimsical side of the poet's nature.

A widely published novelist, poet, and playwright, ALVIN GREENBERG is (as of the most recent available biography) a professor of English at Macalester College in St. Paul, Minnesota. " 'Franz Kafka' by Jorge Luis Borges" comes from the pages of his collection, *Discovering America and Other Stories of Terror and Self-Expression.*

RAMON GUTHRIE (1896–1973) was an American poet, novelist, teacher, and translator. "Springsong in East Gruesome, Vermont" was found in the 1969 collection *Asbestos Phoenix.*

Self-described as a "hunter, fisherman, picker of wild berries, and gardener," Alaskan homesteader JOHN HAINES is also a prize-winning sculptor, a Guggenheim Fellow, a translator, a poet, and has worked on the renowned wilderness documentary, *The River Is Wide.* "And When the Green Man Comes" appeared in the collection *Winter News,* which, according to the author, "grew out of my experience in the Alaskan wilderness. It is poetry of solitude. . . . The subject matter is drawn from nature and its denizens . . . the durable stuff of childhood fantasies of life in the north woods."

SUSAN HEYBOER-O'KEEFE has published short fiction in *New Writers, Period, Circus Maximus, Eclipse, Pulp, Way, November* and *New Oxford Review.* Her first novel received a Goodman Award in manuscript. Heyboer-O'Keefe makes her home in New Jersey, where she works as an advertising copywriter, and currently focuses her attention and "fascination" on her newly born first child.

"As far back as I can remember," writes P. C. HODGELL, "I've been making up stories to tell myself. . . . My parents are both professional artists. I suppose I inherited my interest in craftsmanship and creativity from them, but while they work with paint and clay, my images have always come in words." Hodgell attended the Clarion Writers' Workshop, and is working on a doctorate in English literature with an emphasis on nineteenth-century fiction. Hodgell's first novel, *God Stalk,* is a bizarre and fascinating fantasy adventure. "Bones" is set in *God Stalk's* macabre Tai-tastigon, a city at the edge of the Haunted Lands, "riddled with thieves and lousy with gods. . . ."

Active in poetry since the 1930s, DAVID IGNATOW's reputation has grown steadily for the past thirty years. He is recognized as a major figure in American verse, a chronicler of both realistic and surrealistic aspects of the urban scene. According to James Dickey, "what gives [Ignatow's poems] their unique power is a kind of strange, myth-dreaming vision of modern city life."

British novelist and scriptwriter TANITH LEE secured, while still in her twenties, four separate literary reputations and audiences as a writer of: children's books *(The Dragon Hoard, Animal Castles)*, young adult fantasy *(Companions on the Road, East of Midnight)*, adult fantasy, and science fiction (the impact of her novels *Don't Bite the Sun* and *Drinking Sapphire Wine* has extended well into the cultural mainstream, inspiring works of popular music and art). Prolific and versatile, Lee also writes horror, comedy, and historical novels, and television scripts. *The Village Voice* has crowned Tanith Lee "the Princess Royal of Heroic Fantasy": recipient of both the World Fantasy Award and the British Fantasy Award, a sampling of Lee's varied fantasy styles includes: *The Birthgrave, Death's Master, Volkhavaar, Sabella, Kill the Dead, Lycanthia, Sung in Shadow* and a collection of darkly retold fairy tales, *Red as Blood.*

Born in Cartagena, Spain, FÉLIX MARTÍ-IBAÑEZ (1912–1972) was forced to leave his medical and psychiatric practices and emigrate to the United States when Franco came to power. A prolific medical essayist and medical historian, Martí-Ibañez also wrote *All the Wonders We Seek: Thirteen Tales of Surprise and Prodigy,* which might be described as a magical tour through South and Central America.

The calm of World Fantasy Award winner PATRICIA A. McKIL-LIP's life masks a driving discipline to master both writing and music, combined with—by the author's admission—often restless wanderlust. McKillip's acclaimed novels include three juvenile fantasy books: *The Throme of the Erril of Sherill,* a tongue-in-cheek (literally, when read aloud) pastiche of Victorian fairy tales, inspired by Middle English; *The House on Parchment Street;* and *The Night Gift. The Forgotten Beasts of Eld* followed, and a trilogy: *Riddle-Master of Hed, Heir of Sea and Fire,* and *Harpist in the Wind.* Her most recent work is *Stepping From the Shadows,* describing a woman's odyssey through a life of desperate fantasies conflicting with reality. "A Matter of Music" is her second work of short fiction; the first, "The Harrowing of the Dragon of Hoarsbreath," is available in *Elsewhere* Vol. II. "Storytelling," McKillip writes, "must have begun around a roaring fire inside a dark, safe cave, maybe with a skein of something fermented passing from hand to hand. Unfortunately, small, safe worlds you invent in fantasy—the hobbit worlds—always seem to invite destruction, or at least a good shaking up. . . ."

JENNIFER CAROLYN ROBIN McKINLEY, having spent her life thus far happily ensconced in the world of H. Rider Haggard and P. C. Wren, Joseph Conrad, and Charles Dickens, has entered the latter twentieth century with a crash, by the medium of music videos, especially those of David Bowie and Michael Jackson. When she goes for her long walks lately (she averages three pairs of New Balance shoes a year) she takes her hand-sized cassette player with her and listens to the Eurythmics and Kate Bush. She doesn't know what this may do to her writing, but she looks forward to finding out. (She does still read Rudyard Kipling's *Collected Verse* when she wakes up at 3 A.M. with nightmares. Not everything has changed.) She did thumb down the volume on "Eat to the Beat" long enough to accept the Newbery Honor for her fantasy novel, *The Blue Sword.* Other titles in print include *Beauty: A Retelling of Beauty and the Beast* and *The Door in the Hedge.* She is currently working on a fantasy collection, *Imaginary Lands;* and a new "Damar" novel, *The Hero and the Crown,* is forthcoming.

ROBERT MEZEY, who has publicly listed his political affiliation as "despairing" and his religion as "intolerable," has received a Lamont Poetry Award and a Guggenheim Fellowship; he has been poetry editor for *TransPacific.* About his work, Mezey states: "My poems are largely mysterious to me."

A person of remarkable achievements, Scotswoman NAOMI MARGARET MITCHISON (the sister of J. B. S. Haldane) has played an active role in biology, cattle breeding, social reform (as a pioneer in Britain's planned parenthood movements), politics (ranging from parliamentary elections to the Austrian counter-revolution of 1934 to the organizing of Arkansas share-croppers), anthropology, sociology, philosophy, and polemics, while upholding a writing career that spans more than sixty years. World-famed as an historical novelist, Mitchison has also written two volumes of science fiction. Fantasy elements may be noted in her novels *The Corn King and the Spring Queen, The Powers of Light,* and *Behold Your King,* in her children's fairy tale *The Big House,* and in her collections *Barbarian Stories* and *The Fourth Pig. To the Chapel Perilous* (from which "The Chapel Perilous" is excerpted) is perhaps the most iconoclastic and idiosyncratic Sangreal-redux ever published and has a loyal and growing underground following, despite the fact that the book has been out of print for thirty years.

PAT MURPHY, an alumnus of the Clarion Writers' Workshop, has garnered a growing reputation for her fantasy and science fiction short stories, and is the author of one novel, *The Shadow Hunter.* She is presently at work on a second novel, a fantasy set in the Yucatan. Murphy works at The Exploratorium, a participation-oriented science museum in San Francisco, which she describes as looking as though it were designed "by mad scientists."

A Woodrow Wilson Fellow, winner of the Academy of American Poets Prize, a Robert Frost Fellow at the Breadloaf Writers' conference, LAWRENCE RAAB is a poet and screenwriter whose works range from an opera libretto of *Dracula* to a funny, poignant love poem based on the movie *Attack of the Crab Monsters.*

Dragons, unicorns, wizards, crystal ships, and elfin folk gamboled in unparalleled number across tthe radio airwaves in the late 1960s and early 1970s, helping to introduce fantasy to a generation. Folk and rock lyrics of the period, as variously exemplified by Marc Bolan, Donovan Leitch, Bob Dylan, Jim Morrison, Robin Williamson, Cat Stevens, *Fairport Convention, Steeleye Span,* and others, gently combined surrealism, symbolism, traditional ballad imagery, myth, fairy tale, Edward Lear, Lewis Carroll, whimsy, mysticism, Kahlil Gibran, dream, Freudian nightmare, and psychedelic images. "In the Court of the Crimson King," a 1969 "observation" by British songwriters PETER SINFIELD and IAN McDONALD, members of the band *King Crimson,* is a striking example of this mixture of elements, which Peter Townsend once called "an uncanny masterpiece."

WILLIAM JAY SMITH is a prolific poet, playwright, translator, editor, anthologist, essayist, and children's book writer. Suggestive of Smith's range of interests are the facts that he has served in the Vermont House of Representatives and has been a literary consultant to such diverse entities as Grove Press and the Boy Scouts of America.

JOHN ALFRED TAYLOR was "exposed to Oz books and E. R. Burroughs's Mars stories before I was old enough to know better, so enjoy writing science fiction and horror stories when not in the mood for poetry; though still believe 'A poem a day keeps the madhouse away.' " Taylor's poetry has been widely published; his fiction has appeared in *The Twilight Zone.*

Author (and amateur puppeteer and ventriloquist) STEVE RASNIC TEM grew up in the Appalachian Mountains of Virginia—a background often incorporated into his fiction—and currently lives in Colorado. Since 1979, Tem has published over seventy-five short stories and over one hundred poems. He notes that he has always loved fairy tales—particularly the dark side of fairy tales; most of his work is in the horror field. "The imagination is important to me, and there is no literature that requires more imaginative thought than fantasy/horror/science fiction. It has always seemed to me that there is more truth in fantasy than in anything else." Tem has completed one novel and is at work on a second in collaboration with his wife.

AMOS TUTUOLA occupies a unique position in world literature: a Yoruba tribesman native to Abeokuta, Nigeria, he has become the *akpala kpatita* (professional tale-teller) to the world. Tutuola's books present the most startling, authentic, vivid, and rich visions of west African myth, folk-tale, fantasy, and world-view ever published. Yoruba legend presents a jungle unknown to (or at best tepidly evoked by) Western fantasists: a universe of wild humor, horror, weird magic, and a delirious imagery that rivals Hieronymous Bosch. Tutuola's style is, to many, challenging at first; his work comes into focus as the reader realizes that Tutuola (who writes not with the artifice of a patronizing pidgin dialect, but writes as he must) has captured the cadences, the rhythms, the hesitations, and the exuberance of an ancient shaman tradition. Tutuola was initially championed by Dylan Thomas (who considered Tutuola's first book a "thronged, grisley, bewitching story . . . through nightmares of indescribable adventures") and his work is influential in South America (notably in the writing of popular Brazilian author Jorge Amado). Amos Tutuola presently lives in Ibadan, Nigeria, and has recently visited the United States for an extended speaking, teaching, and symposium tour. Tutuola's expeditions into the heartland of Yoruba fantasy include *The Palm-Wine Drinkard (and His Dead Palm-Wine Tapster in the Dead's Town); My Life in the Bush of Ghosts; Simbi and the Satyr of the Dark Jungle; The Brave African Huntress; The Feather Woman of the Jungle; Ajaiyi and His Inherited Poverty;* and *The Witch-Herbalist of the Remote Town*. This is the first publication of the two stories in this volume.

SYLVIA TOWNSEND WARNER (1893–1978) was a Renaissance music scholar and author of twenty books, including novels whose subjects ranged from a fourteenth-century French convent to the 1848 Paris uprisings. Her first, and best known, novel, *Lolly Willows,* is a comic fantasy mingling witchcraft with British gentry mores. Her last collection, *Kingdoms of Elfin,* contains stories originally published in *The New Yorker* about the goings-on of the elfin kingdoms in England and Europe. The story in this volume is set in this Elfin world, but was not included, because of space considerations, in the collected volume; this is the first publication of "The Duke of Orkney's Leonardo" since its original 1976 appearance in *The New Yorker*.

One of America's most honored living poets, RICHARD WILBUR won both the Pulitzer Prize and the National Book Award for his collection, *Things of the Earth*. Other honors include a Guggenheim Fellowship, the Prix de Rome, and the Bollingen Award for translation. Known for his detached, academic precision, Wilbur's work includes *The Mind-Reader* and "Beasts" (a long poem in which human evolution is viewed through the eyes of a werewolf). The poem in this volume first appeared in *The New Yorker*.

Seventy books and counting . . . the irrepressible JANE YOLEN recently had to slow down her literary output while she designed and constructed a computerized attic studio in her Massachusetts farmhouse. Among her recent books are a pun-saturated children's story, "Commander Toad and the Planet of the Grapes," and an adult collection, *Tales of Wonder*, about which Gene Wolfe wrote: "Most of the great makers of *märchen* are unknown to us. Of those whose names are known, I can think of only four. Of these, only one is a living writer: Jane Yolen. In a better world, we shall hear her tales, with Oscar Wilde's, Hans Christian Andersen's, and Charles Perrault's, over a winter's evening of ten thousand years." Yolen has contributed three very different stories to the three volumes of *Elsewhere:* a poignant fairy tale in the first, a moody adult fantasy story in the second, and a humorous fairy-tale-redux in the third, as well as a poem about creatures of the sea. She is currently at work on a novel based on the story which appeared in Volume II. Dr. Yolen also teaches children's literature at Smith College; her most recent collection of essays is *Touch Magic: Fantasy, Faerie and Folklore in the Literature of Children*.

INDEX TO ELSEWHERE, VOLUMES I–III

404